MICHAEL

Leabharlanna Poiblí Chathair Baile Átha Cliath
Dublin City Public Libraries

IVON

THE GAMES ARE
EVERYTHING
PLAY IS
DEAD

RedDoor

Published by RedDoor
www.reddoorpublishing.com

PB ISBN 978-1-910453-46-9

A CIP catalogue record for this book is available
from the British Library

Cover design: Jason Anscomb
Rawshock Design

Typesetting: Tutis Innovative E-Solutions Pte. Ltd

Print and production managed by Jellyfish Solutions Ltd

To my parents, John and Angela

PROLOGUE

Mumbles seafront, Swansea, 2119

'I think we should call him Ivon,' he says.

'So you finally agree with me about something?' says she.

'What do you mean?'

'Ivon. That was my idea.'

'Was it?'

'Well, yes. I've been thinking Ivon for a while.'

'You haven't said anything.'

The lazy sun warms his shoulders. He is free to put his arm around her here, the way it should always have been. If this is life on the far side of the Fence, he's glad for their exile.

'It just feels right,' she says.

'Yes. Yes. It does to me too.'

'How strange we should both have thought of it.'

'Isn't it.'

'Ivon with an "o".'

'Yes. Yes! Exactly! With an "o". It couldn't be any other way.'

'This is too weird.'

'But what if it's a girl? We're not in England, remember. These things go undecided here. It could be a girl.'

She shakes her head and looks into his eyes, as if suddenly haunted by the approach of something dark and portentous, sweeping in from the east, across Swansea Bay.

'It's not.'

I

London, 25 years later

Deep in the corridors of Parliament, Dusty is ushered into a long, wide conference room overlooking the Thames. The Prime Manager of England, Marcus Apollo, rises from his seat.

'Dusty Noble!' he cries. 'Come in!'

Apollo's smile is warm. He raises his hand, which Dusty takes, their thumbs interlocking. Apollo pulls Dusty's hand towards his breast, then Dusty pulls Apollo's to his.

'Welcome to Parliament!'

Around the long conference table are seated members of the Cabinet. Sunlight filters through the solar molecules of the window wall, burnishing the Managers with a lustre that Dusty finds affecting. He recognises a lot of the faces – the Managers for Football, Rugby, Tennis and Hockey are as recognisable to citizens of England as the Prime Manager himself. So too the Manager for Cricket, Lana Defoe, his old friend. She nods at him. Dusty is surprised to see a smile force its way across her face.

Statesmanship comes naturally to Apollo. He stands imperious in the magenta of the managerial class and addresses the Cabinet in his resonant timbre. 'Comrades, it is rare indeed that we acknowledge the achievements of an individual, for we are all but the products of commune and country – and to celebrate achievement is to look back into the Past, which runs, of course, contrary to the Primacy of the Next Match. Nevertheless, I think we here, in the corridors of power, knew instinctively when Dusty Noble was finally decommissioned two weeks ago that we were witnessing the end of a long and extraordinarily productive career. And it so happens that our instincts are correct.'

Apollo turns to the bank of screens on the interior wall, each showing a live stream of a sporting contest somewhere in the country – at this time of the morning, contests of minor significance, secondary level, possibly tertiary. The screens go blank for a moment, before an image of Dusty as a young man is projected across them, as high as the room, a rendition of the perfect Perpetual Era athlete. He recognises the image as of him, yet somehow not – not quite the face in the mirror, not quite the body. Younger. And an exquisite longing tugs at him, which he fears would overwhelm if lingered over too much. He doesn't understand these irregular feelings. They go against everything he was taught in diminishment training. He is afraid of them.

'If there is one sector of society that is more keenly appraised than we are of the goings-on on the field, of how each match is won or lost,' continues Apollo, 'it is the scientists at the Institute of Improvement. The Eye-Eye have alerted us to the extent of Dusty's contributions for commune and country. Thirty-one years as a batsman at elite level, 95 133 runs, 2015 matches. These figures make him the most productive batsman London has ever known and one of the three most productive England has. The amount of energy raised by his runs alone amounts to 113.08 terajoules. His cover drive has been placed on the national curriculum, and his memory bank of strokes is on order for upload to the archives when he reaches stasis.'

Dusty does not move. Thirty-one years has it been, 95 000 runs, 2000 matches? The last of the statistics melts into his image across the screens. Face-to-face with the young man he used to be, his disquiet does not diminish. 'Dusty Noble, London and

England, 2113–44' the display reads across a chest of perfect symmetry, beneath a face of clean lines and confidence for the Next Match, above a waist of economy, and legs that are slim and muscular in the green day suit of the elite class.

The longing gives way, finally, to what seems like pride, just as he used to feel for London when they were at the peak of their powers. Only this time, as in his dreams recently, it is pride not for his commune or his country but for *himself*, Dusty Noble the individual. As if those statistics were his, as if that aptitude, too; as if he were an independent entity, alone responsible for who he is and what he has achieved. And not an asset, bred, reared and owned by the Commune of London.

'Dusty Noble, you have always been held in the highest regard by Parliament and the scientific community. I know it is not the Perpetual way, but when an asset of sufficient value is decommissioned we in Parliament, who can perhaps see beyond the Next Match, we *want* to express our thanks. It is an indulgence, but happily those very few assets we feel inclined to honour are by definition the ones invulnerable to corruption. Weaker citizens might suffer in the glare of veneration, but a batsman with 95 000 runs…?'

Apollo places a powerful arm across his chest and laughs. Dusty looks at him properly for the first time, as laughter rises from those around the table. The face is wide and strong, made bold by generous eyebrows and a head of shining black hair. This is the first time he has met Marcus Apollo, and yet he knows the face well from countless morale-casts and info-docs. Seeing it in the flesh is a curious experience. He finds himself instinctively liking Apollo, despite having never shared a wicket stand with him or a session's training.

When the laughter dies down, Apollo adopts a solemn air. He turns to his assistant briefly, then back to Dusty. 'We would like to present you with the Iron Joule for services to commune and country. It would not surprise me if you chose never to wear it in public, such is your sense of solidarity with your comrades, but whether you choose to wear it or not the point is, you have earned it.'

Apollo presents the metallic J and presses it against Dusty's chest. He stands back to admire the award. Dusty looks down at it, too, a modest grey symbol, yet signifying so much, perched on the micro-magnets of his day suit, adjacent to his millennion medal. He has never seen one before and is troubled by the realisation that part of him *does* want to wear it, to stride out against convention, to let it be known how productive an athlete he has been. But it will be assumed of him that he does not. For who would want to elevate themselves above the comrades of their rank and class? Who would dare to?

He looks up again to see Apollo smiling warmly at him, as if in expectation of something. Dusty clears his throat.

'Um, when you have lived your life by deeds,' he says, looking down at the floor, then up at Lana, sitting among her new comrades in the Cabinet, and then out at the river and the glinting pyramids of the Institute of Physiotherapy, which rise like teeth from the trees on the other side, 'words don't always come easily.' In the corner of his eye he sees Apollo nodding vigorously. 'I thank you all. You hear rumours of this kind of honour, but you never imagine it will happen to you. I used to wonder if it happened at all. With my commune, London, suffering such a terrible recession, this endless run of defeats across so many sports, it is difficult for me to accept this, particularly since I am now no longer able to help my comrades on the field arrest the decline. But, I vow, when results do start to go our way again, I shall be working the pumps of the stadium generators as vigorously as any citizen – or at least any veteran elite cricketer.' A bubble of laughter rises from the table. 'It is a future I am devoted to. And so, Prime Manager, as grateful as I am, as closely as I will guard it, I will not wear this medal – for it represents achievements that are long in the Past.'

The smile on Apollo's face assures Dusty that his delivery has been convincing, despite the volatility of spirit that has crackled and spat within him since decommission.

'Dusty Noble, truly you are a credit to your breeding programme! I understand you have taken up a new role at ReSure, but should you ever consider a future among the managerial class your application would be entertained favourably, I'm sure.' The Prime Manager holds his hands out wide and addresses his Cabinet. 'Comrades, I urge you to mark this moment with that most esoteric of rituals, that echo from another time, the round of applause. Dusty, this will mean nothing to you, but rest assured we offer the gesture as a mark of our utmost appreciation.'

And with that Apollo brings the palms of his hands together with a crack, and then again, and again, and so on, until the Managers around the table join him in the practice, and the air is filled with a warm, rich waterfall of sound, wave after wave of it, like rainfall. It reminds Dusty of the thunder in the stadium generators, but it is softer, it is giving, it is, yes, *appreciative*.

The effect is hypnotic. And Dusty feels more ground within him give way. When they shake hands again and Apollo pulls Dusty's in to his chest, he is taken by a sudden, maverick urge to bring his left arm round the back of the Prime Manager's shoulders and hold him. He does not act on it, of course, but the mere existence of the thought terrifies him. Where are these rogue impulses coming from? He feels his mind changing, a new personality creaking and unfolding, suppressed till now by the ironclad discipline of the most productive batsman London has ever known.

As he stands before the Cabinet, with England's highest honour on his chest, Dusty fears he is no longer the man who earned it.

Alanis steps into her day suit, pulls on it and sighs as the micro-magnets climb up and around her body, clicking like a swarm of insects into their warm, intimate embrace. It is one of the fondest moments of her day. A vigorous bout of coitus with a dear friend, a shower, a powder and the enfolding of her body back into its own warmth. Not a joule of energy wasted.

'That was quite a bout, Dusty,' she says, breezily. 'We haven't generated as much as that for a long time. We should check our kJ record.'

'Kilojoules?' replies Dusty, with that twinkle she finds so endearing. 'That was a megajoule!'

Alanis laughs. 'True, true!'

Poor old Dusty. He is no longer the athlete some of her other cot partners are, but her fondness for him remains undimmed. It has always been a privilege to couple with so revered a member of the elite, and it is no less of one now, regardless of his recent decommission. She will flare defiantly at anyone who so much as smirks at it.

'Shall we go for an isotonic?' she says, watching as he rises to receive the attentions of his own suit. There is still something majestic about him, as if the suit itself spreads across his body with a kind of gratitude, a deference. He is Dusty Noble, after all.

'I can't, I'm afraid, A. I need to be back at ReSure for a couple of hours this afternoon. Then I'm comping at the Twenty20 this evening.'

'Who have we got?'

'East Anglia.'

'And how are you finding it?'

'What, the comping?'

'Yes.' Alanis hesitates. 'And, you know…life after engagement.'

Dusty smiles at her and shrugs. 'New role, same goal. Decommission may seem abhorrent to you now, but it's just a change of emphasis. You'll learn that in your diminishment training. You learn a lot in diminishment training.'

'Oh, I hope you're right. I'm terrified of it. Imagine not having a Next Match to look towards…'

As soon as she says it, Alanis blushes at her insensitivity, but Dusty doesn't seem to mind.

'The worst part is having to live off rations,' he says.

'But that'll end soon. This recession can't go on for ever.'

'Of course. But to go from elite to managing a calorific deficit in just a few days…that's the tough part.'

They head for the cot door. Dusty rests the palm of his hand on the scanner, initiating that final pleasure of the cot – the low, seething throb of the consolidator, as the fruit of their exertions is banked in the Grid. Energy. Alanis closes her eyes. She can almost breathe it in. Her breast rises slowly and fully, as if she does. The throbbing intensifies, until the door of the cot slides open to turn them out.

Dusty doesn't quite look at her as they walk through the corridors to the foyer. 'I'm happy, A. Really, I am.'

She should have known better than to doubt it. An exemplary Perpetual citizen like Dusty! Bodies may diminish, but the spirit remains in perpetuity! Even in the hard times. Let their results slide further and the energy crisis deepen; Selflessness and the Sanctity of Physical Fitness shall see London through! Sometimes all it takes is one galvanising result. The margin is fine between winning streaks and losing, between prosperity and austerity. The commune may be suffering now, but they must remain positive. Dusty is an example to all!

'I was thinking,' he says, as they reach the foyer, whence she will head to the lounge for some recuperation and he to his new place of work, the Repository of Suspended Resources. 'I've got some travel rights to use after my decommission award.

It hasn't felt right to use any, what with the recession, but the director at ReSure says I should.'

'Oh, you must! Trust you not to! Of course, you must! Austerity's not your fault!'

He laughs that soothing, gentle laugh. 'If you say so!'

His manner changes then, almost imperceptibly. They say Dusty's cover drive has been placed on the curriculum at the Academy for its economy of effort. Elegance and economy of effort – if you could capture him in a pair of concepts... As with his cover drive, so with the shifts in his mood. There is the hint of a stiffening in his countenance, but it's so subtle Alanis cannot be sure it has happened.

'I took the liberty of checking the volleyball schedule,' he says. 'I see your Spring Recess begins tomorrow, and I wondered if you would like to come with me this weekend. I'm thinking of going to Wales, to see the Past. I know it's not for everyone, but I've always wanted to go.'

Alanis is shocked and tries hard to maintain an evenness of expression, but she is unlikely to be placed on the curriculum for anything but the boldest exercises. She hopes Dusty cannot see into her soul, as she often imagines he can.

Wales? WALES?! What did that stand for, again? The Western Assemblage, wasn't it, of Lapsed Era Savages? She didn't even know you could go. What is the Fence for, if not to keep separate those who reject the Perpetual Era, those who live in the Past? Really, a Perpetual citizen is not meant to venture into Wales any more than a savage is meant to visit England.

She reaches for the centurion medal on her day suit and toys with it. 'I...Dusty, gosh. Thank you. What a... Can I get back to you? I just need to check my training programmes. I'll pulse you.'

'Of course you can, A. Do come. It'll be good for you. You never know, it may even be fun.'

They laugh before shaking hands. She stands in the foyer for a moment and watches him through the glass doors as they slide shut behind him. She will say yes, of course she will. Who wouldn't say yes to Dusty Noble? Besides, there's bound to be a programme to protect them from the Welsh natives, or Dusty would never have suggested it. Would he.

But they have had a lot of bouts together recently, and now this, an away break beyond the Fence. As she walks to the recovery lounge, she resolves to go on a holiday of her own sometime and considers which of her other cot partners to invite, for the sake of balance.

❂

That morning Dusty had the dream again. When he was younger it was a featureless dream of speed and rushing air, of being above and yet to the side of things. Recently, it has become more vivid, so that this time he could make out some sort of flying machine, open to the elements, not entirely under his control.

But it's not just the dream any more. His dysfunction may have started there, in his sleep, but now it has found the confidence to walk boldly throughout his head during the waking hours. He can no longer dismiss it, any more than he can these peculiar feelings he's developed for Alanis. He thinks of her now, how she dithered and flushed just then when he invited her to Wales. That touch of rouge on her cheek sat well on a face so big-featured and soft, warm and inspiring, trusting yet bold. He thinks of her in the cot, the sweat gathering on her chest, those strong legs, the lusty cries, the swaying couch and the energy, the prime energy, that will protest against decline. It is true that he has always valued coitus with her above anyone else, which should have served as a warning, but now he finds himself wanting it *only* with her! Of all the cot partners in a citizen's life, to single out one above the others… His is an acute case of Misalignment! How can it be otherwise? If only anyone knew, it wouldn't be the Iron Joule at Parliament he'd be up for but a procedure of Assimilation at the Institute of Correction. It may yet be, if he's not careful.

Wilfully, he draws his hand across the console on his bike and feels the propulsion ring change up a couple of magnet sizes. The greater resistance is overcome by a spasm of power in his quads, and he surges past a couple of secondaries dawdling on the Euston Road. The blast of a siren alerts him to the presence of a security aero behind. He turns to watch the sleek black craft glide past, its front cabin inscrutable, rear windows transparent. A pale-faced young man in the navy of the primary classes sits in the back, his head hung low, as he is delivered to the IC. Dusty looks away.

He enters the gate to ReSure on the Euston Road, parks his bike and crosses the piazza to the main entrance. The ReSure building stands separate from the glass and carbon fibre that is the fabric of Perpetual London. The warm red bricks and sprawling, asymmetric configuration lend it an air of softness, like a smile from Alanis, against the clean confidence of the prevailing architecture. Dusty passes a heavy plinth on his left bearing the statue of a runner in dark bronze. From there he descends a few steps and heads for the far corner, where the entrance lies.

When Dusty passes into the vast white entrance hall, he heads left behind one of the spiral staircases, holds the palm of his hand against the scanner by the personnel entrance and continues on to his chamber. It isn't long before the director of ReSure, Juno Distelle, breezes in.

'Afternoon, Dusty,' she says in a voice deeper than his. 'Ready to file some assets? You'll love it, I promise! There's something very satisfying about keeping the population in check. Meet me in the foyer at 14.25. We have a 14.30 consignment of primaries.'

It's always a 'consignment'. Dusty dislikes the term. He notices that Juno is still looking at him, her head cocked in that faux-sympathetic manner, which speaks either of her extravagant eccentricity or a desire to scrutinise him more closely.

She smiles. 'Trust me, Dusty. Once you've dispatched a consignment, you'll only want to dispatch another. Sometimes I have to stop myself! Repeat after me, Distelle: "The population of London *must* be maintained at two million, no more – and certainly no less!"'

For a second or two after she's gone the corridors resound with her laughter. Juno was an elite wrestler during her years of engagement, a pedigree it would be easy to guess at, even without her frequent allusions to it. The polished vaults of ReSure echo with a personality that extends well beyond her squat frame. She is a peculiarity against convention, isolated for years in the antechamber to stasis, which no normal citizen cares to confront until the day they have to.

Dusty releases the seal at his neck, and his day suit falls away. Stepping out of it, he scans open the slide that presents him with his official suit. The shimmering emerald climbs up and around his body. He feels his pride swell. For a moment he is on duty again for London Cricket; then when he applies the international's sash of white gold across the micro-magnets of his suit, from right shoulder to left hip, he is on duty again for England. He turns the Iron Joule between thumb and forefinger, but consigns that to the slide. No, he doesn't want to put it on, after all. The trappings of his official suit he can still wear with a pride that rises from the collective; this little trinket wants to elevate him above his fellow citizens, worthy and true, just as he ushers them to stasis. Intolerable.

Juno is already in the foyer. When he arrives she smiles, breathes in and stretches her arms out wide, turning slowly in the grand hallway, as if summoning from suspension the countless assets she has filed in her time. 'All this will be yours when I go in there,' she says. She will go 'in there' in three years, seven months and twenty-nine days. There is a countdown clock above her desk.

'Have any of these primaries shown symptoms?' asks Dusty.

Juno nods with exaggerated approval. 'Very good, Dusty! You're getting the hang of this! No. Their dossiers are ready for download. There's a complete surveillance record of the final month for each of them. All model citizens.' She looks up from her tablet through eyes a little too close together for so wide a face. 'Although not as model as they will be in an hour or two!'

Tucking the tablet under her wrist like a discus, she walks off. 'We're in Portal 317 today.'

Dusty follows as she charges up the first steps of Spiral Staircase 2 on the way to the third floor. 'OK,' she says. 'So it's important to affect a certain manner when filing assets. Never forget, it might be a normal working day for you, but for each of them it is almost certainly their last animate day on Earth.' Once on the third floor, Juno leads Dusty through corridors of warm red. 'Generally speaking there are no incidents – but you can get the odd wobble, particularly among the primary classes. When you do, it's important to be sympathetic but firm. It's not often we get a veteran international apply for a position here – those fortunate enough to be filed by you will consider your presence reassuring, just as they do mine. Ah! Here we are!'

It is a standard primary portal they walk into, rectangular and bare, with a console in one corner, an isotonic dispenser in another and, along the opposite wall, ten docking bays, each with stasis pod open and waiting. Dusty shudders at the sight of those vessels towards which they are all gravitating, but he maintains his composure.

At 14.30 precisely, the primaries file in. Five men, five women, each firm of countenance and body, their rank distinguished by navy day suits, their hair cropped. There is a haggard look about some of them – when times are tough, it is the primaries who suffer most – but there are surely more years of service left in those strong limbs. Perpetual policy is to harvest them before their decline.

Dusty and Juno greet each one with a handshake. He can detect not the slightest distress in their faces. Maybe a certain distance in the eyes of some, but this group are prepared. Dusty is relieved. And impressed. He feels uneasy about stasis, yet as an elite he has another eleven years till his. These primaries they are about to consign are forty-five today, four years younger than he is. Inferior at sport they may have been, but some were doubtless intelligent. He has seen their files. Can it be so easy to shrug off animation?

'Welcome, all of you,' says Juno, 'to your future in suspension. Firstly, may I congratulate you on the lives you have led thus far. You may not have been much use at sport, but I can assure you that the exploits of elite assets such as Dusty Noble here and myself would have meant nothing without the base of support that the lower classes provide. You have never tasted action on the field, but your selfless devotion sets an example of citizenship that is relevant to us all, particularly now, when results aren't going the commune's way.'

Juno invites them to take an isotonic before cryopreservation. As they mill about, one of the primaries points at Dusty's sash. 'So, you were an international, were you?'

Dusty nods.

'Which sport?'

'Cricket.'

'That was my field. I had a trial at secondary level. Didn't make it.' He holds his arms out to present himself. 'Obviously.'

Juno clears her throat. 'Now, I trust none of you has taken food today.'

Dusty's new friend leans across to him. 'Today,' she says. Feels as if I haven't eaten this year.'

'No chance of a last meal, then?' says another, to general laughter. 'My calorific deficit has stretched to 23 per cent this month.'

'I'm afraid not,' says Juno. 'I know it's been hard lately, but going into stasis lean is actually the best way. Rest assured, if and when you are recalled, it will be to more prosperous conditions.'

Dusty notes the fine figures as the primaries let fall their suits and climb naked into the pods. For all his confusion since decommission, he feels a layer of discipline return to his withered soul and that old love, once so unquestioning, for London and England. He is proud to usher these citizens to stasis. According to their files, one was a medic, another a scientist, there's a physio, a stadium manager…but a mere accident of genetics has compromised their aptitude for sport and consigned them to roles in the lower classes, working the levers and boards when other people score, filling the air with sound energy. Theirs have been lives led in dutiful service, exemplars of conditioning, never questioning the Sanctity of Physical Fitness.

When the last of them has been dispatched to holding, Dusty breathes out. He and Juno gather the discarded day suits and deliver them to a slide in the wall.

'That's really all there is to it, Dusty. I think you're going to be very good at this. Do you see how pleasing it is? Today, seventy neonates will emerge into the primary class and seventy forty-five-year-olds will leave.'

She looks up at him, and he down at her. Her manner changes. 'Oh, Dusty, I can tell you're thrown by this! I found it a little disconcerting myself, when I was first tutored in it. It's perfectly natural. You know the best thing for it, don't you?

14

A hard, fast bout in one of the ReSure cots. And I can assure you, I go hard and fast, even at my age.'

Dusty does not doubt it. Juno is of no appeal aesthetically, but there is likely to be great power in those sawn-off limbs. There was a time when he might have considered it his duty to draw the energy from them, but such a sense of citizenship has been neutered in him by the peculiarity of these feelings of his for Alanis. So much so, that the prospect of a bout with Juno makes him feel quite nauseous.

'I'm comping at the Twenty20 in an hour,' he replies. 'And I've already coupled once this afternoon.'

'Very well. But we must engage soon. You've been here for a few days now, and you haven't yet coupled with your superior.'

She shuts down the console and sweeps out of the portal.

Dusty takes his pre-match meal at the ReSure refectory on his own. He shovels down his 61-gram ration of enhanced pasta. Personnel come and go around him, primaries, secondaries and tertiaries, but he cannot look any in the eye, thrown as he is by his first brush with stasis. Instead, a troubling vision hangs behind his eyes of the trusting, honest faces of that afternoon's group of primaries, the lid of a pod closing on each.

The vision dogs him as he cycles from ReSure, west along the Euston Road, past the bullet-train station and the arboretums of the Regent's Park Expansion to the right, the long solar panels of the Bloomsbury Sun Farm to the left. He is cycling in the fast lane, surging past citizens whose fate he has become party to. He turns up Lisson Grove and stares dead ahead as he knifes through the neatly arranged maisonettes of the Marylebone Tertiary Quarter. Every so often, the late-afternoon sun glimmers in the corner of his eye, ricocheting off a glass panel, but it does not break his focus.

Soon he is pulling into the bike park at Lord's. This is the edifice he knows better than any other, a second home for thirty-one years. The foreground is dominated by the stainless-steel statue of 'The Cricketer', knees bent, elbow held high some 50 feet above the ground, upturned bat slanting gently down and away from the head, in the pose of a classic cover drive. The heavy lines of the wrought metal at this distance blend into a model of poise and elegance. It could almost be a study of Dusty.

The end of the bat, suspended 45 feet in the air, dips in deference towards Lord's, the mighty stadium generator behind it. From where Dusty approaches, its twin domes appear as one, an arch that peaks 150 feet higher than the raised elbow of the statue below. The aluminium structure is smooth, with a blueish hue. Dusty has always found it a comforting look, but in his heyday it was to visiting teams a fortress without a chink.

Lord's is a monument of simplicity, but the generator seething to the north a chaotic structure of right angles, which rises from the flank of its stadium into a monstrosity of roughly equal size. Already, its menacing hum fills the air, primed for match day.

Dusty takes the gangway that leads up to a concourse running above the turbine shafts on the north side of the stadium. He walks with thousands of other complements now, none of them aware that for thirty-one years he trod the turf they are to gather round. At the appropriate gate, he penetrates the outer shell and navigates the inner concourse, teeming with secondaries and tertiaries, to the veteran elites' block. Out he comes into the arena, which is filling steadily with comps. From the inside, the twin domes create an echoing vault fit to harness the energy of 81 500 people.

On the field, the visiting team's fielders are in position. East Anglia are the evening's opponents, one of the weakest communes, but nothing can be taken for granted these days. London's great clashes with Yorkshire or the North West have long since lost their moment. East Anglia is now the defining fixture.

Dusty does not dwell over the familiar greensward. Instead, he shuffles towards his station, nodding occasionally to an acquaintance as he passes. He takes up position next to Max Innocent, a former comrade of his. The ergonomic seat holds him firmly and tenderly, and he flips it into its active position to start a gentle warm-up, working the pump boards with his feet and the levers with his arms. The stadium throbs as thousands of complements prepare for the match in the same way.

'Afternoon, Dusty.'

Dusty nods. 'Max.'

Max was decommissioned at the same time as Dusty, which has consolidated the bond they'd formed after many partnerships at the crease.

'You ready for this evening's exercise in lost-cause fighting?'

'Come on, Max. That's not the attitude, and you know it.'

'Difficult, though, isn't it?' says Max, who stops pumping and sits forward to hydrate, satisfied with his preparation. 'Watching us lose the whole time. Not being able to do anything about it.'

'It'll come good. We're too big a commune for this losing run to carry on much longer.'

'Let's hope so. I heard that we're now producing more energy from coitus than we are from the stadiums. That's incredible!'

'At least we're still shagging.'

'Well, that's all we've got. I mean, for us to be winning so rarely that these massive stadium-generators are producing less of the sparky stuff than our collective shagging…' Max shakes his head. 'Ridiculous.'

London's batsmen enter the arena, and Dusty eases his limbs to a halt. 'You never know. It may just be that coitus is one thing we're still really good at. It's all relative.'

'Yeah, well, less time in the cots, more time in the simulators, and maybe our elites will start to turn things round.'

'The footballers are doing all right.'

'Mid-table.'

'Don't sniff at it.'

Max grunts, and the two men settle into position, the match about to start. A hush descends as the warm-ups give way to the latency of a stadium generator ready for action. Dusty gazes up at the vault, which arches vastly over them, then closes his eyes.

Within moments, the siren of the stadium computer sounds in steady, staccato blasts of urgency to signal the successful scoring of runs. The pumps are live! Dusty slams his right foot down, then his left, and heaves with his arms. The sound of the siren is overwhelmed by the deafening commotion of 81 500 comps pumping the boards and levers of a Perpetual Era stadium, chanting exhortations to add to the general din. Dusty looks to the rafters and sees by the number of lights that one of the London batsmen has hit a four. For 40 seconds, 10 for each run, the vast turbine shafts turn, and the generator next door roars into life.

'I hate it when we start with a boundary,' says Max, once the last of the green lights goes out and the stadium takes time to catch its breath.

'You can't complain about results one minute, then about how many runs we're scoring the next!'

'No, but I'd rather limber up with a quick single first. It might be all right for those guys over there,' says Max, nodding in the direction of the elite comps in a nearby block, who massage their rippling sinews, 'but they've spent their lives training to do this. I'm a decommissioned cricketer, for joules' sake!'

'That's why you only have to comp once a week. Look, we were grateful for the comps when we were out there; now it's a chance to give a little back.'

The siren sounds again, this time for a single, but Dusty is able to catch Max's last quip as they start to work the pumps again.

'You're so shitting perfect, aren't you.'

Dusty cycles home with a heavy heart. And an empty stomach. There will be no nutrition pouches distributed this evening. London were all out for 123 in the 18th over. Max stopped complaining about the workload at some point in the third over. And the opposition innings was even more restful, with just three wickets to pump through. Dusty imagines the East Anglia comps in the modest stadium generator in Cambridge finishing off their evening's work with the meat of a victory pump, one last, 40-minute bout of energy generation. In time, London will learn how much they generated in their paltry 32 minutes 30 seconds of pumping, but it won't be enough to buck the recent trend.

Even so, Dusty's spirits rise on the climb towards Hampstead and the Veteran Elite Quarter for London Cricket, just beside the heath. The points of reference he has lived his life by are dissolving, but still he finds solace in the return home. That sacred mother of Perpetual society. Let austerity bite, every citizen has a haven to return to at the end of each day, the basic right of humanity, 'a home of your own and for you alone', where none shall trespass, the soul's repose to disturb.

He may not have as spacious a home now as he did when he was an active elite, but it is his, and that is enough, as it has always been. Through the dusky gloom, he can make out its white carbon-fibre frame, low-slung and of one piece, gathering strength from the identical neighbours in its quarter, then the solar roof, angled and convex to follow the progress of the sun, at each end curving down coquettishly to the ground. The same way, it occurs to him, that Alanis's hair falls down the side of her face into an impudent, upturned kink. He smiles at the thought of her, as he holds his hand up to the scanner.

And here she is in his head again – for real this time. When he steps through his front door, a pulse arrives from her. She would love to come away with him.

He catches a glimpse of himself, as he washes his hands in the washroom, and sees a smile. His chiselled face, now scored in places with the first wrinkles of diminishment, looks back at him through steel-blue eyes under a manicured bed of creamy hair. For a moment he looks happy.

II

Rushing air. It's the dream again. Rushing into and past his face. He is above everything and out of step. This is an act of subversion, undermining from on high. He is flying.

Dusty wakes, but not with a start. He knows the dream too well for it to surprise him any more. His heart is racing, but that's the nature of the dream itself, not his reaction to it. It is the exhilaration.

Sometimes it scares him, this idea that he might be a maverick, a rebel even. The world does not accommodate such people. They are dealt with and returned as good as new. He doesn't want to start all over again.

But this time he merely opens his eyes and registers the darkness. It is 3.23 a.m. In a little more than six hours he will collect Alanis from the club, and together they will journey into Wales. He knows he will not sleep again until they do.

With each mile from London, Dusty's spirit lightens, until, a few miles short of the South West's border town of Swindon, he feels at peace for the first time since his decommission. The M4 is wide, undulating serenely through the wind farms and fledgling forests of the South East and, in a moment or two, the South West. The aero spirits him and Alanis smoothly towards Wales.

Conversation has been easy. They have both needed a break from the heavy atmosphere of austerity London, and what better way to escape it. He picked up the aero that morning, pulling away from the compound in Kilburn with a full charge in the capacitor and excitement in his heart. Alanis fits perfectly with his mood and his vehicle. She has chosen a leisure suit enlivened by swirls of navy and vivid cyan. The suit stops at the top of her thigh. It is a pleasure to see her limbs exposed, freed from the possessiveness of a regular day suit. He enjoys the sight of her legs unfolding into the footwell and the sound of her soft, earnest voice.

After a minute or two of silence, she rests her hands in her lap. 'Why did you choose Wales?' she says, just as they cross the border into the South West.

Dusty weighs his words. 'I'm curious. I always have been. I know the arguments against: it's the Past; regress not progress; the Lapsed Era is just that; it has nothing for us; and so on. I see all of that, of course I do. But that doesn't mean that going there can't be…can't be *interesting.*'

He glances at her, but she is looking across him, towards Swindon, and then at a huge agricultural aerofreight twice as wide as their little skim-around and some ten times as long. They pass it, as it slides onto the highway from the north, its consignment dispatched, and makes its return to the fields. These are happier times for the South West.

'Yes, yes,' she agrees without obvious conviction. 'It will be interesting. I can't wait to see it. I mean, we could easily turn off anywhere along here and spend our break visiting the old towns and villages, if we wanted to see things the way they were, but that's not really the Past, is it, because no one lives there. I mean, I've done that loads of times. It's safe. It's beautiful. It's a holiday. But, no, if you *really* want to visit the Past, to *really* experience it, then, well, obviously, you go to Wales, don't you.'

'Exactly! You have to!' The spirit of the moment overwhelms him. Here they are, alone in an aero on a wide open highway, far from the bristling cities, heading west, where soon they will be beyond the Fence, beyond civilisation itself. Free. What harm can there be in a little enthusiasm for that between two old friends?

'I really think this could be an incredible experience for us! We're so lucky to have the opportunity. Most people will never get to see this. They train on, giving their all to their commune and to the Perpetual way, selflessly, *unthinkingly*, pursuing the sacred ideal of physical fitness. And yet there, just the other side of an outsized wall, across a river, exists a completely different way of life. Where being fit might not be the be-all and end-all of human aspiration. They say the generation of energy there is a dirty, haphazard affair, that there is no correlation between sporting achievement and prosperity. Oh, it's funny to think about it, it's ridiculous. But it's...*another way of life*. It's fascinating, isn't it?'

Dusty can see out of the corner of his eye that Alanis is nodding, but no words are forthcoming. For a few minutes, there is silence in the aero.

Nothing now lies between them and the frontier. They have passed Bristol, the capital of the South West and the last settlement before the Fence. In a few minutes they will be in Wales. Alanis is nervous.

She catches her first view of the Fence, sweeping from the north along the edge of the plains until it melds with the docks of Greater Bristol to the south, an opaque blend of steel and solar panelling, remarkable only for its scale. She loses sight of it as the road dips into a valley, but when they climb to within a few hundred metres the wall reveals itself again. It is at its height over the road, some 45 feet tall, but falls away by degrees either side to a regular height of 30, stretching as far as Alanis can see.

As they approach the checkpoint, a border officer emerges. Dusty powers down the aero, and he and Alanis follow the officer inside.

'I'll need your signs, please,' he says.

Dusty and Alanis each place their left hand on the scanner on his desk, and their permits are duly confirmed.

The young officer, proud in his charcoal-grey official suit, refers to his tablet. 'You have applied for, and been granted, recreational permits. They expire at midnight on Monday. Have either of you been to Wales before?'

'No.'

The officer launches into a spiel he has rehearsed well. 'The Western Assemblage of Lapsed Era Savages is to be visited with extreme caution by those from the Perpetual Era. You are advised never to stray from the M4 or other major routes unaccompanied. The sanctioned routes are being downloaded to your central chip now, Mr Noble. Beyond these inroads into the wilderness, civilisation has no jurisdiction. There are hostels along the M4 with viewing stations and Past simulators, in which the depravities of the Lapsed Era are brought to life. Up-to-date alignment certificates are required for entry into these. If you want to travel deep into the Past, beyond the simulators, there are natives at the Swansea West viewing station trained to escort you to the towns and villages of the Swansea Valley. Do you have any questions?'

Dusty is smiling at Alanis in a manner that might be intended to reassure her. He does look handsome. And relaxed, more so than she has seen him recently. As if they were off for an away break of aquasport on the south coast and not going to Wales at all.

'Yes, I have one,' says Alanis. 'Are there cots?'

'Naturally, the hostels are equipped with a full complement of coition terminals,' replies the officer, 'but they are not connected to any grid. You may have heard that there is no grid at all in Wales, at least not as understood by us. The comprehensive harnessing of energy is not practised there, which is the root of their savagery, what separates them from Perpetual society. The Welsh practise coitus for recreational purposes, and quite often reproductive. But there is no energy generation arising. Our advice is to enjoy your coitus but remain aware that no social benefit will pertain from it.'

'Don't overdo it, in other words,' says Dusty, still smiling.

Alanis forces out a little laugh, but she knows she is flushing. Beyond the Fence they will be off the Grid, which is a further twist of discomfort she had not considered. Why couldn't they just have gone to the deserted settlements of the shires? She'd been to some beautiful old places. Dorking, Farnham, Hungerford, Marlborough. All perfectly preserved; all dead; all safe. She'd seen a yellow sign a while back leading off the M4 to Castle Combe and nearly cried out. She'd been there many years ago on a field trip with the other girls on the fast-twitch module at her nursery. It was enchanting, and the name stayed with her. How she wished they were going there. What did Wales have that could not be found in a place like that, other than the rank threat of its living natives?

But she said nothing as they passed Castle Combe, and she will say nothing now, because Dusty has earned the right to visit a place like this if he wants to. She is honoured that he chose her to go with him.

The sun is shining, a condition of comfort to any Perpetual citizen. And yet Dusty derives added satisfaction, somehow, from the knowledge that this sunshine is being allowed to wash over the land and away, untroubled by a people desperate to harness its every ray. This sunshine is of no value at all but for the simple pleasure of its warmth on the skin.

He lowers his window and rests his arm in the void, rejoicing at the freedom to do so. The illicit turbulence that breaks into the aero thrills him. When he glances across at Alanis, she is already looking in his direction. Their eyes meet in a naked instant, before she turns her gaze straight ahead and forces a smile.

Dusty does not share her uneasiness. Energy inefficient it may be, but Wales is setting off little explosions of life inside him the further they venture into the country. Could it be the inefficiency itself? Now that they are past Newport, the M4 is alive with old-style cars, complete with rubber wheels. He chuckles at the outrageous heat and sound loss. The road signs bear the name of each city in English *and* in the old Welsh tongue. The gratuitousness of it! Why is it that Dusty feels he is coming home?

On past Cardiff (Caerdydd) they fly, Dusty laughing at the madness of it all, past Port Talbot (houses on a highway! Ha!), when suddenly, just after a sign to Swansea (Abertawe!), there appears a smaller brown one beckoning the driver to 'Gower'. 'Gwyr!' says Alanis without much conviction, but Dusty is not laughing any more. That sign has touched him somehow, as if he has seen it before.

He has had his fill of the M4 now. The moment the officer told them to stick to the major routes he knew he wouldn't be satisfied with that, nor with a guided tour by a brainwashed Welshman. This is the moment to break loose, so he guides the aero onto the slip road and heads for Gower. A wide expanse of sea and filthy chimneys presents itself as they leave the elevated highway and follow the new road round to the right.

He will not look at Alanis, for he knows she is looking at him. His chip tells him they are still on a sanctioned route, the

A483, as it sweeps them towards Swansea. The sea appears on his left, and in the distance cranes and docks give notice that they are approaching a Lapsed Era settlement.

'Dusty?' says Alanis softly.

But Dusty does not reply. The cars around him stop at a red light. His chip is warning him that civilisation's reach ends here. The red light is joined by another of a yellowish hue, before both are put out in favour of a green one. The cars move on, and Dusty follows them over the crossroad and beyond the jurisdiction of civilisation, into Swansea itself. They are on their own. He thinks he hears a sound from Alanis, but it could have been anything.

Still the brown signs for Gower lead him on, through the hideous, brick-heavy architecture of the Lapsed Era, the noise and the misdirection. To his left, the ill-conceived buildings now fall away to reveal the majesty of Swansea Bay, but it is a commotion to his right that finally inclines Dusty to slow down. A long white wall of corrugated iron shudders almost visibly to the noise that rises beyond.

'Dusty,' says Alanis, with some urgency now, 'what are you doing? This is beyond the pale.'

He looks her in the eye. There is no colour in her cheeks. She is terrified.

'Don't you want to know?' he says, but his adrenaline is high, so that it comes across as a challenge.

His heart racing, he pulls up on a grass verge a discreet distance away from the commotion. Alanis follows him tentatively out of the aero, and together they walk into the teeth of the unknown. The stadium, for that is what he imagines it must be, is growling steadily. 'St Helen's', reads a sign above the entrance, 'Home of the Whites'. The next home game is 'Swansea RFC v Neath', and the date is today's. Access is easy. Following a compulsion he cannot disobey, Dusty slips through an unattended gate into a primitive arena of no focus or coherence. He guesses there are about 10 000 people in attendance, many of them packed into the long white building he had seen from the road, a kind of stand but with simple plastic seats and in some places not even that. He joins those standing in an unseated section. One juvenile with food on its face and a look of aggression in its eye clocks his Perpetual clothing and pokes an adult nearby. The adult is too preoccupied with the match to take any notice. Dusty recognises the sport they're gathered round as rugby.

But he is more preoccupied with the natives themselves. He can make out no pattern, no order to their appearance, young mixing with large mixing with female mixing with male. Many are dressed in white shirts, but the uniform is superficial and ignored altogether by some. Below the waist there is no consistency of attire, some legs exposed, some not. They hydrate from receptacles of different colour and material – metallic, plastic, glass.

It is, however, their attitude, feral and uncontained, that makes the deepest impression on him. He marvels at the unmodulated nature of the noise they make. Not only do these people shout, they do so continually, even when their team are not scoring. There is an emotional quality, as if they can't help themselves. He is frightened by it and exhilarated, just as in his dream.

'Come on, my lovers!' screams one woman, her hands held wide to the sky, a plastic vessel in one of them swilling golden liquid that washes down her naked arm towards naked shoulders and breasts only partially concealed by a dirty grey tunic. Her voice undulates curiously.

'Dusty!' cries another voice, more familiar, behind him.

Alanis is shouting so that she may be heard over the din, but there is an edge of desperation to her cry. He had quite forgotten her for a moment. He turns to see her cowering at the gate.

'Come on!' he urges, then turns again to take in the stadium.

On two other sides of the pitch thousands more jostle on their feet under an open sky, but behind the goalposts to the right the grass widens into another field, which could almost be a cricket pitch, the one patch of grass a kind of deformity on the face of the other. At the far end, the perimeter is bounded by a brick wall, and all around there are Lapsed Era houses, the mean, minuscule windows of some actually looking out over the pitch.

'I feel sick.' Alanis has joined him. She holds her arms tight around her waist and looks about her at the Welsh, as if they were circling crocodiles.

Dusty is too excited to sympathise. The apparent lawlessness of events on the pitch enthrals him now. It is some time before he realises the match is being refereed by a human, albeit in a different coloured shirt. One team is in white, the other black, in an appropriate coming together of opposites, for, truly, there is anger and fury in the contest.

The black team are stronger, but Dusty's final observation, after which he has eyes for no other, is that the white No10 is a contestant unlike any on the field, unlike any Dusty has ever seen. His hair is the brightest blond, so blond it is almost fluorescent. Was it the hair he noticed first, or the way he sashayed through the black midfield just now to score that try, precipitating a thunder from those watching that threatens to tear the old stand to the ground? Either way, Dusty is seduced. He thrills every time the ball comes the way of the No10, who operates with a compelling blend of irreverence and grace, as if he is above the match, or outside it. Dusty is transfixed by the narrative of the contest, by his proximity to it, by the *personality* of it, swept along by the energy of those watching, distressed as they are when the black team score again, a seething swarm of them marching towards the try line.

But moments later the brilliant No10 scythes through once more and arrows in on the full-back. There is a surge of excitement in the crowd. A few metres before the full-back, the No10 holds both arms out wide, waving the ball in one hand like a charm, and mimics a wobble with criss-crossing legs, in response to which the full-back falls over backwards. The crowd bellows with joy as the No10 glides on, but there is a covering winger who has him in his sights. Just before the tackle, Dusty's hero – although Dusty is unaware that this is what the blond No10 has become to him – flings out a long pass, and the white winger scores in the corner.

The roar of the gathering seems to impart movement to the very ground beneath their feet. But it's not like the pump boards at home. The ground here is solid and not designed for energy generation. This energy is intense, and there is a quality of wildness to it. Most of all, though, it is unharnessed – energy generation of a gratuitous kind, which rattles the old stadium and flies off into the air. Dusty cannot help it. He lets himself become a part of the multitude, as they soar ecstatically on the back of their wild ritual, until a perfect stillness settles when the blond No10 lines up the conversion from the touchline.

Alanis glances from face to tautened face. She is gasping for air. Her temperature is high. This has been an appalling experience. She knew it was a bad idea the moment she stepped among these natives, the Lapsed Era garments hanging loosely off their bodies, an affront to the virtues of heat retention. They turn their menacing eyes on her, some horrifyingly withered by excess diminishment, others juvenile and of no organised programme.

She wants to leave, but Dusty is not responding to her appeals. When she cried out to him in her distress just then, he did not come to her aid. He had, by her best assessment, become a wild animal, indistinguishable from the savages surrounding them, his face contorted in a rictus of the most violent aspect, his arms – oh, those masterful, most coordinated arms – shaking the air without method or reason. His face was red, a vein proud in his neck, and he screamed – how he screamed! That model of focused energy had quite unwound, spewing himself uselessly into the general incontinence.

She tries to whisper to him but feels weak and, anyway, does not want to draw attention to herself, now that a terrifying silence has so suddenly descended. The faces of these people are bound up in tension. Some stare intently at the pitch, others can only look away. Alanis is sick, that's what she is, she's sick! She feels oh so keenly the potential energy in the natives and knows it will not amount to anything worthwhile.

There is a thud from the direction of the pitch, a gasp rises up from somewhere, and then it happens. It starts behind the goal to her left, but soon the hopeless stadium is consumed by it. The energy, oh, the energy! Rushing skywards in a torrent, never to be put to use. She cries out to Dusty again, but it is to no avail. She can't possibly be heard above the chaos. People pump their fists against nothing and leap up and down on an unyielding platform that will never impart movement to a turbine. They throw their arms round each other, squeezing no more than the air from their chests. Dusty is among them. He has been seized by a bear of a man and returns his attentions in kind.

Alanis is swooning now amid the indiscriminate release of energy. But, just before she loses consciousness, the surge morphs into something with a kind of structure at least, a discernible coherence. The formless din coalesces into a chant that rises around the stadium:

'Ivon! Ivon! Ivon!'

III

Alanis hovers on the threshold of the women's quarters of the Swansea West Hostel for the English. 'I need to be at home,' she says. 'But, as we're beyond the Fence and you won't take me back, a hostel room will have to do.'

'I'm sorry, A. I'm just… I'm not ready to leave yet. Who knows if we'll get a chance to come here again. There's more I want to see.'

'Oh, joules! I hope I never have to come here again! What a horrible place!'

'You're sure you don't want a bout in one of the cots? Think of the prolactin release.'

'What's the point? We're off the Grid.'

'That doesn't matter. Coitus isn't just for the good of society. It has personal benefits as well.'

'Oh, Dusty, I'm not in the mood.'

He doesn't push it. Dusty and Alanis need some time apart. He leaves the hostel and steps into the aero, while she retires to her room.

He feels bad that Alanis has suffered such a severe reaction to being in Wales, but the truth is he needs some time alone himself. Wales is having a profound effect on him too. He has to return to Gower, and it is better that he does so unencumbered. Indeed, it would be intolerable not to.

Although he did not faint like Alanis, he stepped into that crude arena earlier in the day as if into a kink in his consciousness. When he emerged, supporting Alanis, who quivered in recovery from her turn, it was with an enlivened soul. Enlivened yet unfulfilled, for now he can perceive the vast shadow in his head of a lost personality, just as he fizzes with excitement at its discovery. His brush with Lapsed Era sport feels like the consummation of those little overthrows of discipline that have swept through him since decommission. It's confirmation that he is a new man. Did he, in fact, lose consciousness for just a split second when Ivon won the match for the team in white? He cannot be sure. The intensity of the moment, and the communality of it, transformed him. How could he, after the life he has led, be so suddenly surprised by sport?

A beep in his head signals the arrival of a pulse. But this one has been sent anonymously. He lowers his elbow from the open window. An anonymous pulse. The sender would appear to have something to hide – and, more interestingly, the authority to hide it. 'The white rose mumbles,' the message reads. Dusty is confounded. What can it mean? Who can mean it?

Just as he is trying to remember where he has seen the word 'mumbles' lately, there it appears again – on a road sign. It's a town. Mumbles is a town. And Dusty is heading towards it, towards the very place an anonymous sender has just directed him. He lifts his foot from the pedal. The agency of forces beyond his control has felt powerful since he passed through the Fence. But this is why he did it. The unknown. He presses his foot down again.

The stadium appears again to his right. He dares not stop this time. He will return, but for now he must take what it has given and press on – to Mumbles.

It is warm, and Dusty revels again in the freedom to have his window down while in motion. He lowers the passenger window too and gasps in the rushing air. Soon he is surrounded by grass, from which, intermittently, sprout goalposts, rugby and football, side by side, seemingly interchangeable times. He sees a new beauty in their isolation, and a purity, lifted clear from infrastructure and duty, as if the sports needed no purpose. And, all the while, to the eastern yonder, the waters of Swansea Bay sit serenely, here and there revealing themselves in an undulation of the grassy downs.

A sign announces that he is entering Mumbles at last. The road hugs the coast, and Dusty parks his aero in a space overlooking the bay. He steps out and stretches, taking in the view, warmed by the early-evening sun behind him. Mumbles awaits to the south, heavy with brick and concrete, but honest and tantalising, so hopelessly inefficient and endearing. Dusty longs to be accepted by the town, yet feels too far outside for that to be possible.

A building of brick and wood dominates at the first corner of town. Dusty slows as he walks past, and then stops. That feeling of powerlessness again, headlong inevitability. There, high on the wall, sits a large sign that reads, 'The White Rose'. He has been delivered.

People are sitting outside in postures of repose, as if in recovery but without lying down.

'Dusty?' murmurs one of them in a voice that, impossibly, is familiar to him. And then, more stridently: 'Dusty Noble! It is you! Fuckin' hell!'

Chilled, Dusty turns to his right to see a weather-beaten man sitting at a table. He knows immediately that he knows him, but how does he? How *could* he?

Before he can untangle the strands of his memory, the man continues: 'You don't have a fucking clue who I am, do you?'

He recognises the face, he recognises the voice, but they are not as he remembers. The face is scored and leathery and the hair long, which means this man has not been on Dusty's side of the Fence for years, and the voice is inflected with a sing-song lilt, like those of the natives who came to Alanis's aid at the rugby match that afternoon.

'It's Ricky,' says the man. 'Ricky Tribute. Remember?'

Dusty is dumb. Ricky Tribute. The name is dropped, and after the voice and sight of the man a cascade of memories follows, not called to mind in…well, he doesn't know how long. It *is* him. But how?

Ricky gets to his feet and holds out his hand at an unusual angle, low and tilting straight at him. Dusty instinctively raises his hand in a higher gesture, angling upwards, then hesitates.

'Sorry,' says Ricky and corrects the alignment of his arm, so that their hands meet above their elbows in the Perpetual way. 'We shake differently over here.'

As Ricky pulls Dusty's hand to his breast, he brings round his left arm and squeezes him in a firm hold. Dusty stands stock still with his old comrade's breath warm in his ear.

Ricky lets out a kind of growl, as he shakes him gently. 'It's good to see you, butt!' he says. 'Come on, sit down! Let me get you a drink! What you doing here? Surely, they haven't exiled the great Dusty Noble?'

Slowly, as if beginning to thaw, Dusty takes a seat at the metal table. The chair is metal, too, and he wonders how long he will be sitting in it. Ricky resumes position in the chair opposite. He seems to have no other business here but to sit. It doesn't look as if he has anything else in mind for Dusty, either. Mesmerised, Dusty stares at him and begins to pick out from the disintegration of old age a face he knew well.

'Ricky,' he mutters in a trance. 'They… Where have you *been*?'

Ricky laughs. 'Told you I'd departed, did they? Never did like that phrase, "premature departure". In Wales, death is death, no matter how old you are. Defect of the heart was the reason given out. Which I suppose was true in a way. I fell in love!'

Gazing into Ricky's face brings to mind for the first time their days at London Cricket, the neglected memories juddering up off the floor as if stiff and made of iron. They'd come through the Academy together, the most precocious of the year's batch of London batsmen. But Ricky had always had discipline problems, liable to lose concentration, and sometimes even his temper. Dusty remembers one match at Trafford against the North West. When would that have been? They were young men. Ricky was given out, an edge to the keeper. Dusty watched from the other end of the wicket as Ricky tore off his helmet and raged at the arena, his face burning, his mouth pulsing in a paroxysm of fury, like a fish gasping in air, powerless against the thunder of the stadium. They all knew he was in trouble then. He genuinely seemed to believe that he was right and the computer wrong. Sometimes an edge can be so slight that the batsman himself cannot feel it, but to deny the verdict of the very hardware designed to measure it was chronic Misalignment.

Was that the last time he'd seen him? It may well be that the news of his premature departure came through about then. Defect of the heart, was it? No one thought too much of it at the time. What startles Dusty now is that Ricky was evidently not shut down.

'What happened to you?' he whispers in bewilderment.

Ricky reaches out for the glass of golden liquid in front of him, the same stuff as the natives drank at St Helen's. It is probably not isotonic, Dusty tells himself. He's heard about Alcohol, the Welsh drink.

'First let's get you a pint.'

Ricky calls out to a woman standing at a nearby table. 'Brenda! Can we have two lagers here, please, lovely!' He winks at Dusty. 'You'll love it!

'What happened to me?' he continues, drinking again from his glass. 'Shit. Last time I'd a seen you would be twenty-six years ago, is it? You remember Dee Januarie?' Dusty nods vaguely. 'She was at the Academy with us, 2095 batch, like we were. Short black hair. A little fire-cracker. Middle-order batsman, like us. You must remember! Fuck, she was fit! Still is, mind!' And he tails off for a moment into guttural laughter.

'Anyway, she was left-handed, middle order; I was left-handed, middle order; both elite. So, we applied for a procreation certificate. She qualified for a sabbatical to have the baby. Sorry, infant. It was a no-brainer. They had to go for it. It never even crossed our minds they wouldn't. But did they? Did they fuck! The bastards turned us down! "Introversively inclined", that's how they classified our relationship. It was irregular. Turned out they'd had us under surveillance for a while. They knew about us before we even did. Because, I tell you what, it was only when they denied us that we realised. We hadn't applied for it so we could improve the gene pool, or contribute another infant batsman to the crèches. We'd applied because we wanted to come together and create a new person. Can you see the difference, Dusty? It's subtle. So subtle we hadn't realised. The thing is, it had to be Dee, and it had to be me. Not because of our genes or our pedigree or anything, but because we just wanted to…with each other. Oh, fuck. I'm not explaining this very well, am I? It wasn't a tactical thing, put it that way. We were in love. We know that now. We knew it the minute we got here. But things are different on the other side of the Fence, aren't they? In England, we were just confused.'

'They've done away with procreation now,' says Dusty, simply to ground himself in a conversation he feels he might float away from at any moment. 'It's all done in a lab these days. Deliberate Genetic Fusion they call it. DGF. Taken it out of our hands altogether.'

'Doesn't surprise me. They were always waiting for technology to fix that. Artificial uterus, is it?'

'Partly. Autosome splicing. Gamete cultivation. You can have four or five parents and none of them ever touches another.'

'Neat.'

'I know. Too neat, don't you think?'

'I'm glad you said that, Dusty, as an Englishman. To me, it's fuckin' horrific. Not the Welsh way at all.'

Brenda appears bearing a tray of lagers. She places two of them on the table.

'Who's your friend, Ricky?' she says. 'Or is he your son?'

'Cheeky cow! He's the same age as me, he is! Brenda, this is Dusty. He's from England.'

'I know! I just love those outfits of theirs! So sexy! I'll put these on your tab, is it?'

She picks up the glass Ricky had been drinking from, which is now empty, takes up her tray and moves on to another table.

'Anyway,' says Ricky, 'cheers! Good to see you, mun! What the fuck you doin' here?'

Dusty stares in wonder at his old comrade, as Ricky lifts the latest glass to his lips. They really are going to sit here for no other reason than to talk. And drink. He looks anxiously at the glass Brenda has placed in front of him. It is almost certainly Alcohol. He is troubled by the little bubbles that pulse through it, as if the drink were alive.

'This is lager,' says Ricky. 'Have you had some?'

'No. Why the bubbles?'

Ricky laughs. 'You've obviously never been this side of the Fence before! The bubbles are harmless. Carbon dioxide, mainly. They can mess with your stomach a bit, which is why you'd never find fizzy drinks in your world, but, hey, they taste good, so what the fuck, eh?'

Almost as an affront to his world, Dusty takes up the glass and drinks. It is bitter, cold and explosive. The bubbles protest in his mouth, but the temperature is even more surprising, so far below the ambient that he can feel the progress of the lager even into his stomach. He doesn't like it, but it's new and at odds with his world. And, in that respect, it is perfectly in tune with his constitution now. Isotonic indeed.

'So, you and Dee were denied...'

'Yeah,' sighs Ricky, 'so not only did they deny us the procreation certificate, they put a restraining order on us. Every time we came within a hundred metres of each other, the fucking alarm would go off and some agency cunt would pitch up within a minute. Oh, it killed me! You know I wasn't the most balanced of citizens at the best of times, but I lost the plot then. They took me in, and I was expecting the works – Assimilation and all that, maybe even shutdown. And they did put forward shutdown as an option. But they also offered me deportation to Wales. I kept asking them about Dee, and one day they said they were offering her deportation too. So that was it. We took exile.'

'They deported you? But that's incredible!'

'I know. I didn't stop to ask.'

'You were an elite. One of the best. They wouldn't just send you away for a personality flaw. Assimilation would fix that.'

Ricky shrugs. 'This was twenty-five years ago, remember. Assimilation was a bit hit and miss back then. But, yeah, you'd a thought they'd try. What can I say? They didn't. And here I am to prove it. So's Dee, by the way. We're still together. Best fucking decision of our lives, to take exile. This is the greatest country on Earth.'

Dusty drinks again and holds his face in the vessel for a moment, its bubbles and swirls mirroring the giddiness of his brain. Here he is, indulging in conversation for its own sake, looking backwards without revulsion into the verboten Past. But this is why he came, to sample a new way of life. The more he gives in to it, the easier and more satisfying it becomes.

'You haven't told me why you're here,' says Ricky. 'If they shouldn't a let me go, they sure as fuck weren't going to let you. You must have been decommissioned by now.'

Dusty nods. 'I'm here on holiday. I was awarded a load of travel credits at the end of my service, and I had this urge to come to Wales.'

'I'm impressed. Not many do. And we hardly ever see any Perpetuals here without a guide. Where's yours?'

'Didn't want one.'

'Cool.'

'But I did get some guidance. A message came through a little while ago saying, "The White Rose, Mumbles". That can't have been from you, can it?'

Ricky shrugs and shakes his head. 'Did you get a number?'

'It was anonymous.'

'I hate that.'

Dusty takes another swig and draws in a breath, slow and full. He is free here. Until Monday night, he has no business with England. He can speak his mind to Ricky. 'I've been struggling,' he says. 'Since decommission, I've not been sure about anything. I keep having strange dreams.'

'Oh, yeah?'

'One in particular comes back again and again. It's as if I'm flying, with the air rushing past my head. Defying authority somehow.'

'I've had that dream,' says Ricky.

'What?'

'It's a biplane.'

'A what?'

'A biplane. It's an old-fashioned aeroplane from hundreds of years ago. The first planes ever built, I think. They have a propeller at the front, two wings on either side, a couple of open-air seats, one behind the other.'

'That's it!' Dusty gasps. He hadn't known what it was, or even what it looked like, but now that Ricky's described it he can see it clearly.

'You sometimes see them being flown round here.'

'And you dream about them, too?'

'Always have done. And the moment I saw a biplane I suddenly knew what the dream was. Then when I had the dream again I could see the plane clearly. Still have it from time to time.'

'What does it mean?'

'Never really thought about it. Dee has them, too.'

'*What?* And you don't think it a bit odd? That we all have the same dream?'

'I suppose it is. Shall we go in? It's getting a bit chilly. Welsh clothing's not as intelligent as yours.'

The air inside the White Rose is dark and heavy, with minimal light admitted through the mean apertures of Lapsed Era architecture. A few quaint push-button machines flash in one corner; otherwise the room is lit by an arrangement of lamps on the wall, each inexplicably covered. A sweet, dull smell pervades, making Dusty wary even of where he places his feet. Behind a counter, a bearded man with that distinctive local quality to his voice greets Ricky with some exuberance. He pours two more glasses of lager.

Ricky leads Dusty into one of the darker corners of the room and introduces him to a figure whose face is turned away, obscured by shadow. Dusty comes round to take his outstretched hand, which is when he notices something is wrong. The man is diminished to the point of inhumanity, a bent, wrinkled humanoid without teeth or hair.

'Tom's ninety-seven years old,' explains Ricky. 'He was born and bred here. Lived through the last days of the Lapsed Era.'

At first, Dusty is afraid to look Tom in the eye, and not just because of his debilitation. Those eyes have seen a time before the Fence. To look into them, it seems to Dusty, is to conceive of the Past as something more than a discrete curiosity housed in the museum they call Wales.

All the more disconcerting is the ludicrous defiance of the old man, when his suspicions that Dusty is English are confirmed. 'I was there!' he rails. 'The Millennium Match, January first 2066! What a game! Emyr Delaney! Ryan Pugh! You English couldn't lay a finger on us! Fair battered you, we did! And you've never played us since!'

Ricky looks at Dusty and laughs uproariously, too uproariously. He wants Dusty to like Tom.

'Tell him the whole story, Tom,' says Ricky. 'He's English! He doesn't know! Remember what I was like when I first came here. Give him the history lesson, Tom, like you gave me!'

There is a lustre in Tom's stare, at odds with the degradation of the rest of him. The skin sags hideously beneath his eyes, as if trying to turn them out of his head, but the intensity is unanswerable. Dusty is in thrall.

'The Welshman will always play what's in front of him,' says Tom. 'That's why we're God's people! You English! You never think on your feet! You were never going to beat us!'

'Beat you?' says Dusty, rubbing the top of his head, which seems to grow heavier by the moment.

'They were all like you, before the Earth moved and the air thickened. When I was born, the world swarmed with folk. Too many of them, for sure! Humans thought they'd taken control of the game, what with all their burning and breathing and building. But the Earth, she plays what she sees too, she does, like a good fly-half, and a rolling maul, even of ten billion folk, was never going to pin her in her own twenty-two. Oh no! She broke out! Boom! Volcanoes! The Decade of Fire! And she got a rumble going with her earthquakes. She ripped up the turf and unleashed the foulest vapours into the air, methane, sulphur, carbon dioxide. The seas responded and pounded the shores of the Americas and Asia. Fires raged throughout the world. The air grew hot and thick to breathe.

'And so came disease. The disease to end them all. The Sofa Bug we called it. Devastating it was, attacking the respiratory system, preying on those of inefficient breath, ripping through them like the fires. The old folk couldn't take it. By the time I was a boy, my grandparents and their many brothers and sisters had died. So had my dear father, God rest his soul.

'The fat folk were next. Even boys and girls my own age perished, if they weren't athletically inclined. Humans had grown too much in every way, they had. In my prime I was a good 5 feet 9 inches and nigh on 12 stone, but I would have been *small*, so small, compared to the folk in those days. My size was what saved me and all the others like me. Because the big ones fell. Death was ever-present. The streets became lawless. Folk hallucinated and were nauseous. They threw themselves from high windows and fought each other over the slightest gesture or attitude. By the early 2060s, when I became a man, all but the physically fittest had died. The population of Wales used to be four million, you know! We lost almost half our number. And the English lost three-quarters, so they say.'

Dusty shakes his head, trying to rid it of the fantastical vision, which seeps in to cloud the very corridors of his mind. 'This happened in England?' he murmurs, but his voice feels far away and someone else's. Ricky wears a faint frown as he studies him.

'It happened the world over! Earth lay open now, like a boulder of clay, ready for visionaries to shape.' Tom's eyes close, and when they reopen, a glaze has spread across them, a weariness at the passing years that Dusty can never hope to encompass. 'That was when we broke away. The poor nations were also the least bloated, and we in Wales came out of the trouble OK, compared to everyone else. But the rest of the world had become so sickened by what they had seen – and yet so fit – that peace and physical exercise became the ideals, their only ideals. There was disgust at the lazy ways of the past. They turned their back on history. As for love, for mystery, spirituality... Ha! Gone, they were. Like those poor folk too big for their own good. The games became everything. Play was dead. Soon they were settling international disputes through sport. Oh, I know how it is on your side of the Fence! Life for you is nothing but a competition, a sick, global competition. Prosperity for the victors! Hardship for the losers! Where's the compassion? Where's the soul? We weren't for that in Wales! When the English put up their energy temples across the land, they wanted to take us with them. We refused. Our way of life was at stake.'

Dusty tries to speak, to gainsay the demolishment of his universe, but the words will not form, the tongue will not move.

Tom's mouth is bent in what could be a smile, could be a sneer. 'We chose rugby as the sport to settle the dispute, of course we did! Our prerogative as defendants. And so came to pass the greatest match in Welsh history. January first, 2066. The Millennium Stadium was packed with one in thirty of every person in the land, each with a passion for their homeland that I swear had beaten the dull-eyed Englishmen before a ball had been kicked! No Welshman there ever forgot that day! We won! But not just the match. We won the right to continue in the old ways. We returned to the ancient mines and lived on in love and laughter, while the rest of the world worked their pedals.'

Tears have gathered in Tom's eyes. He is still, but he does not talk any more.

'That was the year of the Great British Partition,' says Ricky quietly. 'The year the Fence went up and perpetuation infrastructure was rolled out across England and Scotland. Dusty, are you all right?'

It is all Dusty can do to nod in acknowledgement. An invasion of his very person is being worked, physical and emotional, by what he does not know. Never has he spent so long sitting for no purpose; never has he stood so squarely in front of the Past and entertained it not just as a hypothetical place and way of life but as a living continuum, running all the way through to the present from what has gone before, that dirty, twisted parody of existence, the Lapsed Era, now being presented to him as progenitor of everything he has known. Not without reason does Perpetual society shield its citizens from exposure to the idea, for, truly, it works a palsy on him now. His body and perception feel as if they are bending. The voices of the others seem loud yet from another place, or dimension; the room, indeed the entire sweep of his vision, lists alarmingly; there is an uprising in his stomach. He panics and rises to his feet, clutching at chairs and tables for the feeling that the earth is swaying.

And then the air is rushing past him again. He feels disengaged, as he does in his dreams. He is in the flying machine. He can see it clearly now: the steel-grey wings, held together by black struts and wires that rattle ridiculously against the air, the furious propeller on the nose of the plane, the angelic dials in front of him, the control stick, which moves as if guided by the hand of another. He is flying low to the ground, close to six stanchions, each bearing a flat, featureless face cocked forwards

45

to the ground, between which the plane dips, before soaring up into a clear sky. The sun is strong above him, and in the distance lies the rich blue sea. He is exhilarated, he is free. The control stick moves again, and with it the plane. He becomes aware of a pilot in the cockpit in front. Through goggles, Dusty can make out blond locks, which flutter in the turbulence. The pilot turns to him and smiles. Dusty recognises him immediately.

It is Ivon.

※

Consciousness descends on Dusty slowly. There is a terrible pain in his head, his brain seeming to pulse against the inside of it. He opens his eyes to find himself in an unfamiliar room, lying on something soft and yielding, which has cultivated an ache in his neck. Time and some painful effort reveal it to be an item of Lapsed Era furniture, long, like a couch but with backing on three sides.

Dusty heaves himself into an upright position, and the musty softness of the couch shifts as if to swallow him. There is protest in his stomach. It begins to dawn on him that he is in somebody else's home. He gasps and leans forward. Somebody else's home?! How could he have transgressed so heinously? He has no memory of it, yet here he is. Somebody else's home. The shame tortures him. But is it just the shame? There is pain too. He doubles up, holding his head, muttering to his restless stomach.

'Ah! He's awake!' says a voice behind him, which he recognises as Ricky's. 'How you feeling, butt?'

Dusty hauls himself round to see Ricky standing in a kitchen the other side of a counter behind him.

Ricky's voice is jocular. 'You made quite a spectacle of yourself!' he says, as if it had been a good thing. 'Here, have some of this. It's basically a caffeine supplement dissolved in water. We call it coffee.'

Dusty takes the cup and stares into a liquid of impenetrable darkness.

'I did wonder whether I should have bought you those lagers,' Ricky went on. 'But sometimes you see an old friend and you can't help yourself, can you? It turns out you're what we would call a complete fucking lightweight!' He roars with laughter, the same way he did the night before. 'Still, I don't blame you. I was the same when I first came here. It's something you need to get used to, Alcohol. All the same. Two pints?! Ha, ha, ha!'

'Ricky,' whispers Dusty, bewildered. 'Ricky. I'm so sorry. What am I doing here?'

'What do you think? You were paralytic. I brought you home, you silly twat!'

'But, Ricky, it's, it's. Ricky, this is…your *home.*'

Ricky laughs again, coming round to join him. 'Oh, we don't worry about that in this country! In Wales, your home is something you throw open to people.'

Dusty stares at him, bewildered. '"A home of your own and for you alone".' He recites the mantra without thinking.

'Oh, please! That "home of your own" shit. It's fucking sad, don't you think? Totally different mindset over here. This place has heart. No conditioning from birth to love a commune. In Wales, you love *people*, individuals – and you do it because you want to. Welcoming them into your home is just one way of showing that.' He flops down on the adjacent couch. 'And you'll always be welcome in mine, butt!'

Dusty has known Ricky all his life, even if he has been missing for more than half of it. He remembers the upturned nose, a picture of impudence in the young boy, but now a broader, duller feature, its pores accentuated, each a tiny indentation. Wispy little purple lines grow out across his cheeks. The hair is as blond as ever, but it is long and unkempt. He has become overgrown with the weeds of age. Yet Dusty can make out the young lad he once knew, and a curious melancholy tugs at him.

He is broken from it by the sound of footsteps approaching, light and assured.

'Here he is!' Ricky cries with evident delight at the coming of someone else into the room.

It's as if Dusty knows who it is before he turns round. He knows, too, the significance of this moment to his life before he girds himself to embrace it.

'All right, Dad!' says a rich Welsh voice that already feels familiar to him. He keeps his eyes on Ricky instead of turning to face the newcomer.

Ricky smiles at Dusty. 'I'd like you to meet an old friend of mine! This is Dusty! Dusty, this is my son. Ivon.'

Only then does Dusty force himself to look away from Ricky towards his progeny, from the reflection to the man himself. And there, standing tall and impressive before him, is the blond fly-half from yesterday's match.

'Pleased to meet you,' Ivon says cheerily, offering his hand.

Dusty blushes inexplicably. He finds himself unable to speak, but takes Ivon's hand in the Lapsed Era way, so as to do something.

'How's yer head?!' Ivon laughs. 'Looks like you two had a good night!'

'It was going brilliantly, until Dusty passed out,' says Ricky. 'Can't take his grog. He's from England.'

'Yeah. I noticed your kit. What you doing over here?'

'He's on holiday. Chose Wales of all places!'

'Sweet! Anyone want a coffee?'

'We're all right, thanks.'

Ivon heads into the kitchen.

'Is Ivon a rugby athlete?' Dusty asks Ricky.

'Oh yeah! And a footballer, a cricketer. You name it. Quite the superstar round these parts. Chip off the old block, I tell ya! He was on fire yesterday against Neath. Practically beat them on his own.'

'Ricky, I was there. Never seen anything like it.'

'You were there! What, at St Helen's?'

'I was driving past. Heard the noise and stopped to take a look. I think it's changed my life. I've never known such, such emotion.'

'That's Welsh rugby for you. It's what they call here the paradox of sport. When it doesn't matter, it matters so much more. I remember what it was like in England. Oh, we wanted to win! Of course we did! It meant everything. It could be the difference between comfort and hardship for everyone. But it was mundane, wasn't it? The people wished for our success, but it wasn't emotional. Like here – we all want unemployment to come down, and we feel more confident and secure when it does. We recognise it as more "important" than beating Neath. But does it move us like beating Neath? Does it fuck! That's what blew me away when I first came here. The sheer passion for sport and its lack of importance.'

Ivon sits down next to his father, blowing into his coffee. The steam rises up in front of his boyish face and into an unruly thicket of the brightest hair. 'What you drivelling on about now, Dad?'

'Dusty was at the game yesterday!'

'Oh yeah? Enjoy it?'

'Course he did. He says he's never seen anything like it in his life! And I know for a fact he hasn't!'

'You should come down this afternoon,' says Ivon.

Dusty feels his cheeks warm again at the mere invitation. He is finding it hard to be normal, conscious of a strong desire to get to know Ivon, to be his friend, to impress him. And yet this impulse is neutered by a kind of fear of the boy.

'Of course!' cries Ricky. 'Ivon's playing cricket at St Helen's this afternoon! Come along!'

'Cricket?!' Dusty replies, very specifically to Ricky. 'But he's a rugby athlete!'

'He's a sportsman! You can play as many sports as you like here. Welcome to paradise! Welcome to Wales!'

'He's contesting cricket today at the very same place he contested rugby yesterday?'

Ricky nods, grinning. Dusty shakes his head in disbelief.

'And tell me, Ricky. How old is Ivon?'

'Twenty-four, aren't you?'

Ivon nods.

'And you came here with Dee how long ago?'

'I see what you're getting at. And, yes, you're right. Ivon was conceived as soon as we got here. He's the child the English denied us.'

'So, Dad tells me you used to bat with him in England.'

A nervousness, light and airy, flares up in Dusty's stomach. Ivon has stepped out of the whirligig of well-wishers in the clubhouse bar at St Helen's to initiate conversation with him. The room is noisy and busy, under the warm gaze of teams gone by, enshrined in murky photographs on the walls, some of them centuries old. Hundreds of people laugh and talk about the tour de force they have watched that afternoon from the man standing before Dusty now. In Wales, a cricketer has the opportunity to bat, bowl *and* field. Ivon was the best at all three today. Dusty could see, for the first time, echoes of Ricky, as he rattled up boundaries with a cleanness of shot uncorrupted by his natural bravado.

'I did,' replies Dusty. 'We came up through the academies together. He was productive.'

'Productive?' Ivon laughs. 'You make it sound as if he worked!'

'Well, he did. We all did. Still do.'

'No wonder he left! He says you were pretty good, as well.'

'I did my bit.'

Ivon looks away for a second and then back, intently, at Dusty. The eyebrows are light and insubstantial, but they arch into a striking pose of mischief and urgency. 'Take me back with you!' he says. 'I want to show them what they missed.'

His eyes appear blue, but Dusty sees now that it is an indigo corona around each that gives that impression. The iris within is a lucent turmoil of light and dark, falling, as if through space, into the pupil.

Take him back? Dusty wants to laugh at the idea. A Welshman in England! It could never be!

But what audaciousness even to think of it! Typical of the boy! And – Dusty's mind is racing – why shouldn't it happen? It never *has*, to his knowledge, but that's not the same. These days London would try anything to improve their situation. Take him back? Already, Dusty is wondering how Ivon would fare in England, how England would handle Ivon.

'Has Ricky told you anything about England?'

'He's told me it's all about sport. Day and night. He's told me I'd hate it, but that's bollocks! I adore sport. It'd be a dream come true. But he doesn't like to talk about it.'

Dusty smiles. Ricky never liked it in England. The revelation ought to send Dusty reeling, but in this curious, melty land it registers as no more than the latest surprise. And is it because he's here that Dusty now wonders if he ever liked it in England himself?

'It's a harsh environment,' he says. 'If you did make it as an elite, the weight of responsibility would be great. And, if you didn't make it, trust me, you wouldn't want to be there.

What you have here is so much more…loving.' Dusty surprises himself with his choice of word.

'Oh! Do you think I could? Make it, I mean? How awesome would that be!'

'It's impossible to say for sure. But I think you have something I've never seen before. Whether that's a good thing…I can run a test to check your cat score qualifies you for elite level, but, from what I've seen, I'm sure it will.'

'Cat score?'

'Coordination aptitude test.'

'Shit. You measure coordination?'

'Welcome to England.'

'Bring it on! I love it!'

Ricky bursts into their conversation, swilling another glass of lager. Dee is with him, and, since Ricky reintroduced them earlier in the day, Dusty begins to remember her more clearly from their days in the Academy. She has aged better than Ricky. A poignant streak of grey runs through her black bob, but she is fresh and beautiful.

'And what are you two talking about?' he says, putting an arm round Ivon.

'I was just speculating on what Ivon's cat score would be.'

'I can tell you what it was with a cricket bat when he was sixteen: six by four at eighty.'

'*What?*'

'I know.'

'And that was when he was sixteen?'

'Yup.'

'What did you use?'

'An old test bat from the Academy. Heat-sensitive technology. I'm sure you use something more accurate these days.'

'But still. Those are the sort of figures the DGF batsmen are producing. For a bred athlete, that's unheard of. I mean, he's not even an athlete. No disrespect, Ivon. On the contrary. If those scores are correct. For a Welshman…'

'I don't know why you're so fucking surprised. Don't forget, Dee and I are both pure-breeds. If it hadn't been for the personality defects, our procreation certificate would have been issued as a priority. Ivon would be batting for England by now.'

Ivon bursts out laughing. 'Whoa! What you two on about?!'

'This is perpetual talk,' says Dee. Her voice, Dusty notices, is unaffected by the local inflexion. 'The mean distance of your points of contact from the sweet spot of the test bat was 6mm with a standard deviation of 4 across 100 balls bowled at 80 miles an hour.'

Ivon laughs again. 'Whoosh!' he says, sweeping his hand over his head.

'It means you're very coordinated, dear.'

'How do you know all this?' Ivon asks Ricky.

'You remember that old bat of mine you used to practise with? It had the sweet spot marked on it, and I told you to always try to hit the ball at the sweet spot. Well, it could measure how accurately and consistently you were doing it.'

'So why didn't you tell me?'

'I did, but you weren't interested. You just wanted to play. And you were right. This is the sort of shit that ruins a player.'

'Ivon wants to come back to England with me.'

Dusty holds his breath. He's not sure why he said that. Is something about Ricky's manner offending him, the one who stayed in England and worked every day of his life to keep the turbines turning? Or is it just that he is falling for the Welsh way, with its accent on spontaneity and looseness?

Ricky removes his arm from round Ivon's shoulders and stiffens. 'You do not want to go to England,' he says quietly.

'Oh, come on, Dad. Let's not do this.'

'Let's not do what?'

'You know. "England's no place for people like us. It sounds like heaven, but it's a hell on earth. Sport isn't everything. Blah, blah, blah."'

The sun has not been kind to Ricky today. He glows red, particularly among the roots of his thinning hair. 'Oh, so Big Shot knows best, does he?' he says, his voice on the rise.

'Ricky,' says Dee.

'You know what to expect, do you? England holds no fears for Ivon. Ivon is invincible! Ivon will prevail! I'll tell you one thing, my lad: Ivon will get chewed up and spat out!'

'Why, Dad? Look at Dusty! He's lived in England all his life. He's come out of it all right.'

'Dusty Noble is the product of a system. Dusty Noble is a machine. You are a free spirit, Ivon. Here! *Here*! Nowhere else!'

'But you heard what Dusty thinks about my…my… fucking…coordination results! He thinks I've got something!'

'Fuck your cat scores, Ivon! And your reflex speed! Fuck it all! Which is what you'll do if you go there! It's your soul you want to worry about. They haven't found a way to measure that, so they'll break it, crush it, take it out of the game. You will never play again. You'll train, you'll compete. You'll spend more time in sport than you ever thought possible. But. You. Will. Never. *Play*. Again. It'll kill you.'

'What? Like it killed you, Dad? Is that what this is about? It doesn't have to kill you, though, does it? Look at Dusty.'

'It does have to. It *does*. The love in your heart will die, and so will you. I know Dusty Noble looks a better man than I do. You probably look at him, then you look at me, and you've made your mind up about which way you want to go.' Ricky laughs. 'Fuck it. I can't stop you. But what does Dusty Noble have now, is all I'll say. Memories of a lot of runs, which he's not supposed to think about. A home of his own and for him alone.

A strong and efficient heart and smart clothing. And in, what, eleven years' time, is it, Dusty, he'll be switched off. Don't do it, Ivon. It'll kill you. And it'll kill me.'

As if it were burning hot, Ricky looks for somewhere to put down his glass, and without a word he heads for the door. He crosses the room as if through his own trail across Dusty's memory. Many years have passed since Dusty last watched that urgent, tortured gait, but how familiar it is! In their youth, Ricky walked away from countless partnerships in just such a way.

And now Dusty is arrested by the stirring of further memories. He is visited by the sense that Ricky and he share a special bond, over and above those distant hours they spent at the crease together. This one is important. He knows it is. But he is too new to remembering to have any chance of calling it to mind.

'I'm sorry, Dusty,' says Ivon sheepishly. He is flushed, too. His father's words have shaken him. Dusty finds himself disinclined to take Ivon back to England now, however intriguing the notion.

'Yes,' agrees Dee, 'yes, you shouldn't have had to hear that.'

Dusty raises a hand to signal his evenness of temper, which is genuine.

'But listen to your father, Ivon,' continues Dee. 'He is right about this. Don't underestimate the joy of what you do out there. And not just out there. In here, as well. The camaraderie, your friends, your family.'

'But I've done it, Mum. I want a new level. I want to see how far I can take it. I want to see how good I really am. Don't *you* want to see it, after the way they threw you out?'

'We will never see it. If you go to England, we will never see you again.'

'Oh, come on!'

Ivon looks to Dusty in appeal. The mere glance triggers that strange nervousness in him again. 'Elites are allowed to visit Wales,' Dusty says.

'And if he doesn't make elite? It takes more than a high cat score.'

'If he doesn't make elite, I'll bring him back.'

'As simple as that?'

Dusty fears it may not be as simple as that, but the imperative to please Ivon is strong.

'Ivon, your father and I were turned away from England because we didn't fit in. No one knows why – we just didn't see things the way everyone else did. But we do fit in here. And what goes for us will almost certainly go for you. Don't go to England, please.'

To Dusty's surprise, Ivon says nothing and hugs Dee.

'Oh, my boy,' she sighs.

'I should go,' says Dusty. 'Ivon, I think Ricky and Dee are right. It is a very different place, England, and I can't say with any honesty it's the place for you.'

He turns to leave.

'You'll come and see us again, won't you?' says Ivon.

Dusty smiles. 'Of course,' he says. And with a heaviness in his heart he picks his way through the busy, laughing room and out into the evening air.

✺

Back at the hostel, Dusty receives another message. It is anonymous again.

'Bring the Welshman back with you. There will be a permit at the Fence.'

He closes the message down. His mind is fizzing. It occurs to him that he hasn't once thought about Alanis. He checks his log. She's been trying to reach him, but he had thought it best to block her comms while he was away. He leaves his room in search of her.

IV

He should have taken a number, an address. Something. How could he have let such an opportunity slip through his grasp?

If you find yourself on the back foot, play your way out of it, like Dad always says. So here he is, just off the M4, on his way to take his chances at the Swansea West Hostel for the English. If Dusty is staying anywhere it is probably here. His bag is slung over a shoulder, just as it was when he first pitched up at St Helen's looking for a game all those years ago, and as it has been most weekends since. He's wearing kit – in this case an English suit. Or a fancy-dress one anyway. His lift has headed back into town. He's on his own. Time to perform.

The stakes are higher now. There's more than just a game to win, there's a life. And Mum and Dad don't have his back for this one. He takes no support with him, not even a blessing.

Last night, he had been decided. He was staying. Gower is home, after all, where his big heart was sculpted, like an unfurling blob of molten glass, by those important to him, Mum and Dad, his friends. Cerys.

Oh, Cerys...

But in the small hours of the morning he awoke. The glow of the weekend's wins had worn off. His stomach was a ferment of despair and hurt. Back in the room he'd grown up in, banished from her bed for the 125th night, her voice ringing through his head. 'It's too much!' The hangers-on, the limelight, his love for her, his intensity – all too much. He's too much.

It isn't getting easier. The small hours. The slump from weekend to the foot of next week.

But now he can see a way out. He is on edge, as if the biggest game is yet to come. He hopes the note he left his parents on the sideboard will explain, but he hasn't stopped to think since he resolved to leave, and the events of the past few hours – indeed, of his life to date – are just dimly discernible to him as outside his bubble. He has his game head on.

He strides into the foyer. It is clean, sterilised – like a hospital. There is a receptionist he notices out of the corner of his eye. She becomes agitated as he continues boldly on his way to the interior.

'Hello?' she calls, as he reaches a door. It begins to open, but a vicious little buzzer sounds, and it closes before it is even half across. He stands for a second, thwarted, his first delivery blocked by the English.

'Can I help you?'

He turns and saunters over to the desk, where stands a petite English girl, neat in her figure-hugging suit. He motions to his own suit and leans on the counter. 'Is it that obvious? That I'm not English. I thought I looked the part.'

'You look very fit, sir.'

'Well, thank you! I try my best. It's fancy dress, see. We all have English suits in Wales. They're not real ones, obviously, but everyone says I could be English, my costume looks so genuine. Woosnam's in Swansea. They do them best. I don't suppose you have Welsh parties in England, do you?'

The girl's complexion remains immaculate. 'Your chip.'

'What?'

'Your chip. You don't have one.'

Of course. The English chip. He should have remembered that. It takes more than a convincing costume to pass as English. Identification protocol extends beneath the skin. There's not much he can do about that. He changes tack.

'I'm here for Dusty Noble. I'm his guide today.'

'In which case, you would have a chip.'

'Really? Guides have them?! Fuck! Can you give me one?'

'What is your business with Mr Noble?'

'So he is here! Brilliant!'

The receptionist's nose twitches, and he senses a small victory.

'Can you just tell him that Ivon is here to see him? Thanks a lot.'

He waits only a couple of minutes before the door that had slid shut in his face opens with a sigh to admit Dusty into the foyer.

'Oh, Dusty! What a result! I'm so glad I've found you!'

'What brings you here?'

'It's decided. I'm coming to England.'

He's very difficult to read, Dusty. Ivon wants to throw himself at him. Here is his passport to England. It feels as if he's known him for years, rather than a few hours. Dusty gives off an air of authority, and kindliness. And precisely nothing. He gives away nothing. His expression is steady throughout it all. Even as Dad was laying into him last night. The product of a system. A machine.

To be switched off.

Dusty studies Ivon. Or is he looking through him, to something further away?

'Let me make a few comms.'

☀

There was only ever one cure for her, and that is the one being administered now. Alanis is going home.

It has been a horrible trip. To witness those scenes on Saturday was appalling, and the hours spent trying to recover since have been torturous. The realisation that she was off the Grid left her feeling isolated and vulnerable. She could draw none of the usual comforts, even though all of them were laid on. Everything was superficial without the security of nexus with the commune. She was cast adrift, her heat signature an insignificant, lonely speck out here in the wilderness.

The hostel room was peaceful and smooth, but it was not home. Her sessions in the volleyball simulator became little more than exercises in time-killing. As for her visit to the Lapsed Era Experience – the viewing platform, high up in the air, had set her recovery back again. Those ill-planned buildings seemed even more grotesque when viewed through a pair of teleglasses, rearing up in her vision like monsters of the imagination. But take the glasses off and the grand vista was no less disturbing, infested with plumes of smoke that snaked up insidiously into the blameless air. She chose not to risk the Past simulators at all. Her alignment certificate is fully up to date, but she couldn't face that level of exposure so soon after her real-life encounter with the Lapsed Era.

Now, though, she feels her recovery picking up as she leaves the room to meet Dusty in the aero park. All day yesterday there had been a block on his central chip when she'd tried to comm, adding to her sense of isolation. Had he imposed the block universally or just on her? Either way, he had returned last night and suggested a bout in one of the cots, a constitutional she agreed might do her some good. But they were off the Grid, and she had never known coitus for the sake of coitus. It didn't feel right. Dirty, gratuitous, no better than the feral ejaculations of those savages in the stadium on Saturday. She isn't sure it did her any good at all. And wasn't there something different about Dusty during their bout? Something, she doesn't know, something, something, well, yes, feral. Selfish. As if he were doing it for himself. As if he didn't care about anything, let alone her prolactin levels. As if she were no more than equipment.

There he is now, and to her relief she is pleased to see him. A new and shocking side of Dusty has been revealed on this trip, but she hopes to consign her experience of it to where it belongs, in the Past, discarded and irrelevant, along with the Lapsed Era. He looks masterful again out there in the sunshine beside the aero. Neat and contained.

And who is that with him? A younger man with the brightest blond hair. Tall, taller than Dusty, but not so economical in his bearing. There is something effervescent about him. He keeps running his hand through that hair of his, pushing it to one side. Alanis cannot understand why he doesn't just cut it. His arms are moving as he talks, his feet never still. As she steps out of the hostel to join them, she can see that the suit he wears is a parody, made of Lapsed Era fabrics. This is when she realises the man is Welsh.

She remains calm, and Dusty welcomes her. 'A, I'd like you to meet Ivon,' he says. 'He was the fly-half from the match on Saturday. He's coming to England with us. Ivon, this is Alanis.'

'Pleased to meet you,' the young man says.

Awkwardly, he takes her hand and pulls it into his chest. His suit really is too funny, but his hand is strong. The man is fit. Alanis likes him. She does not remember him from Saturday, but that is a good thing. She wonders why he's coming to London. She intends to make him feel welcome.

Dusty paces west, away from the Fence, from Ivon, Alanis and Border Control. He enjoys the feeling, however deceptive, that he is heading back to Wales. The pull of duty from the other side of the Fence will out, but for now he relishes being in the hinterland between two worlds. And, if he were free to choose, would he head east or west? He is surprised to find that he couldn't say – surprised and uneasy.

He leans against the quaint metallic barriers on the side of the road and rubs his feet across the tarmacadam, waiting for his comm to be connected. A couple of lumps of grit lie loose, and he smiles as he kicks them, superfluous, into the water many feet below. He looks up and follows the line of the Fence as it runs south and round, hugging the coastline of England, cordoning off its tenants not only from the wild land to the west but from the timelessness of the great river that rolls between them out to sea.

All of a sudden, he is through.

'Dusty, what can I do for you?' The words of Lana Defoe, Manager for Cricket, ring voicelessly throughout his brain.

'I'm at the Fence, about to re-enter England.'

Lana does not offer any comment. Dusty had hoped, in light of the mysterious messages he'd been receiving, that she would know what to say, but instead he can all but see his old friend studying him coolly from under a cocked eyebrow. 'And?'

'I've spent the last couple of days in Wales, and I've seen something extraordinary. I'm bringing someone back.'

'Someone?'

'He's Welsh.'

Dusty is taken aback to hear laughter. Lana doesn't do laughter. He can tell from the resonance that she is laughing out loud, not in her head. But purity of transmission is resumed when she speaks voicelessly after a second's pause. 'You can't bring a Welshman back to England. That's unheard of!'

'I can. I have a permit for him.'

'How?'

'That I don't know. It was waiting at the border. I received an anonymous pulse that said it would be.'

'Anonymous?'

'Yes.'

More silence.

'You've not been briefed on this then?' Dusty resumes.

'No.'

'Well, I have the permit here, but nothing else. Look, I don't know who's sending me these messages, but I'm telling you, even without them, I want to bring this boy back. Lana, you and I have seen a lot of cricketers in our time. Trust me, I've not seen anyone like this.'

'You've never been beyond the Fence, Dusty. They're quite different over there.'

'And his rugby… It might be even better. He contests in *both*.'

'This is highly irregular.'

'We've got to find him somewhere. I think he could be a great asset. If we don't take him, rugby will.'

'That's fine by me.'

'Just have a look at him.'

Dusty kicks more gravel into the river.

After a pause, Lana's tone is softer. 'There will be population matters to address.'

Dusty beams and turns towards the Fence, pacing in the direction of Ivon and Alanis, who talk against the smooth, shimmering backdrop behind them. 'Of course. He'll become an elite. I have no doubt of that.'

'So I assume.'

'But we can start him off in the tertiary class, if that helps with the population management.'

'He'll need to take a central chip, of course.'

'Yes. Yes, I'll talk to him about that.'

Lana sighs. It's another voiced interjection, and this from the meticulously contained Manager of Cricket. 'I'm very uncomfortable with this. The idea of a Welshman in society, it strikes me as dangerous. I don't know who you're getting these messages from – evidently someone in a position of authority.'

'Whoever it is will make themselves known.'

'So we must presume. You have the permit. He can come in. We'll find him accommodation for now, but he'll have to be tested like anyone else.'

'I'll get him tested tomorrow.'

Dusty is back at the border by the time the comm is ended.

'I've spoken to the Manager, and everything's in order.'

There is a glint in Ivon's eye. 'Were you just speaking to her then?'

'Yes.'

He laughs. 'I knew it! I could tell you were talking to someone. But your lips didn't move! So it *is* true!'

'What?'

'You English, you can talk telepathically!'

Dusty smiles and pats the back of his neck. He is pleased that Ivon has broached the subject himself. 'It's all in here. The central chip, which is not the same as the identity chip they'll be inserting into your hand in a minute. Through your central chip, you can communicate neurally with anyone else with a chip. Which means anyone in England.'

'Oh, I want me one of those!'

'Well, that was the next thing. A condition of entry is that you take one.'

'Sweet!'

'They'll need to insert it into your nervous system. It's a delicate procedure, and it's normally performed on three-year-olds.'

'An operation, do you mean? Oh, that's fine. I did my AC joint in '40. I'm good with ops.'

The enthusiasm – the energy – exuding from Ivon is compelling. Dusty looks at him and feels distantly familiar feelings stir. He thinks he felt them once. He recognises them as youthful, joyful, the exuberance that must be tempered by discipline. For a moment, as Ivon stands on the threshold of a new world, Dusty is able to share in his excitement, before he ushers him towards the gleaming Fence that towers over them.

Ivon remembers those long journeys they took to the mountains when he was a boy. He in the back of the car, Mum and Dad in the front. The air would be alive with talk and laughter, opinion and anger, talk and laughter, their tempers rising and falling as seamlessly and beautifully as valley and peak on the swell towards Snowdonia. Oh, how he loves the mountains!

'Are there mountains in England?' he says.

Dusty and Alanis, in front, exchange a glance.

'There are in the north,' says Alanis, looking over her shoulder at him with a smile.

Ivon grins at her. 'Oh, good! Everyone needs mountains, don't they!'

Alanis turns round to face the front again, glancing at Dusty once more on the way.

Ivon fingers the skin on his left hand, where they inserted his identity chip at the border. There is a lesion in the webbing between his first two fingers, a pinprick. He imagines the tiny chip beneath his skin and tries to locate it with the thumb and index finger of his other hand, but can feel nothing. Yet *it* will locate *him* for anyone with the right equipment. And then there's this other chip they're going to insert in the back of his neck. He can't wait to get one of those. He's always hated phones and the way people pace around like robots controlled by them.

'So, how's it going to work, Dusty? When we get to London.'

'We'll find you a room in the Cricket Academy for now. Then we'll have a meeting with the Manager for Cricket tomorrow. She's a friend of mine.'

'Cool! And what about rugby?'

The easy curves of Alanis's body have drawn Ivon's attention on this trip as much as the peculiarities of England, and he wonders if he detected a faint quivering in them for a moment as she looks away from him out of her window.

'Let's just see how we get on with the cricket,' says Dusty. 'My contacts in rugby are not extensive, but we'll see what we can do. You do know you'll have to choose one sport, don't you?'

'No problem.'

Another flare of adrenaline bubbles through him. Ivon takes a deep breath and closes his eyes. They say the crowds in England are 100 000 strong.

He pictures his father shaking his head. 'Don't believe anything you hear about England.' Well, he won't have to now. He's going to see for himself.

Dad. Ivon knows he'll be furious when he finds out where he's gone.

But I'm doing this for you, Dad. Not just for me. Were we not, all three of us, rejected by the English? Me before I was even born. You after you'd helped win so many matches. Turned away. Refugees of sport.

They made a terrible mistake, the English. What might Ricky, Dee and Ivon have achieved if they'd stayed? There can be no nobler crusade than to show them.

Ivon loses himself in such reverie in the back of a silent car, which floats at high speed towards London. Then, as the road flies in from the west, he marvels at the gathering towers of glass that present themselves in the distance, layered but unified, like the pipes of an organ, before the road sweeps down to be among them.

○

'These results are highly impressive. Incredible, even.' Lana looks up from her tablet. 'You're telling me this man was naturally conceived? He's had no formal training? He's from Wales?'

'Yes.'

'And yet these are the scores of a pure-breed elite…'

Dusty hesitates. How can he bring up the matter of Ivon's progenitors without disconcerting Lana – or, worse, offending her? She would have known Dee. They would have been comrades for a while.

'There was a cricketer,' he says. 'In elite women. Her name was Dee Januarie.'

Lana looks up at him. 'Yes,' she says, her face rippling with the effort of recall, or just the surprise of it. 'Yes. She was a prem dep, wasn't she?'

'Except she wasn't.'

Lana sits back in her chair, awaiting enlightenment.

Dusty shifts his weight from one foot to the other. He has set in motion something he cannot control. And yet he relishes the recklessness of it.

'You remember Ricky Tribute?'

Lana looks blank.

'He was also announced as a premature departure. Except he wasn't, either. They are both alive in Wales. This man, Ivon, is their progeny.'

'So he's one of ours.'

Dusty smiles. 'Not exactly. Ricky and Dee applied for a procreation certificate but were turned down. In the end, London exiled them.'

'They sent two elites away to Wales? Together?'

'I know.'

'And tried to pass it off as premature departure?'

'They said Ricky had a defect of the heart. In reality, they were worried about the closeness of their relationship.'

'So they sent them off to Wales, so they could get really close? I'm sorry. I don't accept that. Why would they do that to two assets of such value? Surely they would try Assimilation first.'

'It's odd, but they're out there, alive and well.'

'It's more than odd. And you saw them on your trip?'

'I stayed in their home.'

Lana shakes her head in disgust. 'Of all the depravities practised by the Welsh, the persistence of co-habitation in their culture alarms me most. With all we know now about Crowded House Syndrome. What were you doing staying with them, Dusty?'

'Ricky drugged me with Alcohol and carried me back.'

'You see, if what you say is true, this man – for all these cat scores – comes directly from such a culture. Have you had any more of these anonymous messages? Because I'm far from convinced there's a place for him here. Or even that we should try to find him one.'

Dusty takes this slight against Ivon – against Ricky and Dee – as if it were directed at Dusty himself. 'Lana, you'll have to trust me. I've seen him in action.'

'In Wales, Dusty! In Wales! You're not seriously trying to tell me there's any comparison?!'

'No, of course not. But you've seen his scores. They're even better than I'd thought they would be. He's already on a par with the new DGF cricketers, and they've come through the academies.'

'It's not his technique I'm worried about. It's the mental side. He comes to us as a savage, fully indoctrinated in the ways of the Welsh. If he were a child we might be able to condition that out of him. But, as an adult, these instincts won't be so easy to rectify.'

'Oh, come on! There's always Assimilation.'

As soon as the words are out, Dusty hangs his head for a moment. He could never wish Assimilation on Ivon. Assimilation would mean defeat, because it would mean the end of Ivon *as he is*.

Lana's secretary appears at the door. 'Ivon is here.'

'Show him in.'

'Yes, Manager.'

Dusty walks over to the window wall of Lana's office and looks out at the reassuring curves of Lord's. The statue of The Cricketer holds its elegant pose in the foreground. A cover drive perfectly executed. The angles, the balance, the sense of tension unwound, yet of motion suspended. Dusty will always feel an affinity for that statue, which will remain always a part of him. Around the base a handful of passers-by cross to and fro, lending perspective to it and the even vaster stadium behind.

Dusty turns to watch Ivon's progress into the room. He is fresh-faced from his exertions in the test chamber, the results of which Dusty and Lana have been perusing. The doubts that have been plaguing Dusty since their return from Wales are lifted when Ivon approaches Lana and shakes her hand as if he's been a Perpetual citizen all his life. Dusty knows Lana well enough to see she is disarmed. And for a moment he feels stupidly proud of Ivon, as if the boy were somehow his.

'How are you finding London, Ivon?' asks Lana, inviting him to sit down.

'Loving it! These suits are amazing!' he says, drawing his hand across his chest. 'The bloke told me I'd never have to put a jumper on again, and I laughed. But it's true! I can actually feel it change temperature. How does *that* work?'

'One of the many applications of perfect insulation. Your suit will draw heat from your body and resupply it, as required. It's true – we don't have jumpers in England.'

'What do you do for goalposts?'

'We've been looking at your results. They're impressive. Tell me a bit about yourself.'

With a little glance across at Dusty, Ivon repositions himself in the chair. 'Well, my name's Ivon.'

Lana closes her eyes with a weary smile and nods once.

'I love sport. It's my life. Any sport. You name it; I've played it. I don't know anything else. The rugby club got me a job selling cars, but it's just shaking hands, really. All anyone wants to talk to me about is sport.'

'But you're here for cricket?'

Ivon shifts in his seat. 'Yes. Definitely. If you say so…'

'You've submitted test results across the board, I see, which is unusual. Batting, swing bowling, catching, throwing… Your scores would qualify you for elite status in each, but your batting is particularly strong. Is it as a batsman that you're offering yourself?'

'I'm an all-rounder. Definitely.'

Dusty winces. The room is silent. He sneaks a glance across at Lana, whose crystal-sharp jaw remains unmoved.

'I did tell you, Ivon,' he says gently, 'that you would have to choose a discipline. We operate in a culture of specialism here.'

For the first time, as Ivon turns his eyes on him, Dusty sees a flashing defiance in that boyish countenance. He sees Ricky, and remembers what became of him.

'You told me I'd have to choose a sport. You said nothing about choosing a discipline within a sport.'

'It would be impossible for you to pursue more than one discipline in cricket,' rejoins Lana from behind her desk. 'The academies are separate; the training's separate.'

'How can they be separate? You can't have a batsman without a bowler. You can't have a bowler without a keeper.'

'You can't have an athlete maximise their productivity in more than one specialism.'

'An athlete?'

'The biomechanics of a batsman are totally unrelated to the biomechanics of a bowler, who is different from a fielder or a wicket-keeper. The techniques are separate and worked on separately. In different places and with different people. You cannot be in all those places at once. And, even if you could, you would be sacrificing degrees of proficiency in each specialism to strive for proficiency in all. It would not do.'

'But there are eleven players in a team. They've all got to bat; they've all got to field.'

Lana looks across to Dusty with her eyebrows raised. He's wasting her time. Dusty seethes with indignation at the mere idea, but he cannot deny that Ivon's protestations are making him look a fool, making both of them look fools.

'This is not the Lapsed Era,' says Lana. 'We have a batting squad, a bowling squad and a fielding squad. Every contestant is a specialist.'

'But that's not cricket! It's a fucking abomination! You can't give a kid a bat and a ball and tell him he can only use one of them!'

'Infants in the cricket crèches are given a bat *or* a ball.'

'No, I can't. I won't. Just give me a chance. As an all-rounder. I bat; I bowl; my throwing arm's the best in Wales.'

'I'm afraid that would be impossible. I am prepared to offer you a provisional post at the University of Cricket, London as a batsman, based purely on these cat scores and on the testimony of Dusty here, who seems to think highly of you.'

'You're telling me I'll never hold a cricket ball...'

Lana cuts across Ivon's protest. 'But I have to warn you I'm in two minds. It is clear to me you suffer from the peculiarly Welsh delusion that aptitude belongs to the individual. If you are to have any hope of surviving here, you will quickly learn the fallacy of that conviction. I have tried to welcome you gently by suggesting you might like to volunteer yourself as a batsman, but the truth is that such a decision is not yours to make. This notion that you, the individual, own a range of skills that should be deployed as you see fit is hopelessly primitive and, you will soon discover, offensive to Perpetual society. Because it is society that owns them. You are nothing but the medium through which they are transmitted.'

'Bollocks! I've spent my whole life practising. Hour after hour. As soon as I could walk, I had a bat in my hands or a ball at my feet. *I* put those hours in. Not you. It *is* my decision!'

'And do you suppose the inclination to practise belongs to you, too?'

'Yes!'

'The inclination to practise is a character trait conferred at birth – just like the ability to swing a bat accurately – and the fulfilment of it is a function of circumstance. Either way, it is an inheritance and not something you elected to take on in some sort of neutral waiting room outside life.'

'Whoa, whoa, whoa!' Ivon shakes his head, laughing. 'Are you trying to tell me that it *wasn't* me? When I practised my ball-striking for hours on end because I knew that Dafydd Bennett was doing the same and I wanted to be better, was it not me at all? Fucking society, was it? Or staying out until I'd hit the base of a sapling from 50 metres three times in a row.'

'I don't doubt that you worked hard, Ivon. Or that you believed that doing so was your choice. But I'm sure as well that you couldn't have stopped yourself, even if you'd wanted to.'

'Oh, yes, I could! I did! Don't worry! I know how to enjoy myself. It wasn't all work.'

'Then you worked just as hard as you wanted to. Like everyone. But where that balance lies at any given moment in any person's life is a function of personality and conditioning, both of which are visited upon the individual. To think otherwise is to see yourself as purely self-determining, unaffected by genetics or environment – in other words, outside life. Which is an absurd idea. You can take no credit for who you are, Ivon. It has simply happened to you. And in your case the prime materials were supplied, I understand, by two elite cricketers, Dee Januarie and Ricky Tribute, bred by this very commune. So you belong to London more than you know.'

There is a clatter as Ivon rises sharply enough to send the carbon-fibre chair he is sitting on flying across the room. 'My mum and dad were turned away from London!' he cries. 'I was rejected by London *before I was even born*! Don't you dare tell me I belong to you!'

He turns and strides from the room.

Lana shakes her head and returns to her work. 'We would have to assimilate him, Dusty. You know that. Is this worth it?'

'Let me talk to him.'

As he leaves the room in pursuit, Dusty's first instinct is to wonder what implications this hot-headedness might have for Ivon's future in London. He should not try to become a batsman.

'You don't believe any of that shit, do you?' Ivon says, when Dusty has caught up with him in the stairwell.

'Let's talk about this. I told you you'd find things different here.'

'Different?! That's some fucked-up view of the world your friend has there!'

'It is a fundamental tenet of Perpetual society that we belong to our commune. There is no such thing as acclaim for the individual here. If an athlete is productive, they are serving their purpose. They will not be celebrated, as I saw them celebrate you in Wales. They are just an asset of the commune that has produced them.'

'Look, I don't need adulation or anything. But no one owns me, OK?'

Their fevered descent slows, and Ivon turns to Dusty on the next landing down.

'And what about you, Dusty? You scored how many runs? Did they own you?'

The two men face each other, until Dusty flinches at the younger man's glare and continues down the stairs. Ivon follows.

Outside, Dusty saunters in the warm air. When he looks again, he catches Ivon gazing at Lord's with an expression of wonder on his face. One moment the young lad is staring him down, all fire and shifting colour, the next he is a picture of innocence and wonder, a glow on his cheek.

'It's impressive, isn't it?' Dusty says, as if to remind himself.

'And you play cricket in that?'

'Yes.'

'It makes the Millennium Stadium look like a bungalow. And look at the size of that statue!'

Dusty tries to remember when the statue went up. There was a time before it, definitely. But, no, he can't. Recollection is a skill, like a cover drive. His needs more practice. 'One of the largest of its kind. If only we had the results these days to go with it. I find it comforting, though. Something about a cover drive...'

'Good technique. For a big man...'

They stand in silence for a moment.

'I want to play rugby,' says Ivon. 'I know you're a cricketer, and Mum and Dad were too. I've tried to go along with it, but if I have to choose – rugby's my game. It's the Welsh game.'

'I think you would find rugby in England even more of a culture shock than cricket. It's a brutal arena for someone from the Lapsed Era.'

Ivon grins broadly. 'You're not putting me off, Dusty! Bring it on!'

'The elite rugby athletes here have been bred specifically. They've spent a lifetime in the academies. I've seen the rugby you're used to. Well, they're bigger here. Much bigger. They're ruthless, disciplined, robotic.'

'Ha! I make it my business to play against robots. I make fools of robots.'

'Not Perpetual Era robots.'

'Bring. It. On.'

It's a sport that requires belligerence, thinks Dusty, and the kind of spirit he can all but see now rising from Ivon like the hot breath of a bull. 'I don't know anyone in rugby. At least, not directly. It'll come down to your cat scores.'

'I love a good cat score!'

'What about swing bowling?'

'I want to play rugby, Dusty.'

❋

He won't be a Perpetual citizen until he's taken his central chip, they say. They inserted one two days ago, leaving it to insinuate itself among axon, synapse and dendrite.

'Let's see how we've got on,' says the communications technician, settling down at a console.

Ivon lies in a reclined chair, as if at the dentist. His head and neck are cradled closely in a hollow of unknown substance, white, yielding, yet humming with function. And, like a dentist, the technician dictates notes of obscure meaning, as on a checklist, while, on his console, he flicks through the strata and substrata of Ivon's being.

'This seems to have taken very well. Limited connectivity with some peripherals, but that'll come. Yes, I think we're ready to turn you on. There we are. Welcome to the Grid.'

Ivon waits, but nothing happens.

'So, what does this mean? I can send telepathic messages to anyone I like?'

'This technology replaced the telephone, and it's based on the same principle. You need a person's name to contact them.'

'Go on, then. Let's make a call.'

'Who would you like to speak to?'

Who indeed? He'd like to speak to Mum and Dad, now that he's safely on the other side of the Fence, but that is not a call for a communications technician to sit in on. Otherwise, it would have to be Dusty.

But, no. This is his first call by telepathy. He's got to be able to do better than that. Let's make it a woman, at least. What was the name of that girl who came up with them from Wales? Alana, was it? Now, hers would be a mind worth getting into.

'There's a girl. She's called Alana. Plays volleyball, I remember that much.'

'What class?'

'I dunno. Fit.'

'Elite?'

'Oh, yeah.'

'Let's have a look. There's an Alanis Fountin in the elite volleyball squad.'

'That's her!'

'Right. The first thing you'll learn in training is to make contact with someone, but I'll put you through for now.'

Almost immediately, a voice wafts into his consciousness, filling his head so softly. 'Ivon, you're on the Grid!'

He finds himself bereft of words for a moment. It is Alanis, as expected, and yet there can be no preparation for having her in his head like this. He is nervous, he now notices, like when he called Cerys in the early days.

'They've just hooked me up. You're my first call.'

Her laugh is gentle and soothing when released within his brain. 'We call it a comm,' she says.

'Are you actually speaking out loud when you say this?'

'No.'

'So, what? You just thought the word "no", then?'

'Yes.'

It's true, thinks Ivon. Her voice is clear and blemish-free, burgeoning throughout his soul as in a cathedral. It doesn't sound quite real, but the idealised echo moves him. 'And the laugh?'

'That was out loud.'

The presence in the room of the communications technician starts to play on Ivon's mind. 'So I could continue this conversation without actually speaking aloud, could I?'

'Why not? Give it a try. Tell me how you're finding London.'

Ivon sits up so that his head is lifted out of the cradle that has been holding it. He closes his eyes. 'I feel like a performing monkey but I love it yes tests tests fucking belonged to her she did 190 miles play the sound of you in my head just play Mum never did say…'

Alanis's laugh breaks into his head again. 'OK, OK, slow down! There's too much coming at me! I guess it's hard for you, if you've never used a chip before.'

'Can you teach me?'

'No, but someone will. Just speak out loud in the meantime. It's what we do when we're stressed or unable to focus.'

'You see, you've already taught me something about how it works.'

'Well, I can't teach you any more than that. But I've been meaning to ask if you'd like to meet me at the club. I can show you round there.'

'I'd love it.'

'Good. I'll pulse you the details. Monday, 4 p.m.?'

'What's today?'

She laughs. 'Friday.'

'Monday's good.'

He has a date. And not one with a scientist. London has accommodated him so far – gathered round and pored over him, even – but where is the beating heart of the place? Coolness and impassivity greet him at every turn. In Alanis, he has found a precious pocket of give. Around her, he might build something.

Ricky removes his helmet and shakes out his golden hair. His innings is over, but this time there is no dissent. He is smiling broadly, youthful again. The stadium is celebrating him. He holds his arms out wide, his bat in one hand, helmet in the other, and slowly he turns full circle, soaking up the approbation of the comps, who have stopped pedalling and rise as one to turn their attentions on him. It is rich and warm, the sound they make, a percussive symphony, like the one the Managers put on for Dusty in Parliament, so much softer than the harsh din of the pump boards, levers and turbines. Ricky feeds off it, visibly moved. He is standing still now, arms outstretched, head tilted backwards, eyes closed, chest rising slowly, as the acclaim washes over him.

He lowers his arms and turns to Dusty. There's that smile again, the radiance of a man at peace, who knows who he is and where he is, which is at his labour's end. Now he raises an arm again, but this time towards Dusty, beckoning him to step forward. Dusty does as he is bid, treading into the warmth. Ricky presents him to the stadium. The sound of their approval swells, so that the great vault is full with it. Still it grows, the air thickening until Dusty can make out nothing but the narrow pool of light he stands within, beyond which is a gorgeous chaos of good will and recognition. He longs to let go and plunge into it. He can hear his name rising, over and over again, a melody on the brave percussion. It *was* worth something, thirty-one years, 95 000 runs, a life. He wants to share it, so he turns to his comrade, but the statue of The Cricketer rears up where Ricky had stood, bold, communal and certain.

It is 5.23 a.m. He has another 37 minutes of sleep to observe, but Dusty is in decommission now, so he doesn't follow his programme the way he used to. Why bother? No one checks up on a vet.

He rises from his bed, pulls on his day suit and commands the shutters in his home to lift. The light outside is blue-grey. From his south window-wall he looks to the left and can see the first smudges of dawn above the next home along. He orders up a morning shake and crosses to his dispenser to collect it. A beep in his head alerts him to an error message. There will be no fuel for him today before 9 a.m. Yesterday's defeat to the South West in the elite men's hockey requires further savings to be made. Dusty tuts. It is then that he notices a personal message waiting for him on his chip.

It wasn't there when he went to bed. Why would anyone send a pulse during the sleeping hours? Then he sees that the sender is anonymous again. It was sent at 05.23, a couple of minutes ago. 'Outside', it reads.

Dusty can see nothing unusual out of his south window-wall, but to the north a lonely aero waits on the road. When he spies it, the passenger door, nearest to him, opens matter-of-factly. The invitation is obvious, and Dusty thinks nothing of accepting it, leaving his home at 05.25 in the morning.

Without checking the interior – or the driver – Dusty slides into the aero. Only then does he look across, as the door closes behind. He knows immediately, from the white suit, that he is in the presence of a scientist. What's more, this man is clearly an Exempt, for he is well beyond stasis age. Dusty guesses he must be in his seventies. Diminishment has him. His hair is silver, and an aquiline nose lends him an air caught between the distinguished and the absurd.

'Dusty Noble,' he says, without looking his way. 'One of my finest. You won't remember me.'

The man is right. 'Who are you?' asks Dusty.

'Syracuse Garbo,' he says. If his profile is ambiguous, the voice is rich and authoritative. 'I'm in Improvement. The records tell me you left the Academy in 2113.'

Dusty does not respond.

'You were a most responsive asset. London owes a lot to the work we did around then. We were on the verge of several breakthroughs, which are taken for granted now. They were exciting times. You were at the heart of that.'

'You haven't visited me in the sleeping hours to tell me this.'

A smile breaks out on the old man's face. 'Responsive, but never passive. The secret to your productivity.'

'Why have you been sending me messages anonymously? It is you, isn't it.'

'Tell me about the Welshman.'

Dusty looks across at him again, and this time Garbo returns his gaze. The extra years weigh heavily on him. Dusty can see the extent of it now. As an Exempt in science, he must be one of the finest minds of a generation, but physically he is a grotesque, his face drooping around that defiant, hooked nose. It occurs to Dusty that Exemption is as much a curse as otherwise.

'His name is Ivon. I discovered him on the fields of Wales.'

'I hear he is the progeny of two former colleagues of yours from the Academy all those years ago, Enrico Tribute and Delilah Januarie. Can you confirm this?'

Dusty looks away again and says nothing.

'Dusty, you must know that this is a matter of state security. Not just London. This goes to the top. The PM is to be briefed. A Welshman has been introduced into society, which is one thing, but if the rumours about his provenance are to be believed, Ivon could represent a significant threat to societal stability.'

'What's his provenance got to do with it?'

'Is Ivon on the Grid yet?'

'He successfully took a chip yesterday.'

'Well, that's a start, but I doubt he'll prove a receptive subject. Not at this early stage. He'll have to be watched. There's a lot we don't know about this.'

'You'll leave him alone, won't you? Just let the boy prove himself.'

There is silence in the aero. Dusty is well aware of the authorities' aversion to the unknown. A soft but rising panic has built within him these past few days. What has he done?

'What's his provenance got to do with it?' he says again, more aggressively.

Garbo cocks his head. His thin lips stretch and whiten for a second, part smile, part grimace. 'How are *you* feeling these days, Dusty? Has everything remained regular since decommission?'

'Everything's fine.'

'It was an interesting decision of yours. To bring a Welshman to London. An act of looseness, don't you think? One might almost describe it as reckless. Unconventional, certainly.'

'You told me to do it!'

'And if I told you to jump off a cliff?'

The old man's delivery is quiet and pointed. Dusty stares straight ahead through the aero's windscreen, down the immaculate street. Garbo is right. Dusty *wanted* to bring Ivon back. A properly aligned citizen would never have done such a thing. The messenger simply provided the means. Was it just a trick?

'I think you know why Ivon's provenance is important,' he says. 'You should do.'

'Why should I?'

'Did you talk about much in Wales with Tribute and Januarie?'

'Some things.'

'The TMS procedure of 2111, for example?'

Dusty is seized for a moment, as if by a vision. *That's* what has been niggling at him since his reunion with Ricky, the strange bond he felt they shared beyond their hours at the crease together. There *was* something.

'Ricky and I…'

'You were among the first to undergo Transmigration of the Skill therapy. One of those breakthroughs we made back then.'

Ricky and Dusty were put forward for it from their batch. Of course they were. Dusty remembers now the pride, the sense of responsibility.

He remains motionless.

'Perhaps I've underestimated your discipline,' says Garbo. 'It always was remarkable.'

'What?'

'Have we placed the Welshman yet?'

'We've tried him in cricket, but he wants to be in rugby. The Welsh are passionate about rugby.'

'Let him. He should be indulged for now. Make him feel at home.'

'For now?'

Garbo raises his hand impatiently. 'It's time you were back in your home. The sleeping hours are almost up. But I need you to confirm how he was conceived. I could take him in and do it myself, but it would be easier for all of us if you just told me.'

'It sounds as if you know already.'

'Tribute and Januarie.'

82

Dusty nods.

'That is all,' says Garbo.

'Don't touch him,' Dusty urges, but it is with an air of truculence, defeated truculence. 'Just give him a shift. See what he can do for the commune. That's all I ask. He has something. It's unlike anything I've ever seen. A kind of…of *happiness*.'

The door on Dusty's side of the aero swings open silently, and Garbo breathes in through pursed lips. 'Could it be that your discipline is weakening, after all? I'd feared this might happen. Look into your soul, Dusty. Deep into it. You may find some undesirable inclinations in there. Ivon almost certainly carries the very same, and cares not to bury them so conscientiously. Quite the contrary. But we shall see.'

'What do you know about Ricky and Dee?'

'Bye, bye, Dusty.'

Before he knows what's happening, Dusty is compelled by a sudden instinct to leave the aero. But it's not his instinct. By the time he has re-gathered himself in the street, the aero is gliding away, its door swinging shut.

He lost control of himself for a moment there, which can mean only one thing. Garbo has clearance to use Impulse Manipulation Software. It's the first time Dusty has seen it deployed away from the field. Who is this man? He seems to know more about Dusty than Dusty does.

V

So, he's in. The University of Rugby, London. They really liked the way he stood in a kind of wind tunnel, firing passes at various targets for hours on end. Ivon caught hundreds of balls from all angles with just about the perfect degree of traction between hand and rubber. His ball striking was unerring in its precision, powerful in its timing. Pace off the mark, searing; footwork, mesmeric; physical constitution, robust; fitness, tackling, concentration, blah, blah, blah. When can he just go out and play? Fuck.

It turns out he's a cat-score genius. No idea what all those numbers they read back at him meant, but there were enough people called in to look at them for him to know they were good.

It's been a week since he arrived in London. He's spent most of that time performing stunts for people dressed in white. A lot of it he has spent awake on the most uncomfortable beds known to man. They're sort of wavy in shape, designed to hold you in the perfect posture all night, but you have to sleep on your back, and Ivon has always slept on his front. Last night was his first in URL's student quarter in a place called Shepherd's Bush. Wasn't a bush in sight, just glass and smoothness, outside and in, not a kink of personality anywhere.

And they don't drink, the English. They don't drink. They train, they eat, they rest, they spend hours on interactive video games (except they're in 3D). And they play sport. Apparently. But they don't drink. Fuck.

Still, no one said it was going to be easy. All they talk about here is maximising productivity. Drinking, he realises, is not going to help with that. Lightening up a bit might, though.

That's why he's so looking forward to this date with Alanis at her club. They won't be drinking, he knows that. Although he could do with a jar, just to break the ice, loosen things up. The English go to their clubs for recreation, and Ivon looks forward to a break from all the seriousness. He imagines they play squash or indoor football or something. At least it'll be sport.

The bike he's on has no chain. Riding it started off as a sublime experience. No chain, no grinding of gears, everything is perfectly silent on the sky-blue, rubbery roads that cut between the glass and shininess of London and generate energy just from folk passing along them. He's turning an intricate network of magnets in his bike, they tell him, which is why he feels as if he's floating. Or at least, he did when he started the journey, but now he's labouring. A nifty little screen on the handlebars is showing him the way. The NorthWest3 Club in Belsize Park. The climb from Shepherd's Bush is tough, but if there was one aspect of his constitution that did not set the scientists fizzing with excitement it was his fitness. Not surprising really – everyone in London seems to be going faster than he is. Why don't they just use cars?

When he arrives he is breathing heavily. He can feel a light sweat on his brow, but his body remains cool and dry, somehow regulated by these magic suits they've given him, light like a T-shirt, substantial like a wetsuit, tight yet accommodating. They talk to the little chip they've put in his neck and respond accordingly. Ivon pokes his chest, and the yellow material bends playfully round his finger, like a film of adoring coral. He shakes his head and enters the club.

It is mellower inside than any of the buildings he's been in so far. The foyer gives off a blueish hue, softened by gentle curves in the smooth off-white walls, which seem to grow towards a cavernous ceiling several metres overhead. They are friendly at reception, and when he finds Alanis in the lounge her face lights up. He feels at home for the first time.

'Ivon!' she says, as she leaps to her feet from a chaise longue of lazy curves and warm, glowing redness.

She holds out her hand, the way they do here, which Ivon takes. When she pulls his hand into her, she presses it against her breasts. Is that normal, he wonders, or does she fancy him? On his turn, he is careful to pull her hand in tenderly. He wants to put his arm round her too, but resists.

'Come with me,' she says. 'I've booked us a cot.'

'A cot?'

'A coition terminal. I'll show you.'

Ivon follows her deeper into the complex, down corridors that continue the organic feel, curling overhead like living tunnels. There are doors at regular intervals, and Alanis starts to check each one's number more carefully.

'Here we are,' she says, placing her hand over one of those little screens that open doors. 'You have to scan yourself in, as well,' she says over her shoulder. Ivon does as he is told. 'It's just to confirm that we've gone in together.'

The room glows into life. It is small, lit with that same blueishness he'd noticed in the foyer. He can see two showers to his left, and to his right is an alcove containing a curious chair, or is it a bench? He moves closer to inspect it. Like so much in London it appears to have the property of movement, flexibility, life. There is what looks like a display panel hanging over it.

'Coitus,' says Alanis behind him, 'is how we enjoy ourselves.'

Coitus? The word is familiar to Ivon. Doesn't it mean…?

He turns round to see Alanis naked before him in a crouching position, as if in the middle of a warm-up. She continues to speak matter-of-factly, before straightening up and slipping past him towards the chair/bench thing.

'It's also an important way to generate energy, because it's not linked to sporting productivity. Although, of course, the more vigorous, lengthy and noisy the coitus, the more energy created.' She turns and does not so much sit on the strange contraption as let it take her. This it does elegantly, bending, tilting and *growing* until it cradles her perfectly.

'And there's no better way to get to know people.'

Fucking hell. Even if Ivon knew where to look and found it to be somewhere else, it would be impossible to avoid staring at Alanis, blithely reclining with legs apart on her dais, which holds her out to him like a pearl in an oyster. So stare at her is what he does, amazed.

Then he laughs. He is a long way from home, and she is one hell of a woman, with strong thighs and a firm bosom. Here is the final confirmation. He reaches for the clasp in his collar and flicks it open. His suit falls away from him. Undressing is so much easier here than in Wales. What does that do for passion? No matter. She's waiting. The passion is upon him.

He approaches the cot – for that is what he assumes this equipment to be. Are they really going to do this?

Still she waits. He places a hand beside her shoulder and a knee between her legs. It should be an awkward moment, beset with slip and fumble, but the cot responds to his arrival, morphing and shifting again until his position feels more natural and comfortable than any he has assumed with a woman before. A vision of Cerys flits lightly through his mind, but this won't be the first time he's been with another woman – and he wants to forget, oh God, how he wants to forget! When he joins Alanis, the cot, no, the entire alcove within which it is set, springs into life, humming and swaying in time with its lovers.

But it is the manner in which she bursts into life that makes the deepest impression on him. As coitus ensues, she lets go a long, rising shriek, like a ritual appeal to some goddess of energy, dissolving in Ivon any last vestige of self-consciousness. Her moans and cries fill the little cavern. She implores him to make more noise himself, to thrust harder. Ivon wants to please, more than he ever has. The passion is upon him, indeed. They yell together and sway together, the bed moves, yea, the very cocoon they play in is alive with their crescendo. What a woman! What a concept! What sex!

It is too much. Ivon slumps on top of her. The cot adjusts. She reaches up and pulls down the display that has all the while hovered above them.

'Hmm,' she says, as she studies the figures. 'Not bad wattage, but we're way short on time. We didn't even make it to the first changeover.'

'The what?'

'The first changeover. After five minutes, the woman assumes responsibility for momentum.'

'Oh.'

'Still, it's your first time. You'll improve. Shall we try again on Thursday?'

Dusty and Sonya Trick collect their isotonics and amble into the recovery lounge. He is tingling. They've had quite a bout. For a pair of veterans, they are most productive. Dusty enjoyed it, which is a development, because, lately, coitus with anyone other than Alanis has felt a chore. It's as if Alanis has fallen out of his life since Wales, as if her incompatibility with Wales means incompatibility with him. In her place have stepped Ivon, the brilliant new centrepiece of his preoccupations, and his growing fascination with the Past.

He watches Sonya sigh and stretch out on a recovery couch. Indulging his new taste for memory recall, he tries to think how long he must have practised coitus with her. They would have been cot partners before Alanis even emerged. It's possible they learned it on each other. It also occurs to him that Sonya must have been a contemporary of Dee at the Academy all those years ago. He wants to ask her about that, but a recovery lounge is no place to spring suspicious questions about the Past. Dusty does not want to create a scene.

As Dusty prepares to settle on a couch himself, Ivon and Alanis come into the lounge. Ivon smiles warmly at the sight of him; Alanis freezes. Dusty's first instinct is to dislike seeing them together. At first, he takes it as notice that his preoccupation with Alanis is still strong, but then he realises that it is Alanis herself he envies. Ivon is his discovery, his dream, his hope – his. Yet there must always be distance between them. He thinks of Ricky and Dee again. And Wales.

Alanis strides off towards the dispenser, but Ivon stays to talk. His smile has become a grin, wide and mischievous. His hair is wild and yellow-white, his cheeks glowing and the nose sharper and more impudent than ever. 'Was that…?' he says, gesturing towards the club's interior. 'Is that how we do it? Seriously?'

It takes Dusty a moment to appreciate what he is saying. He nods slowly.

'I don't know what to think. Wow.'

Ivon throws himself on the nearest couch, and Dusty takes up position on its twin. Ivon looks at him properly.

'I tell you what, that business in there will help, don't get me wrong, but, fuck, Dusty, I'm fizzing here! I've got to play. When can I play?'

'You will. Just stay patient. You've been tested now. I know they're impressed. They'll give you a shift soon, I'm sure. It's only university level, which at URL is tertiary standard. So it'll be good rugby, but it's not elite.'

'When can I play elite?'

'Just give it time.'

'All this talking and sprinting and skill–isolation bollocks is doing my head in. It's like the cricket thing. This isn't rugby. It's not even training. It's just focusing in on something until it's so microscopic you've lost track of what it's a part of, or what it's for. Which is rugby. I want to play rugby.'

'It'll happen.'

Ivon seems to accept this, but a new mood quickly comes over him. Suddenly, the sparkle dims a degree. 'Listen, about Alanis. I… Are you two…?' He shrugs and waggles his finger in the air. 'You know, together?'

'What do you mean?'

'Well, she was with you in Wales. I just wondered if you two were an item?'

Dusty smiles slowly. 'Do you mean like Ricky and Dee are?'

'Yeah. Like Ricky and Dee.'

'No.'

'Oh, good. Because, I tell you, she practically jumped on me. I wasn't going to turn her down, obviously, but I just didn't know the form, see. I'm fucking chuffed she's not your girlfriend or anything.'

'You're talking about interpersonal love, aren't you? It doesn't work like that here. Coitus is practised freely between everyone.' Dusty pauses to think of an analogy Ivon might understand. 'It's like drinking a lager with someone.'

'So you go in for free love here. That's what you're saying?'

Dusty nods, but he is unsure.

'Wow.' Ivon puffs out his cheeks and rests his head on the couch. 'Do you know how I can speak to my parents? Can I use this chip they put in my neck?'

Dusty stops himself from giving the answer, which is no – to both questions. 'Why do you want to speak to them?' he says instead.

'Well, I've been here a week. It's time I spoke to them, don't you think? Just to let them know I'm OK.'

'Right.'

Ivon runs his hand through his hair and holds it there. 'My phone won't work here. I want to talk to them. There must be phones in London.'

'I'll see what I can do.'

Dusty hadn't anticipated this. The desire to return to Wales, yes; but the desire just to speak to people there...that is a curious compulsion. He trusts, for now, that its likely denial will not cause too much disquiet in the boy.

VI

At last. Some action. They want him to play. They want him to play tomorrow. The university fly-half has broken his arm in a freak bike accident and will miss the next match at least.

'Do you always play on a Thursday?' Ivon asked the coach, a bloke they refer to as Coach Davis, when he told him.

'You play when you're told.'

'In Wales we play rugby on a Saturday, mainly.'

'You're not in Wales any more.'

He didn't argue. No way. Some proper sport at last. They were throwing him straight in for the home game against the University of Aberdeen. It meant he had to cancel his date with Alanis at the club, but she didn't seem to mind. They would rearrange.

He's already walked round the outside of White City Arena. It was one of the first rituals he performed when they placed him at URL. Check out the ground. He's always done it. Walking the pitch at Mumbles as a boy. Then peering through the railings at St Helen's as a teenager. Dreaming. Or visualising. Engaging the imagination, at any rate, and the soul.

He couldn't see the pitch at White City from the road. And he didn't try to go in. It didn't look as if he could. At ground level the stadium rose first into a forbidding, smooth black mound, impenetrable as far as he could tell. Wide walkways from the north, south, east and west swept up to the top of the first plateau, from which rose a further dome, shiny, glass and of swirling darknesses. He circled it twice that first time, but it yielded not a chink.

For the team run, he and his new teammates – although they keep calling themselves comrades – have been admitted through a modest aperture that has miraculously opened in the north wall. There are twenty-four such entrances around the ground, apparently, but Ivon can't make out any of the others, the glass is so smooth. This one leads them down into a high-ceilinged changing room of no natural light, but a dispassionate flood of illumination, seemingly source-less, leaves not a shadow or nook unlit. Each player has a cubicle of his own, and when Ivon and his teammates gather in the courtyard at the centre of the changing room, on benches arranged in a circle, he is introduced without enthusiasm by Coach Davis.

His teammates are as glassy and cold as the city. The haircuts are of uniform length, which is little longer than a crop. Their studious air holds the changing room tightly. At first, the only hint of personality Ivon can detect is the conviction that his predecessor as fly-half has fallen foul of malpractice.

'He thinks someone got at the transmission in his front wheel,' says the tallest guy in the team, not to Ivon but loudly enough so that he could hear. 'He says he was cycling at high speed when he felt the magnets drift then lock.'

'That's not right. What could have caused that?'

'Magnet misalignment, maybe. A foreign body. He's not even sure there wasn't a little explosion.'

'Someone's taken him out.'

'What? Espionage? At tertiary level? Didn't think Aberdeen had that in them.'

'He's touch and go for the UEA match as well.'

'Well, there's no way *they* did it.'

Suddenly, the intense flanker who has been sitting on a bench on the fringe of the group, flexing his hamstrings incessantly, turns his hollow eyes on Ivon. 'What about Ivon?' he says. 'He's the one who benefits in the first instance.'

The room falls silent. Ivon looks from empty face to empty face.

'What?' he says, plaintively.

There is no reply.

'You think I fucked with his magnets?'

Not a muscle moves in the room, save the flanker's hamstrings.

'But I don't even know how these bikes work! They're a mystery to me. Like magic.'

The silence is broken by Coach Davis's return to the room, and the players retreat to their cubicles. Ivon's kit is waiting for him in his. He wants to rip off his day suit and fling it in the corner, but London clothing does not lend itself to fits of pique. Instead he flicks the clasp and waits as his suit unpeels itself from him. His rugby kit is similar, although he has to pull it up to his crotch before it climbs up and round him. Within seconds it has him in a firm embrace. The kit stops just short of his elbow and at the top of his thigh. It is black with red trim. The boots, when he steps into them, unravel up his calves, before tightening gently round his feet and muscles. The soles will respond, they tell him, to whatever surface they find themselves on and whichever split-second intention flits through the brain. For now, their electric lightness has an inspiring effect, and he flashes up the metal stairs to the pitch as if launching into flight.

When he bursts into the arena, though, he is awestruck for a moment. The place is empty, but, in silence, the threat of its magnitude is vivid. This is where they play student rugby? Through the prism of this great vault, metallic and pregnant, he imagines the scale of the arena they call Twickenham, or Trafford, or Headingley. Already he has heard talk of these

94

places. If the White City Arena is a humble antechamber in the hierarchy of English stadiums, he is impatient to make it his own, on the way through.

His teammates follow shortly and trot onto the immaculate turf. Ivon crouches down to inspect it. The grass is short and thick, unnaturally so, and it protrudes through what looks like soil. It is firm, but there is give. He tugs at the grass, and it comes away in his hand.

'Is this stuff real?' he says to a passing player.

The player looks at him scornfully. 'Well, it's not a simulation. Of course it's real.'

'Yes, but does it grow?'

As the player runs off to take up position, Ivon notices a smaller man approach. His eyes are bright. 'It replenishes itself every six months,' he says, offering his hand. 'But, no, it's not alive, if that's what you mean. I'm Tim. I'll be your scrum-half.'

Ivon is relieved to meet him. 'You seem practically normal.'

'Don't worry about them. They're bred to be hostile to the unknown. But they'll run into walls for you once you've proven yourself. As a scrum-half, I have a more active prefrontal cortex.'

Suddenly, a voice cuts through Ivon's head. He recognises it as his chip at work, but usually there is a repetitive beep to signal an incoming call; here, the voice is inside his head without warning. It is Coach Davis's.

'We have to win this next match. Aberdeen are having almost as bad a season as we are, but they won't be much worse than the South East, and we all know what happened there. Let's make this a good team run. Tim, Ivon, we're working the corners. Everyone else, we're hard and disciplined.'

Ivon shakes his head and turns to Tim. 'Where *is* he?'

Tim points to a spot high in the stand. On a raised platform over the halfway line, protruding from the serried rows of seats and levers, sit Coach Davis and two other men.

'Is he going to be blabbing in our ears all day?'

'Yes I am, Ivon. You're not in Wales now. This is not a game. There is precious energy to be earned.'

'It *is* a game,' says Ivon.

'It's a match,' says another voice, which Ivon recognises as that of the tallest guy in the team. 'It's a contest. It's survival. We stand together and follow orders, or we lose.'

Ivon looks across to the lock forward. He stands menacingly, full square in front of him, 20 metres away, staring him down. And his mouth *does not move*.

'Jesus,' says Ivon, 'are you all going to be in my head for this?'

'You will hear my voice throughout,' says Coach Davis. 'Inter-athlete communication is vocal, unless there is a pressing need for a priority comm not to be vocalised.'

'Fucking hell,' thinks Ivon.

While they've been talking, onto the field have slipped fifteen padded humanoids on circular bases, gliding across the surface as if on wheels. They move in formation and assume position in the other half of the field. A ball, which Ivon had not noticed, is sent skywards from one of them somehow. The tall lock forward rises to take it, and the other forwards gather round to secure the ball.

It is a semi-opposed session, but Ivon is enthralled by these mobile humanoid tackle pads providing the resistance. He lines up outside Tim in a position flat against the gain line with the tackle pad opposite him only a few metres away.

'Ivon!' says Coach Davis in his head. 'Deeper! I want you deeper! You're kicking for touch, D long!'

Ivon remembers from his pitch-quadrant tutorial earlier in the week what this means. Coach Davis wants him to kick for the right touchline, as deep into opposition territory as he can. Ivon does not appreciate being dictated to like this, but, even if he did, he is too fascinated by the overgrown pawns ranged against them to pay any attention.

'I'm flat, Tim!' he shouts. 'I'm flat!'

As soon as the ball leaves Tim's hands, the tackle pads advance, and Ivon can't wait to try his luck. The pass from Tim is good. A tackle pad is up on him quickly, but surely a sidestep would do for it. As he takes the pass, Ivon feints inside. In a flash, the rubber man changes tack and bumps him towards the pads inside, who swarm round. Ivon accepts defeat and turns to present the ball to his forwards.

The session breaks up, as Coach Davis cries out in his head with astonishment. 'Ivon! Ivon! I told you I wanted you to drop deep and kick!'

Ivon stoops to inspect the base of one of the tackle pads, trying to discover what could make them so agile beneath their wide flat bases. He can make out nothing, and when he tries to tilt one of them it moves away from him, as if indignant.

'Ivon!' says Coach Davis again. 'You didn't do as I told you. What happened?'

Ivon looks up at him in the stand. 'I just wanted to test out these giant pawns. They're quick, aren't they?'

'We've set the droids to GSL7, so, yes, they'll give you a good workout. Why didn't you drop deep and kick?'

'A good player responds to what's in front of him. I saw we were playing against a load of Subbuteo figures. I thought they might be weak on the inside shoulder.'

'You ignored my instruction! That's Misalignment!'

'Are you really going to be giving me instructions all session?'

'Of course I am.'

'And tomorrow? In the match?'

'Yes.'

'And what if I disagree with one of them?'

'I don't understand.'

'Well, I might not think it's right to kick. I might feel something else is on.'

'Why would you think that?'

'I have instincts. My instincts are strong.'

There is a pause. Ivon can see Coach Davis confer with his colleagues. Their words are not transmitted. Coach Davis breaks off and turns to Ivon again. 'Think of us as your instincts,' he says, gesturing to the two men either side of him. 'Think of us as your eyes and ears.'

'Who's playing this game? You or me?'

'Why would you think you are better placed to know what's best for the team than we are up here? You are operating in the heart of the action. We are in the stadium eye. Of course we can see things more clearly than you. So we make the decisions. This is standard practice. We have the technology here, so we use it. You're not in Wales.'

'But I have the ball. *I'm* best placed to decide what to do with it.'

'We're not talking about this any more. This is how it is. You and your comrades are the ones trained in Technique and Execution. We are trained in Strategy and Direction. We tell you what we want you to do, how we want you to proceed. You follow. If not, the whole thing breaks down. Let's go from the scrum!'

Just do what they want, Ivon tells himself. His priority is to get onto the field, to play. Against real people. Then they'll see.

Three years, seven months, thirteen days. Juno's stasis looms ever larger. Dusty is beginning to feel its approach as keenly as if it were his own. Juno considers the stasis countdown clock she has had installed on the wall above her desk a sublime cosmic joke. But to Dusty, who sees it on an almost-daily basis, it hangs heavy like an omen.

'I was wondering if you could help me with something,' he says to the woman seated beneath it.

'Of course!'

'We have a filing culture here at ReSure. The record of our people is preserved for...well, for a long time, is it not?'

Juno grins widely. Her neck powers her head backwards and forwards in short jabs.

'So, it occurred to me that this practice might be repeated across society. I mean, in terms of keeping a record of things. I know that scores and statistics from matches are kept on file – I've even seen some of them – but what about the registering of, I don't know, events...and attendances? Enrolment. Medical records. For example.'

She studies him from above fingers that interlock like gear teeth. 'It can be hard working here, can't it?' she says. 'There's something about being around people at the end of their active lives that encourages us to turn away from the future. To look backwards. It makes you feel quite abnormal, doesn't it? As if there's something wrong with you.'

The grin remains set across her face like a sprung mantrap. Dusty knows better than to say anything.

'It's perfectly normal, Dusty. And if you want to see somebody about it there is an adjustment course available to us. I haven't taken it myself, but I have considered it. Otherwise, in answer to your question – yes, absolutely. There is a record of practically everything that happens or has ever happened in London.'

'And are these records available to anyone?'

'Anyone?'

'Well, me.'

Juno blows out her cheeks and stretches back into her chair. She makes obvious the power of her arms, her shoulders, her neck. 'The morning is such a latent time of day, don't you think?

We are at our most coiled. Potential energy courses through our limbs, as yet unwound.'

Dusty smiles dutifully. The time has come, he concedes. Juno bustles round from her side of the desk. 'A morning constitutional,' she says, 'I always find the most gratifying of all. Shall we?'

'I'm sure we shall.'

The cots at ReSure are first-generation, hard and ungiving, but it lends one's exertions upon them a certain purity. Every thrust and grind is accentuated, the transmission of energy without mediation. Not for a moment does the cot feel as if it is helping; rather, it offers itself as a kind of board against which to thrash. There is something bracing about it. And the more so when joined by a woman as powerful as Juno. She is a vigorous partner, louder and more momentous than any he can recall, despite her advanced years. At the height of their exertions she roars and pounds her fists upon his chest, as if summoning her own past as a champion wrestler, as if trying to force another submission. Dusty is invigorated and quite bruised, another megajoule banked, and it not yet 10 a.m.

'So,' he says with a big breath on the way back to their offices, 'I think you were going to tell me how to gain access to London's records.'

'Oh, Dusty,' laughs Juno. 'They're available to anyone!'

'To anyone! But I've always imagined them to be inaccessible.'

'Of course you have. We are conditioned from emergence not to consider the Past. So no one ever thinks to look there. But in theory your humblest primary could walk straight in here and ask to see one of our vaults. If they did, we should show them whatever they want. But, of course, they don't. And if they did, well, we would make a record of it. Alarm bells would ring. So there would be repercussions for a primary. But for a man of your standing, Dusty…you could look up anything you wanted, I'm sure.'

Dusty nods his head with interest. And surprise.

'What is it you're after, anyway?' she asks.

His confidence on the question of his past is growing, and the inclination towards candour that has lately gnawed at Dusty in the wake of coitus has him again here. He chooses to be honest with her. 'I was among the first batch of Academy students to undergo TMS therapy. I want to learn more about it.'

Juno shrugs. 'They'd retain that information at the Institute of Improvement. Have you met the registrar there yet? Martha Havelock. Obviously not. She comes here from time to time.'

'And what about us? Do we retain details of prem deps here?'

'Of course! Have we really not had one since you've been here? There was one the other day. A secondary in handball. Hit by an aero.'

'Don't remember it.'

'Maybe you were away.'

✸

The Institute of Improvement has faculties in each of the many academies across the country, but its headquarters are pleasantly appointed on the banks of the River Thames at Millbank. Dusty joins the river at Blackfriars and cycles south along the flyover, enjoying the sweep of river, parks and gleaming panels. Soon he is on the descent past Parliament, its billowing domes homely yet weighty, an anchor to the proud tower that rises up beside it. He enjoys the perfect synchronisation between the clock on his central chip and that of Great Chronos, from whom they all take their time, the seconds flitting so elegantly from one digit to the next on his mighty face.

At Millbank, he parks his bike and pauses. The Eye-Eye is one of the taller buildings in London, perhaps as many as twenty-five storeys high. More immediately, he is confronted by a courtyard framed by the crescent configuration of the lower, wider proportion of the building. He approaches it from the concave north side, his progress reflected off successive panels of tinted glass, as they watch him make his way to the entrance at the centre of the curve.

In the foyer he is met by Martha Havelock. She wears the navy of the primary class and greets him with a pleasant, gentle smile. Her own stasis is surely imminent, for she looks at least as old as he does, even if she can't be. He cannot imagine London draws much in the way of energy from her limbs, which are slender and hesitant.

'I'm no good at sport,' she explains on the way up to her office. 'Never progressed beyond primary. What I do have is a head for figures. And nimble fingers for inputting.' She laughs modestly, as they pass a descending group of tertiaries, pounding in perfect unison down the stairwell's training lanes. 'Just another flight. They've moved my office down to the fifth floor. I'm in diminishment now, as you can see.'

She takes a seat behind her desk and pulls up the home on her computer. 'Let me put it in the round for you,' she says, and the projection on her desk morphs to throw up a replica interface on Dusty's side.

'So what are we looking for?' says Martha.

'Transmigration of the Skill therapy.'

'Ah, yes. Well, I can certainly help there. We keep a record of every procedure.'

'This one was in 2111.' He hesitates to mention a date so long ago, but Martha is an archivist, he reminds himself. The Past does not faze her. 'I was part of it.'

'OK. Let's see.'

Dusty watches as a succession of menus and figures flashes across the interface at dizzying speed. He is mesmerised. Through the shifting mist of data, the silhouette of Martha beyond is perfectly still but for her hands that skim across the console.

'Well, well – 2111 makes you one of the very first. There was a batch of footballers the day before, but you were pioneers of the procedure.'

Dusty sees his name, the fifth in a list, but he is impatient. He sees Ricky's name, too, just below his. And, there, third on the list is Dee's. A chill runs through him. She was part of the batch, too? This means something, he is sure of it. If only he could remember.

'Can we find out about the others?'

'There were seven of you, as you can see, four boys, three girls, all of you fifteen or sixteen years of age. The transmigrated skill was the cover drive.'

Dusty nods. 'But who were they? Where are they now?'

'Oh dear,' says Martha, from behind the veil.

'What is it?'

Each name on the list is highlighted for a second and flashes as Martha tries to call up the profile. But no profile appears. She clicks on Dusty's name, and a projection of Dusty materialises on the desk.

'Well, you're there in all your glory, but that's it. There are no profiles for any of the others. Daniel Attention,' she says, highlighting the first name on the list, 'nothing. Chad Meninga, nothing. Enrico Tribute. Same with the girls: Angela Hunter, Delilah Januarie, Leanda Wellington; nothing, nothing, nothing.'

'What does that mean?'

'It means they are no longer with us.'

Dusty pores over the unresponsive names on the list. Ricky and Dee he knows about. He can't remember Angela Hunter or Leanda Wellington. Daniel Attention. Chad Meninga. He thinks the names mean something to him, but is that because he realises they should? He must have known them.

'You mean they're all premature departures?'

'I do, Dusty. You would appear to be the only one left.'

'When did they leave?'

'I don't have that information here, as you can see. But you should have it at ReSure.'

'Who was the skill host?'

'For your treatment? Let's have a look. Oh! That's unusual.'

Dusty sees the highlighter labouring on the interface again, this time over the field <skill host>.

'Nothing's coming up. I don't know what to say. It won't tell me.'

'And who was the presiding technician?'

The question is immaterial. He knows the answer before it appears on the interface.

'Syracuse Garbo,' Martha says.

'Do you know him?'

'I do. He's a…shall we say, he's an intense man. Not always the easiest to serve under. But we don't see much of him these days. He's an Exempt. They rarely show their faces, for obvious reasons.'

'Where can I find him?'

Through the interfaces between them, Dusty can see the silhouette of Martha's shoulders tighten. A moment later, the projections between them dissolve into her desk, leaving the woman exposed before him. Her face is drawn – and paler, thinks Dusty, than the cheery one that greeted him earlier.

'The truth is, I don't know where you'd find Garbo. He only ever deals with those he needs to. He's an Exempt. I don't know when I last saw him.'

'Thank you, Martha.'

'I'm sorry I can't be of more help. Let me show you out.'

But Dusty has already left.

The Past has him now. He thought he had developed an unhealthy relationship with it since his decommission, but now he recognises that as nothing more than the flirtatious dance it was. This is what it means to lose yourself in it. A projection merely 12 inches high was all that was needed.

Dusty stares at the image of Daniel Attention that has appeared on his desk back at ReSure. Of course he knew him. Now that he can look into that face again, rendered just as it was thirty years ago, when the young man left them, a swirling cloud of sounds, smells and feelings descends – the sweet, dull whiff of the old willow bats, the pads and guards, the bark of the Academy coach (Dreyfuss was his name, wasn't it). An existence long forgotten materialises as vividly as the little figure in front of him. It startles and bewitches him equally. That such memories exist; that they can have survived a life spent forever looking forward in disciplined devotion to the Next Match, the next bout, the next joule, the next day; that they should have lain all the while neglected in a remote corner of his brain, never to be accessed or even acknowledged. Until now, and the innocuous trigger of a face from his past.

Young men on the brink of achievement. Dusty can feel again the happy buzz of excitement that coursed through him daily back then. Focusing on what came next was natural in those days, without the weight of a long personal history to turn away from, to keep suppressed. He'd tripped lightly towards his life's centre of gravity, which pulled him ever onwards to the next opportunity for excellence, each one presenting itself just ahead, a constant renewal of his raison d'être. When did that dynamic start to lose its momentum? Even when his past grew weightier than his future, he'd stepped steadily onwards. The Next Match occupied him entirely until he competed in his last. That certainty about what is to come has wavered since decommission, but now, confronted with the face of Daniel

Attention, he feels his past seeping into his consciousness, squeezing out concern for the future, like a rising flood.

It is disabling. Apathy, nostalgia, weariness. These are his new companions. He can feel them feed off each other.

Daniel Attention. He was like that. At least, he was listless, reluctant to engage in the training that was demonstrably a prerequisite of excellence. Dusty found his apathy inexplicable. Why would anyone shy away from a simple decision whose virtues were unquestioned, self-evident even? And the decision to extend yourself in training was as simple as any they faced back then. Take it, and you had a shot at excellence; refrain, and you did not. No one so much as considered the latter.

Apart from Daniel, who hated training and constantly grumbled about the monotony of his existence. Dusty remembers feeling...feeling *something* for Daniel, who was in evident turmoil. But Daniel was alone. His plight went unrecognised, and if Dusty felt something for him, somewhere under layer after layer of conditioning and breeding, he never once stopped to consider what or why it was.

He feels for Daniel now, though. There *was* something squirming away deep inside Dusty all those years ago, and now it is raw and close to the surface. He still doesn't understand it, but his relationship with Ivon is illuminating. In Ivon's simple desire to play he detects an echo of Daniel's anguish.

The day they took him away, Daniel had challenged their tutor yet again on the wisdom of another morning in the multigym. This time he refused to take part and sat in the corner singing gently to himself, while Dusty and the others worked out. That was the session they came for him. Dusty pictures it clearly now, that image of the boy on his desk precipitating the memory of the last time they saw him. There was no complaint from Daniel, or comment from any of the other batsmen in the

Academy. One minute Daniel was there, the next he was not. Otherwise, life continued, unchanged.

Dusty wants to reach out to the young man now, to ease him through his pain, but the distance of the years renders that impulse useless and painful. It helps to be able to put a date on it, though, and here it is, in the body text of Daniel's file.

16 Feb 2114 [a month before his nineteenth birthday], 09.17: Taken in, Academy of Cricket, Kennington. Defect: Exaggerated Peripheral Sensitivity. Prognosis: Irreversible. 16.23: Departs.

But did he depart? The files of Ricky and Dee no doubt say the same – he will check them shortly – but Dusty knows what fate befell them. Maybe Daniel Attention lives on. He could be in Wales, too. Or in any of the other corners of the globe unreceptive to the Perpetual Era. Iceland, the Falkland Islands, Australia…

The file on Daniel is absorbing. Dusty loses himself in it, recognising in the progress of a fledgling cricketer's life the same sort of landmarks that delineate his own. Daniel emerged on 15 March 2095 at 17.41 in the London Generation Centre of Bat and Ball Resources, the progeny of Cuthbert Dorrigo, elite, left-hand bat, and Faith Dury, elite, left-hand bat. His names were conferred two days later, and on 22 March he was placed in the Clapham Bat and Ball Nursery. His cat scores from the age of eighteen months were consistently exceptional, earning him provisional tertiary status at the age of four and provisional elite at seven. He was accepted at the Academy of Cricket at the age of nine. Daniel, Ricky and Dusty were the leading left-handers of the '95 batch throughout their time at the Academy. Dusty studies the progression of Daniel's cat scores with pride, knowing that his were much the same – or, actually, always that crucial fraction better. Ricky struggled to accept his lot as Dusty's inferior when the cat scores came through, regularly losing his temper in the early years, or becoming carried away with himself on those occasions he won out. The Academy worked him hard on his temperament. But Daniel was more phlegmatic. Dusty smiles at the memory of his easy-going shrug. 'The next score's the one that counts,' he used to say.

It was after their TMS therapy, on 1 April 2111, that Daniel seems to have become unwell. Dusty is stopped by one entry in his file:

21 September 2111: Surveillance initiated, following irregularity in behaviour of Enrico Tribute, fellow participant in suspended Transmigration of the Skill therapy programme.

Uneasily but in haste, Dusty calls up Ricky's file. He finds the following entry:

15 September 2111, 23.46: Intercepted, Armoury Way, Wandsworth. Irregularity: On bike during sleeping hours. Diagnosis: Impaired Modulation Facility. Prognosis: Manageable.

17 September: Surveillance initiated.

He calls up the files for Dee, Angela Hunter and Leanda Wellington. They were all placed under surveillance on 21 September 2111, as was Chad Meninga, a batsman from the '96 batch. This means Dusty, too, must have been subjected to state scrutiny, as the seventh participant in the TMS therapy programme. He wonders if the file on him at the Institute of Improvement might contain any further information.

What was it about that TMS therapy programme that rendered them all of such interest to the state?

In each case, bar Dusty's, the state's suspicions were borne out, because all six of his co-participants were taken out of the system eventually. Daniel's condition deteriorated the most rapidly, and his indolence was considered too subversive a delinquency to be tolerated. He was taken in for two degrees of Assimilation in October 2112, aged seventeen, with mixed results. In May 2113, he was subjected to all three degrees. There was an initial improvement in behaviour, but by the end of 2113 Daniel was openly contemptuous of his existence as an elite cricketer and, by extension, of everyone else's. It was clear he could not continue.

Time is getting on, but Dusty runs his eye over Ricky's file. If Daniel's problem lay in rousing himself, Ricky's was one of control. Today they would know precisely which areas of the nervous system to target for the Assimilation of such deviants, but things would have been different in those days, Assimilation a clumsier treatment, less readily resorted to. For Ricky, it was a case of management. He seems to have responded well. He made his elite debut for London on 16 July 2114, and he'd achieved it by managing his own temperament without intervention from the state.

But by 2118 he was starting to attract attention for the irregular nature of his relationship with Dee. Illicit rendezvous are recorded in his file, coitus in the field. Dusty smiles at the idea of off-grid coitus, coitus for its own sake – one thing to practise it in Wales, as he and Alanis did only the other week; another to do so in London, where coition terminals connected to the Grid are never more than a few minutes away. Such wanton and useless expenditure of energy amuses the new Dusty.

If only the state had felt that way. Clear evidence of Misalignment.

But another entry disturbs Dusty among those tracking Ricky's relationship with Dee:

Mitigation recognised as participant in suspended Transmigration of the Skill therapy programme of 2111.

It seems grace was extended towards Ricky and Dee. All the more so when Dusty considers they were allowed to take exile in the end, rather than face Assimilation or shutdown.

Consistent with what Ricky told him in Wales, he and Dee applied for a procreation certificate on 22 April 2119. They were denied. Thereafter, the entries for Ricky's erratic behaviour increase and culminate in that fateful innings Dusty remembers against the North West, the last time he'd seen Ricky before Wales, when he left the crease railing against the decision of the match computer. That was on 22 June, it says here. They came for him in the changing room. By the time Dusty had returned from his innings, Ricky had gone.

Defect: Impaired Modulation Facility. Prognosis: Irreversible. 21.33: Departs.

There is not time to study the files of Dee and the others, but Dusty has seen enough to know the sort of tale they will likely tell. High-flying batsmen in the Academy of Cricket, all subjected to a fateful programme of TMS therapy in 2111, all of them in some way or another derailed. All but Dusty.

The progeny of two of them, though, has returned, and London is about to tap into their genotype again. In an hour, Ivon makes his debut for URL. Dusty hurries across town to be there for it.

The rock is heavy in Ivon's hands. It is solid, immutable, of the Earth, Welsh. He holds it on his lap, like a captain might hold a rugby ball for the team photo. This rock is roughly the shape of a rugby ball. That's why they chose it. And on it there are four faded letters, crudely etched, the letters that name him: IVON.

Dad had carved each one, on the same day Ivon and he found the loose rock on Devil's Bridge, out Rhossili way. How he'd clutched it as they picked their way urgently over the rocks from Worm's Head, just before the tide reclaimed the last of the passage home. It was dangerous. The wind was up, and the water frothed menacingly between the last despairing fingers of dry rock. If they'd left it any longer, they would have been cut off from the mainland. That would have meant another eight hours out on the blasted headland, until the next ebbing of the tide, long after nightfall. They were not dressed for a night braced against wind and wildlife. Worse still, Dad would have had to explain himself again at home. They had to make it across, but they laughed all the way as they clambered along the edges to safety.

The letters are worn now, but still there. One bold stroke for I, two for V, and, before the three for N, four pinched scratches to make up the O, which hangs slightly out of line from the others, an arrow head, a diamond, a rugby ball.

He closes his eyes and takes a deep breath, allowing the nervousness to percolate through him, clutching the rock to his chest. It is a ritual he has performed before every rugby match he has played since. This is the first time he has performed it outside Wales. The rock feels weightier here somehow. Through it he can commune with his parents, his friends, the rocks and fields of Gower.

He misses them. On the eve of a game, he would have talked Dad through his vision of the perfect 80 minutes for that match. Then, on the day, Dad would have talked him through *his*, a bundle of nervous energy on the other side of the kitchen table. A hug from Mum, and he would be out the door, picked up by Dai Rees and whisked off to be among a simmering throng of friends to die for, on the cusp of game-time.

Now is his calling to be strong. He's doing this for them. To hold himself high, like the outermost point of Worm's Head, which rises proudly against stormy seas. This is for Wales, sneered at and dismissed by the soulless. This is for Mum and

Dad, expelled by the same. This is for Ivon, a reject before he was born. So much is converging upon him, the lightning rod. In Ivon are gathering the energies. In Ivon must the chemistry ignite.

The changing room throbs. Out there, above their heads, the arena is live and oppressive. The crowd are assuming position and working their levers and pedals. It is a metallic, ugly sound they make, and menacing too, like an army on the horizon. Deep beneath the pounding feet, an expectant call to arms is transmitted to those in the changing rooms. It fills the air with tension and omen.

Ivon's head is bowed as he sits alone in his cubicle, cradling his rock, summoning the spirits of his homeland. He is sick with nerves and shakes his head as if to rid himself of them. Why must he suffer like this? He knows he's good. In Wales, it was the pats on the back that affirmed his talent, the bar-side chats with old men who had seen them all, the looks from teammates when the game was there to be won or lost; and in England, within a few days, they'd supplied the stats to quantify his prowess. Ivon can play rugby. There is nothing to fear. He's played hundreds of matches.

But never the next one. No matter his achievements, no matter the intellectual reasons for confidence, the fear of what is to come will always prevail. Ivon remembers his first game for Mumbles Youth, when Dad railed at him for not eating his lunch. And then on the morning of his Swansea debut he'd climbed into the ground and sat in the stand for two hours, staring at the pitch.

This time there are no superstitions to ease his fear, bar this communion with the smuggled rock of Ivon. London does not allow superstition. Here he has no father, no mentor, no friends, no cracks in the match-day routine to fill with impromptu séances. His teammates are lifeless and distant. Even Tim the scrum-half seemed vacant until they went out onto the pitch to warm up. They have retreated to their own cubicles now to make final preparations and adjustments. He is alone in his. When can it start?

The opaqueness of his little cell twists his mind, with its smooth walls and still, shadowless light. Ivon can bear it no longer. He heads for the door. It swishes open, and he tumbles into the courtyard. Tim is there already. They exchange a look but no words. A horn sounds close by. Tim starts at it and assumes a position outside his cubicle. Simultaneously, each player steps out to stand in file, before the climb up to the arena. The tall lock forward, whom Ivon knows now as Moby Trent, waits until all are ready. Silently, he leads the troop out of the changing room and up the steps to pitchside.

Ivon climbs with head down. The pounding of the stadium is muffled but reverberates thoroughly, as if they were underwater. With each step the noise sharpens and intensifies. Come the final few, the clarity is overwhelming. Ivon and his teammates break through the surface into a new world, which exists only for this, a bubble inaccessible to the outside and not governed by the same laws, into which the chosen few can pass only via that purgatory beneath the stands.

Ivon raises his head. First, he sees the opposition come out in time with them from an entrance on the other side of the pitch. Then, he takes in the great canopy above their heads and the walls around them of countless levers flashing to the rhythm of their operatives, the space swollen with the hard-edged din. The noise begins to abate as they walk towards the centre of the field, until a perfect hush descends, which might have thrown him had it registered. But Ivon's focus has tightened.

Now his nervousness, so crippling underground, begins its transformation into the electric fluidity of being ready. It happens quickly, and by the time he stands over the halfway line with the ball in his hands, the agony of the preceding hours is purged and forgotten. His senses and reflexes are heightened, his field of reference narrow. He is a renewed animal, poised between this moment and the next, purely active, perfectly existent. This is what he is for.

❁

Anonymity is not a convention that comes naturally to Ivon. From up here, high among the 33 000 comps in the White City Arena, Dusty can see clearly which of the contestants below is different from the others. The luminescence of the hair marks out the London fly-half, even before his facility with the ball does.

This university match was not on Dusty's comping schedule, but he managed to arrange a swap with one of the vets at ReSure. A swap to attend Ivon's first match for London! The Welshman he has introduced into society! His presence here will not be viewed as a coincidence. Excessive Interest In Another. Dusty has built up much credit over the years, but credit will run out for even the most respected. The prospect no longer alarms him.

It is not the first time he has comped at a rugby match, but it is the first time he's actually watched what happens on the field. As on the crude stone steps in Swansea, from which he first saw Ivon, he cannot take his eyes off the blond fly-half. Ivon's every touch seems to reek of potential. The thrill of what might happen. Dusty suspects this new spirit moving him is Welsh. How much more ethereal it is, more life-giving, than the preoccupation with what is actual, the achievement, the points on the board.

Now Ivon has his first chance to convert some of the potential into actual. The stadium computer sounds its siren to signal a penalty for London. While Ivon lines up the shot at goal, Dusty prepares with everyone else to begin working the pumps. It's a straightforward kick. But what's this? The waterbot is bringing out not a regular kicking tee, but a bucket of sand!

Ivon takes a scoop and pours it onto the glowing patch of turf that marks the point of offence. He seems to be constructing a platform of his own from which to launch the ball! How delightfully, delightfully…*different*! London really do want to make the boy feel at home. Dusty is impressed. He laughs and turns to the comp sitting next to him, eager to point out the idiosyncrasy, but thinks better of it. Besides, his neighbour is concentrating too much on his pumping position to be concerned with what's happening on the pitch.

The kick is true – Dusty hears it more as a perfectly pitched note – and the ball sails between the posts, initiating the steady blasts of the computer's energy siren. The stadium generator roars into life. Dusty begins to work his levers and pumps, but it is with a smile on his face. Ivon has begun, and he cannot wait to see more.

There's no need to watch. As soon as he strikes the ball, Ivon is turning to rejoin his teammates. A perfect contact like that leads to a perfect trajectory. It cannot do otherwise. Physics. He doesn't need to check with his eyes.

At least that has done something for the atmosphere. It had dawned on him that the stadium had fallen silent, which was beginning to freak him out. Coach Davis's instructions were ringing loud in his head, just as they had at training yesterday, when the stadium was empty. But now the air is thick with sound, harsh and soulless though it may be, like a thousand hydraulic drills. It started with some kind of fanfare from up in the eves, which was immediately drowned out by the noise of this mass workout the crowds are put through in England. Ivon marvels at the steep ranks of pistons surrounding the field, thousands upon thousands of them, remorselessly pounding out their infernal rhythm. From somewhere, deep beneath them, a rumble strikes up whose frequency seems to shake the arena, while on the air Ivon thinks he can hear the sustained note of a human roar sweeping round the stadium in waves. As London prepare to receive the restart, the noise does not relent.

But these voices in his head are bothering him. It's like a running commentary. Coach Davis and his two assistants study their screens and shout their findings throughout the players' heads. No wonder these guys are so dead behind the eyes. They've never thought for themselves. He can see it in his teammates; he can see it in the opposition. How he would like to run at them under his own instruction. Everyone is playing the match by rote. Including Ivon.

He doesn't like it. He responds to a higher power, higher even than Coach Davis, sitting up there on his platform, elevated from the rattling crowd. His quickness of spirit cannot be given over to some technician in the rafters; it must be acted upon directly. Ivon is here to play as Ivon.

The countdown lights in the stadium roof extinguish one by one, and the three minutes are over. Dusty is pleased. It is not easy to watch the match while you're pumping.

The arena is silent again, but for the urgent cries of the contestants and the faint murmur around the stands of citizens catching their breath and talking with each other between pumps. Since Ivon's penalty, the ball has remained mostly in the University of Aberdeen's possession. They are developing a maul, the working chatter of which is now revealed.

Dusty's eyes keep flitting towards Ivon, but for the next few minutes the boy is powerless. His voice is prominent as London's defence marshal themselves against a series of attacks. He looks and sounds confident.

But oh no! Aberdeen are clean through! There was a huge gap in midfield. Now their winger is running for the corner.

Ivon has managed to recover. He hits him into touch as he dives for the line. Is it a try? Yes. The siren wails to confirm it.

Ivon is gesticulating. Just like Ricky.

○

'There's no way that's a try!'

'Of course it's a try,' says Moby Trent. 'Can't you hear the siren?'

'Well, the fucking siren's wrong! I hammered him! If this was proper grass, you'd see the marks.'

'He got it down before he went into touch.'

'Bollocks!'

Moby looks down on Ivon with confusion and contempt. He shrugs and shakes his head. 'The stadium computer says it's a try. Get back behind the line! We've a conversion to face.'

Now Coach Davis joins in. 'Ten, you were at fault for the initial break,' he says in Ivon's head.

'Oh, come on! What is this? Pick on the new boy, is it? And my name's Ivon, not 10.'

'You should have been tighter to 12. Their centre went through the gap you left.'

'Twelve drifted too soon. He followed the dummy runner.'

'I've just run the sequence through the system. It's saying you were at fault.'

'Do you lot listen to anything that's not a computer?'

The conversion is missed, and Ivon trots back to the halfway line for the restart. Strangely, he is encouraged by the try. That was a sweetly timed move they pulled off. So, there is room for artistry over here. Heavily choreographed, mind.

Ivon's restart is well struck. It hangs in the air and teases out a tissue of grasping hands towards it. Moby's rise the highest. He pulls in the ball, and London are on the attack.

Ivon does as he is told while they build some rhythm, but he is no longer listening to the instructions of Coach Davis – 'Inside ball', 'To 6 on your right shoulder'. If he is giving the impression of following orders it is because the orders represent standard procedure, while he waits for the opportunity to break the pattern.

It comes during the same passage of play. Ivon shapes to play yet another inside ball to a frowning forward, when he spots a moment of doubt in the eyes of the flanker opposite, who hesitates as if trying to remember his lines. Ivon does not release the pass, but sweeps the ball beneath the nose of the flanker, who turns towards the man inside.

And Ivon is off. Adrenaline rises in him, as he accelerates into space. For a second or two, his vision widens and as he crosses the 22 he changes direction, drawing the full-back towards the right-hand touchline. He will not score – the full-back reacts with speed and seeming confidence – but a support runner of any kind surely would. There is none. The full-back's shoulder crunches into Ivon's ribs. He tries to go to ground, but the full-back is strong and drives him into touch.

'We've lost the ball, 10!' cries Coach Davis. 'We were building nicely, and you've lost us the ball!'

Ivon is flabbergasted. 'We've gained 40 metres! And if there'd been just one player in support we would have scored. Where were you all?'

His teammates stare at him blankly.

'They were all doing what they were supposed to,' continues Coach Davis. 'You went off-message.'

'But I saw a gap. You're not seriously saying I shouldn't take it, are you?'

'No one takes a gap unless I tell them it's on. We have all the data up here, and the projections. We know how the match is unfolding before you do. If there's a gap opening we'll let you know. And then we'll make sure you have support runners to hand. Not before.'

'But there *was* a gap! I proved that much by running clean through it, for fuck's sake!'

'It's no use taking a gap if no one else is ready for it. You'll become isolated and lose the ball.'

'Well, make them ready for it! If they're that brain-dead, you could have told someone to get in support. But you didn't. You just sat there and said nothing.'

'Stick to your orders, 10!'

Ivon turns to his teammates. 'Lads! You're not telling me you can't think for yourselves!'

His forwards march past towards the line-out. No one so much as looks at him.

Tim the scrum-half follows. He has a twinkle in his eye. As he trots on to the line-out, he whispers. 'Great break, Ivon! Next time, I'll get there.'

It's all Ivon needs. Encouragement, recognition. Sanity. He's through again a few minutes later, and this time he makes it to the try line himself. The relief of more noise to fill the arena is inspiring. Coach Davis seems to raise his game, too, because now he is calling more ambitiously. With his endorsement, the rest of the team start to wake up. Some of them can play a bit, it turns out, and by half-time London have scored three tries. The place is thundering to the workout of 33 000 people.

Oh, the agony! The sweet, sweet agony! Dusty is gasping. It has been almost an hour of non-stop pumping. The vets around him struggle to maintain kinesis, but all are smiling – laughing, even. When was the last time London enjoyed a surfeit of pumping like this? Certainly not since Dusty became a comp. The elite comps in the adjacent block are whooping and hollering as their fearsome sinews thrash at the turbines. Relief has been sent for so that the vets can be substituted, such is their exhaustion. They will have to carry on till the points have been pumped through, which is already set to be beyond full-time. London have been scoring at a rate of more than a point a minute in the second half. The score is past 60 with more than 5 minutes to run. But relief will arrive for the 40-minute victory pump afterwards. Dusty is aware of pandemonium in the wings. The commune of London hasn't needed to supply relief to its comps for a long time.

Ivon. What a contestant! And, what the hell, why not use the Welsh vernacular – what a *player*! Dusty's beginning to see the difference.

Here he is, on the ball again! Time seems to stand still as he shapes to pass to a comrade cutting inside him. The defender opposite is transfixed, and Ivon darts round him like a child at the base of a statue. He closes in on the last man, with another closing in on him. The ball rocks this way and that, as he taunts the defenders with it. But what was that?! How did he get that pass away? Was it behind his back? It was! Almost too quick to see! Try number 10! Ha! It's the best yet! Dusty laughs out loud and looks about him to share the moment with someone. There are smiles everywhere, but it is at the siren for yet another score. No one has seen the try itself. That's seventy up! And another seven minutes of pumping is added on.

The vets are exhausted. Exhausted but abuzz. It may have been only tertiary level, but 72 points! That's a lot of energy by any standards. Where did that productivity come from?

Dusty knows, but it is not politic to point to the contribution of one man. The Perpetual mindset would not even deem it plausible. It is the commune's win, after all. Not long ago, Dusty would have agreed. Now, though, he is alive to the power of something more magical. It is charisma, if only he knew it. But, to Dusty, it is simply Ivon.

VII

Alanis raises her arms and, with eyes closed, turns blissfully amid the jets of hot air. She can feel the moisture leaving her skin. She shakes out her hair and runs her fingers through it, helping the droplets of water towards their end.

'So, what was the score?' she asks Melissa Toni, as they take their conversation from the shower into the dry-off.

'Seventy-two–fifteen.'

'Seventy-two?! Oh, my joules! That's incredible!'

'So, there were 33 000 comps at the match, and the yield was 58.7 gigajoules,' Melissa continues, above the gentle drone of the air jets. 'Guess how many times London Rugby have generated more this season at Twickenham with 82 750?'

Alanis doesn't answer. Her eyes remain closed, as she passes her hands lightly across her body. But she is listening.

'Once,' says Melissa, with some derision.

'I thought URL had been struggling like everyone else.'

'They have been. This has come completely out of the blue.'

'Oh, Melissa! Do you think this could be the turning point the commune's been longing for?'

Alanis looks to her comrade imploringly. Melissa is shorter than she is, but there is such spring in those powerful legs. She admires them now, as Melissa bends down to caress her calves dry. Alanis has always felt grateful for her comrade's prowess on the field – and safe.

121

'If it had happened at elite level, maybe. But tertiary? I don't know.' Melissa straightens up to receive the warm air across her breasts again. 'It's a remarkable result, though. The fact we're talking about it now says a lot.'

Alanis is dry. To stand any longer between the hot jets would be gratuitous. She follows Melissa, who is already marching purposefully towards the dusting chamber. Leaving the sensuousness of the dry-off is a regret Alanis barely notices.

'Oh, but doesn't it just give you hope! News like that justifies all the work we do.'

'It reminds you how good things once were, and could be again. If we keep working.'

'Exactly!'

London *is* one of the great communes! How quickly that can be forgotten! Could you ever imagine East Anglia putting 72 points past someone, or the South East? At any level? Alanis laughs at the idea. No, a prolonged slump this may be, but pedigree is pedigree. London is magnificent, and Alanis is part of that. She turns in the dusting chamber with confidence and a flourish. Today is going to be a good day.

Decisions, decisions. She has a bout booked at the club with Ivon in 1 hour 43 minutes. After her training session and protein supplement with Melissa, Alanis should really take the aerobus to NorthWest3 and pass the time till her bout in the recovery lounge, but it's such a lovely day she wonders if she could get away with cycling there. If she takes her time, it could qualify as part of her low-intensity programme for the week.

She sets max. output at 128 watts and heads off. The roads are gleaming today, and they teem with citizens about their business. There is a new energy about London, no question.

The aerobus glides past her. Alanis is so glad she's not on it. It is all but empty, even fewer passengers than usual, and she smiles to herself at the eagerness of Londoners to propel themselves around town. Truly, with spirit like theirs, a slump can never last long!

Through Finsbury Park and Tufnell Park she maintains steady progress. She would dearly love to go faster. The sun is on her shoulders, the road is clean and blue and seems to impart momentum itself, so joyful is its lustre. But she has a responsibility towards London not to over-exercise. Cycling to the club is already close to an indulgence, what with her high-intensity workout with Melissa this morning and a bout with Ivon to come. And all this in her Spring Recess.

It is Ivon, though, so she is prepared for a light bout. Frank Hiscock told her yesterday that he would likely be around with joules to spend this afternoon. If Ivon comes up short again she'll take a cot with him. Or someone. No matter. She'll somehow bank the sort of energy she intends to. Just looking around convinces her of that. So many citizens; so many joules.

Now, this is interesting. Alanis arrives at the club, and it is clear even from the outside that something is going on in the foyer. When she enters, she can see, indeed, that the place is in a state of rare confusion, a throng having gathered at the desk.

Alanis loiters amid the hubbub, trying to identify the source of the unrest. She is relieved to note that the twenty or so agitants are all wearing the yellow of the tertiary class, for such behaviour would be unbecoming of elites. Alanis knew there would be trouble when the club opened its membership to the tertiaries.

'Please! Citizens!' cries John Garcia, the club manager. 'We cannot accept any more new members today. Our monthly quota has now been filled.'

'So when can we next enrol?' replies one of the tertiaries.

'The first of June.'

'But that's more than a week away!'

Further cries of protest ring round the foyer.

'There's nothing more we can do!' adds John. 'I'm sorry. Why are you all so keen to join? There are countless clubs like ours across London.'

The question is ignored as the unseemly commotion flares up again. Alanis is disgusted, but she notices Jessica the receptionist in a conversation to one side of the desk and slips through the melee towards her. When their eyes meet, Jessica waves at her.

'Here she is now,' she says to two tertiaries, who turn to Alanis plaintively.

'The register says you have a bout with Ivon at 14.30?' says one of them, a brunette with a dimple in her cheek. 'Would you mind swapping?'

'Now, hang on!' says the other. 'I enrolled first! If she's going to swap with anyone it should be me!'

Alanis is taken aback by the request. How odd that someone should want to swap! 'I'm sure there are plenty of men in the recovery lounges available for a bout. Why don't you book with one of them?'

The brunette seems to flex and stand a little taller. 'No, no. I quite specifically want a bout with Ivon.'

Alanis glances at Jessica, who shrugs. She is about to agree – Frank Hiscock is available, after all – when defiance flares in her. No, she will not swap! Why should she, a long-standing member of the club, an elite, pander to the irregular whims of a tertiary?

'I'm sorry, but the appointment has been in the diary for a while. We've already had to rearrange it once. Why don't you just book one with him another time?'

'We've been through his schedule. He has booking requests in place for every viable slot from now until the diary horizon.'

'Well then make a booking with somebody else!'

'I don't want anybody else!'

The tertiary's outburst is piercing. A hush descends among the throng, as the two women face each other.

She doesn't want anybody else?!

'Look to yourself, sister!' hisses Alanis. 'This is Misalignment!'

The tertiary knows it and backs down, glancing awkwardly towards the desk. Alanis, a good few inches taller, sweeps past her towards the lounges.

✹

This is more like it. Not that it's necessarily a good thing, this attention. Ivon hasn't decided on that yet. In Wales, he found it invigorating to be hailed in the street. And warming. A drink was never far away, nor a friendly word. No chance of that here. He senses a different attitude on London's sterilised streets. They're not so easily impressed. No, that's not it. They're not so easily *moved*.

But he is relieved, at least, that some people have noticed his performance yesterday. He thought he played pretty bloody well. So, it turns out, do these folk standing over him now, swarming round in the same yellow suits as his, peering at him reclined on one of these space-age chaise-longue things they arrange so neatly in pairs up and down the lounges. One of them, the first to notice him, has flung herself on the twin of the one he is lying on. She studies him coolly, but with a twist of intensity. She says she has put in for a slot with him next Monday. He doesn't know how to respond to that. The rest have gathered round since, some loose enough to ask him questions, others watching like students at a dissection.

When will Alanis get here? He needs some human contact, some softness, some give. What a release it was just to run out onto a field and play yesterday. And yet has the experience not left him hanging? He felt nothing from his teammates afterwards, and there was nothing. No celebration, no alcohol, no women, no myth-making, no love. He returned to his quarters in turmoil, effervescing without vent, a crescendo without resolution. The upheaval of contest must be smoothed over with festivity. These people aren't human.

'Is it true you're from Wales?' asks the most talkative of his new admirers. He's tall. Ivon tries to imagine what sport he plays. Maybe a fast bowler. Or a basketball player. He laughs a lot, but it bursts from him suddenly, as by a switch. The others are quick to join in each time.

'Yes. From Gower.'

'Tell us about Wales, Ivon. Do they really not observe the Sanctity of Physical Fitness?'

'We're fit!' protests Ivon. Then he slumps back into the couch. 'But it's a means, not an end. Play, live. That's what we do in Wales.'

Just as he says it, Alanis appears. He smiles despite himself. She sees him and waves. There is colour in her cheeks, which reminds him of Cerys during the good times.

'Ivon!' she calls as she sweeps towards him. When she notices his new friends, she pauses and frowns in bemusement. Or is it with disdain?

Ivon reclines luxuriously on his couch and turns out his hands in resignation. 'What can I say? I seem to have picked up some admirers!'

He rises to take her hand. This time he stands close, as she pulls his arm into her breast.

Alanis turns to the girl in yellow on the couch next to his. 'Excuse me, could you move to another couch, please? He and I are waiting for a cot.'

The girl snaps to her feet with what sounds like a squeal. 'My name is Tanya Elg,' she says to Ivon, as if they don't have much time. 'I've put in for Monday, 15.30. Please ratify.'

With that, she retreats with the rest of the group, staring viciously at Alanis as she goes.

'Oh, these tertiaries,' says Alanis, as she takes up position on the couch. 'I knew letting them in here was a mistake.'

'I'm a tertiary, aren't I?'

'I don't know where they're all coming from. There's a crowd of them at reception trying to enrol.'

'What does she mean, "ratify"?'

'She must have put her name down for a bout with you. If you ratify it, that will complete the booking.'

'But I don't even know her.'

'At the desk, they said you have booking requests right up to the diary horizon. It's highly irregular.'

'And I'm just supposed to go with these women, am I?'

Alanis shrugs. 'Unless you have a reason not to.'

'What if I want to go with someone else? You, for example?'

Ivon watches her closely. Is that the same flush on her cheek he noticed when she first arrived, or is it deeper now?

'Normally, it wouldn't be a problem. Subject to my diary, we could arrange it. But this backlog of requests for one person is most unusual. It's not right.'

Is it so unusual, though? What's unusual is that he's expected to honour them all. Ivon is well used to the idea of women wanting to sleep with him, but he's not used to them putting their names down in a diary. And he's always reserved the right to say no. Before Cerys decided she'd had enough of it, he didn't even have to do that. He'd just seek her out and give her a kiss. He's taken, ladies. Sorry. If only she hadn't been away the three times. He's not perfect; he should have been faithful, like Dafydd Bennett, but no one fancies Dai, so it's not a fair comparison, is it? Anyone can be faithful without propositions. Much harder when the place is full of people making a move on you. He always told her, though. He couldn't keep secrets.

He loved her. For nearly half his life. He wants to find love again. Especially here, in a cold place like England. He's not going to find it in a diary of names. Someone real.

He looks across at Alanis and longs to tell her. She doesn't seem to have made the connection. Has she not heard about his performance yesterday? Surely, it's obvious why these women are queuing up.

'It could be to do with the game.'

'Game?'

'Sorry, match. Ours. Rugby. Yesterday'

Alanis beams. Genuinely. Stunningly. The rouge in her cheek, the hair pulled back against an open, honest face, around which play a few whisps, escapees from the hair band's discipline. Shit, she's gorgeous. Older than him, no doubt, but as fresh and hearty as she must have looked in her youth. Cerys had that, the same rosiness as a woman as when they were at school. As if she were always just back from the woods, ever so slightly out of breath. As if there should be sweat on her brow. As if she were too pure for sweat.

'Oh, 72–15!' she cried. 'Oh, Ivon! What news! What a relief! If ever I'm irritated by these tertiaries, I just have to think of that! Do you think this could be the start of a revival?'

He's not sure she even realises he was playing. She certainly doesn't seem to understand that the whole thing was basically down to him. Does anyone seriously think they'd have scored 72 if it had been left to the English? No. He's the 72. She's looking at the source of her own ecstasy.

'It was my first match in London, you know.'

She smiles, but then she was smiling already. Maybe her mouth opens a little wider and her eyebrows arch higher. Either way, it is all offered in a spirit of encouragement, a good-for-you supplement to the main event, not the loin-centric unwinding of her composure he'd hoped for. Alanis is impressed only by that scoreline. The part Ivon might have played in it does not seem to be of interest.

And, to think, they're about to disappear together anyway down a dimly lit corridor to cut to the chase. He should be more excited about that than he is. He looks forward to the feel of her skin, but he hasn't earned it. What about the rituals? The flirting, the drinking, the banter, the off-to-war heroics on the pitch, the peacockery of it all? They've done away with it. Seduction has been bypassed.

Not human, these English.

She won't need that bout with Frank Hiscock, after all. Wow! Ivon! That was momentous! So often it can be hard work maintaining noise levels beyond the second or third changeover, but not that time. That time, it would have been harder not to scream. Actually, there were a couple of intervals there when she didn't want to change over at all. Sometimes it all feels so right and something goes off inside her. She's sure there are more joules arising when it happens.

They reach the recovery lounge – and, after the day she's had, Alanis intends to recover – but her heart sinks when she hears another commotion, just like the one in the foyer earlier on. Sure enough, there is another unruly gathering in the lounge, and the yellow suits of the tertiary run through it like a stain.

'I discovered his name!' shrieked one of the two girls at the centre of the row. It is the same tertiary Alanis had words with at the desk. 'I discovered which was his club! I deserve a bout with him before you! You owe me that!'

The girl she is screaming at is also a tertiary, the one Alanis shooed off the couch when she first sat down with Ivon that afternoon. Both are being held back from each other by flustered club officials. It really is most irregular.

'That information is available to anyone,' hisses the other. 'I was the one who noticed him during the match. If it wasn't for me, you wouldn't even know he existed. You were too busy buffing your triceps surae.'

'You shitting idler!'

'Apathetic, day-dreaming slob!'

'Ladies! Language, please!' cries John Garcia. 'No one is emerging from this with any credit.'

Suddenly, the second of the quarrelling tertiaries spots Ivon. She breaks free from her restrainer's grasp and runs towards him, stopping within inches.

'Please, Ivon, ratify me! My name is Tanya Elg. Monday, 15.30!'

The other tertiary screams unashamedly and thrashes to no avail in a bid to break free. John appears quickly at Tanya's shoulder and tries to usher her away, but, with the faintest hint of a sigh, she flings herself at Ivon. Her arms slip round his back and tighten their grip, so that the side of her head is pressed firmly against his chest. Her face is turned towards Alanis, who can see that it is twisted into an expression of extreme effort, the eyes screwed tightly shut, the mouth stretched unnaturally.

A gasp goes up around the room, soon followed by cries of protest and disgust at the unsanctioned physical contact. Ivon, to his credit, remains impassive. Fancy that, the Perpetual citizen in disarray, the Welshman in control. Oh, the shame of it!

There is a movement in the room towards Tanya, but Alanis is closest to this exhibition of wantonness. She seizes the girl and tries to prize her free from Ivon.

'Get off him!' she cries. 'How dare you! It's disgusting!'

John is soon lending his assistance and together they pull her away, before others converge to subdue the girl amid angry protestations.

'Ratify me, Ivon!' Tanya screeches, quite out of control. 'Just one bout!'

'Save your energy for someone else!' cries John.

'I don't want anyone else! I don't want anyone else!'

That's what the other tertiary screamed at the desk earlier. What is this insidious preoccupation with one man? It must not be allowed to spread any further! It's as if these people see coitus with Ivon as something to yearn for, something more than a drawing off of energy. Alanis fears for the reputation of the club. And, if this unnatural strain of individualism is allowed to develop, for the stability of society. It would be intolerable for such a breakdown in discipline to take hold just as London is showing signs of a recovery. Intolerable.

✸

That was decisive. Ivon enjoyed that. Alanis wasn't taking any shit. What a woman! She really didn't like that girl hugging him, did she? At all.

He was beginning to wonder whether he was getting through to her. She has always shown him smiles and breezy friendliness, but he wasn't sure he'd made a connection. He's feeling surer now. That session in the sex room seems to have loosened her up. And why wouldn't it have? That was a shag from the end of the world. He's still feeling wobbly. And now this, a further show of passion he hadn't thought an English girl capable of. It's taken a bit of work, but she's coming round. Soon she'll be his. The more he realises, the more he knows that this, Alanis and he, is what he wants.

There she stands, flustered and gorgeous, between the two women screaming at each other and wrestling with their captors. The room is noisy with people appealing for calm. Ivon spots Dusty in the far corner – just watching, of course.

Suddenly, four men in black burst in. Without a word they split into two pairs, one heading for each of the hysterical girls.

As the girls are handed over, their screaming and struggling suddenly stop. Was it the touch of the men in black that quietened them, or the mere sight? Ivon cannot tell, but the manner of their submission unnerves him. With heads bowed, they are led away from the room, which is now in the grip of a silence as sudden and complete as the girls' capitulation. Not one of the men in black says a word, their adamant expressions set rigid and severe.

Murmuring creeps round the room once they're gone. Alanis straightens her suit.

'What the fuck was that?' says Ivon.

'Assimilation,' says Alanis without looking at him. 'They'll be taken to the IC and assimilated. Those two were chronically misaligned.'

'What's the IC?'

'The Institute of Correction. They'll be corrected.'

'You're making it sound very sinister.'

Alanis looks at him now. She's not smiling. The eyebrows are up again, though – just slightly this time, enough for him to take her seriously.

'My advice to you is not to ratify any coitus requests for now,' she says. 'At least not from anyone you don't know. Something's not right about this.'

'That's fine by me. You're the only person I know here. Let's clear our diaries and get it on!'

Alanis settles down on a couch and rests a hand across her brow. 'Those two have riled me. I was hoping to have a good rest.'

She closes her eyes, and Ivon is able to admire the length of her. Here, at last, is his home from home.

VIII

Dusty has gone too far. The noise of a cracking fills the air and rents his soul. Something has broken, because the seat he sits on drops suddenly. For a mortifying moment he is falling. Even when he settles again, he knows he is in danger. They are in danger. He looks to his right and by the moonlight sees Ivon, unmistakably Ivon, strapped into a seat, but older than Dusty knows him. At his feet, beneath a steering wheel, a silvery slick of water appears with a brief swirl, a flourish, as if by way of introduction, then begins the urgent business of swelling. Where is the water coming from? Dusty knows only that it is their danger made manifest. His recklessness must yield consequences. He panics and instinctively reaches for a handle to his left. It activates the latch in a door, against which he pushes hard. The door is heavy, but he forces it open against the water outside, which seeps into the footwell, burning him with its coldness. Free, Dusty wades across unstable ground towards a ledge of ice. He scrambles up onto it and sees that the ledge is, in fact, an empire of ice, smooth and unchallenged in all directions, interrupted only by the hole he has climbed out of. He watches now, in horror, as an ancient metal vehicle lists and rocks on a platform that is steadily sinking into that hole. The headlights wave slowly and hopelessly on their descent, until their mayday is smothered beneath the water. But there is another light on inside the vehicle. Dusty can see within its beam Ivon turn this way and that, searching in vain for a way out, strapped in a sinking cage, his mop of hair glowing eerily. Until it too slips beneath the ice.

He sits up with a gasp. It is 3.39 a.m. Slowly he lowers himself back into bed. He thinks about illuminating the room, but that would draw attention in these times of austerity, so he stares into the darkness instead.

He cannot see a way out. For Ivon. How could he have thought this a good idea? As if Ivon would put in a shift in a few matches, impress London in a quiet, understated way, then return to Wales, with all of them, Ivon, Dusty and London, better off for the experience. And Ivon will want to go back. He asked again about 'phoning' Ricky and Dee only yesterday, just after that incident at the club.

This growing storm of attention around him is dangerous, but it was inevitable. Dusty was right about Ivon – too right. London has never known anything like him. For now the unstable and weak of character are being drawn to his flame, but the attention of more formidable agents is sure to follow. Indeed, it has been pricked already. In Ivon, London has found a precious new asset. And London never gives up one of those.

Dusty feels the tug of nostalgia as he cycles through Kennington. With a wicked smile to himself, he decides to go out of his way to ride past the Oval. He relishes the memories it evokes of those early years on the field, where he learned to apply his technique with the Academy team. A flush rises in him as he indulges in these illicit meanderings, not only wallowing in the Past like this but cycling more than is necessary to do it! As he carries on down Nine Elms Lane towards the Academy itself, the nostalgia thickens further. Thirty years ago, when the sun shone on a Tuesday, they used to stretch out in recovery on these green banks rolling down to the Thames. His heart longs for those times.

The closer he draws to the Academy, the more he braces himself for the moment he sets eyes on the old place again. (The 'old place' – just listen to him!) He looks ahead, searching the skyline for the absurd Lapsed-Era chimneys that rose uselessly into the sky from each of the ancient building's four corners. The heavy brick, the four square walls, how he and his comrades used to mock the place for its lumbering antiquity! But he thinks about it now, all these years later, with affection.

He passes one of the Academy's home blocks, sure that he will see those chimneys heave into view – but they are not there! The Academy of Cricket has been rebuilt. In its place rises a new building that glints in the morning sun and means nothing to him. It's for the best. He can go about his business here with a head clear of memories.

He has an appointment with the Academy's TMS officer MacAulay Elsom, who greets him warmly and leads him through a sunny atrium into the opaque corridors of the Faculty of Improvement.

'So you want to attend this afternoon's TMS procedure?'

Dusty nods.

'I imagine you've undergone such therapy yourself.'

'Yes. I'm not sure it had any effect on me, though. At least none that I noticed.'

'Not many do notice much difference on a conscious level – until they next perform the skill in question, when they will have a sense of having performed it many more times than they actually have.'

'I don't remember that.'

'Of course not. But the end result was evidently productive. I see your cover drive is due for upload when you reach stasis.'

Dusty winces to himself. The prospect of that honour troubles him now. A piece of his experience will be carried forward by who knows how many batsmen in a cause he no longer considers sacred.

MacAulay leads Dusty from the pearly glow of the faculty corridor into a small dark cubicle, one wall of which is a window onto a larger room. In that room, a man lies on a table, his head and shoulders couched in a chip interface. A scientist potters round him, taking readings, tending equipment.

'This subject has been prepped,' says MacAulay. 'His existing stock should have been rendered ripe for removal by now. Let me see.'

He sits at a terminal in front of the subject's neuromap, a glowing tree that hovers above the console. He navigates his way to the seat of memory, and the map morphs and seems to rush towards Dusty. It mushrooms into the heart of the neo-cortex. MacAulay swoops through the molecular clusters like a fighter pilot in space, arrowing in on the relevant collection of memories.

'We're looking for the pull shot today,' he says. 'The first part of the procedure is to remove all episodic memories of completed pull shots from his neo-cortex. Of course, the motor memory of the skill itself remains untouched. These are just the snapshots of each execution of the skill that the subject has stored in his unconscious mind. Together, the collection provides a kind of support structure to the motor neurons whenever the skill is executed again. We call it the skill cache. Now let me check the neural coordinates for this subject.'

The neuromap twists this way and that, enlarging and contracting at speeds that leave Dusty bewildered. MacAulay cross-references his navigation with a string of numbers and letters on a tablet beside the console. At last, he unlocks a pressure pad, sits back and slaps it.

'There. In a few seconds our subject will have all memories of the pull shot wiped from his brain. If we were to release him then and expose him to the right kind of delivery he would instinctively pull it with some aplomb, no doubt. But he would feel as if he were doing it for the first time. By the time we've finished with him, though, he will feel as if he's been hitting pull shots for longer than he's actually been alive.'

MacAulay slides across the floor and draws out a rack of w-state memory balls. He runs his eye over them, as if choosing from a box of energy treats, and picks one out. 'Here we are. This is the skill host selected as compatible with our subject. One Titus John.'

'May I?' says Dusty, a sickness rising in him.

MacAulay shrugs and passes him the smooth black sphere, which Dusty rests on the palm of his hand. He stares for a moment at the shiny surface of it, dark and featureless, yet seeming to fall away into a bottomless universe within itself.

Titus John. 'I knew him, MacAulay. A right-hand bat from the middle order. He and I made hundreds of runs together. And here he rests? In this little globe?'

Dusty shakes his head. Titus John was a bear of a man, who smote the ball with power and immaculate timing. He must have been fifteen years older. Why is Dusty assailed by affection for him now that he holds him in his hand? As when he set eyes on the image of Daniel Attention, he wishes he could see Titus again, to talk to him, the way he was all those years ago. The way Dusty was.

'You could find his body in the vaults at ReSure,' says MacAulay, 'but, yes, the sum total of his conscious and unconscious mind sits within that memory ball. We're just after his pull shot, of course.'

MacAulay takes the ball and offers it to the computer's q-drive, which opens up a port to encapsulate it. Another neuromap rises up before him, and he executes more bewildering manoeuvres as he isolates Titus's stock of pull shots. It should be an extensive collection. Dusty remembers the stroke well.

'You're no doubt aware of the theory behind transmigration of the skill,' says MacAulay. 'We're effectively airlifting a stock of vivid memories of a skill, as executed by a master, into a subject's neo-cortex, and this enhances the consolidation of that skill in future practice. The associations are set more swiftly and purely, and myelination is effected more comprehensively along the relevant axons, which is the ultimate aim, of course.'

Again, he slaps a pressure pad and turns to Dusty. 'There we are. The memories are being sent to his chip, which will administer their consolidation into the neo-cortex. This one will take [he leans over to view a counter on the console] 3 hours, 23 minutes. There are around twenty-five years' worth of pull shots to be taken up, after all. But, come, let's see how this morning's subjects are responding.'

Out in the gallery above the training corridors, Dusty and MacAulay watch half a dozen batsmen at work beneath the sunny vault of the new complex. The results are varied, thinks Dusty, one looking comfortable in front of his bowling aperture, others shot-making with confidence but suffering from wayward technique and timing, while one or two look as if they must have regressed altogether, certainly if they have been Academy trained.

'It's important to get them working as soon after the therapy as possible,' says MacAulay. 'The sooner the pathways are exercised between the cerebellum and the subject's new memory stock, the more influence the latter will bring to bear and the more native it will come to feel. You can see now that it's not feeling native at all to some of them, but with time it will come, according to the orientation and conductivity of the athlete's cortico-cortical pathways. Each subject is different.'

'And what's the worst-case scenario for someone who has undergone TMS?'

MacAulay turns to Dusty with a soft frown on his lively features. 'Nothing to speak of. Probably a lack of response. Much like you reported.'

'If I told you that everyone else who took it with me thirty-three years ago departed prematurely, what would you say?'

MacAulay turns away sharply towards the athletes below, exercising in their corridors. 'Look, I'd only just emerged thirty-three years ago. I have no idea what might have happened. These days, TMS is a high-precision procedure of little or no risk to the subject. I can't say if that was the case back then.'

'Do you know Syracuse Garbo?'

'No.'

Dusty offers him his hand. 'Thank you, MacAulay, for your time.'

✸

The ball rolls end over end along the white line.

'Jump!' commands Ivon.

Precisely as he says it, the underside of the ball's point catches the turf, and the ball leaps up into the air like a gymnast, before continuing on its way again, end over end over end. There is a murmuring among the rest of the squad.

'Now, watch this. I'll get it to jump further on.'

Ivon takes up another ball and holds it out in front of him. He drops the ball and stabs his foot onto it, sending it bobbling after the last one. He raises his hand in the air, waits a little longer this time, then brings it down and cries, 'Jump!' The ball obeys.

Tim the scrum-half laughs. 'How do you *do* that?'

'I don't know. It's mystical, see. It's like the ball's a part of me and me of it. The point is,' he says, turning to the rest of the group, waving the next ball with animation, 'I can speak rugby fluently. If someone talks back at me on the field, I can take the conversation where I want it to go. But you guys, you've been taught to recite your rugby. You're given lines and you try to shout them louder than the opposition – when what you've got to do is speak the language off the top of your head. Change when the game changes. So, on Tuesday, let's ask them some questions they won't have prepared for, eh?'

Ivon can't help looking up into the eyes of Moby Trent, which sit highest amid the throng of bewildered faces. At least his eyes aren't dead, thinks Ivon. At least there's anger in them, some feeling.

'And do you think this is helping?' he asks aggressively. 'You showing us how you can talk to the ball. What use is that to any of us?'

'It doesn't have to be any use. I'm just trying to show you that we're the ones who are playing this game. The ball does as *we* say! Us! Not the coaches up in the rafters, not those people doing their workouts in the stands. *We* are in charge of what happens! Let's not wait to be told!'

Moby does not move. 'Don't ridicule us, Ivon.'

'I'm not ridiculing you! Fuck!'

'OK,' intervenes Coach Davis. 'OK. Let's end it there.'

The training session breaks up. Ivon doesn't like this moment. The tackle droids gather together and head off in formation towards their sheds. The balls do likewise. So they *can* move of their own accord. Internal chips, apparently. Or magnets or something. And then, no less without question or personality, the players flock towards the changing rooms.

Ivon watches them for a moment. The sun floods the vast hall of glass they've been training in. As Ivon follows his teammates towards the changing rooms, Coach Davis falls in step with him.

'Actually, Moby is wrong,' he says. 'There must be an application for that ball skill of yours. I've spoken to the lab, and I want you to report to the skills tunnel during your next recovery shift. They'll be expecting you. You've revealed a property of the pedal-ovoid relationship we were unaware of. We need to register and analyse it.' Coach Davis looks up towards the glinting rafters, the vents and the conductors. 'To know that the ball will jump up as a full-back stoops to gather it... Yes. Of course, there will be applications!'

Coach Davis leaves him at the entrance to the changing room. The usual hum, like faint static, emanates from inside, and Ivon steels himself to move once more among the murmurs and furtive glances. It may go against everything he holds to be true about a team, but the cubicle arrangement at the stadium is a relief when set against the iciness of this communal changing room at the university. Ivon strolls as breezily as he can towards his station. His day suit rests on the bench like a coiled spring. Just before he settles into the ergonomic seat beside it, he notices a corner of paper protruding beneath.

A piece of paper! Ivon realises that he hasn't seen one of those since he left Wales. It stands out in this smooth-hard world as quaint, or maverick, or personal. Something you can crumple, at any rate. It speaks to Ivon, and Ivon knows instinctively to keep secret any conversation between him and it. He places his hand on the paper and, checking as best he can that no one is looking, he draws it across the bench and into his lap. With it now concealed between his hand and hip, he glides from the room, back out into the natural light of the training compound.

The paper is folded in half. Ivon's name is written in an elegant script on the outside. It is underlined once with a nimble stroke that tapers from right to left. Ivon recognises in this the agency of a fellow left-hander. He opens the note. The same hand writes: 'We are friends. Our concern is the soul of sport. Yours in style, The Fellowship of Dig.'

Ivon looks up, as if to catch the heel of a retreating figure. All he sees, though, is the stillness of perfect turf under a vault of glass.

❋

Two full matches, one after the other. At elite level. Thirty-eight points scored. One hundred and sixty minutes played. And he hasn't moved a muscle.

Ivon closes down the simulation and opens his eyes. Wow! He was really playing. In his head. Didn't matter if he opened his eyes or got up from the couch, he was still in the game.

Don't ask him how. Central chip, nervous system, retinal projection – they're just some of the words people have been throwing at him lately. But that was more than a computer game. He felt every impact. Some of them really hurt. And yet his body is unharmed. Come to think of it, he played more than two full matches. He had to restart the second one, because, first time round, he picked up a virtual broken collarbone 15 minutes in.

Thirty-eight points, though. Pretty good. They tell him it's not the same, but if elite rugby in England is anything like it was in his head there, he thinks he'll do all right. The players were bigger, but Ivon has yet to have his conviction shaken that wit and instinct will prevail over straight-line muscle, even on this side of the Fence.

These games in the head, they're a way of focusing the mind. Everyone has to play a couple the night before a match. Beats sitting on the sofa at home visualising the perfect 80 minutes. Talking Dad through it. The kick-off, your first catch, your first pass, punt and tackle.

Or does it?

Anyone can play out a video game in the head. It's harder to use your own imagination. And it's dirtier on the sofa at home. Dirtier and saggier. More give. The carpet's colourful, the smells are mustier and tastier, the air thicker with the noise of a Welsh nuclear family. Wales is alive. It has heart.

Ivon looks round his new home. His new accommodation. This isn't a home. It's white. A white floor that feels a bit like leather; white walls as hard as metal; white whiteness. Nowhere to get a hold of anything.

He's trying. He's trying so hard. This *will* be a positive experience. That mental rugby *was* brilliant. Alanis. Sex. Rugby in front of 30000. Maybe 80000, if he makes elite. When…

So much to be excited by. And he will be excited. He must be. He can't slip back into the darkness. The endless hours. The opposite of sport. His temper.

Stay in the whiteness, Ivon.

But just a phone call. Mum, Dad.

Or Alanis. He's getting good at the mental phone thing, but she's never the same on it. Much better in the flesh. Her flesh. He'll try her now.

Stay in the light.

IX

Alanis watches the muscles ripple in her legs as they work the pump boards. The strokes are fluid and authoritative but coiled with potential. Oh, the excitement of a pre-match warm-up in this kind of shape! All they need now is for the University of Rugby, London to give them something to work out for. This, the team that might have kick-started a new surge in London's productivity – 72-15! Wouldn't it be wonderful to be involved in an energy pump like that!

Even in the bad times, a London team would expect to beat one from East Anglia. If URL have struck upon a vein of productivity they could score freely. The strategists have transferred elites in recess to this one in case they do. Alanis senses a buzz in the stadium. London has seen a 23.4 per cent surge in productivity since the 72–15 win last week.

'It's not as if it's an end to our troubles, though,' says Adriana Platt, seated next to her. 'Our base was so low that a 23.4 per cent increase is hardly anything.'

'Maybe not,' says Alanis, 'but it's given us back that feeling of hope, hasn't it? Life feels lighter. *I* feel lighter. And coursing with energy. Don't you?'

'Oh, Alanis! I can't wait for our recess to end! I just want to get back out onto that volleyball court! And I want to smash every last joule out of these pump boards this afternoon!'

A profound rush of excitement rises in Alanis – excitement and joy – but it remains within her circuitry, potential to be tapped, for her discipline is too deep-rooted to let slip the kind of whoop she might have hollered in another age. Everything is channelled for when the pump boards and stadium mikes are live.

The teams are taking to the field. Alanis and Adriana smile at each other, then close their eyes and wait.

❖

'Inside ball!'

Coach Davis's instruction is clear and decisive and what Ivon had been thinking anyway. He turns the ball inside, but that hardly does it justice. He feints left, looks left, makes to pass left, then, at the last minute, flicks the ball out of the back of his right hand. He does it with a flourish, a sense of theatricality. Calculated theatricality, mind. It's all for effect. Make the oppo think that play's about to move left, which they do, leaving a nice hole on his inside shoulder. And, yes, it's also to embellish the manoeuvre, lend it his own stamp, make it more than just the intellectual property of an alien voice in his head.

But, whichever way Ivon dresses it up, what he does is turn the ball inside. As instructed.

Travis, the right-winger, takes the pass and is clean through to the try line. The metallic roar of the stadium starts up. Ivon converts the try, and London have a 7–0 lead after 22 minutes.

It has been a frustrating 21 minutes. Ivon has, for the most part, done as he's been told, kept a low profile, tried to respect their ways. He is appalled that any of his teammates should think he would ridicule them. The image of Moby suggesting as much at training has stayed with him. That upright and very proper bearing of the man. His crew-cut hair, accentuating a skull that is large, wide and ever so slightly flat at the back. He is warlike in his commitment, fearsome in loyalty. And yet there is a hint of the goon about him, too, something a bit clumsy and childlike. For all their differences, Ivon finds him endearing for that. He can picture Moby as a boy in Wales galumphing in for his tea with mud on his cheeks and love in his heart. He would never ridicule that.

But they are from different worlds, Ivon and his new teammates. In Wales, these boys might have become other people. In Wales, they might have become another team, one that expresses itself and plays for the love of playing. But they are in England, and they want Ivon to play within their structures. It is a delicate conundrum. He will not disrespect them, but he didn't come here to play within himself, either.

With the stadium still raging like the inside of an engine, London are defending on their own 22. The penalty siren goes off. Is it in his head or over the noise? The monotone voice of the stadium computer, very definitely inside his head, says, 'Yellow 14, off your feet'.

Too right. That guy just flopped on the ball. And he was a mile offside. The ball pops out towards Ivon. He grabs it and takes a quick step to the nearest edge of the illuminated patch of turf that marks the point of offence.

'Kick for touch,' says Coach Davis.

Tim, the scrum-half, is alongside. So is Travis, further wide on his wing. Ivon sees three defenders scattered ahead of him, and the rest are either lying in a heap where the ruck was or lined up on the other side of it. Beyond the defenders in front of him lies the lush greensward of empty opposition territory; beyond them lies space – lovely, juicy space.

Fuck it. 'Come with me,' Ivon says to Tim. He taps the ball to himself, and he's off.

'Get with him! Fourteen! Nine!'

The thought crosses Ivon's mind for a split second that Coach Davis has given up chastising him when he deviates from the game plan and is now reacting with appropriate instructions for the others. This is progress.

When one of those three defenders sees Ivon running towards him, he holds his position, turning in towards the touchline to cover Tim and Travis. Ivon shows him the ball, grinning, then comes off his right foot with a little dummy. The scrum-half turns and starts to run now towards his own try line. Any moment he will look over his left shoulder in search of Ivon – here it comes – then his body will follow as he tries to unravel himself for a tackle. Just as the scrum-half commits to turning inside, Ivon says 'boo!' and, bang, he comes off his left foot. The scrum-half turns back to his right, but he is floundering, and Ivon accelerates away. Only the full-back is ahead of him now, as he crosses the halfway line.

'Give it to 14!' cries Coach Davis in his head. 'On your right!'

But their winger is cutting off the pass. As he and the full-back converge, Ivon still cannot get the pass away. He thinks he might have to take the tackle, but at the last second he drops the ball onto his boot and dinks it to his right. No instruction from Coach Davis for this improvisation. None even from himself. This comes from somewhere else, somewhere mystical. It is perfect. The winger elects to tackle him just as he performs the chip, just as he is tackled, too, by the full-back. The ball bobbles delicately away from the three-man collision and, pop, with perfect timing it sits up for Travis, who gathers for a free run to the posts.

The stadium is already shaking with its infernal din, which will continue now for a further few minutes. Travis is smiling as he returns the ball for the conversion. Ivon takes it and thinks of Alanis. She said last night she'd be coming. He wonders where she's sitting. That was a special try. He hopes she liked it.

'There's been another try!' shrieks Adriana.

Alanis looks up towards the rafters of the stadium, and, sure enough, another seven green lights have shown alongside the two remaining from the last score. She and Adriana scream with abandon, their legs and arms coursing with the sweet pain of exertion. Seven more minutes! All around her, levers are flashing and the pump boards thundering. She can almost feel herself borne aloft by the waves, supported by the communal surge for energy, and yet a part of it, too. Oh, there's no better feeling! When a commune is empowered to generate energy together! It is the highest virtue, the purest pleasure!

Nine minutes later, the last of the countdown lights extinguishes to signal the end of the pump. Alanis draws in air with long, controlled breaths. Her heart is beating with purpose, an organ at the height of its powers. Her limbs tingle.

She sits back on her chair and looks across at Adriana. 'It might have been 22 minutes in coming, but it was worth the wait.'

Adriana nods. 'Do you think we're in for another bonanza?'

Above the gentle hum of conversation, a strange cry rises from the other side of the stadium. Alanis sits up. Adriana has done the same, and there is a general stirring all around, as people strain to know the source of this renegade release of sound energy.

'Was that someone shouting?' says Alanis.

'I think so.'

'Surely, they know the stadium mikes are not live.'

Another lone cry goes up, this time further round the stand. Alanis cannot quite make out the words. The hum of conversation has intensified.

'What on earth is happening?'

Adriana notices something and points to a block of secondaries lower down in their section of the stadium. Alanis sees a male standing tall with arms outstretched. There is unrest among those around him. The nearest security officers are being alerted. He arches his back and brings his hands together, cupped round his mouth. And he yells into the great void of the stadium. Alanis can make out these words. He shouts them long and slow, as if gathering every last morsel of energy left to him and forcing them out with violence and wilfulness.

'I-von! I-von!'

Anxious faces in his vicinity look about for assistance. Security swoop. The deviant is pacified and escorted away.

'It's a disgrace!' says Alanis.

'Why would anyone do that?' agrees Adriana. 'No one's scored. What benefit can there be in shouting like that?'

From somewhere a few rows in front of the deviant, on the edge by the aisle, another secondary cries out Ivon's name. This outburst is shorter and more spontaneous, as if it could not be helped. There's a hint of desperation to it. The guilty party has not risen from his seat, so Alanis cannot tell who it is, but Security are quick to move in, and a man is led away, head hung low, tears on his face.

Alanis is chilled by these outbursts. She thinks of the scenes at the club the week before and the unnatural booking patterns in Ivon's coitus diary. What is this strange effect he seems to have on people? Uneasily, she scans the ranks of primaries and secondaries, willing the good people to maintain decorum. Come on, London – we are better than this. No more outbursts, please!

It is a relief when the stadium siren cuts across the uneasy atmosphere to signify another score for London, just before half-time. Five green lights go up – it's a try! – followed shortly by another two for the conversion. Alanis slams herself back into the pumping position and works furiously.

She closes her eyes and shouts the name 'London' again and again and again. The noise around her fills the air to saturation.

She can distinguish nothing amid the tumult, which will sweep away the ejaculations of rogue individuals. Let them look to themselves! Individuals have meaning only as part of the commune. Deviants are snapped off like twigs in a storm. She will not hear it. She is true, she is good, she is safe. London is moving again!

London! London! London!

The cryo-pot sighs open. Freezing cloudlets billow round Ivon's head as the iron maiden of ice releases him. He steps out as quickly as he can and roars with relief.

'Fuck! What's wrong with a nice hot bath?'

'It aggravates soft-tissue damage.'

'Gets the mud off, though.'

'Mud?'

'Never mind.'

Moby puffs out his cheeks and runs on the spot, working the cold through his system. He stretches his long frame. Not an ounce of fat on it. Ivon imagines him in a collision with Sumo Simkins back home. Moby's taller, but he must be a few stone lighter. He'd probably cut Sumo in half, though. He was bred for purpose, and his has been a lifetime of conditioning. The same cannot be said of Sumo.

'It's been good having you in the team,' Moby says.

Ivon is stunned and stops mid-stretch. 'I've enjoyed it,' he says, even if this is the first time it's occurred to him.

'They'll promote you to elite after that.'

Ivon doesn't know what to say.

'Times have been tough for this team,' Moby continues. 'Then you come along, and suddenly we can't stop generating joules. The boys are feeling dominant for the first time. I hope it continues when you're gone.'

'It will,' says Ivon, who thinks he might just love Moby all of a sudden, the super-serious, over-sized plonker. 'Of course, it will. There's real talent in this team. You've just got to think for yourselves.'

'You keep saying that.'

'Well, you do! Don't listen to what the coach is telling you! Follow your instincts!'

Moby smiles and shakes his head. 'You wait till you get to elite.'

'Why?'

'They use ProzoneX there.'

'What's that?'

'You wait.'

The blood is starting to course through Ivon's veins again. His skin is pink. He feels fresh and euphoric, as if he could play another match. As if he could drink all night. Even the knowledge that he will be doing neither washes over him for now.

'Keep moving!' says the effectiveness director in the corner.

Ivon continues to stretch out. He wants to give something back. 'What about you?' he says to him. 'You could play elite.'

Moby shakes his head. 'I came through the Academy, but I didn't make the cut.'

'Why not?'

'It came down to me and this other guy. Stanton Jeffries – you'll meet him in elite. He had a slight diligence deficiency, and was able to actualise only 87 per cent of his congenital physical potential. I was graded at 97.6 per cent of mine, but my physical potential was lesser. In particular, there had been an undetected alpha-actinin mutation in the DNA of one of my progenitors, which I inherited. I managed to secure gene therapy for the deficiency, so I run faster now, but by then they've made their mind up.'

'Shit. That's so unlucky! Just one little mutant…thing.'

Moby shrugs as he bends to his left. The effect is faintly absurd, and Ivon's affection for him deepens further. 'We are who we are.'

'But you deserve better.'

'Why?'

'Because you have talent *and* you worked so hard. Harder than he did. That's what you just said, isn't it? I mean, you're basically saying he was lazy, right?'

'I'm saying he was deficient in one area, and I in another. In the final grading, my deficiency was the greater.'

'Yeah, but he could do something about his. There was nothing you could do about yours.'

Moby frowns. 'Why could he do something?'

'Well, anyone can get off their fat arse, can't they?'

'Stanton had a dopamine imbalance across his striatum and anterior insula. It meant he didn't have the affinity for hard work that I have. I'm sure it's been addressed since.'

'Keep working, Moby!'

He shakes his head. 'It's not going to happen for me now. The first generation of DGF athletes is coming through.'

'DGF?'

'Deliberate Genetic Fusion.'

'What?'

'You'll see.'

'Don't you want to be an elite?'

'I have my place here.'

'But you must be ambitious. I've seen you play. You're a competitive fucker.'

Moby's stare is steely. Steely and blank. 'I want to be productive for my commune. That's it.'

'Ivon,' says a familiar voice from behind him. Coach Davis has appeared at the entrance to the cryo-room. 'When you're finished, can I have a word?'

Ivon nods.

Moby arches backwards. 'I told you.'

○

In the heart of Parliament, Dusty gazes towards the Thames, which ripples by as it must have for, who knows, hundreds, maybe thousands, of years, no matter what cricket academies rise and fall along its banks, no matter what matches tomorrow may hold. He is starting to see the thread that runs through things. The commune may outlast the individual, but some things outlast the commune.

'Ah, this must be the Welshman!' The voice behind him is confident and clear. Dusty turns to see Marcus Apollo enter the conference room to greet Ivon, who has been studying closely the screens arranged across the interior wall. The older man is taller and heavier, but Ivon greets him as an equal.

'These screens,' says Ivon, 'I haven't seen any in London.'

'Indeed you have not,' replies Apollo. 'The watching of sport is not a leisure pursuit on this side of the Fence. To allow something too much exposure is to distort it, so our matches are scrutinised only by those who need to know. Here in Parliament we stream footage of every match contested across the state, as they do in the Institute of Improvement. There are many happening at any given time, as you can see.'

Apollo cries out when he spots Dusty by the window. 'Dusty Noble! What a pleasure!'

'It's an honour to be here again, Prime Manager,' says Dusty as they greet each other.

Dusty is moved again to find himself in the man's presence, to experience the width and liveliness of his expression, face to face. There is talk of an Exemption grant for Apollo, such is his facility for statesmanship. Dusty makes a note to investigate his pedigree when he next has the opportunity. He wears a centurion medal, so must have been an elite in something.

They are ushered towards an arrangement of chairs overlooking the Thames. Once seated, Apollo crosses his legs, making obvious through the fabric of his maroon day suit a calf muscle of considerable substance.

'Isotonic?' he offers and then nods to an assistant. 'You find me in a fine mood! Like everyone living in this commune, I am thrilled to see the recent upturn in London's productivity. I am, of course impartial across the communes, but no one benefits when this great engine of our nation splutters and stalls.'

'There's a new atmosphere on the streets,' says Dusty, conscious of an unfamiliar urge to say something, anything, 'in the clubs, the stadiums, the nutrition halls. We're even cracking smiles at ReSure.'

Apollo roars with laughter. 'Well, there's confirmation!'

Ivon allows the good humour to play around him. He is motionless, but for some mischief in the corners of his mouth and a faint narrowing of his eyes, which Dusty catches a couple of times flitting towards the screens over the PM's shoulder.

'Naturally, the scientists have set to work identifying new patterns in this surge in productivity. They keep coming back to the Welshman. Two matches for an under-performing unit; two wins: 72–15 and 56–12. Those are impressive numbers – extraordinary, actually, to win by those margins.'

Ivon shrugs. 'Not in Wales, they're not. We put a hundred past Treorchy in '41.'

Apollo laughs again. 'I don't doubt it, Ivon! You are an unusually productive…how do you say in Wales…"player". Highly unusual. And it is for this reason that we would like to offer you a trial with the elite department of London Rugby.'

'Done.'

There is a moment of silence. Apollo's assistant brings in a tray of hydro-sacs and places it on the table among them. Dusty and Apollo reach over to take one. Ivon does not.

'You will find things different at elite level.'

'Oh, I know. Don't tell me. It'll be unlike anything I've ever known, blah, blah, blah. Listen, I've heard it all before. My parents said it, Dusty said it, that cricket bitch said it, the coaches and the players at URL. And then I get out on the field, and, you know, it's still rugby, isn't it. I'm still good at it. And we win.'

Apollo continues to smile, but his movements are slowing down. His manner has become less airy. He pops another hydro-sac, but Dusty does not.

'Discipline is fundamental to what we do.'

Ivon's composure slips. He lets fly a howl of exasperation and looks to the ceiling. 'This'll be doing what you're told, will it? Following the voices in your head. Not thinking for yourself. Not playing.'

'That word "play" again,' says Apollo, shaking his head. 'I should tell you it has fallen out of use in England. We do not play here. We strive, we achieve, we move forward. In perpetuity. Surely you can see the benefits! We don't look to others to help us, we don't plunder our earthly resources. We propel ourselves.'

Ivon nods slowly, his grin threatening to pierce the edges of his face. 'I'm going to transform the game of rugby in England. And it *is* a game. I will show you how it should be played. I will show you *that* it should be played.'

'You have already transformed London's fortunes in the short time you have been here. You are unique, Ivon, that much is clear, and, I'm sure, as unrepresentative of the average Welshman as you are the average English. We want to harness that at elite level, but it will require…certain adjustments. So far your maverick leanings have been indulged. But, at elite level, to defy on-field instruction is to court disaster, for yourself and your commune. Such delinquency is unheard of. You would be sent to the Institute of Correction. All three degrees of Assimilation would likely be required.'

'What *is* that?'

Apollo takes another sac. 'Third-degree Assimilation? Put simply, it is a reformatting of the brain. A kind of full restore, if I may use the old IT vernacular. It is 98 per cent effective. And – so they tell me – exceptionally painful.'

Ivon's eyes flit towards Dusty, who wants to say something to reassure the young man, but cannot. 'Those people taken away from the club…'

Dusty nods. 'There have been a number of disturbances at our club lately,' he explains to Apollo.

'Ah, yes! I have heard. And at yesterday's match. Most regrettable. An example of the kind of distortions to the natural order I mentioned earlier. The cult of personality is a pernicious thing, but for now at least it is helping us identify those who need help. It cannot be allowed to continue, of course.'

'So, what happens? You cut out my personality?'

'No, Ivon. That would be a last resort. These procedures are energy-hungry. Third-degree Assimilation requires a significant investment of resources. It would be infinitely preferable for you to learn the discipline yourself. Besides, you'll find it harder to transgress at elite level. The interface between the athletes and Strategy and Direction is far more sophisticated, as you will discover.' Apollo pauses to lean in for his fourth hydro-sac. When he reclines again, it is with a kindly smile that makes Dusty wonder if the PM is not beginning to feel the same way about Ivon as he does. Or perhaps this is just his manner with everyone. 'Now, Ivon, do you think you can take all of this on board?'

The ripples of an inner struggle play across Ivon's face. His temples pulse, the muscles flex at his jaw. Dusty wills him to keep his discipline. Don't think you can fight these people, Ivon. No one returns from Assimilation the same person as went in.

'Transgress?' he says. 'Did you really say transgress? Tell me, was I transgressing when we scored 72 points last week? Or 56 yesterday? Was I stepping out of line? Because we wouldn't have scored them if I hadn't.'

'It is true that at collegiate level you have managed to break from the team patterns with notable productivity. Your skills are too advanced for that level. But even collegiate opposition would find ways to counteract them in time. You can be sure that rival communes have already detailed their analysts and espionage teams to investigate you. Individual brilliance is at best a temporary fillip and never a thing to rely on. Long-term success depends upon discipline, structure and adherence to a match-plan.'

'I'm here to play. I'm here to win. Everything will follow from that.'

'We can start from there, I agree,' says Apollo, as if a breakthrough has been made. 'To win is to justify all we do, and all we do must be judged against the directive to win. With that in mind, we may choose to prescribe you certain hormone supplements or genetic modifiers to improve your overall productivity. I believe you have a slight VO_2 Max deficit, for example, and there are various ways to address that.'

'You mean drugs?'

'Supplements, modifiers.'

'Cheating.'

Apollo laughs gently.

'I work with what God gave me,' continues Ivon. 'Nothing more. I will not pollute myself.'

'And did your god give you a rugby ball? Did he give you boots to kick with? You will have noticed, no doubt, the enhancements to productivity in Perpetual Era footwear – did your god supply you with those? No, these too are the inventions of humankind.'

'None of it changes *me*,' says Ivon, pounding his breast. 'I remain the same. In here.'

'I assure you what I'm suggesting is perfectly safe. The technology is far in advance of anything you will be familiar with from the Lapsed Era.'

'It is changing me! Changing my molecules!'

'Your body does change when you become fitter. I cannot deny this.'

'It is introducing alien substances into my body!'

'So is eating.'

Ivon slams his fist on the table, spilling hydro-sacs onto the immaculate glass. 'It's cheating!' he shouts.

Apollo purses his lips and gathers the errant sacs, popping them into his mouth with nonchalance. 'You are from a culture that conceived of sport as recreation,' he says. 'Essentially – how do you say in Wales? – a "romantic" pursuit. You may think you take your sport seriously, but you are…well, yes, you are *playing* at it.' He leans forward to fix Ivon with a glare and pats his chest with a heavy hand. 'We…*we*…take our sport seriously, Ivon. It defines who we are and why we are. You talk of your god; we talk of the sacred directive to go faster, stronger, more productively. We share a common history, your world and mine, in which our ancestors of the Lapsed Era urged their champions on towards similar frontiers of achievement, sometimes with maniacal fervour… then quibbled about how they reached them. With the establishment of the Perpetual Era, we cut ourselves free from such hypocrisy. When we urge our champions on, when we urge *ourselves* on, we mobilise every energy and device at our command towards that end.' He taps his finger on the spotless table. '*This* world is where sport is taken seriously, Ivon. I do believe you want to prove yourself in it, and I urge you to keep an open mind.'

Dusty is disturbed at the way Ivon is staring. Is it at the hydrosacs? He thinks it may be slightly to the side of them. He thinks it may be beyond them. Somewhere way beyond, beyond the floor they're sitting on, straight through Parliament towards the dirty bed of the Thames itself. His head is cocked, his mouth set straight.

'I need a piss,' he says under his breath and rises to leave the room. After a few paces, he turns back. He is tall, flaring and magnificent. 'I can't talk like him, I know it. I don't have the words. But that doesn't mean I'm wrong. And when I talk with these,' he says, holding out his hands, 'and these,' pointing to his feet, 'and this,' beating his chest, before standing defiant and nodding his head, 'I win my arguments.'

He has been gone for a few seconds, before Apollo speaks. 'Do you think he'll come quietly?'

Another pause settles between the two men. Dusty feels sick. He wants to take Ivon away from this. He wants to take himself away. There's no hope for Ivon. Dusty can see that now. Apollo looks across at him. His face has suddenly changed. Gone is the kindliness, gone the sparkle. His eyes are cold and ruthless. They demand a response.

'He is set on proving himself here.'

'Yes, but will he conform?'

'If he wants to make elite, if he wants to strive for England, he'll have to.'

'It'll be harder for him to ignore the instructions of ProzoneX. As long as his chip has fully taken.'

'My only concern is how he'll handle being away from his home.'

Apollo cocks his head, as if he hadn't thought of that – what Perpetual citizen would? – but a man in his position knows something about the ways of the Lapsed Era.

Dusty continues: 'I can see him becoming restless already. Ambition is keeping him focused for now, but at some point he will long for his homeland. The bond between him and his progenitors is strong. He has already asked me about contacting them.'

Apollo is in thought, but waves his hand towards the interior and says as an aside, 'I have a Lapsed Era telephone in my chambers. He can use that if he wants.'

'I just wonder,' says Dusty, before pausing. How can he make the following not sound ridiculous? 'I just wonder, would there be any virtue in letting him return to Wales for a short break? Before he turns elite. If he can relax, it may help his chip complete its insinuation.'

It's a suggestion that inclines Apollo to look at him at least, but there is contempt in his face. He does not deign to answer.

Does he want this, does he want this. Ivon's feet flash across the matt-white bathroom floor. No sound, no slipping, the traction is perfect between footwear and flooring, two surfaces made for each other. Like everything round here. A perfect fit. Nothing wasted. Efficiency gone mad.

He wants to make noise, so he slams his palms against the smooth white wall the third time he paces up to it. The walls are hard. The thud is weak. He will not be made to take anything. He's not a robot. He's not a cheat. He has been engineered once, by a higher power than these pale-faced slaves to instruction. Enough.

He breathes in slowly and fully, head bowed between two arms. Come on. They want you. You've made it to elite. The next stage. They're starting to turn. Those people at the club. The cries of your name at the stadium. That's more like it. Some signs of life. Humanity. A beating heart. These things are eternal.

Like the games. Like play. Bring out the humans. Win back the lost ground. Play.

Ivon crouches in the corner of the bathroom. It is white. He feels the power in his haunches and soon he is bouncing on them. He is in the shape of his life, but if they want him fitter he will train harder. If they want him more disciplined he will smile and cooperate − until he sees the moment, then bang! Let's see them discipline him for winning matches.

They will never have his soul.

As a boy he thrilled to the exploits of legends on the field. As a player he thrills to be on the field himself, to move with the rhythms of a game and to shape those rhythms, the inspiration within balanced against the inspiration without. That, too, is eternal. He will show it to them. There is magic in what they do. Enchantment. Eternal.

'Here he is!' Apollo rises to his feet. The voice is full again, the features animate. Dusty's pall of sickness deepens. 'We'll get you set up with London Rugby tomorrow. It'll mean more tests, but bear with us. You'll see action soon. Possibly as early as Saturday, which is London's next match, I believe.'

Ivon nods once, efficiently. 'Cool.'

'Dusty tells me you would like to make contact with your progenitors. I have a phone in my chambers that is compatible with the relevant pathways.'

Apollo leads them through a door at the far end of the room and down a sunlit corridor animated with faint flourishes of aquamarine. He steps into another wide room overlooking the river, this time offering a glimpse of High Chronos to the left. The room is dominated by a reproduction of The Victor, in acrylic resin by the look of it. Ivon is immediately drawn to the statue and stands silently in front of it, raising his fist to mimic the pose. There is a desk in each of the room's interior corners, one dynamic, one static. And over by the window, proud as an ornament, sits a Lapsed Era telephone. The confidence of its blackness is a delight, as are the bold straight lines. Set against which, the quaint buttons, round and innocent, make Dusty yearn for more forgiving times.

Apollo lifts a part out of itself and offers it to Ivon. The kinked chord attaching the two parts strains at the separation.

'You'll need the right code, of course,' he says.

Ivon is confident with the telephone. He presses the buttons in what looks like a specific sequence. Holding it to his ear, he waits, then turns to the two men.

'Let's leave him to it,' says Apollo, motioning towards the door. Just as it closes behind them, Dusty hears the words, 'Mum, it's Ivon.'

Apollo shows Dusty to a reception room in his chambers. 'Why don't you wait here. I have a few matters to attend to.'

Dusty settles on one of the exercise bikes in the waiting room and begins to pedal, but his heart is not in it. Apathy is creeping over him again. Is this all they are? Slaves to energy. Quantity, quantity, quantity. That Lapsed Era telephone had a purpose once, but it is beautiful, too, isn't it, a quality beyond its function. What quality does Dusty have beyond his function? Once he accumulated runs; now he ushers poor fools to their final resting place; always he has generated energy like the rest of them. Everything has been measured in joules. He sits on the bike, refusing to work it. He realises that as soon as Apollo returns he will pedal as if he has been pedalling all the while. He is pathetic.

But it is Ivon who appears first. His face is blank. 'Dad's not well,' he says.

Dusty stops pedalling. 'What's wrong with him?'

Ivon taps his head. 'He's losing it. Leaves the house first thing in the morning, comes back late at night, drunk. Doesn't talk.

Mum's at her wits' end. Fairly standard, really, in our house. All my fault, obviously.'

The feeling that there is a particular way he should react to this gnaws at Dusty. The relationship between Ivon, Ricky and Dee and these peculiar goings-on within it might be affecting Ivon more than Dusty can understand. It is another reason for him to return home.

'Do you want to go back?' he says.

'I don't think so. Not just now. I'm about to make elite. Dad's done this before. He'll be fine.'

'Do you want me to go?'

That's it! The scales fall from Dusty's eyes. It's not so much that he wants Ivon to return home; rather, it is Dusty who wants to go. He has crossed over. The Lapsed Era is where his heart lies now, in all its seedy glory, with its dirty, haphazard ways. He wants to see Ricky and Dee again and tell them what he knows about the TMS programme of 2111. He feels close to them, connected. Maybe this is how Lapsed Era relationships are meant to be. It reminds him of the feelings he was developing for Alanis before the trip to Wales.

'If you fancy it. Yeah. Sweet.'

'I've still got travel rights from my decommission, and I know someone in Resources. They'll get me a permit by the end of the day.'

A solemn look crosses Ivon's brow. 'Tell them I'm fine,' he says. 'Tell them we're changing things.'

Dusty smiles briskly. Does Ivon think he's changing things? Does he even think he can? He has wrought a quantitative shift in London's joule count. He has turned some of the more vulnerable elements of society, who will be corrected, if they have not been already. Dusty is afraid of the passion that simmers behind the swirling blue eyes. He is afraid of what might happen to a boy who thinks he can change things.

But Dusty has changed, because the idea excites him, too. And maybe Ivon *can* change things. Must non-conformists always be broken? Perhaps they can lead a people in new directions; perhaps they can break the system themselves.

Dusty smiles again, more slowly and warmly.

'I'll tell them.'

X

Oh, momentum! How strongly you gather behind those who work at you hardest!

There is only one week until the Spring Recess for elite women's volleyball is at an end. If Alanis could change one thing about London's upturn in productivity, it would be to have played her part in it by now on the court. She bristles at the thought. The adrenaline when she squares off with an opponent, the sting of a headlong dive across the floor, the release of an overhead smash – these sensations she will soon be able to relish once more. May the turbines turn when she does!

But this is indulgent, to linger on her personal preoccupations. Just being part of a commune whose confidence regenerates – she wouldn't swap it for all the joules in Asia. And hasn't London deserved this resurgence, never once losing faith, though the joules ran low! Now the momentum has swept up more of the commune's units. Three more wins at elite level yesterday, including another for the men's footballers, who have broken into the top four.

There's no way London can be generating more energy from its cots than its stadiums now! Alanis never really believed that rumour, anyway. Still, when it's happening in the stadiums, it so often happens in the cots. Another momentous bout with Ivon. It's as if his coital productivity is somehow linked to London's recovery.

He is slower to his shower than she to hers, but she watches as he strides across from the cot towards the cleansing station. His penis retains its glow and some degree of tumescence, happily flaccid, the assurance of a natural arousal. All too often these days, men resort to manipulation of the autonomic nervous system for their erections. It's perfectly functional, but there is something affecting about a penis that rises without intervention from the central chip. One always gives one's all, of course, but sometimes one's all comes more naturally. Whenever it does, the display's read-out bears testimony afterwards. This afternoon's bout was no exception.

As Ivon steps into the shower next to her, he puffs out his chest and droplets of water begin to fall from the vents above him, dashing themselves on his muscular shoulders, seeping into and through his wild blond hair. He runs his hands through it, and Alanis watches a sleek, glistening orchestra of ripples play through his arms and, when he turns, across his broad back and down through buttocks and hamstrings that are befitting, indeed, of an elite. What a welcome addition to their ranks he will make, too full of potential to remain in the tertiary classes. She is pleased to be able to call him a cot partner. It's time she introduced him to more of her class. Adriana and Ivon would respond particularly well to each other.

'So, did you enjoy the rugby the other day?' he says, turning in towards her, as his first injection of gel is released from the vents.

For a moment, Alanis is not sure what he means. Then she remembers the last rugby match she comped at. 'Ah, 56–12? Yes, what a workout! But then every match lately seems to bring a bonanza for the commune.'

'Yes, but what about the game itself? Sorry, I mean the match.'

They stand beneath their showers, facing each other. He is so close to her that his shower cloud has very nearly merged with hers. Instinctively, she takes a step away from him, and her shower follows. 'It was a wonderful result.'

'But what did you think of the match?'

'I don't know. I'm not a scientist.'

'Did you think I played well?' Ivon says. He smiles and looks down briefly, then back at her again. 'I mean, do you think I… contested…productively?'

'I don't know. I didn't see, Ivon. There was so much pumping to get through.'

Ivon stares at her with a faint smile, but intensity, such intensity, in those eyes of his. As if he were trying to intimidate her from across the volleyball net. But, no, not that. She doesn't feel hostility from him. Just that intensity. His head is angled so that the eyes sear at her from beneath a wicked eyebrow ridge. For a moment she forgets where she is.

'You really must pay closer attention,' he says, as he takes another step towards her.

Now their showers are as one. On every conscious level, her soul screams at her to step away again. But her back is close to the wall and, anyway, something unconscious inclines her to stand her ground. He leans in. She can't imagine what he's trying to do. Slowly he presses his lips against hers. It is a curious sensation, highly, highly irregular, but still she holds steady, as if staring into the sun. She feels his hand in the small of her back. He pulls her in, pressing harder against her lips, now invading her mouth with his tongue. Against her pelvis, she feels his tumescence, fully restored. And warm.

They're off the Grid. She breaks away. His grip on her is firm, but he releases it without a struggle. Was it the unharnessed warmth of his penis that reminded her where they were, what they were doing, who she was? Or was it the unsanctioned physical contact, or that…that thing he did with his mouth and tongue (she can't think how to describe it)? She'll never know, but as she tumbles away from him, out of the shower zone, the thought crosses her mind for a flit of a second to lay herself out on the cot once more. Almost as soon as it is formed, though, the thought has gone, and she ducks left into the dryer.

She is perfectly composed. As the warm jets rise up around her, she turns towards him, standing alone under his cloud.

'Have you met my comrade Adriana?'

Dusty feels as if he can breathe again.

Again? Has he ever felt like this? Focused, invigorated, excited and, yes, happy – these are humours that have defined his life. But never a sense of freedom. Only now, only here in Wales, does he feel light and unencumbered by duty or institutional intimidation. He feels in tune with their ways. He is a Welshman.

Returning is what has done this. He was seduced the first time, but disorientated by the shock of it. Now, in the flush of familiarity, Wales presents itself to him as home. And nowhere more so than the place where it all began, that low-slung, primitive stadium of St Helen's, the playground of Ivon, which appears now up ahead.

There is a gate open in the old brick wall at the cricket end of the complex. Impulsively, Dusty pulls off the road and parks the aero beside it. He passes through the gate onto the cricket outfield, marvelling at the possibilities for life under a big wide sky. To his right, from out of the chaos of Lapsed Era housing rises the clubhouse, the words 'Swansea Cricket & Football Club' set against the white paint in letters of friendly blue. And then, straight ahead, the big field closes in around the rugby pitch. Dusty smiles again at the coming together of sports on one field, just as they come together in Ivon's soul. He walks on towards the turf on which he first saw the boy in action. Over there in the corner is the gate where Alanis and Dusty slipped in to watch the remarkable rituals unfold. The rugby posts are down, but the pitch is clearly marked, and Dusty walks upon it. The smell of the natural grass drifts through him blissfully. Under foot, the turf is pleasingly solid and without spring. He is stirred by the living green of it.

Someone is sitting towards the back of the stand, the rickety old metal stand, where he was first embraced by a Welshman. He walks towards it. The man is blond and rises slowly to his feet. It is then that Dusty realises the man is Ricky.

Dusty calls his name and raises his hand as he enters the shade of the stand and starts to climb. Ricky is expressionless on the way down. The tier shudders with each heavy step he takes. Just as Dusty is wondering which handshake to use, Ricky lets out a roar and hurls himself at him. His shoulder thuds into Dusty's chest, knocking him off his feet, but as they fall together they turn in the air, so that each of them lands on his side on the sharp metallic steps, Ricky taking the brunt of the impact. They bump down to the bottom of the stand, but, before Dusty has time to take stock of the angry pain in his right shoulder, ribs and hip, Ricky is flailing at him.

'You fucking cunt!' he screams between the blows. '*Traitor!*'

Dusty manages to parry the worst of it and is quicker to his feet. He springs back into the sunlight on the pitch and turns to face Ricky, shocked at the sight of his old comrade, who stumbles slowly to his feet. His long, ragged hair is already stained with blood from a wound that disappears into it from the side of his forehead. A dirty, sparse garment across his torso reveals a livid graze on his left shoulder, which oozes more blood down his arm. Around his loins, the clothes are torn and stop at his knees. One of his feet is naked, the other shod in a flimsy article that scarcely clings to it, whose pair lies discarded in the stand, at the point of impact.

He lumbers towards Dusty.

'Ricky? What are you doing? It's me, Dusty! Dusty Noble!'

'I know who you are, you fucker! You've ruined our lives! You've ruined Ivon's life!'

'I have not! He's thriving. He's made elite.'

Dusty will not retreat any more. When Ricky comes at him again, he deflects his assault and pins him in a bear hug. Ricky bursts into tears.

'Have they assimilated him?'

'No!'

'Have they tried?'

'No,' says Dusty, but this time less strident.

Ricky is now leaning against him, quivering with emotion. Dusty releases his grip, and Ricky sits upon the ground. His head is bowed. His shapeless arms draw in his knees.

'What sport?'

'Rugby.'

Ricky half-smiles.

'I'd watched every game he'd ever played. Cricket, rugby, football. I remember the excitement in the early years. In all of us, him, me, Dee. He had it. That was obvious. What would the future bring? How far would he go?' He shakes his head. 'Too far, it turns out. But then how could he stop? Once *you* opened the way to England for him, how could he stop? If you're good enough to keep going, you keep going, don't you? Until you're so far away from where it all started and you wake up one day and you're fucking lost. He's not a stable kid, you know.'

On the left side of his head, Ricky's hair is now streaked with dirty red. The blood has reached his shoulder and clothes. He looks wild.

'Your head, Ricky. It's bleeding.'

Ricky waves his hand dismissively.

'Why did you do it, Dusty? You knew there'd be no coming back. You knew you were taking him away from us.'

'I didn't do it! He came and found me. He wanted to come.'

'He didn't understand.'

'He's doing fine.'

'He'll never come back.'

Dusty turns away. He catches a glimpse of the abandoned footwear in the stand and bounds up to it. A dark brown strap that could be of organic matter is all that passes across the top of the foot, leaving exposed on the sole the very imprint of Ricky's foot, his toes, his heel, the ball and arch. It is black in places, filthier even than on the underside. Dusty presents it to him. He takes it with a grunt and slips it back on his dirty foot.

'Why did you come here, Dusty? You put the idea in his head.'

'Did I? You think it hadn't occurred to him?'

'You know they would never let a savage through the Fence. Not without the endorsement of the great Dusty Noble.'

'Doesn't stop him wanting to go.'

'Oh, fucking hell! I want to go and live on Kepler 22b, but it's not going to happen. And, if I did, there'd be no coming back, so I'd better be sure.'

'I think we should get that head wound looked at.'

'Bollocks.'

'Where's the nearest medical centre?'

Ricky laughs bitterly. 'This is Wales, Dusty. Linda has got enough on her plate without me cluttering up her surgery.'

'I'll take you.'

'I'm not going. You must have some angio-gel with you.'

'There'll be some in the aero's first-aid kit. Haven't looked.'

'We'll put some of that shit on it. It's opening time in half an hour.'

MICHAEL AYLWIN

Ricky lies back on the grass and closes his eyes. He stretches his arms out wide. With the blood and the wrinkles of diminishment picked out by the sun, he looks for a moment as if he's departed. He sighs, drawing it out into a wail.

'But then I think maybe he's right. Maybe *they're* right, in the Perpetual Era. Why let this,' he says, pounding his breast, 'have any concern but to pump blood round your body? Why not strive to make the rest of you the most efficient machine possible? Fuck knows, it's easier that way. No love, no anger, no sadness, no doubt. And then they switch you off. And if you're a fucking genius like our Ivon, why wouldn't you want to keep on improving and improving and improving until there's no more improvement left to squeeze out of your dead eyes, until you're a ruthless, invincible, fucking robot.'

'He'll never be that, and you know it.'

'Why have you come back here?'

'I don't know. I…I love it here.'

Ricky roars with laughter, so loudly and suddenly that Dusty, who has been crouching on his haunches, rocks back into a sitting position. Ricky, still laughing, still spluttering, raises himself like a choking man onto his elbows and thence to his unsteady feet. 'Dusty Noble! Dusty Noble, champion batsman of the Perpetual Era, loves it here! In Wales!'

Dusty looks up at Ricky, placing his hands on the ground behind him. 'I'm changing, Ricky. I can't explain it.'

'You will NEVER be one of us!' Ricky spits. 'Ivon will never be a robot! You will never be a Welshman!' He walks away a couple of paces then turns, as if to strike like a cat. There are tears in his eyes again. 'You took our son away from us! You have no children, you have no family, you can't know what that means!'

'No. No, you're right. I can't. I would never have done it if I could. But he wanted to come, Ricky. I couldn't turn him away. He'll come back. I'll bring him back. I swear it.'

'They won't let him back.'

'Yes they will,' Dusty forces himself to say. 'Elites are allowed to visit Wales. When I came here the first time, I brought an active one with me.'

'They'll never let him.'

'If they trust him, they'll let him.'

'If he remains the son I love, they'll never trust him.'

'I'll bring him back. Somehow.'

Ricky's watery eyes seem to give a little as the two men hold each other's gaze. Dusty doesn't know how he'll do it, but he vows to himself that he will.

'Let's go to the aero,' he says, scrambling to his feet. 'We need to put something on that cut in your head.'

Ricky stands his ground defiantly, pathetically, bloody and dishevelled.

'Come on, Ricky. Now.'

He takes his arm. Ricky shakes it off with a snarl, but he starts walking.

'I've been doing some research in London. Do you remember the TMS therapy we took in 2111?'

There is silence.

'Of course I do,' Ricky says quietly, after a few paces.

'What do you remember?'

'It's when Dee and I first spoke to each other. In the lanes later that same day. I was frustrated because I couldn't hit the bloody thing. She was just so fucking serene. "Don't try so hard," she said, which was advice I'd never heard before. Neither had she, it turned out. She said it like she was in a trance or something. That was the beginning of it all. Us, Ivon. All this.'

He drifts off. Dusty is afraid to look at him, the blood, the dirt, the tears of the boy he grew up with. He is in awe of him.

'Ricky, there were seven of us who took that therapy. I'm the only one left. All the others have gone.'

'Talk to Dee about it. I don't want to know any more. Take me to the Rose.'

✺

Welsh juveniles pass to and fro. Dusty is mesmerised by the chaos. The juveniles wear the same clothes, at least, dressed in the Lapsed Era style, an assortment of garments of differing shades of blue, each with the school badge on the chest. The exuberance is loud and chaotic. None of them walk in formation. Some spot Dusty sitting in the corner and point in his direction, giggling as if they found him funny.

Dusty's shoulder and elbow ache from the fall. He has spent more time than is natural inspecting the riotous comings together of paint on the wall, some of humanoid form, or the yellow wooden swing doors that lead from the corridor he sits in, or even the slippery smooth floor the juveniles squeak around on. He tries to look anywhere but in their eyes, until, at last, he meets those of the person he is here to see, he longs to see. Dee is dressed natively in loose-fitting clothes, of a darker shade than her charges', apart from her shoes, which are white and, thinks Dusty, designed for sport. The contrast she cuts with Ricky is stark. She is neat in manner, graceful in movement, and young, much younger-looking than Ricky.

She holds his gaze for some time, stock still, remote and inaccessible to him across the stream of juveniles shifting and surging around her. He rises to his feet, but she does not react. Instead, she turns to a collection of little wooden boxes in the wall and rifles through the paper in one of them. She pulls out a few sheets and, studying them, walks in his direction.

'Take a seat in there,' she says without looking at him. 'I'll be along in a minute.'

Dusty steps into a room full of tables and chairs. More bright colours adorn the walls. He closes the yellow swing door behind him, but it has panes of glass in it, so he does not feel any more comfortable. He paces up and down the aisles between the tables.

There is a click at the door. Dee crosses the room and sits in a chair behind the largest desk. She studies Dusty coolly.

'How is he?'

Dusty sits on one of the tables in the first row. 'He's fine. He's, he's incredible. London's never seen anything like him. He's sparking a transformation in fortunes. It's funny how an entire commune can galvanise around a couple of uplifting results.' He smiles nervously.

Dee is unmoved. The reunion with his fellow Academy graduates has not been the uplifting affair Dusty had imagined. Lapsed Era ties are strong. He had not foreseen how upset with him Ricky and Dee would be for taking their boy to London. He feels lonelier than ever. What a peculiar torture, to walk in this inspiring land and be shunned by it.

'Did you never think to find out about him, before you took him away? He's not cut out for it.'

'Oh, Dee, I think he is! He's been fast-tracked to elite. 72–15 and 56–12: those were the scorelines in the two matches he played for URL. And that in a side that hadn't won all year. It's sparked a commune-wide resurgence. He and I had a meeting with the Prime Manager earlier this week.'

'I know. He rang me from his chambers.'

'Of course. How do you think he sounded?'

She smiles for the first time. 'Very Ivon. Excited, passionate. Loving. Defiant.'

'Momentum is with him.'

'But it's not always going to go well, is it. And there's too much of his father in him. You know what Ricky was like, even before he came to Wales.'

'I've just been with Ricky.'

Dee's countenance changes, her cool defensiveness slipping. 'Where?'

'At St Helen's.'

'What was he doing?'

'Just sitting there.'

Dee shakes her head. 'He was at home when I left this morning. He's not been well since Ivon left. He can't take it, Dusty. He's an alcoholic.'

'He threw himself at me in the stand. We took a fall down the steps. He cut his head open.'

'What?'

'I've treated him. He's fine.'

'Where is he now?'

'I dropped him at the White Rose.'

She holds the palm of her hand against her forehead, then runs her fingers through her hair, pulling the grey streak to one side. The hand finishes cupped around her chin. 'He told me he wouldn't today,' she says quietly. 'He's taken Ivon's departure badly. I'm not surprised he went for you. He holds you responsible.'

'And you?'

'This was Ivon's decision, not yours. If only he knew what he was doing. But he had to do it, I understand that.' For the first time, she looks at Dusty openly. Her eyes are rich and vulnerable. 'Our life is falling apart, Dusty. If London swallows him up, if he never comes back…' She looks away.

'I'll bring him back, Dee. I promise. I'll get him out of there.'

A silence hangs in the room. Resolve and, he thinks, love are surging through Dusty now. Ricky and Dee, he will do this for Ricky and Dee, because of love for them – yes, love – for two individuals. And not for any commune.

Dee turns her head back towards him. Her eyes are glistening red, but she doesn't look at him. 'Ivon had a girlfriend here for years,' she says. 'Cerys. A lovely girl. He adored her. But it's not easy when your boyfriend is a national hero. She didn't want to do it any more. He didn't want to let her go. He wouldn't.'

A pile of Lapsed Era books sit on Dee's desk. She straightens them absent-mindedly before continuing. 'Well, Cerys threatened to involve the police. She would have done it, too, if we hadn't got him through. He was distraught. He may play without a care in the world, but he has very dark moods. And you can't be playing all the time.'

The atmosphere is delicate. Dusty is aware that he is upholding something precious for as long as he partakes of it. And to partake of it is to be in Wales. It is a privilege not to be broken.

'I can see how he resembles Ricky,' he says. 'But he is young, too, and strong, like Ricky was. He has boldness and vigour.'

'If Ricky were to go to London now…' Dee laughs softly at the idea. 'We've lived in Wales for twenty-five years now, just like Ivon. Even if he could be young again, Ricky would never cope. We're different people now.'

'I was talking to Ricky earlier about a TMS procedure that we underwent, the three of us, in 2111.'

'You were part of that, were you?'

'Yes, and I've been investigating it. Something went very wrong. There were seven of us. Within six months we had all been placed under surveillance. And I'm the only one who survived. Daniel Attention, gone by the age of nineteen, less than three years later. Chad Meninga, Angela Hunter, Leanda Wellington, all gone within a few years of that. You and Ricky, gone in 2119. But we know what happened to you.'

He has Dee's attention now. A precious connection is being formed.

'I remember Leanda,' she says. 'She took an aero out and drove it too fast on a windy day. It flipped on the M2. Killed her instantly, they said.'

'Angela Hunter?'

Dee shakes her head. 'Rings a bell…'

'I can't remember Chad Meninga, but Daniel Attention suffered from a failing work ethic. He couldn't bring himself to train properly. And eventually he was flat refusing to. They took him away. And I remember the final straw with Ricky…'

'The stadium computer giving him out. I know. He still goes on about it.'

'And what about you, Dee? What happened to you?'

She sighs and sits back in her chair. 'No specific incident, I don't think. I just remember my attitude changing, as if we were missing the point somehow. That we'd achieve a lot more by slowing down a bit, smelling the roses, you know. Engaging with the spiritual side of what we were doing, the joy, the laughter, the timelessness of it. I mean, none of this made any sense to me at the time, but we came here and I soon understood, by which I mean I developed a language for my disquiet. Ricky's always said this country has let us be the people we really are.'

'And they let you come here, just like that?'

Dee shrugs. 'They released us at the Swansea West Hostel. We soon found work as coaches, Ricky at the cricket club, me in the local schools, and we settled down in Mumbles.' She laughs at the memory. 'We were just drawn to the Gower Peninsula somehow. I can't explain it.'

'Yes!' says Dusty, leaping to his feet and pacing in front of Dee's desk. 'It was the same with me! Exactly the same! The moment I saw the signs from the road, I had to follow them! How strange we should all feel that way. And then there are the dreams. Ricky told me you both have them. So do I! The flying machine!'

'The biplane.'

'Exactly!'

'The safari.'

'The what?'

'Safari.' Dee sits forward with purpose and energy, trying to make herself understood. 'Um, it's a kind of, well, it's being out in the wilderness, Africa, the wildlife, leopards in particular. Ricky and I both dream about it. Then there's the champagne dream!'

Dusty's enthusiasm is checked. These dreams mean nothing to him, but he presses on. 'There's the dream where my prowess with the bat belongs to me. You know, it's something to be cherished and *I* have the right to be proud of it, not the commune!'

Dee laughs and claps her hands. 'Oh, yes, of course! I have that one all the time. Although I can't say whether it started before or after Wales. It's a perfectly normal thing to feel here. Then there's the sinking-car dream, of course.'

Dusty stops pacing abruptly. 'I had that one just the other night! Ivon sank with it.' He winces at his own insensitivity, but he must sustain the conversation's momentum. 'And then there's Ivon. I know it's not the same as it must be for you, but I *feel*, I feel something for him. I'm not alone in this, it's true. There have been a number of strange displays of intense feeling for him among the populace recently. But the moment I heard his name chanted at St Helen's that first time, it moved me so powerfully.'

'That was another thing,' rejoins Dee. 'His name. It's quite unusual, but I remember feeling strongly that we should call him Ivon, with an "o". And Ricky swears blind he felt the same way, independently of me.'

As if a thought has occurred to her, Dee raises a hand, sliding her chair into a corner of the room. 'Let's just see if there *is* some connection with all this.' She positions herself in front of a Lapsed Era monitor, which springs into life when she touches a key. 'Right. Let's try Gower and Ivon.' She types at the keyboard and waits for the results. 'No, it's no good. All that's coming up is articles about Ivon, the boy from Gower.' She thinks again.

'Try putting in "flying machine",' suggests Dusty.

'I'll try "biplane".'

She hits the search button. A second later, she manoeuvres a device by her hand, and a second after that she gasps.

'What is it?' asks Dusty.

Dee does not respond. Dusty walks round to look at the screen over her shoulder.

'Oh, shit,' he murmurs to himself.

Dee looks up at him, and he down at her. She is wide-eyed, as if she has just glanced into the deepest recesses of her soul. He knows he must look the same.

There, on the screen, in a two-dimensional photograph that makes Dusty's heart ache, is the flying machine, and from out of it, his arm resting casually on the fuselage, a man smiles at the camera with a languid mischievousness that makes Dusty's heart want to break. Another picture, softer of focus but ancient too of provenance, depicts the same man, bare-headed and in the loose white garments of the time, frozen in the flourish of a cover drive, the bat in his hands like a wand. His hair is golden and curly, luxuriant and untamed. And on his face, even at the point of execution, he retains a hint of that same mischief, that same smile, that joy. 'David Ivon Gower was a former English cricketer who became captain of the England cricket team during the 1980s. Described as one of the most stylish left-handed batsmen of the era, Gower played 117 tests…'

Dusty stumbles away from the screen, into the middle of the room, into the middle of his being, which opens up now to claim him. A thousand blinding lights go off in his head, memories he never knew he had. And yet none will yield to registration. It is a personal history he cannot apprehend, a life he will never be able to call his own, residing, though it may, in the firmament of his brain.

His skill host. This man is his skill host. *Their* skill host. He feels something inside him give way and a gentle turbulence muster at his eyelids.

For the first time in his adult life, there are tears, soft and warm, in the eyes of Dusty Noble.

XI

Ivon stops.

What the fuck was that?

'That wasn't me!' he mumbles to himself, stunned.

The ball that he has just kicked spirals away to the touchline on halfway.

'That wasn't me!' he says again, louder this time, to one of the purposeful forwards striding past him in the direction of the line-out. He is ignored.

'I didn't mean to do that!' he says to Brandon, the full-back.

'Yes you did,' Brandon replies matter-of-factly, as he runs past as well.

His teammates and the droids adopt formation for a line-out on halfway, the silence eerie under the Twickenham roof, some 200 feet above them.

'Ivon. Assume position,' says a voice in his head.

'What was that?' Ivon says, shaking his head. 'I didn't… I was going to throw a miss pass to 13 then. And…and…*something* made me kick for touch. It was like someone else controlled me for a second.'

'This has been explained to you, Ivon. This is ProzoneX, the most advanced Strategy and Direction software in use today. If you get on the field on Friday, you will find it directing the team. If you want to get on the field on Friday you will follow those directions. It is essential that you do. Everybody else will be. And our opposition will be following theirs. There is no room for delinquency.'

Ivon stares at a blade of fibre-grass on the Twickenham turf. It is white. The one next to it is green. Neither has been painted. They just *are* those colours. He has been told about ProzoneX, but he wasn't listening. He's heard talk of impulse manipulation software, but never paused to consider it. He thinks of taking a knife to the back of his neck. Cut out that central chip. Back home, there is grass. You paint on it, and then you play on it. Players and grass, alive and distinct from each other. Here, his teammates are as much a part of the pitch as the lifeless green and white, like those droids that line up opposite them and formation glide across the turf.

They want him to become a part of it. They want him to give up his separateness.

'Ivon.'

He twitches his head, irritably. 'So we no longer count. The players…the athletes. It's a clash between computers.'

'Of course you do. You kicked the ball, not the computer. Assume position.'

The rise and fall of Ivon's breast increases. He wrestles with the urge to scream. And, as he does, the same strange impulse that made him kick just then inclines him to start jogging towards the line-out. After a couple of paces, he overcomes the instinct and digs his feet in, the way he did as a boy.

'Ivon.'

He grits his teeth against the voice in his head. Don't look up at them, he thinks to himself, in case you race up there and smash to fuck the computers and the coaches.

After a pause to make clear that it is of his own accord, he walks towards the line-out. His teammates are in position, some of them crouched, others poised with feet in perfect alignment, ready for the signal. Not one of them looks in his direction, even though they wait for him.

✺

'Put this on and KEEP IT ON. Leave the counterpoint on your bed. There'll be an aero outside at 18.00. Get in it.'

It is signed by the 'Fellowship of Dig' again. Ivon recognises the handwriting from the note that had been slipped under his day suit in the changing room the week before. This message is written on a piece of paper, too.

Someone's been in his lodging. He thought that was against the rules, even if he'd invited anyone in to visit, which he hasn't. There is what looks like a white glove lying on his bed, but when he picks it up he can see that this item has that Perpetual Era quality of seeming more alive than some of the humans. It obviously does something. He pulls it over his left hand. When it's on, a small white disc on his bed, like a gambling chip, starts to glow, as if it too were alive. This must be the counterpoint.

Ivon checks the time: 17.53. He is excited suddenly – that light, uplifting sort of excited that he knew when he was young. It's only a piece of paper and a glove, but Ivon knows that in this environment these represent subversion. In this mysterious intervention he senses an opportunity for relief from the drudgery, the monitoring, the formulas, *the mind control*.

He paces through the house. It's more of a bungalow, really, his new elite lodging, or 'home' as they keep calling it. But it's much like the last place, only bigger, with a patch of fake grass out the back and his own in-home simulator, next to the bathroom. Rather than walk to the communal simulators at URL, and sometimes queue, he can step into his own, as he does now, and let off some steam whenever he feels on edge.

For kicking practice, he doesn't even need to set anything up. He grabs the training ball and fires off a quick three punts into the vortex of his simu-wall. The second is measured at 65 metres.

At 17.58, he steps outside the front door. As always, the streets are quiet, the same in Richmond as they were in White City. Bang on 18.00, one of those weird floaty cars ghosts round the corner and pulls up outside his house. The rear door nearest him opens silently. Ivon climbs inside.

The interior is decked out just like the Bentleys that Reesy sold on his forecourt on Carmarthen Road – when he could source them. Pale leather seats and walnut-veneer trimmings. And a chauffeur with a hat on.

The chauffeur says nothing as the car pulls away and drifts through the streets of London.

'Where we going?' asks Ivon, after a good five minutes' staring out of the window at the neat, hypnotic sameness of residential London.

'Canterbury, sir.'

'You called me sir?' Ivon laughs. He likes it.

'Sir.'

'So, are you from this Dig lot, then?'

'I am just the driver, sir.'

'And what's this?' says Ivon, waving his left hand in the air.

The driver half-turns to see the glove on Ivon's hand, which is when Ivon notices that he, too, is wearing one.

'It's a deflector, sir.'

'And what does it do?'

'It allows you to travel without detection. There should be a counterpoint.'

'Yep. Left it on my bed.'

'That's where you will show up on the Grid.'

Ivon nods approvingly. 'Can I keep it?'

185

'Regrettably, sir, you are to return it to me this evening. Officially, such things do not exist.'

Once the streets of south London have been negotiated, the car flies out into the countryside and the commune of the South East, along the M2, says the driver, past the cities of Gillingham, Maidstone and Ashford, and the dead towns of Sittingbourne and Faversham.

Canterbury is dead, too, maintained only for the visit of tourists to the Lapsed Era. Ivon feels at home immediately, as they ease past houses of substance and antiquity, colour and irregularity, past an old church on a corner. Then, round that corner looms a magnificent gatehouse of two turreted towers that puts him in mind of Cardiff Castle. They pass beneath its arch and on down narrow streets, oozing history and personality, until he is dropped off outside another gatehouse, smaller but more ornate.

'You will find the meeting through there, sir,' says the driver.

Ivon thanks him and climbs out of the aero. Already he can see the corner of a greater building beyond the gate. When he walks through it, he is confronted by the grandest cathedral he has ever set eyes on. To think the English hide treasures such as this! If this were Wales, an entire city would be thriving around it. In England, it stands in silence.

There is an iron gate set into the nearest tower, surrounded by elaborate carvings, and beyond that a door, both of them open. Ivon follows where they beckon.

Once inside, he stands in front of the cathedral's long sweep and gasps. The English might tell him that the vault of Twickenham is higher than this when measured scientifically, but Ivon tilts his head at the steepling arches in the ceiling and thinks they might mark the very frontier with God.

He becomes aware of a voice, deeper in the cathedral, through an arch some 50 metres away at the top of a wide flight of steps. He presses purposefully on towards the sound. Sceptred dignitaries watch his progress from the walls, as he bounds up the steps, shiny and uneven from the centuries. Through the arch, the cathedral opens up again into another breathtaking stretch of columns and arches, as long as the first. Ivon sees rows of dark brown pews, peopled by men and women in clothes he might expect to find back home.

They are listening to a man standing at a pulpit, framed by the billowing splendour of the arches and vaulted ceiling behind him, where the polished stone rises up further steps to its height at the altar beyond. Not only is this speaker dressed similarly to the others, he is notable for his age. Ivon finds it reassuring to come across a man of advanced years in England. He is fit and commanding and delivers his speech with animation and movement, but his presence is a reminder that old age is not tolerated in this country. Ivon sees him and feels comforted, as if he were at home. He stands in the archway and listens to the man speak.

'Thomas Carlyle, the nineteenth-century philosopher, wrote of the Vikings: "What we now lecture of as science, they wondered at and fell down in awe before as religion." He was a man who railed against the passing of a more magical, more unknowable time, when stories and heroes were enshrined in the workings of the natural world, which was explained by those legends. What heroes are there left to us now? What magic, what legend? Long after Carlyle passed, sport — our precious sport — began to succumb as well to the creeping tentacles of science, hauled down from its lofty perch, where it had shone as something sacred and unknowable, magical and beautiful. It had been a source of joy and colour. A story. A drama, whose contestants knew of a life beyond the games and loved those games the more for it.

'But soon it became a thing to unpick, to dissect, rationalise and explain, like a rat stretched out on the laboratory table. No corner of it remains unexplored. We know sport and its workings so intimately now that indifference towards it is universal, even if it powers the world we live in. And those few of us who care to dig deep in search of our souls must languish in this monochrome prison, seeking to undermine it whenever we can.

'We are alone, my friends! For which of our people can conceive of sport today as a thing to be savoured, where winning is not a solemn duty, but a happy fillip to the higher spirit of fun, style and excellence? Why, that spirit was once so strong that our ancestors from the Lapsed Era used to turn up in their thousands to the games, not to pump boards, but to *watch*, purely and simply! No scientists they – just men, women and juveniles marvelling at the feats of free spirits. Yet their equivalents today, whether elite or primary, cannot so much as move from here to there but that it fits in with the relevant programme.

'And what if we were relieved of our duties to pump at the matches we attend? Would we even want to focus on events on the field, as our ancestors once did for joy, when we would have nothing more to watch than athletes following the vectors and algorithms laid down by higher intelligences, all personality, independence and freedom cut out of them like a dangerous disease?'

Ivon is emboldened to take a step or two forward, emerging from out of the arch into the choir. The speaker notices him but continues.

'Ours is a struggle without end. Early in the twentieth century, the German sociologist, Max Weber, described the rationalising process of science and technology, which was well under way by then, as "Die Entzauberung der Welt", the demystifying of the world, or Disenchantment. It took longer for it to take hold of sport, but, insofar as there ever was a struggle between the forces of Disenchantment and the cavalier spirit of the Corinthian age, that struggle has long since been lost, the latter swept away by its ruthless, indiscriminate nemesis. But I urge you to remember that the Fellowship of Dig predates the Perpetual Era, for all that we must exist underground as the last bastion of that Corinthian ideal. We have done no more than to look deep enough within ourselves to find the last flickering of a romantic soul. Our mission is to coax it back to life in others, to re-enchant the world.'

His manner changes as he looks for the first time directly at Ivon, across the ancient stone. He ushers him nearer.

'Finally, I present to you Ivon…'

Before he has a chance to continue, a spontaneous round of applause breaks out. Ivon looks round at the faces, a few hundred of them, and sees glove after glove, like the one he wears, one per pair of clapping hands.

'We shall call him The Emissary,' the speaker continues when the applause has died down, 'for he comes from Gower.'

There are gasps and murmurings among the congregation, but Ivon notices a smile on the face of the speaker, as he raises his hands for calm. 'Gower, in this instance, is a region of South Wales. As far as we know, there is no connection. But it should be obvious that the spirit is strong in him!'

The old man comes out from behind his lectern and approaches Ivon with an arm extended, enfolding him in his gown. Ivon is happy to be led.

'Before we repair to Ye Olde Beverlie for our libations,' he says loudly, 'I invite you, Ivon, to be the first today to touch the Relic and thus confirm yourself as one of us.'

'Sweet,' says Ivon.

'That's a yes!' cries the old man with a rich peel of laughter, and the congregation rise to their feet with a cheer.

Ivon looks across at his guide and begins to appreciate in profile a remarkable hooked nose. 'Who are you?' he says in gentle bewilderment, as they begin the walk to the high altar.

The old man turns to him with a smile and offers his hand in the Welsh way, which Ivon shakes. 'I am Syracuse Garbo. It's an honour to meet you. You are everything we hold to be true made flesh. A triumph of Nature, as a thing wholly miraculous, stupendous and divine, over the forces of Disenchantment.'

'Nice to meet you.'

'When we reach the Relic,' he says more quietly, 'you might give the others a chance to gather round. Then our ritual is simple. Touch the Relic and declare the words, "Fun, style and excellence".'

'I can do that.'

They climb the steps towards the high altar, past a stone throne of great substance and incalculable age, then on through the tombs of ancient English kings and queens. When they reach the altar, Garbo turns to wait for the congregation, which is filing up to join them. At the appropriate moment, he nods encouragingly at Ivon, who approaches the Relic. It is mounted on a simple wooden stand and is, as far as Ivon can tell, an old cricket ball. The stitching is neat but aged and the leather worn. And on its surface are inscribed, with the flourish of a human hand, the letters 'DIG'.

Ivon lays his hand on the ball and states clearly and loudly: 'Fun, style and excellence!'

There is another cheer, and the men and women of the Fellowship of Dig turn to each other in a flurry of Welsh handshaking and a murmuring of mantras. Garbo approaches Ivon with hand outstretched again. As they shake, he dips his head slightly and says: 'Dig deep for your soul, brother!'

Ivon nods, and soon he is surrounded by friendly well-wishers.

– ☀ –

Dusty pulls away from the Swansea West Hostel for the English. Within moments, he is drifting serenely along the M4, in and out of the Lapsed Era cars of the Welsh, soon to leave behind their endearing sturdiness for his lonely journey into England.

He is tingling from the events of the day before. If the ramparts of his discipline, built up over a lifetime in the Perpetual Era, have been crumbling these past few months, yesterday cracked open the soft core at their heart, the essence of something delicate they had been protecting from the outside world – or imprisoning, deep within himself. He cried. It was tentatively at first. The little droplets in his eye and on his cheek confused him. But then, just as Wales felt like home after his first visit, so he settled into tears, once he became familiar with the curious relief they seem to provide. Now he feels he could slip into them at any time.

He and Dee wept in each other's arms for long stretches of the afternoon. She, with all her experience in emotion, gently eased him in. Dusty had felt naked and vulnerable, but she helped him see the natural, eternal truth of what they were doing. Her tears fell on his shoulder, and his in her hair. It has created something between them. That and the years. Mutual recognition of the long history between them, which isn't there in the eyes of his old acquaintances in England. He can't get Dee out his mind, or the afternoon they spent in each other's tears.

And then there's the figure presiding over it all, this Lapsed Era cricketer, David Gower. It makes sense – to a degree. They read the biography of his life as if it were the biography of their own, the life they never knew they'd led, because they hadn't. Only the memories of it must have been lying all those years in their minds, and the spirit – the noble, subversive spirit – that had all the while tried to infiltrate Dusty's consciousness, no matter how model a Perpetual citizen he became. Now, it floods through him.

Dee and he had nodded in recognition at the details of that life. The Tiger Moth Gower had flown low over his teammates in defiance of authority. Of course he had. The car he'd driven across a frozen lake and lost beneath the ice. The childhood in Africa, the adolescence in Canterbury, the afternoons under a wide sky, the shots, the laughter, the revelry. And, underpinning everything, the notion that it should be fun, stylish and beyond analysis.

This man was the skill host for the ill-fated TMS procedure of 2111. Dee and Dusty knew it immediately. Ricky would know, too, or Daniel Attention or any of the others, if they could see what Dusty and Dee have seen. But why? Why would the Institute of Improvement have chosen a man from the Lapsed Era as skill host? It was the very first Transmigration of the Skill procedure. Surely there were more suitable candidates from the Perpetual Era. This is where the sense runs out.

'And why did we receive all this stuff from our host, these memories and attitudes?' asked Dee, banging her head with the heel of her hand. 'We were only supposed to get his cover drive.'

Dee.

He will bring Ivon home to her. He must. He imagines her reaction to seeing him again. The tears. Could Dusty be there to share in them?

He comms Ivon now. The voice at the other end is faintly hoarse.

'Why are you vocalising, Ivon?' says Dusty.

'I feel rough as a dog.'

The roughness fills Dusty's head. 'What's happened?'

'Oh, Dusty, I got shit-faced last night. Absolutely wrote myself off.'

Dusty has no idea what he's talking about, but he is anxious suddenly. Ivon's gravelly voice, twisted with the contortions of his vocal chords, is very Welsh, far from the perfect sonorousness of a voiceless comm. There are many obstacles to Ivon's repatriation, not least the threat of summary apprehension. London is tolerating his eccentricity for now, but patience could run out at any moment. If there is to be any hope, his very Welshness must play itself down. Dusty's instinct tells him that this latest affectation is the result of activity quite the opposite of that.

'What do you mean?'

'I got drunk. I'm hungover. I've got to play today.'

'You'll be all right, though,' says Dusty, more in hope.

'Yeah. Course I will. It'll be like the old days.'

'What were you doing?'

'Ah, these people! It was like being back at home! I got picked up and taken to Canterbury last night. They were all sitting round in this cathedral, and they welcomed me like I was, I dunno, a long-lost brother or something. There was this old geezer going on about the way sport used to be. The way it still is in Wales, I told them. Then we all went to the pub and drank. What a laugh! This is more like it! English people who are fun!'

'Who are these people?'

'They call themselves the Fellowship of Dig.'

'Never heard of them.'

'They're a bunch of reprobates, I tell yer! Proper laugh. It's a secret society dedicated to the undermining of Perpetual values. Brilliant! They have meetings around the country. It's got regional branches and everything. All run by this old man.'

A chilling thought dawns on Dusty. 'An old man? What do you mean? How old?'

'Proper old. Welsh old.'

'You mean he's an Exempt?'

'If you say so.'

'Did you get his name?'

'Sicarus, or something.'

'Syracuse Garbo.'

'That's the one.'

Dusty vocalises his next words, as he tries to remain calm. 'I should very much like to speak with Syracuse Garbo.'

'Not a problem. We have an arrangement. If I ever need him...'

'Be careful, Ivon. Be very careful.'

○

He is drunk no more. Where his head had been awash only a few hours ago with the bubbling currents of a long night of revelry, now the waters have receded to expose the hideous pulsar of fear, heavy and intense. The transition from drunkenness has been inexorable and is now complete, uninterrupted by anything so sensible as a night's sleep.

He has eaten pasta. Not as much as he'd have liked, but hopefully enough. In Wales he had found eating pasta the most effective way to conceal alcohol on his breath. For his lunch at the refectory today, he tried to sneak in an extra portion, instead of his match-day quota of fruit, but Perpetual Era technology scuppered him again. He'd had his 207 grams of enhanced pasta, 3 hours, 47 minutes before game time; the dispenser would not let him have any more. At least he was on his own. His teammates have more efficient digestive systems than he does, and the first of them were coming in for their allotted lunchtimes just as he was leaving his. He was careful to turn his face away, or at least his mouth.

Not that it made much difference. His new teammates are so indifferent to his existence not one of them would voluntarily look him in the eye anyway, still less smell his breath. He's beginning to miss the guys at URL. At least they were hostile towards him, showed evidence of feeling. Some of this lot are as impenetrable as the shiny glass fabric of their city. Ivon swears he can see a field of vision shine forth from each pair of eyes, like headlights from a car. The young ones, these new

DGF athletes they keep going on about, don't seem to register anything beyond their raison d'être, rugby.

Only a few of the older ones have acknowledged his existence of their own accord. A couple of them on his first day went so far as to be aggressive.

'You're the one who won't take his genetic modifiers, aren't you?' said one of the front-row forwards, a man of formidable width, with a swarthy, handsome face.

At the time, Ivon had groaned inwardly at yet another display of hostility towards the Welshman, but, in light of the indifference since, he looks back at it now almost with affection. 'That's right,' he replied.

And another of the older players, a No. 8 by the name of Mike Bulstrode, came over to join the conversation. 'Why would you do that? A chain is only as strong as its weakest link. You're putting us all at risk.'

'I'm not going to be your weakest link. You'll see.'

'You'll take them eventually,' said Bulstrode.

'I will never take performance-enhancing drugs,' said Ivon, the blood rising within him.

His two inquisitors studied him for a moment, looked at each other, then walked away conferring with each other.

He can't find any purchase on his new teammates. He's been an elite for only three days, but there are no promising kinks in the team's uniformity for him to wheedle his way in through, no Tim the scrum-half among this lot. The half-backs here are as serious as the forwards, as serious as the coaches, as serious as the computers running the show.

There's not even a captain for him to appeal to, or be chastised by.

'We don't need captains in elite,' said Doug, one of the scrum-halfs, on Ivon's first day. 'We have ProzoneX.'

Now the indifference is starting to close in. Ivon is hungover. He is ill at ease. He is in pain. He sits deep in the bowels of Twickenham. The ominous rumble from the crowd warming up throbs throughout his head. It is not as harsh a transmission of sound as at the White City Stadium, but it is more diffuse, all around, part of the walls, the floor, the air. He is afraid of emerging from his cubicle. This is not Ivon. He is on the bench today, although no one has put it to him like that. He is part of the elite squad. They are all here, all available, with fifteen of them starting the game. He can discern no hierarchy, no personalities. They are all London Rugby. And, today, Tyne and Wear are the opposition.

The fear is strong in him now. When they come out into the stadium, he and the other forty-four members of the squad not starting the match take their place on ergonomic seats, down by pitch-side. The stadium is vast. Ivon guesses there are more than ninety thousand people present, but it's hard to tell with the levers flashing round the four steep tiers, like arms brandished against the fainthearted. When the teams take to the field, the levers are brought to rest, and a hush descends, forcing Ivon to confront his situation.

He has never been a reserve before. How can he prepare when he doesn't know if or when he'll be on? What should he be doing, what thinking? He can't think. He can't focus. The Rhossili stone felt alien in his hands when he tried to commune with it earlier in the changing room. He is cut adrift. His mother and father are far from here. His father is a drunk. He is a drunk. Why didn't they run a fitness test on him before the game? They should have run one. They just assume he's fit. Like all the other elites around him. But he's not. He's not fit. Not for this. The bench. He should be great on a bench. Just play. As and when. Fuck it. No pressure. Be brilliant. His head is sore. Sore afraid. This is not Ivon.

He looks to either side of him. Square jaws and eyes set with focus. Not a fidget or tremor. The line of elites is strong, and oblivious to him.

※

An hour into the game, he is called. The voice of one of the coaches is in his head. Neither of the other fly-halfs in the squad are fully fit. He's going on for the last 20 minutes. Just follow the instincts, the coach tells him, whatever they may say.

Ivon rises from his seat and is admitted into the transition compound where he begins to warm up. London are losing, but their performance is improved. Their starting fly-half, Spencer, approaches the transition compound, clutching his elbow. His collarbone has snapped. Out for two weeks. He is short and powerful, in contrast to Ivon's longer, more languid bearing. Ivon watches him enter the compound. No words or glances are exchanged. Ivon is released onto the pitch.

His fear recedes, as he walks onto the stage. But this is still not Ivon. It doesn't feel like his stage today. He is a guest. There is meekness in him. That is what it is. The will is missing.

He receives the ball from a line-out, his first touch, and knows before he knows that he is to throw a miss pass to his outside centre. It is executed immaculately, for this is still the body of Ivon. His array of skills remains extensive and of a premium grade. It will be put to good use in the minutes that follow. ProzoneX knows precisely what its new asset is capable of. Ivon's head is fuzzy and unsure, but no matter. He has ceded control of it to the computer. The body responds. Smoothly, the ball is sent to those areas of the field the computer targets in its shifting engagement with Tyne and Wear's Strategy and Direction software.

At one point, Ivon sees the eyes of a defender drift from him to the man outside. He knows what this means. He has seen it many times. Where the eyes lead, the focus follows, and with it the body. The defender inside doesn't have him covered. A dummy, a step, and Ivon would be away, no matter how strong these new opponents, no matter how quick. But ProzoneX has other strategies, and Ivon turns the pass inside to set up the next ruck. He does not resist, even though he will lie awake in the nights to come despairing over the opportunity missed.

With five minutes remaining, London trail by six points. They are awarded a penalty, when the Tyne and Wear No. 12 is offside. Ivon steps forward to take the ball. The kick at goal is straightforward, and he is aware of an instinct to gesture at the posts for the attempt at three points. This time, though, he stops himself.

'Wait!' he says in appeal, if not to ProzoneX, then to the coaches at least. 'Surely we go for the corner! I'll put us close, then we go for the drive.'

'The decision's been made.'

'But we're six points behind! We need to score a try!'

'Take the kick, 10!'

'This is the fucking computer again, isn't it!'

Ivon is visited once more by the impulse to point at the posts. He follows it. The kick is successful, and the thunder of 90 000 workouts strikes up. He turns to jog back into position, urgency gathering within him. He knows he must win them this game now or suffer the agonies of his darkest mood when next he is alone. Even if he does win it, will he ever forgive himself for ceding control to a computer?

Two minutes to go, and Ivon shapes to punt for the corner. The contact is sweet, and the ball erupts from his foot with that special propulsion, seemingly greater than the force he has imparted on it. It spirals towards the corner, some 60 metres away, over the head of the covering winger, lands just a few feet infield and scuds poetically into touch. Ivon imagines the lyrical roar from the St Helen's faithful at so divine a kick, but the din from the Twickenham crowd does not fluctuate, as they continue to pump through the points from his penalty.

London's forwards run towards the corner bellowing exhortations at themselves, which Ivon can barely hear above the noise. Tyne and Wear win the line-out but are unable to gain much ground with the clearance. When London secure the next line-out, they develop a rolling maul. Tyne and Wear collapse it 10 metres short. Penalty to London. Thirty seconds remaining. The stadium falls silent, the latest points pumped through.

Ivon feels the alien inclination again. ProzoneX wants him to kick at goal and settle for the draw.

'No!' he cries, in protest.

The forwards jog past him towards the halfway line, the penalty won, the decision relayed. Ivon runs up to a few of them, trying to make eye contact.

'You've got these fuckers on toast!' he yells. 'Let's go again! The corner! We can win this, boys!'

None of them responds. He runs in front of Mike Bulstrode, determined to force his attention. With a fearsome fist, Bulstrode brushes him aside and jogs on.

'Ten!' says a voice, loud but steady in his head. 'We're taking the kick. It is decided.'

The impulse to point at the posts overtakes him one last time, and he gives in.

'But we can win this!' he pleads. 'You're settling for the draw! And that's if I land the kick!'

'ProzoneX computes that, on this form, there is a 73 per cent chance of you doing that. The probability of a try from this position is 23.2 per cent. We are on a losing streak. We will take the kick and bank a much-needed pump of 20 minutes for the draw. If you convert it.'

A corridor of light has lit up under the turf from the point of the offence, leading away from the try line, parallel to touch. From anywhere along it he may take the kick. Ivon lines up the ball, 30 metres away from the try line, 10 metres in from touch. There are 90 000 people in the stadium, but he does not feel their eyes upon him. Most are not watching. There is murmuring, conversation. His soul is disengaged. Going for goal is not his decision. This game has not been his, even if it lies within his compass, and his alone, to secure the result. He takes his regulation steps away from the ball – three back, two to the side. He pictures the ball leaving its tee, turning end over end on its ascension, the poise at its height and the sighing descent towards a resting place beyond the posts. He commences his run-up and strikes. It is good.

The stadium pumps roar into life, but Ivon is already heading to the changing rooms.

There are Perpetual handshakes all round. In Wales, a room of this size would be steaming with the sweat and mud of so many rugby players, but here the air is clear. Ivon still doesn't know how they do that. He sits on the bench, away from the earnest congratulations being passed about among his new teammates.

In Wales, Ivon would have had his first slug from a can by now. Kit would be strewn across the floor, the air thick with steam and song, shirts off, lesions livid and untreated, the pain throbbing blissfully through wracked bodies at the end of their ordeal, soon to shower, soon to dress in shirt and tie, from the primeval to the civilised in 45 minutes, with just a hint of trauma maybe, on the brow, or across the cheek, to wear as the reminder of what they'd been through that afternoon. He should be going from here up to the bar to meet Cerys, Mum,

Dad and carouse the night away with teammates and loved ones – is there any distinction? – in that happy Welsh haze.

He should be going from here to meet Alanis.

Physical pain is all he recognises in this parody of the post-match ritual. He may have played only 20 minutes, but he feels as sore as if it had been 80. These English are fearsome specimens, and they hit hard. His body is rattled. And the inside of his head aches, as the last of his hangover is purged.

Ivon looks around at his teammates with despair. They are sober and earnest. He knows how they feel – he almost prefers losing to the irresolution of a draw – but why does he get the feeling that this is his new team in celebration? They shake hands and murmur to each other. Now the head coach breaks it up and sends them all to the benches along the walls of the room, where Ivon is already sitting. He is pleased. They have avoided defeat. He talks them through the statistics of the match, drawing attention every now and then to a notable performer. The accolades – if that's what they can be called, for they are no more than the recital of dry numbers – are received in silence, no discernible pride in the recipient, no approval voiced by his teammates.

In time, Coach White looks straight at Ivon. 'And, finally, when the commune needed him to, Ivon converted the penalty that earned us the draw.'

For the first time, Ivon has the attention of his teammates. He does not return the gaze of any of them, but looks instead at Coach White with a hangdog, sullen air, his elbows resting on his knees. Ivon is ashamed of his performance. They should have won. He could have won it for them. He would have without that computer in his head.

Coach White looks down at his tablet. It's almost as if he is reading from it when he says: 'That was an impressive debut. For an athlete new to elite sport, without the enhancements provided by genetic modifiers and hormonal supplements, without even the benefit of an Academy education, a PST quotient of 77.9 is encouraging.'

'What does that even *mean*? PST?'

'Purity of Skill Transmission.'

Ivon sits back and leans against the wall. He looks up at the ceiling, searching the featureless white for something, anything, a fleck of peeling paint, a smear of condensation. 'And what does *that* mean?'

'ProzoneX measures the end result of each skill as executed by an athlete against the intention as transmitted to the athlete by ProzoneX. The weight and direction of every pass, the force and angle of every tackle, and so on. A figure is generated for each athlete as a percentage of the ideal. More detailed breakdowns will be made available. Your PST for passing today was 87.3, which is…' Coach White hesitates, as if something were caught in his throat, and looks down at his tablet, 'exceptional. Although it was only for 20 minutes.'

Ivon is now slouching against the wall. 'That wasn't rugby,' he says.

And there is silence.

'You think I was good? I was shit. That's the worst I've ever played.'

Laughter breaks out among a few of his teammates. Ivon ignores it, though it surprises him.

'We should have won that game, boys! Instead, we let a computer take it away from us.'

Those that had laughed now begin to murmur. Coach White speaks out across them. 'This is Misalignment, Ivon. You continue to speak as a Welshman. It was explained to you on the field why you were to kick for goal.'

'That wasn't an explanation. That was a maths lesson. Look! I know when a team is broken. Any player knows it. They were broken. We just had to win the line-out and keep our composure.' Ivon looks around at some of the forwards. 'You must have realised that,' he implores them.

Ivon is confronted by hard, unmoving faces. Not one looks of a mind to reply, and Coach White speaks before any can.

'The probability of scoring the try was 23.2 per cent.'

Ivon scoffs. 'We would have scored! I know it!'

'ProzoneX computes data from every match that has ever been contested. It has a precise, statistical measure of how we are faring against our opposition not only in any given eighty-minute match but across any given five minutes of any match. *It* knows. And, when it issues a directive based on a precisely calculated balance of probabilities, it is right that we follow that directive and not the emotion-led hunch of a Lapsed Era Welshman.'

'Ha! You're right! I work on intuition, not data. I should have taken control myself. Kicked for the corner. Forced you all to do the right thing.'

'There would have been profound repercussions for you if you had.'

Ivon flushes.

'There is no need for this,' Coach White continues. 'Why would you rebel against a consciousness that can hold and appraise far more information about the match than you, as a human, ever could, and can make decisions based on it far quicker? You did as ProzoneX instructed today, and you put in a shift that was really, really…good.'

Suddenly, there is a bellow of exasperation from the other side of the room. 'Oh, come on!' cries one of the players. Ivon looks to see which one. It is Mike Bulstrode, who glares at him aggressively with mighty arm outstretched. 'Why are we bothering with this Lapsed Era rhetoric? "Really good", "exceptional", "encouraging", "impressive". Idling hell! Let's just assimilate him! He can do a job for us. He can kick, pass, run – anything ProzoneX wants. Let's make sure he does it.'

The room settles into silence once more, its natural state. Ivon can't remember how he came in, can't see where he goes out. The four walls of the square are lined with men he barely knows, men he can barely tell apart. Dead, sourceless light fills the room.

Coach White rises to his feet. 'Let's end it there.'

XII

Dusty has decided to take steps. For two days, Ivon has not been receiving comms. And he didn't show up at the club this afternoon for a bout with Adriana Platt. If Ivon is ever to see his homeland again, Dusty must act now. He has left messages, but he can't be sure Ivon knows how to pick them up. He closes his eyes to study the address he has taken from the Resources database. Ivon is currently living at 23 43rd West, Richmond.

Dusty is resolved to seek him there. Can he do it? After his recent trips to Wales, the idea of entering another's home no longer appals him – indeed, he warms to it as an affirmation of his new-found Welshness, his affinity for the Lapsed Era. And yet...

He has not left his own home. He paces through it, he presses his hands against the glass, he fizzes intolerably. But he has not left his own home. Social norms are powerful, even to those who no longer want to be governed by them.

He is being ridiculous. He can leave his home, at least. Go for a cycle. Head south, follow the river west. Find himself in Richmond. Who would ask questions or interfere? He is Dusty Noble. He wears the green of elite. He has walked with managers, scored 95 000 runs. Why must he keep reminding himself of these things?

✺

Olympus Dan.

Ivon opens the message sent to the whole squad by Coach White. Their 'Next Match' is on Wednesday against Yorkshire, the league leaders. It's a four-day turnaround from the last one, their shortest of the year, and there is an injury crisis at fly-half. Coach White is fielding a new team. Ivon is to start.

'Olympus Dan is the first DGF athlete to break through in elite rugby,' the message reads. 'He is nineteen years of age and, at 6 feet 8 inches, the tallest man in England. View his file. The scientific community is pleased with the successful application of DGF technology and with this contestant in particular, who best represents it. He is the league's most productive athlete and a significant factor in Yorkshire's success this year.'

Ivon opens the file. His eyes are closed. The vision of a for-midable man fills his head. He looks years beyond his stated age. His bare forearms, folded across his chest, seem to come at Ivon, rude slabs of muscle and twisting vein. They look in no way elongated. None of him does. Isolated in Ivon's brain, this man's height is impossible to gauge, but he is in perfect proportion. If he really is 6 feet 8 inches, he is bigger than any man Ivon has ever seen. There is a look of amusement on Dan's face, sneering, impregnable amusement, the look of a creature at the top of the food chain. His forehead is heavy, his jaw clean and wide, the eyes large and pinched in each corner, as if Oriental genes had been among those deliberately fused in this man.

A column of stats runs down the side of his image. They mean nothing to Ivon, a jumble of numbers and 'g's and 'm/s's and all that. Ivon plays the footage that accompanies the file. Olympus Dan bursts from the base of a scrum. The footage pauses, and a series of arrows and numbers and 'g's appear. The viewing angle swoops round him, isolating him, magnifying him. Glorifying him, thinks Ivon. Then the film runs on to show Dan's lowered shoulder crunch into an opposition flanker who has gone too high on him. The footage pauses again, as the flanker's jaw breaks away from his head, a finger of blood just beginning to spew. More arrows, more numbers more 'g's.

Ivon stops the footage and opens his eyes. He thinks again, for the umpteenth time in the last 48 hours, of that moment in Saturday's game, when he saw the defender's eyes leave him, when he felt in that instant, that precious, vital instant, the certainty that he could break the first line, create havoc in a regimented defence. You have to act in those moments. No one is better than he is at acting in those moments. But he didn't. He let it go. He let the computer invade his head and change him, make him a worse player. He could have overruled it, he knows he could.

This Olympus Dan. He's a human, isn't he? He follows orders, plays to the rhythms of a dead computer, like the rest of them. Ivon can take him. He leaps from out of the naked white corner he'd been crouching in and runs in tight circles round his house. A pulse, lither than electricity, tingles through his body as he shimmies off his right foot, then another sends him off his left. He ducks into the simulator, grabs a rugby ball and fires another punt into the simu-wall. Sixty-nine metres. Bosh! He is manic again. He wants to beat people. He suspends his mania as best he can, trying to programme his chip to present him with the biggest, ugliest rugby players known to science. Can he ask for Olympus Dan himself? His mind is racing, so that he fumbles the controls, as if operating them with tremulous fingers. He closes his eyes and forces himself to be still, breathing deeply, flitting more accurately through the options in his head. No Olympus Dan is available, but there are others. Soon he is dashing lightly past a succession of muscular clones in his head, occasionally scragged by one of them, as represented by the morphing droids in the simulator. The droids are quick, they are strong. Why don't they just do away with players altogether? Set up a game between London's computer and Yorkshire's, transmitted through the droids. Because Ivon is quicker, Ivon is stronger. He is alive. Another beaten. And another. Then, bang! He mistimes a shimmy and is knocked off his feet. He lands on his back on the yielding surface of the simulator and looks up at an iron-faced athlete leering over him, its shoulder bonier and more sinewy than whatever it was that just hit him then.

He flicks off the simulation. The ceiling above him is like any other in this sugar-free world. It is white. Not white the adjective; White the noun. A distillation of what it is to be White. Whiteness personified. Any ceiling-ness a subsidiary property, easily overlooked. They should have won on Saturday. He should have won it for them. He sees the eyes flit across to the next man along. He feels the ethereal flicker of opportunity rise up in him. And the sick horror of its passing without action. He is nothing without the facility to act.

The ache of longing now takes a turn on him. And where there's longing there is Alanis. How he wishes he could see her face light up at the news of another vital win, a win inspired by him. How he wishes he could see her face. He received a message from the club yesterday. She had pulled out of their date in the sex cot today and someone else was stepping in to replace her. Just like that. No explanation, no consultation. The only comfort that had helped him through the agony of yesterday was the prospect of seeing Alanis, and even that was removed at 17.58 when the message came through. 'Alanis Fountin is unable to fulfil…' The message appears in his vision again – there, floating against the Whiteness, the letters, the numbers, commonplace and inoffensive, yet arranged in such a way as to devastate him. Get them away! He shakes his head, furiously trying to rid it of the words, then holds his breath to calm himself and take the steps to delete them.

Maybe it was the result. The draw. His failure. Would she have cancelled if London had won the match the day before? If he had stayed true to himself?

But he hadn't. He missed his moment. Which others went with it?

Seize every opportunity. Act. Mum used to tell him that. All she ever told him, really. It was her thing. Quiet, insistent, pertinent, amid all the other stuff from Dad.

Mum. Dad.

Alanis.

Home.

He will not yield. He will not take no for an answer. Not from Alanis, not from ProzoneX, not from Olympus Dan.

He will impose himself. There is something in him. He is Ivon.

It is getting late. Dusty has done away with the original plan to approach this great taboo by a circuitous route of no suspicion. The river can wait for another day. He has charged headlong at his destination, instead. South-westwards through Maida Vale, Ladbroke Grove and Shepherd's Bush, joining the Great Western Arcade at Hammersmith, pedalling through its airy pavilions, on to Kew, and thence south across the river through the Kew Arboretum and Deer Park to the foot of Richmond Hill. He climbs it now, engaging his hybrid navigator. A bold red line leads him onwards up the blue road, through neatly arranged formations of south-facing homes, curved to follow the sun.

Ivon's home is on the next street but one on the left, just below the brow of the hill. For the first time, Dusty slackens his pace. Is he really going to attempt this? This is Ivon's home, his sanctuary, for him alone. What right does he have to violate the sacred haven of another? He slows again, as he turns the corner. And there, just 77 metres away, the red line halts, rearing up into a beacon outside 23.

He stops. A lifetime's immersion in the Perpetual Era. 'A home of your own, for you alone'. How would he feel, even now, if someone invaded his? 'I'd be fine,' he thinks. 'Of course. I welcome it. It is the Welsh way.'

Enough. He faces more urgent issues than to fuss over questions like this. Besides, Ivon is Welsh. To him, it would mean nothing. Dusty must see him. And then devise a way to take him back to Ricky and Dee.

He rides on. Ivon's home lies on the westward side of Richmond Hill. It sits, like those nearby, on an embankment, in order to retain its southerly aspect. The entrance is set into the side of the house. Dusty must ride past the sweep of its up-tilted window wall to seek access. As he stops to dismount, he wonders how he might get in. There is little chance of Ivon answering his comm all of a sudden, but he prepares to try him. Otherwise, he will see if he can catch his attention from outside.

'Dusty Noble!'

Dusty is startled. It is a powerful voice, and it rings inside his head. The shock of an unexpected direct comm alarms him. Out here, it can only have come from a security officer. He looks around, and on the road a few steps behind stands a man dressed in the black of the security class.

'Dusty Noble!' he says again, this time voiced, as he strides slowly in Dusty's direction. 'Veteran elite cricketer. Archivist at the Repository of Suspended Resources. Resident of the Veteran Elite Quarter for London Cricket. Hampstead.'

Dusty's chest rises at the introduction. His heart is fast, but boldness gathers within it, as it did when he stood strong in the cause of commune and country.

'What brings you here?' says a new voice to his right.

Another security officer is approaching in the same manner from further down the road.

'I'm on a ride. I fancied a trip south of the river. Lactic acid levels were medium-low, I have joules to burn this week, so I decided on some repeats on Richmond Hill.'

The first officer smiles and looks to his comrade. He moves in closer to Dusty, while the other continues his approach.

'You know whose home this is, don't you…'

The enquiry is pitched halfway between question and statement.

'Do you?' says Dusty.

The officer smiles again curtly.

Dusty races through scenarios. His first thought is that these officers have been detailed to shadow Ivon. For what? To watch him? To protect him? Ivon's an asset, but not yet so important that he be a target for that level of espionage. Dusty doesn't know where these officers came from – perhaps a concealed aero, perhaps nearby homes – but he is sure they were here already.

He considers remounting his bike and pushing on without explanation. They know who he is, so they must have called up his file. They will know from it that he is a veteran of high standing. But the higher the better, as far as some security officers are concerned. He doesn't want to risk the indignity of an immobiliser to his central chip. Or the pain.

Dusty decides to stand his ground and come clean. He can see no reason why he shouldn't be here. It's not as if he has crossed any threshold yet.

'I've been trying to get hold of the man whose home this is. He has been off-comms for two days now. I came to try to effect a meeting with him. Out here, of course.'

'What is your business with Ivon?' says the second officer.

They *are* shadowing him.

'Ivon is a unique athlete,' says Dusty, stalling for time as he gathers his thoughts. 'He is of great interest to the scientific community.' Dusty thinks of Syracuse Garbo. 'There's a scientist I need to speak to. He's an Exempt, but Ivon knows how to contact him.'

The officers exchange a look, but it is enough for Dusty to notice.

'You know him. Syracuse Garbo. You know Syracuse Garbo!'

The first officer smirks at Dusty and steps aside. 'On your way, Mr Noble. On your way.'

Dusty takes a breath to lobby them further, but then lets it out again. If they really are in league with him, Syracuse Garbo will be informed of this encounter.

'Tell him I know about Gower.'

The first officer's smirk develops into another smile, but otherwise he remains unmoved.

Dusty has been offered a dignified retreat. He decides to take it.

XIII

'More comms from Ivon?'

Alanis opens her eyes and sees Adriana standing over her. Is her distress as obvious as that? She notices now that her hand is resting, palm upwards, across her forehead. She removes it and levers herself up on the couch into a more upright position.

'Five times yesterday, twice in the evening. I've blocked him, of course. But still…'

Adriana throws herself on the adjacent couch. 'Wow! That is seriously misaligned.'

'I know. I can't think what to do. I suppose I should report it. But, well, it's Ivon. He's new here. He doesn't understand.'

'What's there to understand?' scoffs Adriana. 'You don't invade an individual's personal space. I mean, we've all had days when we've made a few comms. But never to the same person. Next, he'll be trying to get into your home!'

Alanis laughs, but she is not in the mood for jokes. 'It's such a shame. He's so productive in the cots.'

'And just imagine how productive he'd be if he were properly aligned. You owe it to the commune to report this.'

Alanis squirms. The threat of Assimilation for Ivon has preyed on her mind. 'Oh, Adriana! He deserves the chance to align *himself*, doesn't he?'

'Why?!'

'He's new! He's an elite!'

Adriana looks at her askance. Almost as if she suspects Alanis herself of Misalignment. Should she suspect her? Alanis has asked herself the same question. Why does she feel protective of Ivon?

'He never turned up yesterday for the bout you booked us,' says Adriana, leaning back into her couch.

'What?!'

'Didn't even ratify it.'

'Oh my joules!'

'I'm an elite!' cries Adriana, sitting forward again, before composing herself. 'I had to go with Harvey Cockerill in the end.'

'Adriana, I'm so sorry! I thought the two of you would be so productive together. You *will* be!'

'Well, he'll have to get himself in alignment first. If he's so productive, he has a responsibility to everyone. Not just to you.'

Alanis sighs. 'Maybe I should report it. But it just doesn't feel right.' She clocks another sceptical look from Adriana. 'It's not as if I'm afraid to do that kind of thing. You know Dexter Eco. I was the one who had *him* fixed.'

Alanis notices Adriana's eyes widen further and flit urgently to somewhere above her head. She nods in the same direction.

Alanis turns round to see Ivon himself standing over her. She jumps to her feet and splutters his name. He does not reply or move. Something about his bearing makes her glad there is a couch between them. The green of elite suits him, she finds the presence of mind to notice. He is looking fit.

'You cancelled our date yesterday, Alanis. I'd been looking forward to that.'

He's looking at her in that same way he did under the showers a few days ago. As if he's trying to see into her.

'Oh, I know! I just felt we'd been seeing a bit too much of each other lately and that it would make sense for you to have a bout with someone else. Now that we've cleared your diary of all those suspicious bookings…' She tails off as he begins to come round to her side of the couch, his eyes fixed on her. 'Adriana, here, is an elite of the most impeccable credentials. I thought you'd go well together. Why didn't you even ratify her?'

He is standing barely a metre away now. He wears the faintest hint of a smile.

'How could we ever see too much of each other? You helped me clear the diary so we could spend more time together. You've got me, Alanis. Here.'

He pats his chest lightly, but the movement is fast enough to make Alanis jump.

'But you haven't tried a cot with anyone else. Why don't you try now? Adriana's free. Aren't you?'

She turns her head in Adriana's direction, without quite taking her eyes off him.

Ivon laughs. 'I don't want anyone else!'

Alanis blushes. She is aware of others in the lounge, so many elites, so many role models. She hopes none has picked up on this outburst from Ivon. Her eyes flick to Adriana, whose face is shot through with astonishment.

Ivon breathes out a heavy sigh. His chest falls; his head flops for a moment. Alanis enjoys the freedom of the break in eye contact. When he lifts his head again to look at her, it is with a vulnerability that strikes her as absurd.

'Let's take a cot now. You and me. Not for…that…just to talk. Let's just go…*somewhere*.'

He takes her hand unannounced, unsanctioned, from the underside. She snatches it away as if electrocuted and squeals at the transgressive contact. 'No, Ivon! No, I will not go with you! I cannot! I have a bout booked with Andrew Catt. It's too much!'

She breaks away from him and heads towards the foyer, although it could be anywhere for all she cares. Andrew Catt appears at the far end of the lounge. She likes Andrew, even if middle-distance runners tend not to be the best for wattage. They greet with a proper handshake.

'Are you ready?' he says.

She nods. He leads the way to the corridors, but before she follows an instinct makes her turn to Ivon one last time. He is where she left him. Adriana is saying something to him, but Ivon stares fixedly in Alanis's direction, a brilliant-haired figure of strength, tall above the murmuring elites on their couches. He shakes his head, softly, slowly.

There is something about the way Ivon looks at her. And the look is changing. She walks away from the lounge troubled.

❀

Dusty sighs as he watches the pod close on Austin Michael. It's the first time he has escorted to stasis a citizen he knew personally. Austin was a tertiary-level batsman, who occasionally trained with the elites. He might have been an elite himself, and thus granted another five years before stasis, but for a deficit in his trajectory-imaging processor speed. In particular, this manifested itself in a tendency to be late with his pulls and hooks. But he was a good man, who loved the commune.

'Farewell, brother,' says Dusty softly, as he places a lingering palm on the lid of the pod, before it slips away to holding. A tear swells in his eye, which he wipes away with the back of his hand.

'It must be hard,' says a thin but jaunty voice behind him.

Dusty spins round. Silhouetted against the window that looks out across ReSure's great entrance hall stands Syracuse Garbo.

'To be constantly in the presence of comrades on the brink of stasis. For them, it's a once-in-a-lifetime transition. But you. You have to go through it with them... How many times a day, is it? I'll bet facing the Yorkshire attack was positively uplifting in comparison.'

'I faced them then. I'll face this now.'

There is silence. Did Garbo notice the tear?

'You weren't really going to enter Ivon's home, were you, Dusty?'

Dusty stares dumbly at him. Finally, he has an audience with Garbo, and he stares dumbly at him.

'Could it be that your discipline has finally given way?'

'Who is David Gower?'

The light is behind Garbo, but Dusty can hear him chuckle. He steps into the room, and Dusty catches a glimpse of that nose and the hideous wrinkles as he saunters over to one of the portals and the track leading into it.

'I wonder when it'll be my turn,' Garbo says. 'There's a lot to be said for the conventional route. For knowing when your end will come. Once you're exempt, you go from year to year. I've got my annual review in August.' He leans over and peers at the point where the track disappears into the portal. Then he straightens up sharply and quips: 'I'm confident!' He nods his head, as if convincing himself, and repeats more thoughtfully: 'I'm confident. There's a few years left in me yet!'

'Gower.'

Garbo laughs again, more heartily. 'Ah, yes! Gower! Well, you tell me, Dusty! What do you know of the great man?'

'I know he's in here,' says Dusty, tapping his temple.

'And how do you know that?'

'Because I've seen him. I've read his story. He was our skill host, wasn't he? The TMS procedure of 2111. You were the supervisor. What happened?'

Garbo sits down on the end of one of the pod tracks. 'I suppose you're owed an explanation. Sabotage. Sabotage is what happened. It was a delicate period for TMS. You were guinea pigs, to be blunt, for the most advanced cerebral procedure of the time.'

'So why was a Lapsed Era batsman chosen as the skill host?'

'Oh, he wasn't, he wasn't! We'd identified as skill host an exemplary citizen with an immaculate cover drive. We had to be careful. Although we'd learned to isolate the skill back then, the procedure was not perfect. At the turn of the century we had discovered the seat of memory, the location in a human brain of the continuous record of a person's life – in essence the recording of everything that person had seen, heard, touched, tasted and smelled. But every instant of that record is rooted in a myriad of different places. Crudely speaking, to extract a coherent memory is like trying to pluck a flower whose roots spread deeply into the soil and in many directions, intertwining with many other roots. One isolated memory – of a cover drive, for example – might contain within it traces of interference from others picked up either from its place in the seat of memory or from its journey there through the hippocampus. When you're downloading thousands of cover drives from a skill host's memory bank, the potential for contamination becomes significant. The Swanton-Axelby screen has purified transference since, but in 2111 that technology was not available. That's why we were so careful with our choice of skill host. We thought we had eliminated most of the risk of contamination, but you could never be sure. In the event of any transferral interference, our skill host had to be devoid of thoughts or personality traits that might corrupt our subjects.'

'And a batsman from the Lapsed Era was not what you had in mind.'

Garbo shakes his head. 'The skill host we chose was of sound temperament, but my assistant turned out to be less than the model citizen we had taken him for. It later transpired he had been recruited to an underground cult dedicated to the undermining of the Perpetual movement. An ancient cricketer by the name of David Gower was the figurehead of their cause, the representation of all they held dear. Fun, style, excellence…' Garbo drifts off for a moment, before resuming his tale with urgency. 'And these people had an upload of Gower's brain! It had been captured right at the dawn of the neuro-archiving age. Gower was by then a very old man. You can imagine how crude the rendition was.'

'We didn't stand a chance.'

'I'm afraid you didn't. When it came to transmigration, Konig – my assistant – substituted Gower as the skill host, and I think we can safely say he had been less than meticulous in isolating the relevant skill. Indeed, he had wilfully polluted it. The transmigration was contaminated with all manner of impurities from Gower's soul. Every one of you on the tables that day inherited something of his subversive nature. As well as his smooth cover drive.'

Dusty can feel the tears begin to visit him again. The faces of his former comrades swirl through his head. Dee, Ricky – how innocent you were of your deteriorating attitudes! Daniel Attention, your Exaggerated Peripheral Sensitivity was that of another man from another time. Dusty wants to weep for them, so blameless were they. And yet he recognises, too, what that corruption of personality has done for the lives of Ricky and Dee. He recognises what it has done for himself, his thickening whimsy more precious to him the more it overtakes and undermines him.

'What happened to us?'

'Most of you were hopelessly corrupted. Lapsed Era attitudes are insidious. Their twisted tentacles reach into your soul. Once they have you, they are incredibly difficult to remove, even with today's technology, more so than memories. Assimilation thirty years ago was clumsy and brutal, at best a temporary solution.'

'So you offered exile.'

'We waited to see how things panned out. This was new to all of us. To a scientist, it was fascinating. To the authorities, it was a potential crisis, the release of a virus into the system. Konig was removed and shut down, but the rest of you – you were too important.'

Garbo shifts his weight further back onto the track, sitting like a kindergarten coach on the edge of his desk. 'Daniel Attention was the first to threaten the integrity of societal order. We tried to assimilate him, but it was hopeless. His indolence was so ingrained, our procedures seemed no more sophisticated than torture. They wanted to shut him down, but I'm pleased to say I won him an alternative. He was offered exile.'

'So Daniel Attention is *still active*?!'

'Oh yes. He chose Australia. As did Chad Meninga.'

Dusty wipes a tear from his left eye, but another forms to replace it immediately. And now his right hand is needed at the other eye, which is also brimming. He leans back against the window and looks towards Garbo. A softness has settled across the corners and crevices of the old man's face, so that he seems open to Dusty for the first time. It is the prompt for further tears, which begin to arrive with more confidence now. Dusty can no longer hold out. He buries his head in his hands and feels his body tremble with those same convulsions that seized him when he was with Dee in Wales.

'As I suspected,' says Garbo, but his voice is gentle, the sneer smoothed out. 'It has you too. Finally. Even Dusty Noble has succumbed.'

'I don't understand!' cries Dusty between his sobs. 'Why wasn't I affected before?'

Garbo shrugs. 'Maybe you were. All we know is that you managed to handle it. Channel it even, which is what I hypothesise you did.'

'But it had no effect on me.'

'You have always been a remarkable citizen, Dusty. If we were given to the elevating of individuals, as the Lapsed Era was, everyone would know your name. The authorities, certainly, hold you in the highest regard, as does the scientific community. You are a pillar of the commune – more than that, a wellspring. Your cover drive is on the national curriculum and your mind on order for upload come stasis. You know all that. But what you might not realise is the extent to which your progeny populates the ranks of London cricket.'

Dusty removes his hands from his face and peers at Garbo through bleary eyes. Why should this surprise him? He has lost count of the number of procreation certificates he has been issued with over the years, or the number of sperm deposits he has surrendered. He knew what it was all for, and yet to be confronted with the reality is to fuel his tears further.

'You know some of them,' says Garbo. 'Marius Amstrad?'

Dusty nods slowly as he recalls the elegant youngster. They shared a century partnership against the East Midlands, he thinks.

'Yours. Percy Sabatini, John Lawes, Vernon Goff... I could go on.'

Another paroxysm of weeping overcomes him.

'The point is,' Garbo continues, 'you have always been strong – the very model of a Perpetual citizen. An infusion of Lapsed Era impurities did not seem to shake your constitution one iota. Your discipline was ironclad. It is only now, after decommission, with the ills of diminishment creeping upon you, that we find it wavering. Six other elite athletes suffered the same dose as you in 2111. To greater or lesser extents, they were all corrupted, all taken out of the system.' Garbo hesitates. 'Well, apart from Leanda...'

'Killed in an aero,' says Dusty. 'So that was true.'

Garbo nods, his focus glazing briefly. 'She might have flourished. She'd acquired a certain bravado from the infusion, a wickedness, which enhanced her productivity. But she drove the aero far too fast. Couldn't help herself. Misalignment.' He shakes his head at the memory. 'But you, Dusty, you were never thrown off course. What's more, it's my hypothesis that you were enhanced by the spirit of Gower, by a hint of the unconventional. As if you knew that this was not all there was. Did you *ever* feel that?'

Dusty dries his eyes as best he can. His fit has passed physically, but it leaves hanging over him a dreadful pall of melancholy. He wants to believe that he was a maverick all along, just as he wants to believe that that tendency was his alone and not just an inheritance from a Lapsed Era cricketer. He has been corrupted, as if by a disease, but how elegantly the disease corrupts its victims by rendering them possessive of it. If only he could say he'd had mischief on his mind.

And then it occurs to Dusty that Garbo is pleading with him. 'You're one of them, aren't you?' he says.

Garbo sits with his hands resting under his thighs. His shoulders are hunched forward, accentuating a hollow chest. He studies Dusty, a faint smile on his lips, his head tilted to one side.

'This underground cult. Ivon's told me about it. You gave him Alcohol. The night before his elite debut.'

Garbo eases himself off the track. He walks to the window and looks down over the entrance hall, lit through the skylights high above by the last rays of sunshine a London citizen will ever see.

'After the sabotage was uncovered, I was part of the working party set up to investigate this cricketer, David Gower. The more I researched him, the more I could see how incompatible his values were with those of the Perpetual Era, how much of a disaster to society the infusion of his spirit might become. And yet the more I researched him, the more intrigued I became. Oh, I was never much good at sport myself. I made it to secondary level as a high-jumper. It was my IQ that marked me out. And in my life as a scientist I have encountered the entire spectrum of what we know, from multiverse to preon. Set within that great sweep, how can sport be conceived of as anything more important than a game? How can humanity? We are fleeting, contingent, ephemeral. Like laughter.'

'Don't you dare speak like that in here!' Dusty's fury strikes him like lightning. He strides towards the portals, eyes flaming at Garbo. 'Every day I help people into boxes and send them through this wall. Sport is no less than the justification of their brief time in this world. And you come in here with the weight of the universe on your shoulders and cheapen what they live for!'

Garbo is in silhouette again, but Dusty can make out the return of his provocative grin. 'Oh, Dusty!' he laughs. 'What a contradiction you are! One minute you're weeping like a Welshman, the next you're puffing out your chest and spewing Perpetual rhetoric! Maybe I'm wrong. Maybe there can be no synthesis between the Perpetual Era and Gower. The one has subdued the other in you all this time, and now that its work is done the other emerges to stake a claim. You're a walking experiment! A fascination to me!'

'And what about you? A scientist so highly valued by the state that they granted him Exemption. And by night he heads an underground cult whose purpose is to undermine the very system that venerates him.'

'You should come. To one of our gatherings. I think you're ready. Ivon loved it. You will too.'

'Ivon needs to go home.'

'Ivon is happy here. He's like a juvenile in a multi-gym with all this sport he can immerse himself in.'

'It can't last. You say Gower's incompatible with the Perpetual Era. So are the Welsh with the English.'

'We don't know that. Ivon is of interest precisely because of where he comes from. He is the progeny of purebred English elites, yet has been lifted clean out of the English system, conditioned by a diametrically opposed set of values. To the scientific community his case is a unique and precious experiment. But now the Managers are interested too – in what kind of an asset he could be. If it were up to them, he'd be taken in for Assimilation right now. We are trying to fight that. Rest assured, a lot of important people are watching.'

Panic consumes Dusty once more. It is the same each time he discusses Ivon with a figure of authority. London will not let him go, nor will England. 'You cannot stop him returning home! Please! It will kill Ricky and Dee. And what about the effect on Ivon? If he's troubled he won't be productive. He's Welsh.'

'That's a very Lapsed Era way of looking at it. I congratulate you on your conversion. But I haven't been infected by Gower the way you have. My admiration for him and the Lapsed Era is intellectual. I do not share your conviction that Ivon must be reunited with his progenitors – sorry, his family! I do not understand that impulse.'

'You do understand it. You just choose not to engage with it.'

'Well, that *is* the Perpetual way, Dusty. Surely you've not forgotten! So much more is achieved by the disabling of feelings. The experiment with Ivon will proceed.'

'And when they assimilate him?'

'Then the experiment will be over, and London will have acquired a fully integrated new asset. But I do not consider his Assimilation inevitable.'

'Of course it is! And once it's happened, he'll never return home. He'll no longer want to!'

'Then his pain will be over.'

'And Ricky and Dee's?'

'He will not be allowed home, Dusty.'

Two quick strides forward, and Dusty forgets his distinguished history as a Perpetual citizen. He seizes Garbo by the upper arms and makes to shake him. The arms feel brittle in his hands. He is sure he could break them.

'You will stop this experiment now!' he roars in Garbo's face. 'Ivon must return home!'

Garbo's face is blank. He remains passive. 'You're talking to the wrong man. Marcus Apollo might be able to help you there, not I.'

'And I'm sure the Prime Manager would be interested to hear about your alternative life. Head of an underground cult? Dedicated to the undermining of Perpetual society?'

Garbo smiles wearily, and Dusty loosens his grip.

'I am an old man now. My time could come as early as August. I'm ready for it. You, though, you have a decade at least left to you. I doubt anyone has called up the security file on Dusty Noble for many years now, so model a citizen have you been, but there will be a record on it of your exposure to a contaminated TMS procedure. Coupled with the sort of things I could reveal about your behaviour recently – and now in particular – you might very suddenly find yourself subject to correction.'

Dusty has felt bold and fatalistic about the consequences of his changing personality, but he is disgusted to find himself hesitant at the prospect of Assimilation, now it is voiced by someone who could bring it about. He surrenders his grip on Garbo. 'If you go down, your cult will go with you.'

'I doubt it. We are not a serious threat. In 2111, the Fellowship of Dig was taken apart following Konig's act of sabotage, but it was a far more aggressive sect in those days. I played a part in its revival over the years that followed. We are more about celebration and escapism now.'

'Your purpose is to undermine the Perpetual movement. That's what you told Ivon! That's what you told me!'

'We like to sound more subversive than we are, but the new incarnation of Dig is far less threatening than the old. We are tolerated.'

'The authorities know about you?!'

'There's not a lot they don't know about. The deteriorating discipline of the great Dusty Noble might be one lacuna; otherwise, their infiltration is pervasive.'

Dusty turns away and paces between two tracks to the transition wall. He stretches his arms above his head and lays the palms of his hands against it. For a second, he is closer than he has ever been to the holding bay and the stasis that lies beyond. 'You're bluffing,' he says. 'The authorities would never tolerate something that celebrates the Lapsed Era.'

'Don't underestimate us, Dusty. We are more broadminded than you think.'

Dusty turns into the room. 'Us? We?'

Garbo lowers his eyes and smiles.

'You're more than a scientist, aren't you. What's your relationship with Marcus Apollo?'

'Oh, but I *am* a scientist, Dusty, a humble scientist. One so diminished and weak, he can't show his face in public.'

'You're the Prime Manager.'

Garbo barks out a laugh.

'Marcus Apollo is just a front. And you're the Prime Manager.'

'Marcus Apollo is a highly capable statesman, for whom Exemption awaits.'

'And there's no Exemption review for you at all.'

'I can assure you, there is a reckoning higher even than Marcus Apollo's whose findings on matters of life and shutdown are final. In August, the review panel will assess how close I am to that last great defeat and advise accordingly. I will accede to their findings. I have made that known.'

'Marcus Apollo answers to you,' murmurs Dusty, shaking his head.

'Marcus Apollo is the Prime Manager and his own man,' rejoins Garbo in earnestness. 'Don't underestimate him. He understands there is an alternative to the Perpetual way. He doesn't believe in it, but he is conversant in the debate. And it is a debate that has intensified in recent years with the development of Deliberate Genetic Fusion. There are those in science and the state who are troubled, and I include myself among them. Twenty years ago, when the introduction of artificial assets into competition became a live question, the Primacy of Organic Assets was asserted. And the POA is, in essence, a Lapsed Era sensibility. DGF was science's response to that, but we are encountering the same issues again. They have developed artificial gametes now, which begs the question, at what point does an organic asset become artificial? Where will it all end, and what will be left of sport and the human race when it does?'

Dusty slumps to the floor. His disillusionment since decommission may be due to the rise in him of a Lapsed Era spirit, but Garbo's words are giving form to vague fears that have been gathering in his mind anyway. The sense of things running out of control. Perhaps it is the kind of concern they warned him about in diminishment training, the preoccupation of those whose end is approaching. The sureness of attitude he used to know is discernible to him now only in the eyes of the young. As if the young know where they are heading. As if he once did.

'Ivon represents the counter-revolution,' Garbo continues. 'He is the first savage to be admitted to Perpetual society. I want him to succeed here. I want him to become a productive asset while remaining true to who he is, which means no Assimilation. But I am in a minority. Most believe he will fail, and want him to. It would be less complicated that way. All are agreed, though, that he must first be allowed to try. And that would not be possible if he were to return home. I'm sorry.'

Dusty's head is now hanging, as he contemplates the floor between his legs. His forearms rest on his knees, and beyond them the hands that guided London and England to terajoules of energy flop like empty gloves.

He wants to fly to Wales. He wants to spend the days left to him with Ricky and Dee. And Ivon. He wants to take Ivon home. For the boy's sake, but for his own too. Return Ivon to his people, and Dusty will be welcomed. Without Ivon, there can be no Wales.

Dusty lifts his head. He blinks into the light streaming from ReSure's entrance hall. He cannot make out Garbo at all, not even a silhouette. It is then that he realises Garbo has gone.

❖

'It's too much!' Alanis's words ring in Ivon's head, as if she were saying them again and again over the telepathy phone. 'It's too much! It's too much!' Her voice has established its line, and now that of Cerys joins in. The very same words. 'It's too much! It's too much!' The two lines harmonise, their wavelengths criss-crossing and fluctuating then merging, until both sing out their chorus in unison.

Too much this, too much that. He's a handful, all right. Always has been. No one goes with Ivon expecting a quiet life.

The wheels of his bike describe an eight. He cycles over the same patch of ground in Finsbury Park, going round and round, over and over. He wants to carve an imprint in the blue, rubbery surface, make his mark on London somewhere, cut out a niche. But the surface yields nothing, not even a scuff. He will keep going until she appears. He is loitering, circling. Like they used to in the old days, at the top of Overland Road.

Cerys said that. 'It's too much.' Eight years, three months and eleven days after he'd kissed her for the first time. Thirtieth December last. The bleak midwinter. One hundred and forty-something days ago. What was it now? One hundred and forty-six. No, seven. One hundred and forty-seven days ago. The front porch of her little home. It was too much. Didn't want to share him with everyone else. Couldn't. That's Ivon's girlfriend, titter, titter. It would never be just the two of them.

Yes, it would, it would. He never chose the limelight, he never chose all the hangers-on. He chose her. It would end, it would.

But not yet.

No, not yet.

He screams in silence, still on his hypnotic sashay back and forth, back and forth. It's not like this with sport. The game is getting away, so you act. If you're good enough you get it back. Nothing can stop that. But when the girl goes… The game is taken away altogether. You act, but it makes no difference. Act and act and act again, under a cold moon and unfeeling sky. A window that will never open, curtains that will never part. He'd just wanted his girl back.

'It's too much.' He sees Alanis as she stood in front of him at the club this morning, tall, strong and angry, so suddenly angry, a frown where there had been only smiles. Shutting him out. Retreating towards the cots with that other bloke. Trying to pair Ivon off with one of her friends. The promiscuity of it. She deserves better. He knows her. She is too like Cerys to be happy here. He looks again towards the exit of London Volleyball. The door shut against him.

When do they finish? They're meant to have finished.

They must talk. Not out here, not at the club, not any place where people may see or distract. She needs to focus on him. He pictures her on the seafront in Mumbles. The clubhouse at St Helen's. The dinner table with Mum and Dad. In Cerys's chair.

He looks up again. He stops his figure-of-eighting. She's there at the door. A group of three girls. Alanis is the tallest. They talk and look confident and relaxed, expectant of nothing in particular. They slip round the side of the building. Ivon prepares to follow, but then remembers. The bike park. They're collecting their bikes. Sure enough, they reappear moments later, cycling in formation, Alanis in the middle, her legs long and strong enough to pull away from the others, he's sure. They set off down the blue road out of Finsbury Park. He waits. Lets them get ahead. Then follows.

They cycle out of the park and head north. He doesn't know where she lives, but it's not far. They climb a hill. When will the other two go away? Alanis and Ivon have much to discuss. He is ready.

❁

Their conversation continues as they reach the brow of Crouch Hill. The view from here is a favourite part of Alanis's journey home. The green sweep to the north of London inclines her to fill her lungs as much as does the climb itself. From the great wind farms atop Highgate to the west, she runs her eye along the contours of Muswell Hill ahead of them as it falls away into the forests of Tottenham to the east.

Melissa and Adriana are as excited as she is about London Volleyball's next trimester, which begins at last with the visit of the South West tomorrow. The inactivity of their Spring Recess is about to end!

'My maximal vertical displacement has improved by 5.3 per cent,' says Melissa, who has been trialling a new genetic modifier. 'So quite good, but not remarkable.'

Alanis tuts. 'But, Melissa, your vertical displacement has always been the best. A 5.3 per cent increase in your max is equal to seven or eight in mine.'

'Yes, but you have such limb length.'

'I know. But a few extra cents on my MVD wouldn't go amiss.'

'Well, you'll be trying it yourself soon enough. They're downloading the GM to everyone's inoculators in the next few weeks.'

Ah, her inoculator! The mere mention of it makes Alanis think of home. She will be there soon. A couple of cerebral simulations on the couch, a nice easy physical one in the simulator, maybe a quick leisure doc over a long isotonic, then bed. She needs it all the more after the day she's had. That bout with Andrew Catt was prolonged in the extreme, and she doesn't think their wattage ever rose above 175. It was so drawn out she had to skip a much-needed recovery session to avoid being late for the team meeting. And all this with match-day tomorrow. After the business with Ivon earlier, it has been a stressful day. At least he seems to have stopped comming her now. Or maybe he hasn't. She has to remind herself that she's blocked him. She'll check the log when she gets home.

And now the Elite Quarter for London Volleyball appears on either side of them. The astro lawns are neat and uniform. From them rise home after home, like comrades standing united, a configuration to warm the heart. Alanis's is among the first.

'I'll see you tomorrow!' she says to the others as she turns off to the left.

'Can't wait!'

'Rest well!'

'You too!'

She likes to slow her pace along the road to her home, as soon as she can see its soft, smooth curves. She relishes this moment each day.

○

At last. They've gone. One of them was the girl Alanis had tried to fix him up with earlier in the day. She was making him feel angry just by being there. Just by being. He's all right now, though. Alanis is on her own. Ivon and Alanis are on their own. He likes it.

He pedals a little harder and closes to within 70 metres, maybe. He thinks about calling to her, but, no, this is not the place, out here in the street. Someone may turn up. Ruin everything. They need to be alone, undisturbed. He wants to take her away from all this.

Yes, he wants to take her back to Wales. He wants to go back to Wales. He can see that now. It is Alanis who has made him realise it. He yearns for the warmth. She is his home.

She turns down the side of one of these space-age houses. It looks very much like the one they've given him, perhaps a little smaller. The entrance seems to be round the back. He pushes down hard on his pedals. They're funny about their homes here. She's unlikely to invite him in. But maybe if he could get in…

He knows the door to his house stays open for a few seconds after he's opened it. If he's quick, he could slip in behind her. Yes, hers would be an excellent place to talk. She would be relaxed and on her own territory.

He hurtles down the slight slope leading off the road to her house. He is grateful for the perfect, soundless traction between tyre and surface. At the corner of the house he jumps off the bike and lets it fall. Her door is still open, but he does not know for how much longer. He runs to it and just as it is swishing shut he ghosts through. The first line of defence is breached.

She is not visible from the doorway. The interior is an inverted replica of his, a little white corridor leading to a white room, which will have a low white chaise longue just to the right, out of sight, and an alcove to the left where food and drink is dispensed.

There she is. She crosses from the right to the alcove and stands a few feet away. His heart is racing.

'Alanis, we need to talk.'

◉

From emergence until now, Alanis's has been a life of structure and blissful predictability. Variations in her life are measured out by the quantity of things, never the quality. Only that recent excursion into the Lapsed Era might be accounted a qualitative shift in her experience, but it was a lone aberration and she was able to chart each sickening step of her descent into it.

In extremis, the human mind, she is now discovering, works at an accelerated rate – and yet the body responds before consciousness can fathom the nature of the trauma. That is Ivon's voice, is her first thought. But it can't be. There was no alert to notify her of an incoming comm. And anyway she has blocked him. And that was not a comm. But it must have been. She is at home. To hear a voice outside her head would require the speaker to be present. It would mean another person in the same space at the same time. And she is at home. The paradox is confusing. The voice was certainly not in her head though, because it came from an external source – yes, it definitely did – off to the left, slightly behind her, from the direction of the door. It was certainly Ivon's, too, for no one else speaks with that distinctive inflexion. The resolution to this paradox is hardening in her mind.

Ivon is in her home.

In the time it takes her to spin round in response to the shocking violation, her heart accelerates and a cold, tingling shockwave sweeps through her. She sees the arm. Then, in microseconds, her eye follows its line up to the face, which confirms Ivon as the invader, but the petty specifics of identity are lost amid the storm the crime has unleashed upon her. She loses control of her head first. It breaks into tiny oscillations round its pivot, side to side, side to side, a hint of up and down. Her mouth goes next, trembling, murmuring, muttering, 'nonononono'. She stumbles backwards, away from the desecration, and collides with the wall. Against it, she can feel her entire body convulse. Her arms close round her, and her hands grasp again and again at whatever they can, the opposing shoulder, the upper arm, the torso, up and down her body they go, desperately trying to shield her, desperately trying to fold her up within herself, to withdraw again, now the sacred haven of withdrawal has been invaded.

She hears him speak of home, but not hers. He wants her to go with him to his. The violence the depravity the ABOMINATION. She must defend herself. What use the shutdown of her systems into shock? She must overcome. Turn the invader out. She must fight within her own home.

She screams and hurls herself in his direction. He braces, but she knocks him back against the door, then slams the heel of her hand against the underside of his jaw and jerks his head back. She tries to reach for the door's release panel, when he fights back, seizing her arms and holding her away from him. His grip is strong, and they struggle against each other, when suddenly his grip relaxes. His whole body relaxes. She recognises the latest generation of immobiliser at work. Security must be here. But how so soon? She imagines her home flashing up on the Grid as desecrated. She wails at the shame of it. The very least she can do now is to expel him herself. She reaches for the release panel. The door opens, but he has re-gathered himself quickly and resists when she hits him again, shoving her back into the room. And yet he does not follow. He suffers a seizure, as if electrocuted, and yells in agony. The immobiliser has been intensified. She notices two security officers at her door now. They wait at the threshold, their gaze averted. Ivon about-turns, still shouting out his pain, and with two impulsive strides he is with them. The door closes.

Alanis sinks to the floor. This violation is a trauma too hideous and outlandish to understand. She will carry this with her. In time, she will consider, quite seriously, turning herself in for Assimilation, the agony a price that must be borne if she hopes to recover equilibrium.

For now, though, she trembles against the floor, her arms spread wide across it. She is homeless, quite lost.

Ivon breathes heavily. His hands are on his knees. The surface beneath his feet is sky blue. An ant crawls on it, just like the ones in Wales.

Alanis.

He notices a pair of feet on either side of him, shod in uppers of matt black.

'Who are you?' he says without looking up. 'What was that in there?'

It takes several seconds for them to reply. 'Come with us.'

He straightens. The men are dressed in black. He has seen such figures about town. It was men like these who took away the fighting girls from the club last week. Their faces do not invite conversation.

He doesn't know what agony it was that seized him in there, but the sense that it emanated from these men is powerful. Neither of them moves, as Ivon comes to terms with what just visited him, and the fact that it has gone without, incredibly, leaving a twinge behind. A few seconds ago, he was shot through with it, a white-hot pain that seemed to live in every fibre of him, as if it had always lain there, as if it knew the entirety of him, mobilised for a moment, then quietly slipped back to lurk among his trusting molecules. It leaves him in peace now, but its threat remains vivid.

'Where are we going?'

One of the men is looking away, towards the street. The other studies Ivon out of the corner of his eye. 'Come.'

Ivon follows. He is disengaged, walking where others tell him. He has lost his girl; he now cedes control of himself, as they want him to on the field, as he did just then when some searing impulse made him march out of Alanis's home to this bleak encounter with two sentinels in black.

Alanis. He doesn't understand.

He is ushered into the back of one of their black and wheel-less cars. Through the streets of London they glide, past the colour-coded citizens, some on bikes, some on foot. Ivon catches a glimpse of a few of the faces. Disengaged, he and they.

Onwards into the green heart of the place they ghost, where the road rises above the parks and river below, into a lattice of converging routes that sits over the water like a spider. They take a road towards the east, skirting along the southern riverbank, until the people and buildings run out, replaced by a sudden forest, whose trees are arranged densely and precisely on either side of the road that knifes through it. After a few minutes the trees end as abruptly as they start, and Ivon notices a lonely building ahead of them, which stands tall and heartless against the reappearing river.

He steps from the car and follows as his escorts guide him towards the silvery smooth curve of the southern wall. A door opens from nowhere, and Ivon is admitted into a circular atrium, whose mirrored walls rise the full height of the tower's interior into an apex of glass. There is a desk, manned by an operative, and a smattering of men dressed in the black of his escorts. No one reacts to their arrival. Ivon is led straight to an elevator. It climbs to the eleventh floor, where the doors opposite those he stepped in through open into a wide window-lined room, which gives views across the river and trees to the proud glass of the city beyond.

'Ivon.'

The voice that hails him is neutral.

Ivon turns to its source, on his right. 'It's you,' he says. His voice is neutral too, even though he should be pleased to see the old man who entertained him so well in Canterbury. He had that funny name. And the nose. Cirius, or something.

The old man is sitting on a jade couch. He invites Ivon to join him on another. The view from here is comprehensive – not only of the expanse outside but the length of the bare room, a desk at the far end and Ivon's inscrutable escorts, who stand on either side of the elevator doors.

'Welcome to 1, Greenwich, where we senior Exempts live and conduct our business, away from the eyes of the population.'

'Like an old folks' home.'

He does not respond.

'Are we going to start drinking now?'

The old man sighs and leans forward, resting his elbow on his knees. 'What have you done, Ivon?'

Ivon pauses to consider. For the first time since it happened the swirling traces of what just passed between him and Alanis begin to gather into something coherent in his mind. His numbness flecks and spits into a reaction against the suddenness of it, the brutality and hostility. She was his anchor, his haven, his home from home in this sinister, soul-free land.

'She flipped. That wasn't her. I just wanted to talk.'

The old man shakes his head. 'I want to help you, Ivon. I want this to work. But you're not making it easy for me.'

'It was like she went mad.'

'You entered her home!'

'I just wanted to talk to her.'

'That's not how it works here. You should have learned that by now.' He looks briefly in the direction of the men in black. 'You're an Assimilation waiting to happen, Ivon. If my officers hadn't been shadowing you just then, you would have been taken in as a matter of course. And you would not have found the machinery of state security as careful to preserve your identity as I am. I have managed to persuade them to let my people in Improvement deal with this incident. The injury crisis at fly-half has made your release for tomorrow's match a matter of urgency. But if you keep transgressing you will be corrected.'

'This is the brainwashing, is it?'

'Assimilation, Ivon. They will change who you are. Your conversion to Perpetual citizenship will be complete and irreversible. You will no longer be the Welshman. Just another fly-half. The experiment will be over.'

'What are you talking about? Is that all I am to you? An experiment? Was I an experiment when you welcomed me to Canterbury like some kind of messiah?'

The old man smiles and rises from his seat. 'We shall have to place a restraining prompt on you. That is the very least that would be expected.'

'What do you mean? What is that?'

'It's nothing to worry about. It merely prevents you from approaching to within 100 metres of the girl.'

'Fuck that! I'm patching things up with her. I can't enter her home. I get that. But I am going to make it work.'

'It won't be as simple as that. I believe you have just experienced the shock of an immobiliser to your system. With this restraint, your chip will be programmed to deliver such a charge if ever you breach the 100-metre radius.'

Ivon rises to his feet. 'This fucking chip!' he cries, slapping the back of his neck. 'No one said it was for controlling me!'

'New applications for it are continually coming to light. You should think of this as cutting-edge technology.'

Ivon shakes his head. A fury is rising in him. 'No. No. That's enough. I've had enough. I want to go home.'

The old man looks out over the river. 'It's too late for that.'

The rage in Ivon takes a surer hold. How could he have left his homeland for this? A rage and a panic. He turns to the nearest stretch of glass and, roaring, he hammers his fists against it.

His consciousness is switched off like a light.

XIV

'What do you mean, he's travelling separately?'

Dusty tries to calm himself. The head coach of London
Rugby is a man of presence, but his focus is elsewhere, his eyes
tuned in to a retinal projection, probably perusing the blueprints
for this afternoon's match-plan against Yorkshire. Dusty has
cycled from Hampstead to Richmond, setting off as soon as
the sleeping hours were over, to intercept London Rugby's
elite squad as they gather to depart for the north. It is his most
overtly irregular act so far. He cycled past Ivon's home again, but
didn't stop this time, nor was he intercepted. There was no sign
of life inside or of security guards among the shadows outside.

Now Dusty mingles unobtrusively with the London Rugby
squad, clad in the green of elite. The head coach has barely
acknowledged him, except to tell him that Ivon is not travelling
with them to Yorkshire.

'Has something happened to him?' Dusty says, pressing him
as gently and urgently as he can.

'There was some incident last night. He's travelling up in a
sealed aero. Precautionary.'

'Incident?'

'Entered another's home.'

'They've not assimilated him…'

'No. We need him today. Situation to be reviewed
post-match.'

Dusty backs away, looking around him, as if in hope of catching a glimpse of the boy. What has he done? If security around him has been tightened…

He decides to try him once more. This time, to Dusty's surprise, Ivon answers.

'Dusty, what the fuck's going on?'

He is vocalising again. The panic and fear resonate in Dusty's head.

'Stay calm, Ivon. Where are you?'

'I'm in a… I don't know… It's a…they've put me in a van. I'm in a box.'

'They're taking you to the Headingley Dome for the Yorkshire match.'

'They won't let me see Alanis. They won't let me go home.'

Thoughts rush through Dusty's head. Ivon must be brought home. To London and then, somehow, to Wales.

So it was Alanis, was it?

'Dusty?'

Their conversation is probably being monitored.

'Just get through the match, Ivon. Don't do anything irregular. Follow your prompts. Do not go off-plan. Just get through the match.'

Dusty breaks off the comm.

He doesn't have the stone with him. He has never prepared for a match without the stone, nor travelled to a match alone in a windowless box. He has never played in one without the prospect of love or a return home.

Coach White had released him earlier from the cell they'd held him in deep within the stadium – another first – waiting for the rest of the team to arrive. He was cool and practical as he and a pair of security guards escorted Ivon to his cubicle.

'You are required for this match,' he explained, 'but your temperament is under investigation. Transfer in solitary is a standard precaution. You will link up with your comrades now.'

His kit was waiting for him in the cubicle. He sits in it now, staring at the empty space between his hands. No stone. No spirit. No desire. The thunder from the stadium above has built to a climax, just as it does in London. The air is saturated with it. They will not be admitted to the arena until game time. Their warm-ups and team runs have taken place in a hangar adjacent to the cubicles.

Ivon is numb again. As he was in the car from Alanis's to the old man's apartment. As he wishes he'd been in the box to Yorkshire. There may be nerves in him, there may be rebellion, anger or conformity – he does not know. The whiteness has him. The white noise from above, the white walls in his cubicle, the white canvas across his soul.

He steps out of his cubicle before time. He needs clearance above his head, in front of his face. No more small rooms. The communal area between the closed doors of the cubicles is empty, except for Mike Bulstrode, who strides across it from the direction of the toilets and sneers when he sees Ivon. He passes close to him, then pauses, looks around and turns. He places the outside of his forearm across Ivon's chest and drives him back against the wall. Ivon does not resist.

'So you entered another's home?' he says. Then shakes his head slowly. A white scar cuts diagonally across the stubble on his chin, from the corner of his mouth to somewhere under his leaden jaw. There is moisture on his brow and in the roots of his hair. His pupils are wide and pulsing. 'They say you'll be assimilated when we get back to London.'

Ivon manages a smile. 'Olympus Dan getting to you, is he, tough guy?'

Bulstrode leans up and into his forearm. Ivon can feel the wiry hairs on it catch against his own stubble, even as the vice is tightened across his windpipe.

'You savages disgust me,' he says, spitting the words into Ivon's face. 'If I had my way I'd assimilate you myself.'

Ivon's eyes bulge as Bulstrode presses his forearm deeper into his throat. The pressure is released. Bulstrode opens his mouth like a lion and expels a hiss of air. He walks away, flexing his neck right and left. The siren sounds to summon the others from their cubicles.

Dusty's joules for the week are burned, but still he has to run. He has ditched his bike. He's always liked running. It is, along with coitus, the purest of the major exercise types. Humans have always run. They must have. Just as there must have been a time before bicycles, swimming pools and cross-trainers. Coitus and running – it was ever thus.

He has no appointments at ReSure this afternoon, but an afternoon's quiet recovery is an intolerable prospect. He must run. Through these streets he knows so well because they are so easy to know and he has run them so thoroughly. He remembers now a time when the roads weren't sky blue and uniform. He remembers dusty orange. And isn't there even a recollection of grey streets deep down under his memories, trying to raise itself from beneath all the others?

Is there any way he can watch the match, watch Ivon?

No. For a viewing screen he would need to be in Parliament or the Institute of Improvement. It would be impossible to secure an appointment in either at such late notice and on suspicious grounds like the non-scientific watching of a match. And, anyway, no, no, intolerable. The match is taking place now and Dusty has to keep running. To stop and expose himself to it… No.

Just get through the match, Ivon. It may already be too late, but if he can survive this latest incident with personality intact he may yet see Wales again – and so might Dusty. They would need to remove the identity chips from their hands. There's a device at ReSure that removes them neatly from premature departures. Why wouldn't it work on animate citizens? That would take their central chips off the Grid, free them up to be Welsh with impunity. They could commandeer a boat from one of the aquacentres across the water from Wales. He has seen a map at ReSure. The Fence stops at Woolacombe. Any one of the aquacentres round the corner, along the far coast of the South West, might offer up a boat within reach of the coast of Wales. Dusty's memorised the names. Bude, Bideford, Padstow, Newquay. Or there's the northern end of the Fence, which stops at Preston, so the aquacentre at Blackpool, maybe, St Annes, Fleetwood… To want to flee from England to Wales, to do it *willingly* – the idea is unheard of. Who would expect it? They'd be away and gone before anyone realised.

Just get through the match, Ivon.

No words are exchanged on the march up to the arena, just the odd comment in their heads from Coach White. 'We will be working the fringes. We will be operating off 8 and 9.'

Ivon has been excluded. What kind of a team treats its fly-half as a peripheral figure? The insult is bracing and ridiculous.

'You're to kick goals, 10. Kick goals and tackle.'

They step out into the arena of the Headingley Dome. Ivon bristles, despite himself. The people in the stands wear the same colour. It is white. Is this place bigger than Twickenham? To Ivon it seems so. He can garner no sense of the numbers in the stands, but the whiteness is vast, rising up all around through four tiers of white and flashing metal. High above them,

244

stalactitic cables drip from the rafters. That metallic thunder fills the air.

From out of the ground on the far side, the Yorkshire squad file out. Most file towards seats in the stand, but fifteen of them take to the field. The two teams line up either side of the halfway line, black against white, each man facing his opposite number. The Yorkshire fly-half is shorter than Ivon, but his eyes are quick and intelligent.

Ivon's attention, though, cannot but gravitate towards the man two to his left. Olympus Dan, the Yorkshire No. 8, is indeed the biggest man he has ever seen. As the two teams step in to shake the hands of their opposite numbers, Ivon can see the air exhale in short bursts from Mike Bulstrode's chest. Ivon takes the hand of the Yorkshire fly-half, but he watches Bulstrode shaking the hand of Olympus Dan. He pulls the hand of the taller man into his chest, holding it firmly, flexing his muscles, staring up into the eyes of his opponent. Olympus Dan is unmoved. When it is his turn to pull his hand in, Bulstrode comes with it, refusing to release the lock in his elbow. The heads of the two men collide, Bulstrode's scar-swelled brow butting gently against the mouth of Olympus Dan. As quickly and as eerily as in London, the stadium falls silent in advance of the match. The otherworldly panting of Ivon's teammate intensifies.

Yorkshire have been assigned the kick-off. The ball hangs high in the air before descending on Bulstrode. He takes it safely and a maelstrom of converging players crashes round him. His head and shoulders jut above the seething maul. The match is under way. Oympus Dan waits in the open field.

Ben the scrum-half clears the ball into touch – no chance of him passing it to Ivon. It's the last London see of the ball for the next five minutes. Yorkshire bombard them with ball-carriers, granite-hard, dispassionate ball-carriers, who do not utter so much as a whispered oath in contact or in the lawless moments after it. Not a dig, not a fist, not a hint of personality. Neither Yorkshireman nor Londoner indulges in the nefarious. Even Bulstrode seems clean. Why doesn't he treat some of the opposition the way he did Ivon just before they came out? Ivon knows the answer. Because he would be penalised. It would cost his team.

Plenty of pain, though. These men hurt. Coldly, relentlessly, legally. Olympus Dan takes the ball only once in the early exchanges, crunching into Michael the centre. (Doesn't anyone in England have a nickname?) Ivon is a couple of feet away and hears the weighty slap of flesh on flesh, the exhalation of air. Michael has gone low and brings the gargantuan down, then leaps to his feet and resumes position with the exaggerated eagerness of a man in pain.

Yorkshire are pounding their way to London's 22, but the London line is holding. It is not long before Ivon must play a part. His first tackle is on the Yorkshire inside centre, a three-quarter of the bristling, pugilistic kind. He reminds him of Chunk Jordan, the Cardiff centre who sees the ball as a permission slip to charge at someone and performs a little jump whenever he is given it. This guy does not jump, but charges at Ivon as if he has been pre-programmed to do so, which he probably has. Ivon tries to hit him in the midriff with his shoulder, but the centre's forearm is like a weapon of war and strikes him in the face. Falling backwards, Ivon manages to grab the centre's torso, pull him low and take out his legs as he rampages through. He takes another blow to the face, the centre's knee catching him on the nose, but he brings the man down, even if it is his opponent who has dominated the collision. Yorkshire have won a few more precious metres, and Ivon knows he was the one to yield them.

He scrambles to his feet, his brain reverberating like a struck bell. He sniffs hard on his smarting nose and tastes the blood in his mouth. The world lists for a second. He sees Olympus Dan patrolling behind the frontline. The point of engagement has moved infield, and Ivon is taken by a powerful impulse to sprint round to the other side of the next ruck. It is ProzoneX. He is already sprinting before he has time to think about it. As he arrives in position, his opposite number is darting for the gap between Ivon and the next man along. Ivon is just in time to tackle him round the knees and avert a defensive crisis. Without ProzoneX's instruction, he would never have made it.

A heat is rising in him, his disengagement dissolving. All avenues to warmth and home may be closing down off the field, but his despair recedes now, forced out by a deep-rooted instinct. It is pride. It is competitiveness. He is weak like this, reliant on a computer to keep him up to speed. He will sink into mediocrity, anonymity, if he does not respond.

A Yorkshire ball-carrier knocks on. The ball is hastily whipped out by one of London's flankers to Ivon, who follows ProzoneX's prompt to boot it into touch, just as he is clobbered by Yorkshire's punchy centre. He is ruffled.

Yorkshire build another attack from the line-out. Ivon starts to bark orders to his teammates, trying to marshal the defence, but he is wasting his breath. These men respond to another calling. Their silence is unnerving him.

Mike Bulstrode manages to rip the ball from a Yorkshire ball-carrier, but he knocks it on. A metallic voice in Ivon's head announces a scrum to Yorkshire. The two packs gather on the London 22, left of centre. Ivon takes up position a few metres away. He looks around the stadium for a few seconds, the vast, still whiteness of a crowd larger than any he has ever known. And quieter. They murmur gently, minding their own business. Around the mouth to the changing rooms, Ivon sees a phalanx of security guards, striking a contrast in black. They are, at least, looking towards the action. Ivon recognises among their number the men who accompanied him earlier in the day.

The scrum is formed, the ball fed in. A hiss of exertion rises from the struggle. The scrum twists, so that the London back row turns away from Ivon – and Yorkshire's towards him. Olympus Dan picks up the ball at his feet and erupts off the base. He is coming at Ivon. Don't look at his face. Don't look at his arms, his torso or the ball. Just focus on the legs. Bring him down. The legs are mighty and ripple as if something inside wants to get out. Ivon crouches on the balls of his feet. He closes his eyes and throws himself in the path of Olympus Dan. His left shoulder takes the blow. The pain explodes across his chest, into his neck and down his left arm. He feels himself tossed backwards and to the side. He cannot hope to cling on to whatever part of Olympus Dan might be within his grasp, because for a moment he cannot be sure where he is. By the time he has hit the ground, he knows his man has gone. He knows that Olympus Dan has scored. A siren sounds and is almost immediately drowned out by the roar of the stadium.

The searing pain down his arm subsides after a few seconds. Ivon lies on his back, gazing up to the rafters high above and the cables that droop down from them like the timeless vines of a jungle. He imagines for a moment they are lifelines, by which he might lift himself out of here and away to Wales. If only he could reach them. But his arm is numb and weak.

'You have suffered transient neurapraxia of the brachial plexus,' says a voice in his head he does not recognise. 'It is trivial. You may resume.'

Ivon sits up slowly. With a speed that does not feel natural, the strength returns to his arm, which he lifts to shoulder height and rotates gingerly. He looks towards the London enclosure for clues to his recovery but sees only the security guards, some of whom have begun to agitate. He wonders if they can arrest him for missing a tackle.

Back behind the posts, no words are spoken. Some teammates crouch on the line, ready to charge at the conversion, others stare into the middle distance. Ivon looks towards Mike Bulstrode, but he is turned away from the team and stands stock still. The thunder of the stadium dominates them all.

As the minutes tick on, Ivon's passion builds. It is clear he does not feature in London's game plan. He has learned to appreciate when the ball is due to come his way — a kind of déjà vu gathers in his mind, which is consummated by the arrival of the ball in his hands and the execution of the skill he has been tasked with. No such impulses are forthcoming now, other than the occasional positional prompt from ProzoneX. Ivon's prison is closing in. Frozen out off the field and now on it. His temper rises. The soul-renting din from the stands buffets him on all sides, tightening its grip, heightening his mania.

London have the ball on the halfway line, but the passage of play that Ben the scrum-half has been developing among the forwards has come under pressure from the ferocity of the Yorkshire hits, and the move threatens to unravel. Ivon knows he is being called into play, because an impulse moves him to drop deep quickly and provide Ben with an option behind. He feels a premonition that he is to kick for the corner. He is to kick his life away.

He follows the impulse, quickly retreating behind the pack. He sees Ben prepare to whip the ball to him. There are Yorkshire forwards in close attendance, grappling for the scrum-half. As Ben picks up the ball, one of the Yorkshire forwards breaks rank to charge at Ivon. Ivon sees an opportunity behind the defender's aggression and with a monumental force of will he overrides the impulse conferred upon him.

Roaring with the effort, he drifts to the left, calling to Ben that that is where he is going. But this is not the mystical relationship he has with Ceiron Reeves at Swansea, where words are no more than the casual confirmation of what they both know the other is going to do. Here he screams at Ben from the depth of his soul.

'Left! Left!'

Ben is too taken with ProzoneX instruction to be able to respond, and the ball comes back to where Ivon is meant to be standing. Ivon knows this and has left some of his balance behind him, so that he can reach back to take the ball one-handed. He has to break his stride. The Yorkshire defender is on him, but Ivon's manoeuvre is so improvisational, so outlandish to rugby by computer, that the defender is thrown, and Ivon steps boldly out from under his nose.

The Yorkshire computer is manoeuvring its defence in expectation of a kick. The calculation has been undone. Ivon has breached the pattern. He has beaten the first defender, and in so doing he has beaten his own computer. He feels free all of a sudden. That fleeting, precious freedom that is granted maybe just once a game against the best. He is back at home, in Gower, by the sea. The ball is in his hands, like a flaming sword. The opposition start to turn this way and that. He offers the ball to a teammate, bamboozling one defender. Bang! He comes off his right foot, then ghosts between two more off his left. Going away, he tucks the ball under his left arm to fend off the flailing arms of another. Olympus Dan crouches before him, his massive arms spread wide. Ivon sees the try line beyond. He shortens his stride and slows to confront him, holding the ball out again in two hands, daring him to strike, then with a hitch-kick he arcs away to his right. The acceleration is devastating. He calls on full power and full power responds. As he sweeps past him, he sees Olympus Dan frozen, as if shot, his mind wanting to go both ways, his body a hapless victim of the warring desires. Olympus Dan puts one hand to the floor, his balance tipped, and Ivon is past him.

The try line awaits, 30 metres away. Ivon looks round. One winger and the full-back are closing in on him from the sidelines. He thinks he can beat them, but he searches for supporting teammates, just in case. One of his centres is working hard to get with him. For now, though, he is too far away. The rest are still coming to terms with the broken pattern. Olympus Dan has regained himself and joins the gathering tide of players in pursuit.

Yorkshire's points have been pumped through, and abruptly the stadium falls silent. Ivon turns to the try line again. He will do this alone. No one is going to catch him. He crosses the 22. He is inspired by the feeling that beyond the try line his freedom awaits. Wherever he may go, whoever he may take on, it will always come to this. Ivon, the ball, the imperative to play, the talent. Let science seek to dissect and smother, nature will not be contained. With this try he will prove it. With this try he will free instinct from its chains. He will free sport. He will free himself!

Ten metres out, he is taken very suddenly by the impulse to slow down and look for support. It catches him unawares.

'NO!' he screams, as he turns his deceleration into a sidestep.

The covering Yorkshire winger buys it and flies past. The try line is still open to Ivon, and, summoning every last fibre of body and soul, he accelerates again.

His efforts are futile now, and he knows it. He hears the crescendo of the full-back's feet behind and is sick at the inevitability of his felling, even before the peremptory cut of his legs from under him. The sting of the full-back's weight across his knees is sharp, but as nothing to the damage inflicted on his soul. He tries to reach out for the line, but it is five metres away. He brings the ball back within his bosom and cradles it tightly, as if it were his life. His eyes are closed, as he curls up on the ground. Two mighty hands seize the ball and pull. Ivon will not let go. The hands pull again, ruthlessly, unanswerably. The ball is lifted clean off the floor, and Ivon with it. He opens his eyes, as Olympus Dan raises him skyward and holds him to the air above his head, like a weed uprooted.

A harsh buzzer sounds in Ivon's head. 'Penalty,' says an automated voice. 'Tackled black 10 not releasing ball.'

Ivon is brought to ground. He looks about him imploringly. 'What the fuck was that?! I was in! You know I was! Did you not want me to score?'

'You were not in, 10,' says Coach White. His voice is firm and amplified in Ivon's head. 'ProzoneX calculated that the 11 would cut you off.'

'Bollocks!'

'We needed you to look for support. We needed to keep the ball.'

'There was no support!'

'It was coming, but you didn't look for it. You went for the line again. And all this after you defied ProzoneX's instruction to make the break in the first place. There's nothing I can do for you now.'

Ivon looks around him again, like a hunted animal. 'What? What? What does that mean?'

He walks a few paces towards the sideline, towards four security guards who wait for him, but it is not of his own accord. 'No,' he says, and he makes himself change direction to fall in among his teammates, as they wait for the penalty. Again, he finds himself turning towards the sidelines; again, he overrides the impulse and stays among his teammates. The security guards are coming towards him now. 'No,' he says once more, a whisper this time. He runs – to where he doesn't know – but he turns and runs.

He has taken barely five paces when it strikes. A seizure of unimaginable pain, like that which pulsed down his arm for a few seconds when he tried to tackle Olympus Dan earlier, only more intense, constant, and everywhere, throughout every nook and cranny of his body. It is the pain that visited him in Alanis's flat. He screams in agony, but there is nothing to grab at, because the pain is all over him, a white sheet of suffering, so he sinks to the floor and brings his hands round the back of his neck to where the chip is, to where he let them in.

The pain subsides, leaving him weak, and two pairs of hands hoist him to his feet. He is escorted from the field, his head hung low. His replacement jogs the other way.

Yorkshire kick for touch.

It's over. Ivon lies on the floor, his cheek against the white. His legs are tucked under his arms. He is travelling at high speed towards London in a floating box. No noise. No motion. It could be an underground cell. He will never play again.

He will be transferred to the Institute of Correction. And there taken for Assimilation. He will be turned into one of them. The perfect sportsman. The dead human being.

A premonition of finality crushes him. The end. He doesn't know why he feels this way. The perfect sportsman. Hasn't he always striven for that?

'You will never play again,' says Dad, over and over again in his head.

'You are playing at it,' says Marcus Apollo.

His mood is black, just like on the worst days. The paralysis is upon him. A sickness sits in his stomach. The emotional grown physical. He is unmanned, about to be perfected. It is the end of all that he has known. He will never play again. The dark nights under soaking floodlight. The sunny afternoons. The breeze. The song. The love that runs through it. His teammates. His girl.

It's over.

Dusty saunters to a stop a hundred metres away from The Cricketer. The mighty statue is always best viewed from the edge of Regent's Park. Just here, the poise between substance and elegance is at its most exquisite.

He allows himself to sink into reverie. He can remember now the very year The Cricketer was erected – 2125, their third title in a row. Dusty was at the peak of his powers, or the high plateau, for wasn't it the case that his excellence endured season after season? He thought nothing of it at the time. When an athlete's focus is forever on the Next Match, he doesn't mark the trail he leaves behind. There are no matches ahead for him now, but he clings to the new dimension he has discovered in the things behind him, as if to let go would be to unravel. He remembers how the smooth, bulbous walls of that stadium-generator beyond used to thunder with the runs he scored. What productive times they were! Could it even be that The Cricketer is a tribute to him?

He turns away. Misalignment. Do they not have a point, the forward-seeking architects of the Perpetual Era? What is there for him in these memories? Had he a future, they would not wield the pull they do. Were he as responsible as he should be to the needs of London, indulging in their recollection would be abhorrent.

Had he a future. Were he as responsible. He does not and he is not. These memories are all that is left to him.

He runs again. Across the road. These memories are not all he has. He has Ivon. He has a future in Wales. And he has, yes, he has, a part of him is…there must be a way of expressing it that justifies his delinquent longing to make contact. There are in Regent's Park, exercising in the elite training corridors of London Cricket, examples of Dusty's progeny.

Along Park Road, through Hanover Gate and onto the Outer Circle, he scuds across the sky-blue roads. He is Dusty

Noble. He is off to see his progeny. To do so is a thought that has occurred to him, an urge that has visited. He will not dismiss it as an irrelevance; he will not belittle the impulse. Here is the possibility to – what? – meet, touch, look at his progeny, which arises from his knowing about them, from his living in the same city. It is as simple and as innocent as that. Through the tree grid he pounds, left over York Bridge, until he reaches the Inner Circle and the high conservatories of London Cricket's Elite Centre for Batting.

For a moment – for more than a moment – it's as if he's never been away. He strides through the doors of the ECB with the air of a man who has done so for more than thirty years, head high, back straight, arms swinging naturally.

'Hello, Todd,' he says to the secondary at reception as he sweeps past.

Todd does not reply.

On Dusty strides, into the grand central corridor. The skies above are clear, and the gills are tilted to diffuse light throughout the height and length of the gallery. Off to the right are the portals for the training corridors, but Dusty turns left, halfway down the hallway, into the recovery lounge. Men and women in the green of elite wander and recline across the lounge. Dusty makes no eye contact, heading directly for the notice-face. He scans the training schedule. Who did Garbo say were his progeny? Marius Amstrad was definitely one of them. Percy Sabatani another. Dusty racks his brain and scans the names. Jake George? Was he one?

He notes Marius's corridor.

'Dusty?' says a voice behind him.

It is Patrick Desolay, opening bat. Dusty cannot hold his gaze. He looks past him and catches sight of Miranda Leaf with her hands in her hair, then back at Patrick and down to the curve of his bicep, which seems more pronounced than it should be. Losing streaks – why do they send rational athletes straight to the multi-gym?

'What you doing here?' Patrick's tone is not unfriendly; neither is it welcoming.

'Appointment. I have an appointment.'

'Oh? Strange place to have one.'

Dusty moves away, back towards the training corridor. 'You keeping productive, Patrick?' he says over his shoulder, without quite turning his head.

He doesn't wait for the reply, slipping into one of the training portals and up the off-white moulded steps to the viewing gallery. The air hums with the arrhythmic clicks of bat on ball and the sighs of ball along simu-wall. Dusty marches along the gallery, flicking through the batsmen in their corridors as through the pages of a book. Marius Amstrad is in 1-23. Dusty can see him now and in a few more strides is over his corridor.

This is his progeny. Of course. How had he not seen it before? Dusty is bewitched by the young lad's elegance and economy of effort. The balls fly from his bat with speed and deference, again and again. The authority of movement, the grace, the sureness of shot. The sureness. It is Dusty looking at Dusty, at how Dusty was, at how Dusty can be again through this progeny of his. He can feel the tears prick at his eyes. He wants to claim ownership of this boy. Is he not his? Reared by London, yes, born of its breeding programmes – but made in the image of Dusty Noble from Dusty Noble's seed. Dusty can perceive the link now, direct and timeless, between progenitor and progeny. He can appreciate the individuality of it. He wants to know who *his* progenitors were. He wants to know who Marius Amstrad's other progenitor is. There is somebody else in the boy. He is in the image of Dusty, yet not. But how to draw out the strands that are his and those of someone else? He watches him as if in strobe lighting, snatches of mannerisms and bearings and angles of profile flash across the boy's body like the projection on a simu-wall, each speaking anew of an influence or trait that is Dusty's, someone else's, familiar, on the tip of his tongue, just out of reach. Dusty knows his co-progenitor but cannot identify her. Of all the girls he successfully applied for a procreation certificate with, which are you?

He wants it to be Dee, but he can't remember if they ever applied. If they did, it might explain his tempestuous relationship with Ricky. But, no, he cannot see Dee in Marius Amstrad. Lana Defoe, Manager for Cricket? The authority of stroke would be consistent, but, equally, none was more authoritative than Dusty's. Sonya Trick? Teresa Southfield?

Marius ties his feet up facing a leg-side delivery and offers a catch to short leg. A chink in his technique. Amid the masterclass it is a sudden and surprising flaw. Dusty had trouble with the very same shot! He knows exactly what Marius is going through. He understands! A warm surge overtakes him, tenderness, empathy, a hint of melancholy – confusing new conditions for a Perpetual citizen, but Dusty feels alive with them. There is hope and excitement too, the prospect of a connection, the opportunity to help.

He bounds down the stairs and scans his way into the training corridor. The simulation powers down, the bowling aperture suspends operation. Marius and Dusty stand face to face in a blank oblong box. Dusty's momentum wavers as the young man's eyes turn from surprise at his arrival to suspicion.

'Dusty Noble,' Marius murmurs, as if to confirm it.

Dusty's son is taller than he is. He knew that already, of course. Now it strikes him as overwhelmingly significant. But, no, it is not that. It is the word 'son' that is overwhelming, ancient, obsolete, discredited and suddenly in his head from nowhere, a smithereened relic from deep within the human registry, rising up and coalescing to form a new star in Dusty's firmament,

257

a new body of gravity to order himself by. He looks down, away from the intense focus of his son's gaze. His eyes settle on the forearm, then the gloves, the latest generation of intelligent cricket suit. Dusty suddenly remembers the last days of pads and guards. Batting was harder then with all that extraneous weight about one's person, but wasn't there something noble about it too, nobly inefficient? Isn't there something noble about this – memories popping through into his consciousness like an infestation, impossible to contain, the overrunning of a neat, future-leaning mind?

He focuses on the bat, which Marius holds so effortlessly, as if it too were an intelligent extension of his very person. Dusty reaches out for it. He thinks he wants to offer Marius a few tips, but he is reaching out as well for his past, for his purpose on Earth, for his son. Like the teeming memories, tears burst forth from his eyes as he holds out his hand. He is not bold enough to take the bat; he is not bold enough to look anywhere else.

'Are you *crying*?' says Marius. The contempt is unmistakeable. He takes a step backwards. The bat is whipped away.

'Dusty Noble!' says another voice from the aperture end of the corridor. It is Anthony Penn, Head of London Batting, a former comrade. 'I heard you took a post at ReSure. You having second thoughts?'

Dusty is stranded, unable to look at his son, unable to look at Anthony Penn. The tears have marooned him. He pulls his hand back in and bolts for the exit, his head half-turned against Anthony, in full against Marius, his son and heir.

'Get yourself on a coaching programme,' says Anthony, as Dusty sets off. 'I've always said it.' Then he pauses. 'Are you…?'

'He just walked in here, Head,' says Marius. 'Walked in and started crying.'

'*Crying*?'

Dusty plunges on through the grand central corridor and away.

✺

Ivon opens his eyes. He sees whiteness, of course. He sits – no, he lies – in a featureless, infinite expanse of white. The whitest yet. He can make out no ceiling, no walls. No corners, no edges. The light and white hang perfectly around him, so intimate with each other as to dissolve all points of reference.

His body stretches out, held in a half-mould that could have been custom made. The smooth edges of the casing – he immediately thinks open sarcophagus – are all he can make out of any substance. He thinks he is lying down in it, but he could be vertical, he could be on an angle. His torso must be raised slightly – or his head – for he can see the extent of his body. He is naked. His body hair has been removed. He tries to lift his head, but he cannot move it.

Something else is not right, and when it dawns on him he is sick with terror. There are no visible restraints binding him, so he tries to lift his arm. He cannot. He tries his other, then his legs – to no avail. He tries again. His fingers and toes too. There is no response.

He is paralysed.

He gasps.

'No need to panic,' says a voice behind him.

His eyes flit to all points in their sockets, desperate to lock on to something fixed in the outside world. He strains again to shift his position.

'We have placed a hiatus in your somatic motor neurone network for now,' the voice continues, undulating, with a faint lisp. 'Your peripherals have been disengaged. Full function will be restored once the procedure is complete.'

A figure steps into his field of vision. Ivon is able to orientate himself – he *is* lying down – but this man, in the black suit of security, remains discrete in a void of whiteness. He is smaller than the men of his class Ivon has encountered so far, and when he turns towards him Ivon can see that he is younger, too, possessed of a lively, impish face and movements that are swift and precise.

'Your limbs are immobile, but they should retain full sensation.'

Pain swells in Ivon's thigh as the man presses down on a bruise. His fingers are thin and strong. Ivon seethes; then, when his tormentor turns to look him in the eye while digging his fingers in deeper, he cries out. In his mind he is thrashing about, in his mind he is breaking free, protecting his thigh. But Ivon's body does not respond, save for transmitting its pain.

'Good!' says the man, jerking up to full height. 'It is all in order.' He smiles sharply. 'Forgive me. My name is Ignatius Andrew. I am an Assistant Director of the Institute of Correction. I shall be assimilating you today. Call me Nate.'

'Where am I?'

'In the IC.'

'Where is that? I want to see the outside. I want to see *something*.'

Ignatius sucks in through pursed lips. 'That will not be possible, I'm afraid. We are some way under the ground. You will see the outside again in time.'

He studies Ivon for a moment and cocks his head, then brings it in nearer, studying Ivon's nose. The skin of his face is without blemish, without stubble or discernible pore. He tuts. 'That nose of yours is a mess. Quite broken.' He inhales, as if a thought occurs to him. 'Let me straighten it for you.'

A big fat pain erupts across Ivon's face. The fingers are nimble and, yes, immensely strong. His head must be held in a vice, for it does not move as his nose is repositioned. A hideous crunch and grind releases shockwaves through his cranium, as tectonic plates might across the Earth. Ivon bellows with the pain and helplessness.

Ignatius stops suddenly and holds his palms up to his handiwork, as Dad used to after he'd balanced the bails on the wicket. 'There. I think that's better.' He winces. 'Or is it? Maybe we'll leave it to the experts. Sorry.'

Tears are streaming down Ivon's face. The iron tang of blood is in his mouth again. He is desperate to bring his hands up to his nose, but they lie uselessly by his side. The pain pulses round his face and into his head.

'What are you doing to me? What is this?'

Ignatius eases one buttock onto the side of the casing and lifts one knee to rest there. He holds his chin between his thumb and forefinger, as if in mockery, his other arm across his midriff. He pauses for effect.

'This is your Assimilation, Ivon. You've been heading here for a while. All three degrees, I'm afraid.'

'What does that mean?'

'It's a question of how deeply into the strata of your consciousness we need to delve. In your case, we cannot hope to undo the damage to your personality wrought by a lifetime in the Lapsed Era without removing the entire register.'

Ivon is exhausting himself with the mental effort to move. He strains every neuron in his head, and when his body yields no response he breaks out into a roar of frustration. He hurls abuse at Ignatius, every violent imprecation he knows. Ignatius jumps to his feet, a look of horror on his face.

'I don't think I've ever heard such aggression from an assimilee!' he says. 'You speak of fucking and the cunt as if they are bad things. Really, I think gratitude the more appropriate response. We're going to provide you with the mindset to become the best you can be. I've seen fear in a subject before;

I've seen tears. But I've never known anyone rail like this against their own improvement!'

'You're going to wipe out my memory! That's what this means, doesn't it! Destroy my mind!'

'Oh, dear joules! No, of course not! Everything removed will be reinstated. You'll feel very different towards it all once the procedure is complete, but we will take nothing away.'

Ignatius turns away and walks purposefully to the fringe of Ivon's vision, where he stops to perform a task. Ivon strains frantically to see what he is doing, but it is hopeless.

'First of all,' Ignatius continues, 'a distinction. We are not talking about your conscious memories, although it is true they will come out with everything else. This is third-degree Assimilation, Ivon! We will be delving far deeper than the surface. Your memories are superficial, malleable, a conversation between your conscious and unconscious minds, with the conscious always in control, bending and shaping the details of what actually happened to fit its ever-shifting requirements. No, we will be removing the very seat of memory itself. The register of everything that has ever happened to you, as experienced by you. It is rooted in the unconscious. The human mind is incapable of retaining such data on a conscious level. Can you imagine being able to replay in your head every second of your life to date? Or, worse still, being unable to change the details of any of it? It would be intolerable! Which is why the human mind keeps the seat of memory well away from the conscious. But it is all in there.' He has returned to be by Ivon's side and leans in again to his face, tapping him playfully on the forehead. 'And that is what we shall be removing. For now.'

'For now.'

Ignatius straightens up and begins to peruse what looks like an opaque sheet of glass in his hand. 'Yes. It is temporary. We need to wind the scoreboard back to nil–nil, as it were.

Once we have removed the register of what has made you you, we can start to tinker with the hardware. We will install the Perpetual Starter Pack.' He shrugs and cocks his head. 'It is a bundle of hormones and regulators that helps to foster a personality consistent with Perpetual values. All citizens are fitted with it upon emergence these days.' He laughs. 'It is true that in a few years we shall have little need for the IC! Our juveniles are reared so meticulously under the new technology that we expect Misalignment variance to be all but eradicated in the latest generations. But you represent a very different case. We will not know the extent of the underlying faults in your circuitry until we have removed the seat. Then we shall to work. Once we are satisfied that the necessary adjustments have been made, we will replace the register in its entirety. Your personal history will remain unaltered. But, of course, it will now be repellent to you, as it should always have been. Indeed, I doubt you will care to summon it to consciousness at all. You will be set free from Wales! Free to focus on your productivity!'

Ivon screws his eyes shut. He is no longer taking in what the man is saying. If only he could move. If only he could be home.

His breath quickens to a pant. His mouth is dry, his nose a wall of blood and swollen tissue. He cannot move. Hatred burns inside him for the spineless English who have rendered him thus. For those who made him stop just short of the line. For the computer. The cunts who let the computer do that to him. He roars again.

Stop. Breathe. Persuasion. Persuasion is all he has left. He tries to calm himself.

'OK. OK. I'll change!'

Ignatius looks up from his glass tablet, his eyebrows arched, his head cocked again, a half-smile on his lips that gives Ivon a fleeting sense of hope. 'You'll change?'

'Yes. Yes, I'll change.'

He tucks the tablet across his midriff and brings his other hand up to his chin again, spreading forefinger and thumb across the front of it. He is listening.

'I will control my individualism. I will stop making decisions that do not conform to the game plan. I will place my abilities in the hands of...of ProzoneX. I will be guided by...by...him. It.'

A new voice breaks into the conversation. It is loud, it is strong and profound. Ivon cannot tell if it is in his head, or in the room, or on the air, or up on high.

'These abilities ARE NOT YOURS!' it booms.

Ignatius brings his shoulders up to his ears, as if to take cover. He winces at Ivon, but it is in mockery, cowardly, contemptible mockery.

'You betray your on-going delinquency when you speak in such terms,' the voice continues. 'You are no more than what has happened to you. You are no more than what you have been given.'

Ivon's breath quickens again. He closes his eyes and wrestles with the instinct to scream. He tries to remain onside; he tries to imagine what they want to hear. But the will is too strong in him.

'No!' he cries. 'No! I have been given nothing!'

'You are a bundle of genetic instructions to which things have happened,' rejoins the voice. It is calm, but it fills the room completely. 'That is all. The genes are an inheritance from your progenitors and the rest a function of what has happened to you. You have been shaped by the Lapsed Era, but you cannot claim responsibility for that, any more than your progenitors can for the organised programmes they came through.'

Ivon's breast is heaving against the futility. The blandness and collusion. The emasculation of heroes, the smoothing over of boldness. His body may lie on a slab, taken out of the game, but there is a spirit in him still. He knows not from where it came, inherited or acquired, but he knows that it is vivid and it is his. 'This is madness!' he cries. 'Fucking madness! I have acted! I have changed things in my world! I have changed things in *your* world!'

'And after Assimilation you will continue to contribute. But these ejaculations of pro-activity are mere exchanges between you and the external world, which created you in the first place and continues to shape you. That world is permanent; you are ephemeral, like a spark leaping from the turbines, like a fly-half breaking from the game plan. You are not independent. You are not self-determining. On your own, you will fizzle out.'

A faint buzzing begins in Ivon's head. Actually *in* it. Not like the comms that fill the space between his ears. He can place this sound within his head, two precise spots, either side of central, on a level towards the top of the ears. It slowly builds. Ivon senses a tide rising. He is panicking. In his mind he is thrashing again.

The voice in the room continues: 'Your progenitors were bred by the commune of London, whose gene pool belongs to the commune. You are a part of that great programme. Your aptitude was conferred by London, and London here reclaims you.'

The buzzing is louder and has grown beyond its origin, into the top and front of his head. It has stabilised, and now the frequency begins to build towards a pitch. Ivon knows that its purity of focus will have consequences, like the note that shatters glass. Something is impending. He is about to burst.

Ignatius reappears in his vision. His palms are held together as in prayer. 'The hippocampus and the relevant strata of your cerebral cortex are being prepared. I'm afraid it is necessary for you to remain conscious for this part of the procedure. You may experience some discomfort. It will soon be over.'

Ignatius steps out of view. Ivon's eyes dart this way and that; his breath bursts forth in staccato surges, part pant, part wail. His brain is vibrating, the buzz crescendoing. It is almost here; something, the moment, is almost here. The not knowing is torturous, the dread unbearable. A very precise pain sizzles into life, deep within his brain. Then, as if a flame, it sweeps throughout the region of the buzzing. Ivon cries out.

The pitch is reached. He stares into the space above him. The pain is white. It has surpassed the physical. He stops screaming. His brain unfolds, tearing itself open and unravelling, lifting him out of himself and into the white, through the white and beyond.

He is at St Helen's on a sunny day, the turf is firm, the crowd in good voice, Ceiron just ahead of him, Jenks alongside, Dafydd Bennett on the bench, ha! Or maybe at 15. The promenade to Mumbles, with Cerys on his arm. She is above, hair tumbling towards him, lips flared. Then so is someone else. The Llanelli game. Then Cerys, beneath him this time, body arched against the dirty, cold stone. Beside him. He is beside himself. The curtains drawn, the door is locked, the walls a sleeve between him and the insistent world. His father yells. Then laughs, then cries. His mother lost in thought. She smiles. There's something on, it opens up, his life, the field, the goal, the stumps. Ivon, Ivon, Ivon. He has something. He's home, he's in hell, he's among stars. The table is his, the room and laughter, the possibilities endless. The fields, the surf, the seagull yelps. You have something. Yes. Yes! You *are* something. A piece of work. Be still, my sweet. The cool, dull whiff of boots and Hefin Stevens stabs his hand and fires are lit, the coals aglow in the dark days before Christmas. A ball turns and turns and turns seeking completion seeking home. Want it. Reach. Have. Home. Darkness at last. It surrounds him. Warm giving walls that live, do not demand. It is organic. He is home. It is over. He is home.

XV

Dusty checks his course towards Juno's office. Two black suits step out only a few seconds before he is due to arrive at her door. He turns sharply away and loiters. Everything feels out of joint. He pretends to preoccupy himself with something, anything, on his neuro-face.

When the security officers have passed, he resumes his course. Juno seems subdued. Or is it disconcerted? Either way, it's not flamboyant, it's not wicked. It's not Juno.

'Dusty,' she says neutrally, suddenly cool, suddenly inscrutable.

He takes it as an invitation to speak. 'Have you heard anything from Headingley?' He should be more circumspect, but he can't remember why he should, nor can he straighten his head out to remind himself. Then when Juno does not respond, he presses her further. 'The rugby match yesterday. Against Yorkshire.'

Juno takes a short breath. 'We lost. Badly. 49–6.'

Dusty's shoulders slump. Inside, he wants to scream Welsh words like Ricky. Fuck. What the fuck. What the fuck has happened to Ivon. He wants to hammer the floor with his fists. He wants to rage. But the slumped shoulders have it.

'I can't access the match packs.' Should he be admitting that? 'Can you?' He doesn't want to hear the answer, which he knows must be yes.

Juno studies him over those interlocking fingers. But there's no grin, not even a twinkle in her eye. Something is wrong. Very wrong. Dusty is being marginalised.

'What happened in the match?' he blurts out.

Excessive Interest in Another. He knows it, but he doesn't want to correct himself. He can't.

'How should I know?' she says.

'You've seen the score!'

'Of course I have, Dusty. I check the scores every morning.'

'So you can access the match packs!'

Why can't he?

'Yes! But I haven't gone into any of them! Why would I? I'm not a scientist!' They stare at each other, as if about to engage in a wrestling match, the sport in which Juno was a champion. 'And you're not one either.'

She is offering him nothing today. London is offering him nothing. He has nothing to offer London. The relationship is collapsing. He feels the chill wisps of rejection play round his ankles. If he stands still they will billow higher. Privileges rescinded. The security officers earlier.

'What were Security doing here?'

Again, the hopeless question is blurted out.

Juno shrugs and raises her eyebrows.

That's something. The slightest hint of ambiguity. Could it have been a playful gesture? This is Juno, Dusty tells himself! The most momentous woman he has ever known. He does have more to offer. Of course he does!

'Shall we see if a cot's free?' he says, the spirit in him high.

Juno lowers her hands and reaches for her tablet. 'I've had my constitutional this morning.'

She does not look up at him again.

※

Lana happens to be facing away, as she pulls up her day suit. The legs are still sleek, but as she straightens he notes a slight heaviness of buttock before she is cupped and covered by fabric. Manager for Cricket she may be, but there is less wattage in those buttocks than when she and Dusty were among the leading cricketers of their respective genders. There is less in his.

She looked sad when she pulled down the monitor after their bout. Diminishment is a reality for them now, but there is always the next bout to look towards and the aspiration to make it better than the last. When it's not, there is a brief pang before the mind turns to the next again, to the shower, the powder and the return of unravelling body to day suit.

Dusty leans back against the wall, stretching his legs. 'Do you know, I don't care that we don't register the same figures as we used to!'

And he doesn't. His heart is racing as he says it — another outrageous unorthodoxy. The journey in discovery of himself goes on. It is liberating to feel the real Dusty bubble through what is left of his discipline; it is thrilling to express it, to allow it to express itself. He knows it cannot last.

Lana turns and looks down at him. When was the last time she sat with him on a recovery couch? She doesn't need to say anything. Gone is the sadness he saw a few minutes ago. There is astonishment, perhaps even shock. Did he really just say what she thought he did?

'I mean, yes, I'd rather we were banking a megajoule each time, like in the old days. But let's think more about how much we must have generated together over the years. And I don't mean at the crease. I'm talking in here. You and me.'

She pauses before slipping her feet into her shoes. A tress of hair breaks from behind her ear and brushes her face as she watches the shoes fold round her feet. She tucks it back in place, quite thoughtfully.

Dusty wants to go on. He wants to tell her he doesn't care that the grip of her thighs is not what it used to be, the gyration of her loins less momentous, her audio a little strained and dutiful. He's not the dynamo he used to be, either. But isn't there something else now, something about this hint of gentleness in their coitus? The numbers may be down, but there's a new quality to it that strikes a chord with the new Dusty. He knows it must be Welsh by nature. Yes, he looks at Lana and he sees Dee, their slippings a poignant echo of the bold, clean assets that went before – and all the more beautiful for that. He wants to tell Lana these things, but he chooses not to.

'Diminishment is hard, Dusty,' she says. 'This inclination of yours to look backwards instead of forwards – it seems to me you are suffering. There are people you can talk to.'

Dusty is irritated by her impeccable alignment. After all they've been through, all they've contributed to London and England over the years, with nothing now but administration left to them before stasis, can they not be allowed a moment's mischief in the post-coital wind-down? Irritation provokes him further. Recklessness leads him on. 'And not just the joules, Lana,' he says, with no thought or care for tomorrow. 'What about the cricketers? How many of those do you think we've generated? I saw Marius Amstrad yesterday. Did you know I'm his progenitor? Something about him reminded me of you. Could it be…?'

Lana gasps and heads sharply for the door. 'No. He's not one of mine.'

She heads sharply for the door without Dusty.

'What? You *know*? How do you know?'

Lana does not look round but, on her own, she initiates the consolidation. She initiates the consolidation without her coital partner by her side, without Dusty. 'We just know.'

Dusty is too stunned to take his place next to her. The consolidator rumbles, their potential now actual, and she stands alone at the door. She doesn't look for him. She's going to leave the cot without him. The door sweeps open. She looks to the floor for just a moment. (Did she?) Lana strides out of the cot without a backward glance.

○

In all his thirty-six years of coitus, no one has left him behind in a coition terminal like that. He's sure of it. On his path back to the recovery lounge, he passes a pair of cot partners, who eye him suspiciously. Why wouldn't they? He's never seen anyone alone in the corridors of a leisure club either. This pair must have just seen Lana though, a few moments ahead of him, striding in the magenta of the managerial class, who walk without care wherever they want. That must have struck them as unusual. Now Dusty presents himself as the reason. What must he have done? And he a veteran elite…

It occurs to him that he should summon the bearing of the elite he once was, who generated terajoules with his prowess, but such assurance has deserted him. He has lost the momentum of agency. He is a burst balloon, defined by what is left of him, blown on by the eddies what is left of him can catch.

The recovery lounge is busy. Lana has gone, which he notes with relief, but he scans the room for Alanis. Maybe she can tell him something about Ivon, now they are seeing so much of each other. Alanis and Dusty have not taken a cot together since that bout off the Grid in Wales, not since Ivon came to London. Have they even spoken?

Melissa Toni is in the lounge. Even stretched out on a couch she slugs from her isotonic with focus, a study in bristling potential energy. He wanders over to her, then hesitates the moment she spots him. The isotonic is at her lips, but she has stopped gulping. She lowers it slowly at the sight of Dusty and sits up, swinging her legs round to the floor.

'That Welshman of yours,' she says, shaking her head menacingly.

'Have you seen him?'

'No, but he's seen Alanis.'

'Where is Alanis?'

'That's a good question, Dusty,' she says, rising to her feet, growing into her instinct for a fight. 'In the IC, probably. Or an infirmary. She may need to be assimilated. A model citizen, an elite of impeccable standing and service. For her to have to go through an ordeal like that, the humiliation of it, the pain, through no fault of her own – it's disgusting!'

'Wait a minute! Assimilation? What are you talking about?'

'He entered her home, Dusty! Your man! Ivon! The Welshman *you* introduced into society! What were you thinking?!'

'It's part of his culture. He doesn't understand. In Wales, they *live* in each other's homes.'

'And in the jungle they eat each other, which is why I would never let a tiger loose in England. *You* understand, Dusty! You should have seen where this was going.'

'Alanis understands too. She's been to Wales. She brought him back with me.'

Melissa throws her isotonic to the floor. The bottle bounces a couple of times, spewing what's left of its contents around their feet. The violence of emotion comes as a surprise to Dusty. Alanis has told him about Melissa. She's an outside hitter; aggression is integral to her role on the volleyball court. She's probably on a programme, Dusty tells himself – encouraged to lose her temper once or twice a week. That's all this is, an exercise. He tells himself that, but it's not so easy to let the hostility roll off. It might have been when he'd been active himself, but no one ever behaved like this to Dusty Noble then. The recovery lounge has fallen silent, but Dusty can see or hear nothing beyond the seething pugilist opposite.

'Don't you dare implicate her in this sick experiment of yours! She trusted you, you flagging clock-watcher. And she trusted him. Now look where that's got her!'

'There's no reason for her to be damaged by this. If you think about it, what's wrong with entering another's home?'

A murmuring breaks out round the lounge, if only Dusty could register it.

Melissa cries out, half-laugh, half-shriek. 'And you've let him into *your* home, have you?'

'I've been to Ivon's home in Wales!'

'Have you let him in to yours?'

'I would.'

'But you haven't, have you?'

'No.'

'Ha! You stand there, uttering these Lapsed Era depravities, but you don't even have the balls to be exposed to them yourself. It's pathetic!'

'I do!'

'And how long has the Welshman been in London? A month? Six weeks? And he hasn't once entered your home in all that time! Why don't you admit it? You could no more handle it than any of the rest of us. You shouldn't be surprised that Alanis couldn't either.'

Dusty is overtaken, quite suddenly. Not by the tears this time, but the sense of something he can't control is no less vivid. He falls back onto the recovery couch behind him and holds his head in his hands, but it is not enough. He needs words, a word perhaps, and he finds from somewhere a visceral syllable from the Lapsed Era, yes, it has to be something Welsh. He cries, 'Fuck!' Except he draws out the vowel into a prolonged scream, so that it sounds more like 'Fuuaaaaaaaaaaaaak', a scream from the depths of his soul, book-ended by an f and a k. Ghostly white pimples appear in his vision, dance hypnotically for their moment, then fade into the reality of the way things are – like Ivon, like Ivon.

He appears to be trembling. She's right! He never let Ivon in to his home, and not just because a Perpetual citizen would never do that, not just because it is forbidden.

It was a matter of fear. Dusty Noble, afraid. All those years his bravery was a given, a starting point from which he built his life as a batsman, a rock on which London built a dynasty, erected a statue. But that wasn't bravery, his defiance of all-comers, all missiles. That was mastery of the known. Perpetual citizens cannot be brave. Everything is too *known*.

Ivon has been brave. To stride into a new world with so little knowledge, so ill-prepared. So incompatible. Dusty is half the man Ivon is, half the man he thought Dusty was. It's a revelation that yawns beneath him, a chasm where once there had been fathoms of rock.

'She didn't turn up for our match yesterday.' Melissa's voice is softer now, but Dusty cannot look up. 'Our re-engagement after the Spring Recess. Joules, she was so excited about it! We all were. But she didn't turn up. Too traumatised. She's been given compassionate leave. I don't know when we'll see her again.'

Oh, Alanis! If only Dusty had the time, the emotional space, to consider what his actions have meant for you too. He might, in his nostalgic frame of mind, weep in remembrance of the magnificent young woman who glided into the club one day and of the intervening years in which – yes, as a would-be Welshman he can say it – her relationship with him grew. But his mind is too full with the roar of Melissa and his own conscience, with fear for the future – for himself, for Ivon and for a Wales without him.

The net is closing in. In the streets and clubs and refectories, he feels the eyes of people turn on him. When he was of genuine value to the commune he walked without fear of glance or whisper. Now each day is a gauntlet of lingering eyes and dark looks. Recognition at last. And from the black suits, who populate his landscape at every turn, dark, inscrutable, half-turned away.

Down here in the bowels of ReSure he is free from it. He sits in what they call the Shed. Dusty asked Juno what the word meant. She shrugged.

He looks about at the tools of their business. The quaint strips that illuminate the Shed are tucked out of sight, above architraves and beneath surfaces, but they are clear sources of light that might not look out of place in Wales. All around him are labelled shelves, drawers and containers neatly cataloguing equipment for the handling of suspended assets, some of it still in use, most of it obsolete now the systems have been automated – trolleys, magnetic handles, rope, cleaning agents, cylinders, valves, handsaws. But it is the item in his hand that holds his attention – a chip-pull. Dusty turns it over. He holds it to the webbing between his forefinger and middle finger, as if about to perform the procedure. His finger hovers over the trigger. Could he do it? Would he do it if the moment came? Will he. When.

It'll sting, most probably, but that's the least of the issues. A puncture of the skin, followed by the drawing up of his identity chip through the flesh, to be presented at the end of the needle as a grain of metal. From puncture to retraction, 53 milliseconds, from integration to isolation, a citizen to an outcast.

The device is smooth and black, light and innocuous. Ergonomic in the right hand, ergonomic at the aperture, the nozzle fitting perfectly between fingers. It would be impossible to miss its target, or to bend this device to any other use. He pictures himself on an aqua-trainer with Ivon, well out to sea. Punch, and he's off the Grid; lean over to Ivon and, punch, so's he. Then onward, onward to Wales. What a rare opportunity – to work in ReSure and be of a mind to desert. Without the latter he would never have thought to remove his identity chip; without the former, he would never have known it to be possible. Perpetual citizens are claimed at birth, a grain of metal in their hand and a set of values in their soul. Few pause to consider either. None know of a life without them. To remove all that…

'I wouldn't do it if I were you.'

Dusty is jolted from his reverie. There at the doorway, face dripping from that aquiline nose, is Syracuse Garbo.

'I think you might find that the final straw,' he says. 'The file on you is building. Nothing decisive yet, but becoming the first animate asset in Perpetual history to take himself off the Grid – that would certainly clinch it.' Garbo takes a few steps into the room. 'Surely, if you were serious about this, you would perform the procedure somewhere they couldn't swoop on you within minutes.' He idly pulls open a drawer marked drill bits. 'In Wales, for example.'

Dusty stares at the chip-pull, frozen in his hand. He considers making an emergency show of good citizenship, but why bother? Garbo probably knew about his plans before Dusty had even dreamed them up.

'Do you really think they'd just let you go? Dusty Noble, the batsman of a generation.' He leans over and taps Dusty on the forehead with a drill bit. 'There's too much they want in here. And it is theirs, of course.'

With an irritable swipe of his hand, Dusty brushes the drill bit away. 'They,' he sneers. 'Them. Why do you always try to act the neutral? You *are* one of them.'

'If I were one of them, you'd have been taken to the IC a long time ago. If they knew what I do. Or rather, if they could make the connections that I am in a position to; if they could apprehend the broader picture of what has happened to you. I don't suppose even you have quite worked it out.'

'I know I've been corrupted by Lapsed Era sensibilities. Like Dee, like Ricky and the others.' Dusty snaps to his feet. 'In fact, no! Not corrupted! Enhanced! Empowered! To see colours and shades, cracks, quirks and opportunities! To see the Past. I want to join Ricky and Dee. I want to go.'

'They'd come for you.'

'Not if I had immunity.'

'If. But, even then, England would go to sport over you. Imagine it, Dusty! You batting for Wales in one glorious final stand for independence from the very country that created you – *against* the very country that created you! The poetry of it! That would be something to tickle your Lapsed Era sensibility! You'd lose, of course.'

'You think?'

Garbo roars with laughter. 'You and a rabble of Welshmen against the latest generation of English cricketers? Of course I think!'

'It would be cricket the Welsh way, remember, on a Welsh field. Eleven-a-side, people having to bat *and* bowl. A team fired by passion and a love for sport versus one custom made for it. With humans officiating. I'm not so sure we would lose.' And if I ever make it to Wales, he wants to say, Ivon will have come, too.

With a smirk, Garbo replaces the drill bit in its drawer. 'Freak results have been known to happen, I suppose. But by definition they are one-offs. Order is always restored in time.'

'One win is all we'd need.'

The smirk broadens into another smile. 'There's just one small problem. You'll have to do it all without Ivon.'

For as long as the details evaded him of what befell Ivon at Headingley yesterday, Dusty could stumble on in hope. But hope is a baseless ephemeron. It is lack of achievement made animate, inspiration for those with no points on the board. There is no place for hope in England. It's why he hoped so to make it to Wales. Why he dreamed of a life elsewhere, his identity cut out from the webbing between his fingers.

Now, though, he squares up to the truth. He squares up to the old man who smiles and is frail, as airy and insubstantial as hope itself. 'What's happened?' he says.

'Ivon was taken to the Institute of Correction yesterday. There was nothing I could do, I'm afraid. My people managed to step in when he entered the girl's home, but when he defied an on-field instruction in the service of London Rugby it was out of my hands. He was removed from the field in the eleventh minute and transferred in a secure van to the IC. There he underwent third-degree Assimilation last night. The procedure was a success. Early indications are that London – and no doubt England – are set to benefit from a fully conditioned new asset of considerable productivity. There are many in the scientific community who are already excited by his addition to our armoury – and, accordingly, by the loss of the Welshman. As you know, I rue the passing of an opportunity to assess the merits or otherwise of another way of life. But I am old, and the exigencies of the Next Match are considered more pressing than my speculations. It is a loss from a scientific point of view – and I suspect, for you, a personal blow. I regret it.'

'Let me see him,' says Dusty, but it is softly, as if lost, in a daze.

As soon as Dusty sees him, he knows. Ivon is a bona fide elite at last, a Perpetual citizen, a sportsman perfected. He is gone.

The projection on the teletable is scaled down in thirds, but the definition is precise, so much so that it enhances the impression, which Dusty knows is being made flesh in a skills tunnel somewhere in the same building, that Ivon has been transformed. There he stands in miniature, lean, still and intensely necessary. Gone is the constant movement. The energy that spewed from him, as if from a loose length of hosing, is nowhere to be seen, turned off, or more likely turned inwards, harnessed and contained. Could it even be that the accent has been smoothed out? Difficult to tell – he's not saying much. Certainly, the wild, brilliant hair has been removed, leaving skin stretched aerodynamically across the skull, as smooth and focused as the walls of the skill tunnel, as smooth and focused as the man.

A member of the IC's coaching panel is with him. Together they are working through a kicking drill. 'So, try to make the next one kick up after twelve rotations,' he says to Ivon.

Ivon takes the ball and stares at it. He seems to be thinking things through. With a brief intake of breath, he drops the ball and brings his foot sharply down upon it. It turns end over end along the skills tunnel, jumping up a few metres away before bobbling to a standstill.

'Not bad,' says the coach, consulting a tablet. 'But that was after eight. Here, have a look at this.' The two of them gather round the tablet. 'This is a snapshot of your boot striking the ball when you demonstrated the skill to us a few weeks ago. This is the same just now. Notice how the vector quantity applied by your boot to the ball this time is 18.43 newtons lighter than it was before and 0.97 of a degree shallower in its angle of attack. Try again.'

Ivon nods solemnly and takes up another ball. He goes through the same routine. The ball turns across the ground for a little longer this time before kicking up.

'Excellent!' says the coach. 'That was on the twelfth. Do you feel you're mastering it?'

Ivon nods.

'Now, this is nothing you couldn't do before,' continues the coach. 'You were the one who alerted us to the skill, after all. But you were unable to explain how you did it then, and for a Perpetual citizen, as you are now, that is an intolerable situation. What we have done is to capture the skill, analyse it and return it to you fully anatomised. The aim is for you to perform it without relying on instinct, which may desert you on a bad day. In other words, you own the skill, rather than the other way round.'

Dusty looks away from the projection and up at Syracuse Garbo. The old man continues to watch the teletable, like a troubled god.

'He's gone,' says Dusty. 'That's not Ivon.'

Garbo doesn't look up. 'Of course.'

'What have I done?'

'What have we all done.'

A great weight pulls on Dusty. It is the weight of things that have happened to him. The effect is heightened by the sight of the old man looking downwards, the tug of gravity on his drooping face a perfect expression of what Dusty feels. The sabotage that was perpetrated on Garbo's watch all those years ago – an injection of the Lapsed Era, the spirit of this man Gower, into a world that has no place for it – has worked its way through to this terrible end.

'Give me exile,' says Dusty. 'You could do it. Let me be the last from 2111 to leave.'

Finally, Garbo looks up from the tableau in front of them. He studies Dusty with a kind of sympathetic indifference. 'Where would you go?'

'Wales.'

Garbo winces. 'Really? Do you think you'd be welcome?'

He's right. Dusty has always known it – no Ivon, no Wales – but he resents being told, especially by the man responsible for it all. And he cannot bear to accept it. Or afford to.

'I could find Ricky and Dee. Explain everything to them. We could plot. Maybe gather a team, challenge England to return Ivon to Wales. Do *something*.' Garbo mocks him with an incredulous grin. 'Please. I cannot stay here.'

'And suppose you could persuade Ricky and Dee even to listen to you, let alone accept you as a friend, or just refrain from making a pariah of you among the Welsh. Suppose you manage all that, then raise a team and persuade the English to accept your challenge. Suppose you then manage to defeat the English – and this time it would be cricket the Perpetual way, officiated by computer – what will you do with Ivon himself? He is, as you say, gone. Wales is anathema to him. Ricky and Dee repulsive. You can be sure they will have turned him against you too, the man who wants to take him back there. Assimilation in the mid-twenty-second century, it is irreversible. This was the danger. This was where we were heading all along. You've always known it.'

'They've never tried it on a Welshman,' Dusty murmurs, a last spasm of hope, but it is with no conviction. His horizon, so briefly extended during this heady, reckless flirtation with the Lapsed Era, is closing in on him again, tighter even than it was during his days in service, when at least he had a boundary to aim at, gaps in the field and a throbbing corridor down which the ball would fly. Now he can see nothing.

He glances down at the teletable. It lies empty. Ivon has left the skills tunnel. Dusty turns and flees the pod, out into the stark corridor, along its tunnel to the IC's central stairwell, down which the light floods from the day outside, many flights above. He pounds up the staircase in search of the exit. The ground floor is five storeys higher. On he plunges towards the foyer.

Two figures walk ahead of him, tall and shaven-headed. As he passes them, he is taken by an impulse to look in their direction. He stops in his tracks. There is no mistaking the taller of the two men, even without the brilliant shock of hair, even with the bruising across his swollen nose.

'Ivon!' he gasps.

Ivon's face is blank and remains so.

Dusty is short of breath, but he no longer cares about social embarrassment. 'Ivon! It's not too late! Come with me, back to Wales!' He pauses to catch his breath, his breast heaving as Ivon's gaze remains steady. 'For Ricky and Dee, if nothing else. Please!'

There is not a flicker across Ivon's face, or in his eyes.

The coach from the IC steps forward. 'He's going nowhere. He's just been assimilated.'

Dusty remains focused on the son – that word again – of his old friends. 'Ivon!' he insists.

The boy – the man – slowly shakes his head.

His companion interjects again. 'I'm sorry, brother. He has to go for his next round of hormone supplements.' And sharply he leads Ivon away.

'Hormone supplements? Ivon, you wouldn't!'

Ivon stops. He turns round, so slowly that Dusty has time to regulate his breathing. The gaze settles on him and is steady throughout. 'They will make me a more productive asset. Why wouldn't I take them?'

'You swore you wouldn't!'

'That was when I was playing,' Ivon replies with deliberation, his accent painstakingly neutral. 'Just playing.'

He looks off to the left for an instant, at what Dusty does not know. Then he turns and hastens away with his companion down the corridor. Dusty watches him go, his chest rising and falling, his past deserting him as surely as his future.

By the sound of it, London are having a good day. The thunder from Lord's has been almost constant since he arrived. Dusty is glad of it. Those guys in the London cricket team, he's seen service with them all, some for many years – and of the younger ones, quite a few, it turns out, are his sons. He wishes them all well. Their shared past history means something to him at least, if nothing to them.

It had to be this way. Dusty and The Cricketer. Alone. The great, steel statue rises directly from the paving that surrounds Lord's. Access to it is unrestricted. No barriers, no plinth. How sad, he thinks, that he should leave it until now to make his first proper approach and inspection of it. He has never had cause to break from the thoroughfares and walk up to it, nor has he ever thought to. He wonders if anyone ever has. How typically English! How Perpetual!

With the match underway, Dusty can begin without fear of interruption. He is excited. Gone is his despair. The solution he has struck upon for his predicament is quite brilliant – creative, Lapsed Era, Welsh.

He puts down the magnetic handles he has borrowed from the Shed at ReSure and sizes up the right heel of The Cricketer and the lower leg that runs roughly parallel to the ground, just above chest height, towards the bent knee. Dusty runs his hands over the upturned surface of the calf muscle, as if planning where to build his home. The expanse of it is broad and matt, but not quite smooth. From this close, he is able to note the undulations and ridges in the brushed surface that run across the statue's entirety and ought to offer assistance. He takes up the magnetic handles, presses them against the statue and pulls the switch on each, pleased to note that their grip on the metal seems as sure as it was on the pods they were designed to lift. Using the handles as purchase, Dusty swings his legs up and onto the upturned calf, the first base of his ascent.

Once up, he gathers the handles and walks towards the back of the right thigh, which presents itself as an almost sheer incline. The left buttock bulges beyond the vertical, but the right is more or less flat, up to the bend forward at the waist. He places the handles on the buttock and heaves himself up, his feet and knees scrambling for purchase. The micro-magnets in his shoes offer extra grip against the ridges in the steel, and he is able to release the magnet in the right handle and swing it higher up, before following with the left.

As he scales The Cricketer's back, a broad 18 foot slope, falling away to the right, he exults at his ingenuity. No Perpetual citizen has ever thought of this! By merely dreaming of it, Dusty proves how far he has come. It is not for Perpetual citizens, the property of their commune and nation, to decide what they do with themselves. But Dusty... Dusty is showing how he is free at last! He is showing that there is freedom at all!

Just behind the left armpit, he swings his feet round to find purchase in the crook of the neck and left shoulder. He takes a moment to regroup, then hauls himself up on to the top of the head by the magnetic handles. That these devices should once have conveyed assets to and from stasis. And now they bear him here.

A vague giddiness he hadn't bargained for wobbles the edges of his consciousness – he has never found himself so high and free – but it only enhances in him the rarity of what he is doing. Steadying himself, he rises to his feet, leaving the handles behind, their purpose served. The stadium, which he turns away from now, continues with its thundering. He is presented with the left forearm of The Cricketer, running along from the raised elbow, waist high to him and parallel to the ground some 40 feet below. He is able to lean forward, swing his left leg over so that he is straddling it. Here he is, at the very top of the statue that has towered over them all for so long, inspiring awe – a concession, was it, to the spirituality of the Lapsed Era, which no citizen thought or dared to approach, still less touch, less climb. But this is not his journey's end. He is bound for the bat at the end of the forearm, towards which he inches now.

He cannot, quite, banish thoughts of Ivon from his mind. The cold eyes, the focus, the containment. It is as the wild-haired spirit that he should remember him, but that too conjures sickening feelings, those of loss and remembrance of Wales, of Ricky, of Dee. He had hoped to join them, how he'd hoped. There can be no Wales for him now. Oh, Lapsed Era, are you any less cruel than your monochrome successor? To breed unregulated impulses, encourage such hope for how things could be – and to deny it all!

At the statue's glove, Dusty gasps. A pair of letters are carved into the strap, identifiers of the kind they used to wear when this statue went up in '25, the player's initials. Tears start to well again, as he considers them. Here, on the highest plane of The Cricketer, safely concealed from the impressionable eyes of those below, turned up towards the sky, reads the simple inscription: 'DN'.

So, it *was* meant to be him all along. It *is* him. The Cricketer. He knew it. Dusty Noble is sitting astride Dusty Noble. Who sanctioned this tiny detail, tucked away from view? Was it the Commune of London itself, or a rogue operative working on the left glove, who detected in himself the forbidden admiration of an individual and indulged it where no one would see? Ha! In this way, the Perpetual Era winks at Dusty at the very last. All those years of unflinching coldness, of means–end rationality, all those years and the Perpetual Era had a heart somewhere after all, whether renegade or institutional, it matters not.

It matters not.

Dusty climbs over the fingers of the left glove, then those of the right, out onto the bat itself. *His* bat, he can now say. He sits cross-legged on the blade and looks along its gentle downward slope. He had thought he might do this at the end of the bat, more obviously isolated, but, no, he might fall. No statement was ever made by an amorphous stain on the floor. And, besides, his sense of theatre and panache, which he fancies was always there, is more heightened now. Such an end would never do.

He pulls the rope from off his shoulder and over his head. How grateful he is to ReSure for these arcane devices, and for its archive of information on how ends were met in the Lapsed Era. It is possible that without it he might not even have conceived of this brilliant solution. He is crying openly and relishes the thought that he is now beyond all fear of show.

From crèche to decommission, the cricket bat has defined his existence. He swivels round onto his front and lies along the length of this magnificent representation of it, his cheek pressing against the blade as he looks out over London. He slips his arms round the bat and with his left hand swings one end of the rope under it, catching it with his right. Sitting back up, he threads the rest of the rope through the loop he has tied at one end and pulls it tight round the blade. Then, through the loop he has tied at the other, he slips his head and gently closes the noose around his neck, as the footage described. The engineering of the knot is exquisite. The parts move smoothly, without resistance.

The stadium turbines roar into life again. Could this be the start of the upturn they have been yearning for? Hopeful signs have been there for some time. Ever since Ivon arrived, now Dusty thinks about it. That match at the White City Stadium, 72–15! Oh, what a pump that was! It occurs to Dusty that Ivon might be London's lucky charm – and he smiles through his tears at the very thought, settling into a comfortable position facing Lord's, his legs dangling over the side of the upturned bat.

Yes, he will remember Ivon as that – a lucky charm, a gift from another time. And if London had to appropriate him, so Dusty will travel the other way. Fancy bringing about your own premature departure! The audacity of it, the individuality, the dislocation of thought, the genius! Dusty Noble does not belong to London, what though they bred him and reared him. Dusty Noble will not surrender himself to London. He belongs to Dusty Noble, and he will take with him his cover drive and the myriad other shots he has played in his forty-nine years.

In a few hours, thousands of citizens will file out of that grand old stadium generator. The first few, perhaps, will look up routinely at the mighty statue and for once see a new message. And so the word will spread throughout the multitude. There are new possibilities; there are new ways to live! Look at Dusty Noble up there! To think, he might have trundled on to his stasis in eleven years' time, surrendered all he'd had or known! To think we all might!

Yes, there is another way. Dusty pushes down with his hands against the bat and eases himself off its edge, as if slipping into a rock pool on the mystic coast of Gower, as if slipping into his freedom.

Acknowledgements

Crowdfunding is an increasingly popular path to publication, with good reason, but it does rely on the generosity and faith of potential readers. I hope I've already thanked profusely those who pledged their hard-earned towards Ivon without seeing so much as a dust jacket, but you can't be thanked enough. So, thanks again. The phrase 'it wouldn't have been possible without you' is a staple rhetorical device in acknowledgements, but to crowdfunders it applies literally.

All books, whether crowdfunded or not, need publishers. Many thanks, then, to Clare Christian, Anna Burtt and Heather Boisseau at RedDoor for agreeing to take on Ivon with such energy and creativity. Your hybrid model, marrying the selectivity of traditional publishing with the democratising verve of self-publishing, provides a much-needed outlet for those books that might not fit easily into any of the mainstream genres. I think it will prove as important a development in the publishing industry as crowdfunding.

Readers are important, too, even before publication. My thanks, then, to James Perry, Richard Warlow, Dan Morrish and James Cunningham for their comments on the early drafts of the all-important opening pages. And, for their comments on the early drafts of the full manuscript, still more to Hugh Godwin, Gilbert Simmons and Ben Roome, in particular the latter, who read it twice, apparently of his own accord.

This book was also expedited to its current state by Richard Beard and his class of happy (sometimes) scribblers at the National Academy of Writing: Lesia Scholey, Sally Hodgkinson, Eamon Somers, Laura Ashton and Sue Blundell. It's a curious experience to have your work pulled apart line by line by a randomly thrown-together group round a table – and, of course, never easy. Friendships are forged or killed at birth by it. I'm so pleased we're all still talking, let alone such good friends. See you at the Pineapple.

Finally, thanks and undying devotion to Vanessa, Max and Francesca. They say families are the death of creativity – and there's no doubt they can get in the way – but neither is there anything like a noisy, loving house for seeing how people tick. Writing this book would have been possible without you, but it wouldn't have been as much fun.

About the Author

Michael Aylwin is a sportswriter and an award-winning, bestselling author. This is his first novel.